Million Dollar Question

Million Dollar Question

Ellie Campbell

Cover design by Design for Writers

ISBN-13: 978-0-9915381-4-0
ISBN-10: 0991538145

Also by Ellie Campbell

How to Survive Your Sisters
When Good Friends Go Bad
Looking for La La
To Catch A Creeper

Thank you!

As always, we are indebted to our agents, Caroline Hardman and Joanna Swainson at Hardman Swainson in London for their invaluable assistance and advice. Thanks to our too often neglected and ignored husbands Ian and Gary who have to put up with burned dinners, messy houses, and distracted wives caught up in hour-long phone conversations or glued to their laptops as we burn the midnight oil and forget to go to bed.

And thanks again to our lovely readers and reviewers who have supported us on our journey and all the wonderful bloggers and indie authors who have become friends along the way. There are too many to mention but you know who you are.

Prologue

The battered old transit had been on her tail since she left the office. Humming, the woman cut deftly in front of a rust-riddled Renault, screeched into a side street and watched the van fly past. Paranoid, maybe but she had a good reason for staying anonymous. Her eyes flicked to the briefcase on the back seat.

An extremely good reason.

Still she was more excited than nervous. Closing in on her target.

Even with its challenges this job fired her blood. She sang with the radio as she steered her elderly silver E-class Mercedes through the traffic. She adored its 'birdseye' maple trim, two-tone leather upholstery and quirky seatbelt that snaked round her body at the touch of a button. And being a bit shabby, it didn't attract attention, which suited her perfectly.

Her boss asked once if she ever felt regret. She stole another peek at the innocuous-looking briefcase, so full of dangers and traps. No, being the messenger suited her fine.

The late spring sun pierced through the clouds, alloy wheels chewing up the miles as leafy North London avenues gave way to grimier streets. She spotted a boarded-up shop, a broken window in a litter-strewn yard.

Somewhere, close now, her unwary quarry was drying dishes or pegging out washing, never dreaming of the approaching tempest. She smiled. Like sex, the anticipation was frequently—

'Go left on the roundabout,' Ozzy ordered.

What reaction would she get? Shock? Tears? Prayers? Once a husband had burst through the door and furiously berated her for upsetting his wife.

Little did he suspect.

She began practising her patter as her eyes scanned house numbers. 'Hi, my name's Agent—'

Again Ozzy Osbourne interrupted. 'You have reached your destination.'

Chapter One

Rosie Dixon perched herself on the hard plastic chair, watching the drawing take shape. A line, followed by a squiggle. Snake maybe? Then what looked like a head of a person with ears on top. And was that a saddle on its back or—

'Do you like it, Miss?' Emily asked.

'Oh yes, it's good.' Rosie smiled encouragement as the young girl plucked another crayon from the Tupperware box and worked earnestly, tongue curled stiffly against her cheek in concentration. 'Extremely good. I love the bright colours you've chosen.'

Finished, Emily pointed at the purple object. 'What do you think that is?'

'Um. Let's see.' Rosie peered closer. It vaguely resembled a bear, although how that fitted in with the 'My Family at Home' project, heaven knew. She didn't want to offend but... 'What's his name?'

'Bruno.'

Ah yes. 'Bruno the bear. Of course.'

'Bear?' The girl shook her two perfect bunches and wrinkled her tiny freckled nose. 'It's not a bear, Miss, it's a chocolate Labrador. Mummy's boyfriend has one. Durr...'

'Well it's lovely.' Rosie stood up. 'And I'm Rosie, remember?'

Not that Rosie didn't appreciate being called Miss, she did. Made her feel like a teacher, although the rather less grand title of 'Teaching Assistant' suited her fine. She'd been working at Avondale Infants for eighteen months now, supporting primary-aged pupils in classes of thirty-plus without needing to fret about parents' evenings, lesson plans and the mountains of paperwork expected of a real teacher. She loved the small children and the hours meant she could still collect her own two sons from junior school.

'Miss?' Max, angelic curls disguising an impish spirit, frowned at his latest creation. 'Can you help me?'

'Shove over then.' She nudged him playfully, as she squeezed beside him. Who'd have ever thought that she, shy little Rosie, always too timid to raise her hand in class, would be making a difference, however small, in the world of education? Just showed that good could come from the direst of situations. Even if it had taken a broken heart and some other God-awful trials to get her here.

She tucked a lock of shoulder-length hair behind her ear and handed Max a glue stick.

All things considered she really was incredibly lucky.

Mid-morning, the kettle in the staffroom had boiled and Rosie's fellow teaching assistant, Gemma, was handing round the custard creams. Also in her early thirties, Gemma was recently divorced and had a secret obsession with *The X Factor*'s Simon Cowell that Rosie was sworn, on pain of death, never to reveal.

'Anyone got an astrophysics degree?' Carol, teacher of Orange Class, leafed through a stack of forms, eyebrows furrowed. 'Certainly need one to fill in all these bloody risk assessments. Talk about 'elf and safety!'

Rosie joined in the laughter as she dropped a teabag in a smiley face mug. She was about to ask her colleagues, flopped onto chairs for their short break, if they were all right for beverages when Pauline Dawkins, Admin Officer, sidled up, a giant birthday card tucked under one paisley-clad arm.

'Barry's fiftieth. Whip-round,' she hissed, spy-like from the corner of her mouth, as if the sole male teacher might burst in and discover the dastardly plot. 'Drinks and cake at four.'

Pauline took her charge of The Birthday Book extremely seriously. Rosie had suffered the same ordeal when she'd turned thirty-three in March.

'Oh, I'd love to be there, but I've my sons to pick up.' Dutifully she scribbled, 'Have a great day, Barry!' unable to conjure anything witty or mildly original.

The envelope under her nose was stuffed with pound coins and larger notes. Rosie opened her ancient leatherette handbag, pushed aside her soggy egg sandwich and peeked inside her purse.

A lonely fiver lay folded next to a single fifty pence piece.

Her heart sank. That cash had to last the next two days until her monthly salary reached her bank. The twins, being eleven, always needed money for this or that and Charlie's cheque was late again.

But then again poor Barry had recently lost his wife. Fifty pence seemed so stingy and she'd never dare offer the five pound note and ask for change.

There was an uncomfortable beat. Rosie's fingers froze. Nobody was paying attention but still damp pooled in her armpits and along her hairline, her insecurities running rampant under Pauline's scrutiny.

Was she assessing the havoc a runaway husband could create? Maybe worse – thinking it no wonder he'd strayed? If Rosie had once felt young, pretty and loved, it had all vanished with the end of her marriage. She cursed herself for not finding something smarter to wear than the skanky black cords pilled from the washing machine and a faded cotton blouse (Selfridges Sale 70% off) which sagged where it used to cling. And she'd totally messed up her hair attempting to add subtle honey-gold streaks from a Superdrug box to her mousy-brown frizz and ended up with tiger stripes instead.

Blow it, she thought, and handed over the fiver with a flourish, smiling to silence the warning pang from her gut.

'Ta ever so.' Pauline stuffed the note in the envelope. 'We want to buy him a special present. Poor devil's all on his lonesome...' She broke off, fiddling with the plastic ID badge dangling from her neck. 'I didn't mean...well, it's different for you with those darling boys, never a dull minute in your house, I'm sure.' Her eyes fired with matchmaking zeal. 'Now there's a thought. Don't suppose you and Barry...?'

'No. Really.' Rosie tried looking appreciative instead of appalled. Bearded bespectacled Barry was even more tortuously shy than Rosie and any attempts to speak made him extra nervous. They only had to reach the kettle at the same time and Rosie could feel her hands sweat, watching him twitch and stammer. As for fireworks, there'd be more sparks with two squibs in a rainstorm.

'Just an idea.' Pauline shrugged it off. She was basically a kind woman, Rosie thought, whatever catty things people said – just maybe a touch too blunt for the fragile sensitivities of a mostly female environment. And it must be excruciating asking people to hand over cash.

Pauline left to corner someone else and Rosie slumped onto an empty seat, tea forgotten. Two years since Charlie had walked out and no one – except Rosie in the secret corners of her soul – believed he was ever coming back. The beautiful home they'd spent ages lovingly doing up had been sold, Rosie and the boys now installed in a tatty two-bed terrace in a scruffy housing estate, where luckily the neighbours had welcomed her as one of their own.

Better off without him, everyone declared. What self-respecting woman stayed with a cheat after all? Outraged friends wanted him to suffer and occasionally Rosie did too. Not in a nasty, vengeful way, but at least to experience a few twinges of her own devastation.

She had fantasies in which he came crawling back, grief-stricken over what he'd carelessly tossed aside. She'd imagine herself on the arm of Colin Farrell, wearing a fiery-red figure-hugging dress, strikingly elegant, flawlessly made-up, her belly flat and her legs mysteriously three inches longer. She'd be ice-cool, telling him it was too late but usually in these daydreams – and she knew it was wrong – just as Charlie left, dejected, her stony heart would relent, she'd apologise to Colin, kick off her heels and run to Charlie's joyful arms.

Other times her sleep betrayed her. She'd walk in the kitchen to find Charlie cooking spaghetti bolognese, wearing only a chef's apron and an endearingly rueful smile. Silly stuff. Like last night – they'd sat in the bath together, him soaping her back. So convincing was this dream that in the morning she'd lazily stretched out her arm to him, forgetting that his side of the bed was empty and cold. He'd been her best friend and lover for so long. Not easy persuading her subconscious to switch from love to hate. Or even indifference. And he'd been such a caring father to Luke and Tim. Were they truly 'better off without him'?

Determined not to submerge into despondency, she jumped up and tackled the backlog of crockery clogging the staffroom kitchenette.

Damn. She'd thought she'd got past all those predictable emotional stages, familiar to her as commuter stations. Denial. Shock. Anger. Depression. Last stop – Guilt – where she still lingered, scolding herself for not leaping to action the second Charlie's secretary warned her about the female customer who showed more interest in the showroom's Sales Manager than the vehicles on sale.

And why hadn't she? Jumped? Leapt? Fought?

Because it had been unthinkable. Laughable even. With the red flag flapping inches from her face, Rosie had brushed it away with a smile, too certain of her husband to fall for that alarmist nonsense. This was Charlie, after all, her soulmate, who'd rescued her in her darkest hours, made her believe in her own worth after years of her mother's jibes. He loved her even if she had grown two dress sizes finishing the kids' meals, barely ever wore make-up, slumped around the home in baggy sweatshirts and couldn't stay awake to watch an entire film when the boys were finally in bed.

'...first out. Hey, what's so fascinating about that sponge? You've been staring at it ages.'

Rosie hadn't realised Gemma had joined her at the sink, let alone that she'd been speaking.

'Sorry, Gem.' She came out of her daze. 'What was that?'

'I was saying that as long as it's not last in, first out, 'cos technically speaking...' Gemma pushed her glasses up her nose and gave Rosie a meaningful glance before picking up a tea towel.

'Technically speaking…?'

Gemma sighed as she wiped a saucer. 'Rosie, you dingbat, did you hear a word I said? That meeting with the union reps yesterday, Carol's just filled me in. They're talking staff cuts. Redundancies. Teaching assistants in particular. Some of us – God knows how many – are for the chop!'

Chapter Two

'. . . Well, after I'd bumped into him in Cannes airport, a Geneva tea room and the British Museum,' the heiress flourished a knuckleduster of sparkling rings, light bouncing off a rock the size of a chandelier crystal, 'I said, Rupert, sweetie, this is positively karmic. If you weren't such a hottie, I'd swear you're stalking me.'

Olivia, idly calculating the evening's takings at $1,250 per head, felt neck hairs stir as her brain snapped into gear. Coincidence? Hardly likely. Not with Rupert Mandrake, her deviously intelligent boss. Besides, if karma did exist, she and this crowd of celebrities, blue bloods and social climbers were in deep, deep doo-doo.

Sensing impatience, she smiled at the man beside her, her tawny-gold eyes conveying amusement at their mutual suffering. Still, she doubted Ethan Goldstein, the famous movie producer with his ponytail, leather jacket and too-tight jeans, would be any more scintillating a conversationalist. She recognised that anxious look – probably hoping to quiz her about falling stock prices or some shaky investment.

She could feel her iPhone whispering to her from her clutch purse. But, no, she'd already taken far too many trips to the restroom, scanning the internet for untimely leaks about a couple of deals that were causing her sleepless nights. Keep that up and they'd think she had a bad case of cystitis.

She shifted on her three-inch Camilla Skovgaard stilettos, smile muscles stiff, throat uncomfortably raw. Overuse? Or the beginnings of a deadly virus, one that all her doctors had yet to discover?

She'd been here long enough, surely? Schmoozed every single MC Capital client. She was itching to leave, to zoom to the perfect chocolate-box village of East Hampton in her scarlet Lamborghini, wind blasting her expensively styled russet hair. She might even catch up with Brad in their favourite hangout, Rowdy Hall.

And then to bed in their darling cottage, next to her handsome, golden-haired fiancé, the billionaire's son that *Time* magazine had listed in America's ten most eligible bachelors.

They'd bought the little clapboard house, two blocks from the ocean, just last year. It was modest enough, compared to his parents' nearby fifteen bedroom summer retreat, with tennis courts, golf course, boat dock and helicopter pad, but it made the perfect weekend getaway and Olivia adored it.

The producer seized an opportune pause. 'So where is the so-called Wizard of Wall Street, our young Nostradamus?' His bleached white smile looked strained. 'The slippery son of a bitch swore on oath he'd be here tonight.'

'Some international crisis.' Olivia shrugged slender perfume-scented shoulders. 'You know how these things go.'

'Involving a blonde, his mega-yacht and no cell phone service.' His laugh was as taut as his surgically altered skin. 'If you talk, tell him it's crucial we speak. Urgently.'

'Ab-so-lutely.' She flashed a lighten-the-mood grin. 'Anything in the auction strike your fancy?' She brandished her bid number. 'Besides the Bora Bora spa vacation? That's mine.'

'Hah,' an arm came around her waist, making her jump, 'I know you, girl. You'd be on a plane home after two days.' The benefit host, Arthur Cottrell, of CRAWL (Care and Rescue Animal Welfare League) bowed his balding head over her hand.

Alas, true, probably. Vacations weren't her thing. Who else found themselves bouncing on a jeep in Masai Mara Park, scrubbing their hands with antiseptic wipes and searching for a satellite connection while everyone else took lion photos?

'Mind if I steal this foxy lady, Ethan?' Arthur laughed, obviously convinced that Olivia found his comparison to a feral scavenger original and delightful. 'Dear girl, I've someone dying to meet you.'

Hell! She was never getting out of here. She sensed an incipient migraine – or possible brain tumour? – as Arthur steered her past the featured poster boards. Horrific images: emaciated horses; a baby tiger immobilised in a cruelly small kennel; a cow marooned on a roof by flood waters. Those huge bewildered eyes made her feel guilty about the mouthful of hanger steak, which was all she'd found to eat tonight, thanks to her stupid diet. Perhaps she should go veggie again – ignore her nutritionist's insistence on Paleo?

African safaris be damned. She dealt with blood, guts and murderous predators every day at MC Capital. And unlike most in their cutthroat little universe, Olivia hadn't had to claw her way into Rupert Mandrake's legendary wolf pack. Irresistible Rupert, five years her senior, had actually courted her, wielding charm with the precision of an endoscopic knife, convincing her she was indispensable to 'the team'.

Naturally half 'the team' assumed they were sleeping together and undoubtedly loathed her guts.

'CRAWL's biggest fundraiser yet,' Arthur gloated, as they passed temptingly close to the marble hotel reception lobby. 'Tasting stations from every celebrity chef in Manhattan. We sold out weeks ago.'

'You might need a ballroom with a higher ceiling.' Joking, she glanced up at the soaring frescoes overhead. 'If it has to contain all those enormous egos.'

'And here we are.' They'd reached a looming Mount Rushmore of a man with a massive sculpted face, escorting a willowy girl, impossibly glamorous in wide-legged satin trousers with matching braces over a cream silk sleeveless top. 'Olivia Wheeler, meet William and Lucy Shipton.'

'Delighted.' Olivia's fine-boned hand was swallowed in a crushing handshake that emphasised obvious wealth and power. Fleetingly she wished for her business suit and sensible heels. It was hard enough to be taken seriously in office garb, let alone dressed in a simple Donna Karan sheath and looking much younger than her thirty-three years.

'Arthur's been bending my ear about you.' Shipton's voice boomed to match his frame. 'Says you're Mandrake's new secret weapon. Taking the financial world by storm.'

'Well, I'm learning from a master.' She twinkled up at him. 'Rupert made his first hundred grand in grade school while most of his classmates were attempting model airplanes.' With practiced grace she snagged a vodka martini from a passing tray.

'And of course he's been a legend ever since,' he stated, dryly. 'This is my niece. Graduate student at Stanford. Lucy, Olivia here works in the infamous hedge fund industry.'

'But don't hold that against me.' Olivia stabbed at the olive. 'If you believe the media, we've caused every disaster from the troubles in Iraq to the melting of the polar icecaps.'

A strident voice rose above the conversational hum. 'Truthfully, darlings, it's positively our first outing for weeks. We're on the *strictest* regime – no wasteful extravagances, simple dinners at home. In this uncertain economy we must make sacrifices.'

'Frugality still the latest fad,' Olivia informed the others as ice cold vodka did a happy dance on her tongue. 'She just stole Nicolas Delacroix from Le Lapin Doré in Paris to be her personal chef. I doubt there's anything simple about those dinners.'

Lucy giggled charmingly. 'I *totally love* your accent. Are you English?'

'My father was. Mother American. I was mostly raised in Spain. But then between boarding school, Oxford and a stint in the City of London…' Olivia shrugged. 'The jolly old accent stuck, don'tcha know.'

Well, perhaps her vowels may have grown just a *teensy* more cut-glass. Never waste an asset after all.

'How fabulous,' Lucy gushed. 'I'll be in Europe this summer. Sailing round the West coast of Scotland on a volunteer project. Studying dolphins.'

'Olivia here is a true animal lover,' Arthur interjected, puffing up like a proud parent. 'Heart as well as brains. She was one of our first volunteers during Hurricane Katrina. Hardly older than you, then, Lucy.'

Lucy's eyes were gobstoppers. 'Oh God, was it awful?'

'It was no Mardi Gras, I can tell you.' Why in God's good graces did Arthur have to bring that up? Olivia's headache magnified as unwanted images crowded in. Despair. Rage. Wading through stinking polluted water. Stumbling into waterlogged corpses. Breaking into houses to find starving dehydrated survivors among the 250,000 pets abandoned by owners who expected to be back in days, not weeks. The stench. The hopelessness. Her skin itched at the memory.

Awful? It was the seventh circle of hell. Nothing in Olivia's sheltered upbringing had prepared her for such horrors. Yes, she *had* been an animal lover but your heart could only be broken so many times. The experience had left her with nightmares and a host of phobias that only grew worse when she was stressed.

There was a loud crash and a shriek. They whirled to see a famous supermodel, a stick insect with cheekbones, tugging vainly at a harness attached to a three-legged pot-bellied pig.

Olivia blinked. Standing on a chair, a voluptuous dowager mopped food from her tent-sized gown while at her feet the mobility-challenged porker gobbled Grade A sushi among shards of broken china.

'Oopsie.' Arthur tutted. 'Better get that cleaned up.'

Olivia's mouth snapped shut. 'Live animals? Oopsie?' She glimpsed an exotic leopard-printed black girl gingerly parading a very real, equally unhappy, leopard.

'You gotta be kidding me!' Olivia's mind conjured disasters. That leopard loose… Teeth. Claws. Blood. Screams. 'Surely the attorneys… Insurance… Health codes…'

'Only Arthur!' Shipton shook his gargantuan head, indicating a group of men. 'He's even got the Mayor eating out his hand.'

'Until he gets food poisoning,' Olivia muttered. 'Or some weird cross-species disease.'

'Precisely. Look, is there somewhere private—?'

There was another yell, guests scattered and a black shape hurled itself across the room. Shipton grasped Olivia's arm just as a gigantic drooling Rottweiler bounded towards her, nose happily seeking her crotch. The smell of dog made her want to vomit. Drool landed on her hands, spattering over designer silk. Billions, no, *zillions*...of disgusting germs, microbes, bacteria...partying on her skin. Someone giggled. Eyes stared. She felt herself gag.

'Excuse me.' Olivia pushed the brute away as Shipton grabbed the beast by the collar. 'I have to—'

And with that she bolted.

'Honeychops!' The words were slurred. 'How's the charity bash? Hey, everyone, 's my workaholic girlfriend. Hello workaholic girlfriend.'

'Hello yourself.' Outside the plush ladies' room, phone held in pink-scrubbed hands, Olivia winced. Brad would laugh himself sick about tonight's fiasco, all those animals on the loose. He knew she hadn't particularly wanted to attend but he'd still been pissed off that she hadn't cancelled. Despite his Harvard law degree and partnership in his uncle's firm, Brad and his trust fund buddies found the whole 'work' concept rather strange.

Whereas Olivia loved it. She was addicted to the pulse. So many weeknights she fell asleep on the condo sofa to the Tokyo and London stock exchanges blaring from CNBC. Then up at four-thirty for her power yoga class. No wonder these days she was often too tired for sex, not in the mood or yawning, half-comatose, as Brad got the job done and rolled over, spent. It was a gruelling schedule but there was an endless line of wannabe Gordon Gekkos eager to take her place. The constant need to prove herself was immense.

'Ted and Muffy invited us on their boat tomorrow. First sail of the season. Muffy wants to know when we're getting married. When *are* we getting married?'

'Hi Olivia.' A giggling drunken screech assaulted her ear. 'Set a date yet? Tick-tock, you know. We can't wait for you to have kids too.'

Muffy. Hardly mother of the year, spying on her nannies with the teddy-cam, outraged when they spilt her most intimate secrets. Her kids were shunted to school by helicopter and showered with everything except the thing they most wanted – their parents' attention. Olivia knew what it was like to be shoved aside for convenience sake. She could never do that to a child. And Rupert would hardly let her bring a squalling baby to the office.

But did that mean she didn't want any?

Irrelevant. She had years before she need worry about the biological clock.

'Yes, wouldn't that be peachy, Muffy, darling,' she cooed. No point in alienating Brad's closest friends. 'Tell Brad I'll catch him later.'

She clicked off as she reached the revolving doors. Cameras flashed, obviously expecting a celebrity. A uniformed doorman opened the door to a yellow cab.

Someone grasped her elbow and pushed her in, enclosing them in the tiny space. An involuntary scream bubbled in her throat, choked back when she recognised Shipton.

'Sorry, Miss Wheeler,' the big man growled, 'we need to talk. Cabbie, drive us around the block.'

'No, Cabbie, take me home.' Olivia gave the address and slammed the partition. 'You have to accost me? This couldn't wait?'

Shipton rested his silver head against the leather seat as the cab pulled away. 'Answer me this. Where exactly is Rupert Mandrake?'

'Grand Cayman. Flying home tomorrow. If you'd like to set up a meeting…'

The man pulled out a packet of thin cigars, took one out and with a small grimace at the No Smoking sign replaced it. 'Unlikely. Considering he was spotted last night exiting Caracas airport.'

'That's ludicrous. Why would Rupert be in Venezuela?' She thought about it. Then shrugged. 'Then again why not? He doesn't tell me everything. And that's the thing about private jets – people get around.'

'You're right. He doesn't tell you everything.' The box disappeared into the jacket. 'You've worked for him...how long?'

'Almost two years.'

'Arthur mentioned you're both invested in this latest fund of Mandrake's. That's a heavy commitment. $750,000 minimum.'

Olivia shrugged. 'True but it's paying big. CRAWL plans to expand into another 3,000 acres of land this year.'

Despite her splitting head, she felt a surge of pride. She'd initiated the introduction after all. If only her parents had lived to see the results of their only offspring's inexplicable love of mathematics. Granted she wasn't musical, passionate or as beautiful as her mother. Nor had she inherited her father's artistic ability. But it was her talent and daring that had multiplied her inheritance and turned it into a virtual goldmine.

Of course, between Brad Winton and Rupert Mandrake, good fortune had favoured her beyond her wildest expectations. Maybe hers wasn't the 'working-class barrow boy to mega-tycoon slash peer of the realm' inspirational story but she was on a hell of a ride. If things continued, one day it might be the Wheeler fund dominating the market, the Wheeler limo meeting Olivia's private jet, the Wheeler yacht lying in some tropical harbour...

'And you?' Shipton was watching her face.

'Gotta play to win,' she chanted the MC Capital mantra. 'Yep, I cashed in every bonus, stock and cent of equity I could muster. Me. My fiancé, Brad Winton. His family. And a very select few friends. Rupert's golden. Turns away investors all the time. And you know what they say – only a moron leaves money stagnating in the bank.'

'They do, do they?'

It hit her then. Morons. Banks. Her face flushed.

'Oh God. You're *that* William Shipton. Shipton's Investment Bank. I'm so sorry. I'm such a big-mouth sometimes.'

The banker frowned. 'No, but you may not be as clever as you think. You don't see anything strange or secretive in Mandrake's activities?'

Olivia's embarrassed cheeks paled to ice. 'Secretive? Strange?' She folded her hands, forcing professional courtesy. 'I assure you our compliance procedures are a hundred per cent… Of course there are always jealous vultures hoping to profit from—'

'No nastier than usual rumours then? No discontented clients or unpleasant scenes?'

'Of course not! Bloody hell!' She recalled the strain on the producer's ultra-tanned face. 'What are you…?' Immediately she was hot again. Boiling, even with bare shoulders and the lightest of wraps.

'*Come on,* Miss Wheeler. Exclusivity is the oldest trick in a con-man's book. Make it hard – no, impossible – to get and the fools flock round in a feeding frenzy. And Mandrake's luck in this volatile market has been nothing short of unbelievable. When *did* you go to work for him? Shortly after your engagement to the Winton boy, wasn't it?'

She wouldn't listen. Why was the journey taking so long? Stuck in a dirty old cab with the stink of fake pine making her want to puke. She fumbled for the window button but the driver had it locked. The dread feeling was back in spades. She couldn't breathe.

'Rupert Mandrake is an unscrupulous thief.' Shipton was too loud for the cramped space. She wanted to smack his smug presidential face, pummel against his big fat old chest, call him a liar. Bile rose in her throat. 'This latest sham fund is under investigation by the SEC and my contacts are fairly certain he's gone on the run. Your magician plays with a marked deck, Olivia.' He finally used her Christian name. 'I'm afraid you, CRAWL and all his other victims will end up returning all illegal profits. Wait! Don't be insane!' He grabbed her arm as she fumbled for the door handle, heedless of the cab's speed, before seizing her wrist as she turned and lashed out. Then she was trying to punch him and he was fending her off.

'Olivia! Olivia, calm down… *Stop!*'

Chapter Three

Outside the bright turquoise door of No 9 Forge Street, Rosie inserted her key and felt stubborn resistance. Shutting her eyes, she counted slowly to ten, put down her carrier bags and prepared for battle.

'Hurry up, Mum,' squirmed Luke, her eldest son by six minutes two seconds. 'I'm bursting for a wee.'

'Hold on a mo.' She wiggled the metal, left, right, in two millimetres, out one millimetre, like a safecracker searching a combination. If she stuck her ear to the panel, she wondered, might she be guided by tiny clicks?

'Let me try.' Tim reached out an eager grubby hand.

'No way. If it snaps we'll have to call a locksmith.'

Rosie twisted the key again, ruefully reflecting that the five pounds donated to Barry might have fixed the problem. Much as she hated being stingy, as a single parent she needed to learn ruthlessness. Charlie's child support was late, her credit cards had maxed out and last night her poor oven had gasped its last smoky breath, resulting in a pasta bake more raw than al dente.

And now redundancies at work? Talk about a bolt from the blue.

A movement. Abruptly the lock succumbed and the door flew open.

'See.' She smiled with relief. 'Is your mother brill-i-ant or what?'

She might as well have been whistling in the wind as the boys thundered up the stairs, flinging off jackets, racing for the bathroom. She followed them in, looking forward to a hot cuppa, remembering another bolt from the blue – her ex-husband's desertion.

Mind you, there'd been clues. Late nights at the showroom. That second mobile phone 'for business only'. He'd grown aloof, irritable, complaining about the kids' noise, the messy house, her mediocre cooking. He'd accused her of giving him the third degree if she innocently asked about his day, turned his back when she snuggled up to him in bed. But still, would he actually have left if his secretary hadn't spilled the beans?

She was staring blankly in the fridge, trying to envisage a quick and easy meal when she heard the knocking.

'Mrs Dixon? Mrs Rose Ann Dixon?'

A young woman was on her doorstep: chestnut chin-length bob, pretty face and wearing a simple navy suit with lace-up blue suede boots that probably cost more than Rosie's monthly salary.

'Yes, that's me. Although it's Ms now. I'm divorced.' Rosie knew she was destined to disappoint. The peach-toned foundation and pale terracotta lips were a definite giveaway.

The girl cleared her throat. 'May I come in?'

'Er, yes, OK.' Rosie led her into the small sitting room. 'Excuse the clutter,' she apologised, booting a football out of their path. 'I'm a bit behind.'

'Know what you mean,' the girl sympathised. 'I've a stack in my in-tray this high.' She held her hand at thigh level.

Rosie felt an immediate rapport. 'Honestly, you're probably wasting your time with me. I'm a fraction short this month.' She gestured her visitor to sit. 'And I've everything I need cosmetic-wise.' Everything being dried-out mascara, lipstick that doubled as a blusher and an eye-pencil so short she kept losing it in the sharpener.

'Don't worry. I'm not selling anything. Quite the reverse.'

Not the Avon lady? Then who was she? Save the Environment with a petition to sign? Rosie hugged suddenly-chilly arms as her mind flashed to grimmer scenarios. Inland Revenue? Debt agency?

Charlie always nagged her to not let people in until she'd found out who they were.

The stranger had her head down, rummaging in her briefcase. Remembering the hoard of unpaid bills, Rosie's stomach lurched. She hated even mild confrontations…so much so that several neighbours thought her name was Rachel, the postman called her Roxy and the woman in the bakery greeted her as 'Susan'. She'd never liked to set any of them straight, although Christ knew how 'Two Belgian buns and a jam doughnut' could be mistaken for 'Hi, my name's Susan'!

'Tea?' she asked, watching her guest pull out an official-looking folder.

The girl glanced up. 'Yes thanks. White, no sugar.' She took off her jacket and laid it on the sofa arm, unwittingly covering up a chocolate stain.

Waiting for the kettle to boil, Rosie was now convinced something was very much amiss. The building society, probably, wondering why her standing order had been late twice in a row. Against all good sense she wished Charlie was beside her, his big strong hand holding hers, facing trouble together.

They'd all noticed him in that Knightsbridge wine bar, the girls filing in for a night on the town. Cornflower blue shirt that matched his eyes, tiny cleft in a chiselled chin, hair like waves of wheat just begging some lucky lass to run her fingers through it. The lucky lass that night had been an amazingly slim toothpick with platinum hair flowing to a waist he could have encircled with one hand. The life and soul of his small group, he was unaware of Rosie and her mates, but she kept finding her eyes drifting in his direction.

Stepping out into the night in driving rain, she'd spotted him again. The platinum toothpick was holding his jacket over her head, shrilly berating him, and Charlie, drenched, was on his mobile beside a Saab immobilised by a yellow clamp. As they all splashed by, Rosie and Charlie's eyes had made contact and he'd winked, making her heart skip.

She could still feel that pleasurable thrill when her loser boyfriend had crawled in on unsteady legs, stinking of booze, at four that morning. The next day, on courage borrowed from who knows where, she'd finally told him it was over.

How many times after had she dragged her friends to that wine bar without seeing Charlie again?

Then came that hen night, a magical evening when the Gods of mirth shone down, making everything they said hilariously funny, every venue fabulous. No one noticed the tall, broad-shouldered man as the future bride and bridesmaids stumbled up the nightclub stairs. Then a waitress handed Rosie, of all things, a honeydew melon. Wiping tears of laughter, Rosie spluttered out that she'd made a mistake – the bride-to-be was the one in veiled tiara and leopard thong, gleefully cracking a phallic-looking whip.

The girl's expression said it had been a long night. 'Other side, love.'

Peering bleary-eyed, they saw a carved message. 'CAN I BUY U A…' with a crude sketch of a glass. Minutes later, to everyone's delight, a bottle of Dom Pérignon arrived. No clue to the sender. It wasn't until she passed the downstairs bar on her way to the toilets that Charlie had greeted her. She never did understand why she'd been the chosen one.

The day he'd asked her to marry him was the happiest of her life.

'Won't last,' her mother had announced. 'What is he, thirty? Too old – and far too handsome. Been around the block a few times, I'll bet. You'll never keep a man like that.'

'He's only twenty-eight.' Nineteen-year-old Rosie refused to let her mother's cynicism spoil the best thing ever to happen to her. 'And he's ready to settle down.'

Of course her mum was now happily saying, 'I told you so', even though for so many years they'd proved her wrong.

But in the end she hadn't kept him, had she? Charlie was firmly ensconced in the expensive house near Highgate he'd jointly bought with the female customer now known to their old friends as 'Charlie's new fiancée'.

The credit crunch had hit them too. Charlie's dealership was practically offering cars at cost; so desperate were they to shift them. Hadn't he sat and explained his financial struggles to Rosie on that very sofa just a few weeks ago, declaring he still thought of her as 'his very best friend'?

Was it so wrong to feel just a mite sorry for him and to be pleased, in her most secret heart, that he still cared for her at all?

'Before you say anything,' Rosie returned with two mugs on a tray and a pre-rehearsed speech, 'I'm expecting a substantial payment from my ex-husband, which should sort everything out. I'm usually exceptionally, er, meticulously monetarily aware of the importance of fiscal record-keeping and, um, usually extremely efficient about paying bills and this brief hiccup is by no means—'

'What?' The visitor took the mug, looking startled. 'No, it's nothing like that. I'm here because...'

...because I need to evict you? Rosie held her breath, imagining an absurd scene straight from her beloved historical romances. She and her sons trawling through cobblestoned streets, pushing a wooden cart of meagre possessions as she rasped, 'Any room at the inn for two little 'uns and their sick old mum?'

'Because...' the stranger repeated, eyes twinkling, mouth suppressing a grin.

'Yes?'

Perhaps the girl was crazy? Rosie clasped her hands tightly in her lap, feeling a touch crazed herself with the suspense. A mad young woman who wheedled her way into random homes then refused to leave. Or even finish her sentences.

The bailiff-cum-lunatic leaned forward, smiling. 'I'm from the Premium Bonds.'

'But...I haven't...bought...any...' Even as she spoke, Rosie's mind flicked to her twenty-first birthday. A friend handing over a card with a certificate inside. 'I didn't think Premium Bonds still existed.'

'Oh they most certainly do. Safer investment than the banks after the way they've been behaving.' The girl crossed her shapely legs, opening a folder. 'And I'm pleased to inform you, Mrs Rose Ann Dixon, that you've won a prize.'

'You're kidding!' Rosie's jaw dropped.

'Luckily I'm not.'

'But that's...well...very good. Thank you *so* much.' Rosie laughed for the first time that day. How much was it? she wondered. Fifty quid? Hundred? 'I've never won *a thing* before. And your job's to go around informing all the winners?'

'Only the ones who've won the jackpot!'

'The...the what?'

'I'm Agent Million.' She laughed at Rosie's stunned expression. 'Ernie's picked out your numbers and I have here,' she brandished a rectangular slip of paper boldly printed with the initials NSI, 'a cheque for one million pounds!'

Chapter Four

'Livvy! Livvy!'

God, she felt like crap. Olivia's skull pounded, her arms and legs were tightly bound, nausea sweeping in a wave when she moved her head. Why couldn't she move? Had she been kidnapped? Drugged? And why wouldn't that awful banging and shouting go away?

Twice her eyelids fluttered open, only to be skewered by harsh daylight. Finally, she succeeded in freeing one arm from a tangle of sheets and shoved the pillow over her head. Everything hurt.

The door opened and Beth's voice penetrated her cocoon.

'Come on, Livvy. I've brought you up a coffee.'

So that's where she was. England. London.

'Go away. I'm dying.'

'Not surprised after the state you were in last night. You looked like you'd done ten rounds in a cage fight. What in heaven's name happened?'

'Don't know. Don't care.' It was all coming back now. The horrors. The humiliation. The days she'd spent, shut up and crying in her apartment, until she'd decided to flee. She buried her head even deeper under the pillow. Her friend pulled it away.

'It's gone eight. I have to get to work and drop Jessie at nursery. Rise and shine.'

'Shine?' Olivia croaked, covering her eyes. 'You got to be joking.'

'You can't spend your whole life in bed.'

'Why not?' Let the next twenty years go by, today's scandal sinking into the muddy pools of ancient history, and then maybe she'd be ready to face the world. Totter out of the bedroom with hair to waist, unshaven legs and pits, and see if humankind had succeeded in destroying the planet or if they were all whizzing around like the Jetsons in robot-controlled hovercars.

Meanwhile uninterrupted oblivion, no memories, no pain.

Was that how her mother had felt when…? But no, she skittered away from that dangerous line of thinking.

'Look,' Beth gave her a gentle shake, 'it's not as bad as all that. It's only money.'

'*Four billion dollars? Only money*?' Olivia rolled over, hand shielding her eyes like a visor. 'Tell that to the stock exchange, the plummeting market. Or the people who've lost everything they've ever owned. Including me. Oh Beth, it was dreadful. They had crime scene tape everywhere. They kept us in a room, took away our computers and cell phones, asked questions for *hours*. They treated us like…like criminals.'

'Poor thing. I know. It was a nightmare.'

'Did I tell you what Brad said?' Olivia flopped over again.

She nodded. 'So unfair. He sounds like a creep.'

'He thinks it's all *my* fault,' Olivia moaned. She could still see his white angry face, eyes red-rimmed and hate-filled, the jerky clumsy movements with which he pulled drawer after drawer on to the floor, cramming her expensive designer outfits into supermarket boxes. 'I gave him his engagement ring back. Threw it actually. I didn't force him to stick his stupid money with Mandrake. He *begged* me to introduce him.'

But then why *would* she expect Brad to charge to her defence? He'd always seemed more like an indulged carefree young boy than shining knight, his emotional growth stunted by a surfeit of privilege and lack of obstacles. It had been part of his appeal, a happy contrast to her own cynicism and driving ambition. So naturally he'd let her down. Just like her dad, all those years ago. And every man since.

'And then his dad pulled up in his car, waving his shotgun. Said if I didn't clear out that instant, he was going to fire.'

Beth's round cheerful face looked troubled as she stooped to rescue a crumpled scrunched-up sleeveless top that had cost Olivia $350 at Neiman Marcus. 'I'm sure he didn't mean—'

'You bet he did. He's probably hired hit men to track me down. Old man Winton's bloody ruthless and he blames me too. They all do. Brad's parents, their friends and—'

Olivia wriggled to a sitting position, reaching for the hot drink. 'Even my own friends... I couldn't stand it, Beth, everyone hating me, my phone ringing off the hook, reporters pestering me for statements. I had to leave New York. I'd be evicted eventually anyway. I'm...' Putting the coffee down, she swung her legs over the side of the bed, clad only in camisole and skimpy thong. 'I'm broke!'

'So you mentioned. A few hundred times.'

Olivia missed the sarcasm. She ran her hands wildly through her hair, leaving it standing on end, elbows on knees, eyes fixed on the floor. 'The Connaught said my American Express was refused. So humiliating – I had to leave.' Panic rose again. 'I've never been broke before. Or hungry. Except perhaps when my great-aunt Winnie tried to feed me some gross old canned meat, probably left over from the Crimean war.' She almost gagged at the memory. 'And even then Dad sent me an allowance.'

She sprang to her feet, staggered, and caught the bedpost to steady herself. 'I'm going to get a gun, that's what I'm going to do. And when I see Rupert...'

'Oh for Pete's sake,' Beth reached the end of her patience, 'you're in England, not the Wild West. Besides no one knows where Mandrake is. There's an international manhunt on.' She stooped as her foot connected with something that clinked. 'Oh no! Olivia! Not the last of Simon's eighteen-year-old Glenlivet. If you're going to drink yourself to death, could you *at least* stay out of his booze?'

Eek. Olivia winced, hands clutching tighter at her skull. Not the husband's stash. 'Did I? Oh shoot. I'll pay him back. When I get on my feet again. Promise.'

Oops, perhaps she was still a tad drunk. Her only clear memory from the fog that was last night was Simon's too-audible whisper, 'How much longer do we have to put up with this?'

Poor Beth. The look on her face when she'd answered the door over two weeks ago and saw Olivia sitting on the larger of two oversized suitcases. She'd actually rubbed her eyes, mouth slack like a shocked goldfish.

'Livvy? Oh my God?'

'Look what the wind blew in.' Olivia had grinned sheepishly. And well she might be sheepish.

How long since they'd been in touch? Olivia was sure she'd sent a Christmas card, well…a while back…and at least one Facebook message. Besides, that was the great thing about old friends. Beth had always been her faithful shadow in the abysmal days Olivia spent with her elderly Aunt Winnie, and even roommates for the first year of college until, well…maybe they'd drifted a bit then too. But you couldn't break that kind of bond. She hoped.

With a shriek of delight, Beth had pulled her into a bear hug that Olivia – not a touchy-feely person – suffered with stiff awkwardness, and dragged her two heavy suitcases into the narrow hallway.

Olivia's childhood companion had put on a whole bunch of weight since their last meeting. She'd always complained that slight, undersized, sharp-boned Olivia had made her feel like a jolly green giant with her hockey player bulk, round cheeks and squashy nose – Little and Large, they'd joked. But now her face was flushed, her hair a mess of wiry curls and she looked positively maternal.

She'd bustled Olivia into the living room, where a slump-shouldered man in a shapeless cardigan and sheepskin slippers – yes, actual slippers, darling, seemingly people do still wear them – was watching TV. He was fair-haired – as far as his marginal hair went – sunk in a gloomy expression that made him look decades older than forty or whatever he was. One of England's defeated grey men, Olivia's father would have called him. The husband.

Peter? Simon? Matthew, Mark, Luke or John? Embarrassingly, Olivia couldn't remember. She'd turned down the honour of Chief Bridesmaid and skipped the wedding with a humorous note saying she'd come to the next one.

On the TV screen a red-faced man was bellowing at the camera. '...ought to be hanged, the lot of them. MC Capital...parcel of crooks...'

Moving swiftly, Beth switched the channel, flipping to a *Simpsons* cartoon. Oh well, it was too much to hope there was anyone left on the planet who hadn't heard the bad news.

'When did you get in? Oh it's great to see you.' She glanced down at the dirt on her knees. 'Sorry I'm such a mess. I've been potting geraniums.'

'I'm broke.' Olivia had blurted it out without thinking. Pathetic. She changed tactics. 'I mean...I'm planning to spend a few days with Aunt Winnie.' Trying to sound excited by the prospect. 'Thought I'd pop in and say hello before I went over.'

She glanced around the modest sitting room, dominated by the corner TV. There was a pastel sofa and two armchairs obscured by flowery cushions, lace curtains, buttercream walls, a vase of dried flowers on the boarded-up hearth and a few cutesy figurines of baby animals and kissing children. It was all so...Beth. Probably she'd made the colourful rag rug too. Amazing that Beth had opted to stay in the neighbourhood Olivia had so despised, mere yards from her parents' home. If Olivia hadn't remembered the address, the riotous flower garden would have been a certain clue. Beth always had green fingers. Though her nails were distinctly black right now.

'You don't know?' Jaw dropping, Beth wiped her hands on her unflattering sweatpants. 'The old lady got admitted to Helmshott Manor last August. They found her wandering around Morrisons in her nightie.'

'Oh my God!' Shocked, Olivia sat on the arm of the nearest chair. 'Why didn't anyone tell me?'

Beth stared. 'I'm sure they did. You're next of kin, after all. Someone must have written. Or phoned. But don't worry. You can stay here as long as you like. Can't she, Simon?'

Eyes glued to the TV, Simon grunted without a hint of his wife's eagerness. Possibly he was shy – or depressed – or maybe stoned out of his mind with a few too many hits on a hidden bong but it was hardly a rousing welcome. Since then he'd barely said two words to his uninvited guest.

As Beth bustled around, putting discarded garments into her laundry basket, Olivia glanced down at her naked leg. She had a bruise the shape, and almost the size, of China on her pale toned thigh. Vaguely she remembered falling off a bar stool? A bar? Or was it a pub? Yes, although she loathed pubs, nasty dirty things, crushes of people pushing against you, toilets you'd be crazy to sit down on, and never an available table. She'd been drinking elbow to elbow, talking to someone. Then – crash. On her back, legs sprawled, laughing hysterically. Hands had helped lift her up. Unwashed labourers' hands for all she knew. Nasty germy hands. Touching her.

Oh God, anything could have happened. She'd been so drunk, so vulnerable. Alcohol might have replaced the tears which had soaked her pillow in the first days after that fateful meeting with Shipton but it hadn't removed the pain.

Beth looked worried. She paused in her attempts to tidy and put her hands on her hips.

'You need to get it together, Livvy. You've been here over a fortnight and you haven't done a single interview. And Simon… Well, you can't stay forever and he's understandably upset about that red wine on the hall carpet. This might all seem like the end of the world right now but think how much worse off you could be. At least no one's out to arrest you.' She frowned. 'They're not, are they?'

Olivia shook her head. Another mistake. Her brains continued to slosh even when she'd stopped. 'Well, the Feds may have mentioned being a witness. It's all a blur. I'm sure I wasn't told *not* to leave the country.' She focussed on her once-immaculate nail polish, now chipped. 'Anyway there can't be a trial until they catch Mandrake.'

'They could try his accomplices though. Not that you're an accomplice,' Beth added hastily. 'Look, all I'm saying is – you haven't even visited your great-aunt yet. When was the last time you saw her?' She paused, looking awkward. 'I hate to ask but...all that money you were making. Didn't you help her out?'

'I offered. I even sent her cheques but she returned them. Said she was doing quite well, thank you very much. Dad left her quite a lot of money. She had that companion, Edith, who lived with her. And I... Well the last few years have been so hectic.' Olivia squirmed with self-loathing. Unforgivable. There simply was no excuse. Even if she and Aunt Winnie had never seen eye to eye. Or even, as a child, eye to vast Victorian bosom.

'Yeah.' Beth gave a heavy sigh. 'She's always been a stubborn old bird. I stop by and visit when I can. We social workers see it all the time. Pensioners losing their savings, even their homes, to pay for nursing care. Meanwhile...' bitterness crept in, 'all these refugees and no-good slackers get it all for free.'

Another change. Her friend had been so liberal in college. A bleeding heart as Brad's father, the staunch Republican, would say.

Olivia reached for a t-shirt, strangely self-conscious of her revealing camisole, trainer-moulded abs and flimsy lace thong. Beth had always had legs like sturdy young oaks but her stomach had expanded to something even Spanx couldn't save. Of course, she also had a (presumably) loving husband, a doting daughter and a job that obviously didn't expect her to dance along an ever-changing tightrope between feminine but not provocative, sexy yet professional. If Olivia wore a shapeless tweed skirt like Beth's to MC Capital, that prick Rupert would have accused her of wearing a horse blanket and hustled her home to change.

She rubbed her face, yawning. 'I thought you were book-keeping?'

'Not for the last three years.' The hurt was obvious. 'Didn't you read any of my letters? Oh, forget it.' Beth added some dirty mugs and plates of barely touched food to her overflowing laundry basket. 'Just clean up before we're overrun with ants. I don't want Jessie to see this mess – or get freaked out by Mummy's scary friend.' She gave a hard stare. 'It's pasta for dinner tonight. Is that on your weirdo diet?'

'I'll find something to nibble on. I don't mean to be a pain.' Olivia wanted to say more but the words choked in her throat.

'It's OK. You'd do the s...' The platitude withered. Olivia had the uneasy feeling they were both thinking the same thing. Selfish, self-centred Olivia Wheeler.

'Better make it up to me, that's all,' Beth finished with a grim smile. 'Here.' Stripping off the bedding, she loaded Olivia's limp unresisting arms with sheets and pillowcases. 'Throw these in the washing machine. I suggest a hot bath and then ringing a few employment agencies. And for God's sake eat some breakfast. If not cornflakes and toast you can do fruit, at least. Last thing I need is you getting ill on me.'

Olivia's eyes filled with gratitude. 'Thanks, Beth, you're a pal.'

She made a move to touch her hand, burdened though she was. To her surprise Beth pulled back. 'Don't bother, Livvy. We both know you'd be miles away if you'd anywhere else to go.'

They stared at each other. Beth's eyes were dark with emotion, Olivia's face flushed with shame. In the dresser mirror she glimpsed a frightening apparition. Dirty hair in a greasy tangle, hollowed eyes black with encrusted mascara, green-tinged features clownishly smeared with make-up.

'That's not...' The word 'true' hovered on Olivia's lips but she couldn't finish. Clearly their two paths had veered off in a dramatic V, another casualty in the Wheeler quest for better and brighter things.

Beth swallowed, biting her lips, backing off with a visible effort. 'Just try a bit harder, that's all. You'll get over this Brad, and what's a little cash in the scheme of things? The Olivia I remember was a fighter. Honestly, you say you're skint but Simon and I work every day and we can't afford to go drinking every night. You still have your health. Brains. Even your looks, damn it.' She gave a hollow laugh. 'The trouble with you, Livvy, is that you've always been so lucky. And you don't even realise it.'

Lucky? Well, it was all in the way you looked at things, she supposed. At this precise moment she might have been luckier if Brad's father *had* fired that shotgun.

Then again… Beth hadn't *had* to take her in. Or Simon could have stamped his slippered foot down and refused. And what had been their reward?

Vomit.

Spilled wine.

And stolen scotch.

The sad truth was Olivia knew she was here on sufferance, an unwelcome, barely tolerable intruder. Nobody out there gave a toss if she lived or died.

And, really, could you blame them?

Chapter Five

'I could *so* easily get used to this.' The cocktail's skewer of fruit chunks nearly pierced Rosie's left nostril. Which one was it – Sex on the Rocks or Brazilian Crush? She'd lost track.

'Best digs on the beach.' Her friend, Anya raised her Frisky Diva with an ear to ear grin. 'Cheers.'

'Well, if I can't splash out for once in my life,' Rosie signalled the barman for another round, 'what on earth's the point of it all?'

Was there ever a better recipe for happiness?

Sunshine: bright.

Sea: azure.

Golden sands dotted with comfortable padded loungers.

And a bevy of free and lethal cocktails.

El Gran Palacio Del Oro, Marbella's newest, most luxurious all-inclusive resort, boasted four acclaimed restaurants, three gigantic dazzling pools, and a multitude of activities, from windsurfing to parasailing, all at their disposal – if they could ever tear themselves away from the drinks list.

They sat under the shade of an enormous straw parasol, Rosie in a tie-dyed tangerine t-shirt and faded denim shorts beside a bikini-clad, cowboy-hatted Anya, whose chair was turned sideways to face the full force of the sun. Unlike Rosie, rubbing another dollop of Factor 50 on her reddening shoulders, Anya's gorgeous olive skin seldom suffered sunburn, lucky thing.

Was it truly less than two weeks since Agent Million had swept into Rosie's life like a modern-day fairy godmother, changing everything with three small words?

⚜ ⚜ ⚜

One Million Pounds.

The woman continued to speak but she could well have been lecturing on Latvian lace-making for all Rosie heard.

One...million...pounds. Staring open-mouthed, Rosie's head reeled as she tried making sense of the amount. One thousand thousand pounds. A hundred would have been fabulous, thousand a miracle but one *million*...

She'd seen the films (*Slumdog Millionaire*), watched the documentaries (*Secret Millionaire*), sat through the TV game shows (*Million Pound Drop*) – even hummed happily away to *Who Wants to Be a Millionaire,* never envisaging for a moment that she'd ever come near to that much money in her entire life.

The events that followed were a blur. Later, she remembered looking for hidden cameras or someone to leap out and scream, 'Fooled ya.' She'd stammered questions. Could there be another Rose Ann Dixon? Was it absolutely a hundred per cent totally certain? There'd been a second cup of tea, this time made by the Premium Bond representative while Rosie went upstairs, scrabbled through her battered filing box to unearth her bond and shakily checked her numbers against Ernie's.

Afterwards Agent Million recommended they visit the bank together, so Rosie left her sons next door with Anya, who'd just come off early shift, then it was into this flash silver car to her local Lloyds branch to deposit the cheque. The popping of the teller's eyes, the ten-second pause as he scrutinised the flimsy piece of paper – Rosie holding her breath and sucking in her stomach for some subliminal reason. But he never handed it back, saying ha, good try. No, instead he simply slipped it into the slot in his small cream-coloured machine, ran both hands over his keyboard like a concert pianist performing the 'Flight of the Bumble Bee' and then it zipped anti-clockwise, came out the other side, he placed it into his drawer and that was that.

Next please.

Except…

That as she was leaving, the Bank Manager, who'd been harassing her lately with threatening letters, hustled to the exit, pumped her hand and tried to coax her to his office for a friendly chat. And it was with great delight that she turned him down.

Back outside Rosie's house, Agent Million joined her on the pavement. 'I know this is a shock, Rosie, and it's your money so you can do what you like but if I can suggest three small things…'

Rosie stared, feeling that she'd entered a fairy tale.

'One,' Agent Million handed over a clipboard for Rosie's signature, 'choose wisely who you tell. Less people at first the better, perhaps – you'll get some funny reactions, not all pleasant.' She passed Rosie a copy of the document, stashing the other in her briefcase. 'Two, it often helps to stick to routines.' She grinned. 'Wait a day or two before jacking in your job and buying a string of racehorses. And three, any problems, call us. We've a whole investment team to help you and I'm here if you need a friendly ear. We don't just throw your life in turmoil and run.'

She slid into her car and waved.

'Enjoy. Have fun. Be happy.'

As the silver car pulled away, a stunned Rosie walked up to Anya's door. It opened and instantly fat tears rolled down her cheeks. She saw alarm on Anya's face and flapped a hand, trying to catch her breath, hiccupping, which made her laugh, half-choke and sob again. It took five minutes, her worried friend passing over tissues, for Rosie to recover enough to explain.

After all she had to tell *someone.*

And Anya couldn't have been more thrilled. Screaming, jumping up and down, smothering her with kisses and hugs.

'You need a fabulous holiday. Right away. To celebrate.' Anya chinked white wine glasses filled to the brim. 'The Seychelles. Or the Caribbean. Or…' Her big Bambi eyes were alive with excitement.

'Whoa, hold on.' Rosie raised her hand, slightly giddy. 'You're forgetting something. 'Charlie's taking the boys to Cornwall this half-term.'

'Can't you go without them?' Anya had changed from her green uniform required for the nursing home where she worked, into a colourful dress, dark hair loose and feet bare. 'You deserve a break.'

'On my own?' Rosie grimaced. 'Charlie got most of our friends in the divorce. You're my only real mate apart from Gemma.'

And thank God for Anya. She'd been an absolute lifeline when Rosie, shell-shocked, grieving, newly divorced, had moved next door, forming a strong supportive friendship over borrowed milk, babysitting emergencies, and lots of takeaways and wine.

'Yeah, well,' Anya's wiggling eyebrows suggested Rosie had just hit another jackpot, 'I was saving for a new roof – but hey...'

The idea took root, blossomed. In a few weeks' time it would be Anya's big 'three-oh'. And after so much scrimping, how tremendous to do something wild, something that'd blow the constant struggle of always making do into well-deserved oblivion.

'Let's go for it!' Rosie was suddenly enthusiastic. 'After all it's not exactly a string of racehorses.' She explained Agent Million's advice to her friend.

'Quite right too,' Anya said soberly. 'People aren't always as nice as you think they are, Rosie.'

Luke wandered into the kitchen, followed by Tim.

'What people aren't nice?' he asked.

'Everyone's lovely.' Rosie rushed to hug and tickle them, an ordeal to which Luke submitted unwillingly and Tim quite enjoyed. 'Listen, guys, I'm taking us all out to dinner. Anywhere you want. Italian. Chinese. Indian. You choose.'

'Burger King,' Luke declared, sweeping back his long floppy fringe. He'd recently acquired a 'girlfriend', insisted on growing his hair long and dressing like a stylish dude.

'Maccy D,' Tim argued. He was still her baby boy, Rosie thought fondly, a scruffy good-natured tyke who thought the girls in his class were lame.

'Oh well,' Rosie shrugged helplessly at Anya, 'not what I had in mind but... Want to join us?'

'Maybe next time.' Anya drained her glass and hugged Rosie goodbye. 'I couldn't be happier for you, babes,' she whispered, close to Rosie's ear. 'Madly jealous, naturally but it couldn't have happened to a sweeter person.'

'Oh Anya,' tears welling, Rosie squeezed her hand, 'it's not going to change things between us, is it?'

'Change things, babes?' Anya playfully tapped her cheek. 'Bleeding better.'

So here they were. Marbella, jewel of the Costa del Sol. She'd tricked Anya by paying for the whole thing in advance and refusing to accept a penny. Such unfair tactics had sparked a hail of protests, but stepping into the eye-popping marble lobby brought instant forgiveness. By the time the golf cart had driven them to a darling little casita, secluded by tropical shrubbery, they knew they'd arrived in paradise.

And why not? It was Rosie's first splurge. Even once the cheque cleared, she'd found it hard to cut loose. Besides buying the boys two longed-for mountain bikes it wasn't until Gatwick airport that she'd first splashed out, twisting Anya's arm to make her accept the La Senza knicker and bra set that she'd drooled over. Smiling, Rosie adjusted her new Gucci square-framed sunglasses, still shocked by their £190 price tag.

She'd only been abroad twice before. First time was her honeymoon in Turkey where she'd dragged a wilting Charlie through San Sofia, the Blue Mosque and the biblical ruins of Ephesus in a forty degree heat wave. The second, a waterlogged camping holiday in Brittany where even Rosie had been unable to persuade her sodden, shivering family they were all having a whoopee time.

Feeling the heat more acutely now, Rosie shyly slid off her shorts to reveal the sexy royal blue bikini Anya had persuaded her to buy from the hotel's very expensive boutique.

A waiter, carrying a pitcher of Sangria past their straw parasol, gave her an appreciative look and something stirred inside Rosie, something new and possibly dangerous. She struggled to interpret the unfamiliar symptoms. Palpitations. Dry mouth. Was it fear? Apprehension? Guilt at leaving her sons – who'd jumped into their dad's car without a backward glance?

Or was it this whole new life opening up before her – a world of possibilities hitherto unimagined. Luck could turn in an instant. One minute financially strapped, besieged by problems. The next…

'Did you tell Charlie yet?' Anya adjusted her hat to cover half-closed eyes.

Rosie shook her head, bare feet resting on an empty chair. 'No. Nor the kids. Too big a secret for them to keep, especially visiting their grandparents. Agent Million's right. I want time to adjust.'

'I'd love to be a fly on the wall when Charlie hears the news. If he hadn't run off with Vile Val, he'd be here, lazing in luxury, instead of his parents' crummy cottage. He'll be sor-ry.' Anya chanted the last word.

Sorry? Rosie had sensed regret in Charlie several times. When he'd dropped off the boys. When he lingered for a hot drink.

But now…wow, she actually had one up on her handsome, fickle ex. A million dollars up.

Yes, the bikini, the glasses and this holiday were only the start. She had money now. She wasn't the shy, mousy frump who'd lived in the shadow of a far more glamorous husband or the harassed working mother trying to scrape by. Perhaps she *could* transform herself? Turn into a suave, sophisticated beauty. Someone who'd bring Charlie to his knees, someone he couldn't help but fall in love with all over again. Oh yes, he'd be sor-ry. And she might even make him suffer before she took him back.

With a whoop of joy she dragged Anya to her feet and together they ran shrieking to the sea.

Chapter Six

Olivia's high heels tapped past the Slug and Lettuce, scene of last night's misdemeanours. Bits and pieces of the evening's debacle were returning, each more unsavoury than the last. Drunkenly spilling her story to some unknown creep, hair falling over her eyes as she got louder and sloppier. Falling on her ass. Arguing with the barman when he refused to serve her another drink. Being kicked out into the street.

Hastily she crossed the road, ducking her face away, hoping business suit, styled hair and make-up would prove sufficient disguise. She saw a coin shining on the pavement and stopped to pick it up.

Heads, the Angel tube station would take her to the City.

Tails, she'd go North, visit Aunt Winnie.

Her heart was thumping, fast enough to bring on a stroke, her blood pressure probably sky high. Nervously she smoothed her ineptly ironed suit skirt. Once upon a time head-hunters had come courting her, keen to appropriate her talents. But that was before she'd hitched her rising star to Rupert Mandrake's fiery comet and the market was still reverberating from that particular meteoric crash.

No, she was too nauseous for humble pie.

Winnie it was then. Poor old dear. Thrifty and reclusive she may have been but when Olivia still lived in London, on her rare visits to her great-aunt, Aunt Winnie would inevitably hobble to her tea caddy for a gift of five pounds. Which Olivia, hardly lacking with her extremely well-paid City job, would have to secrete somewhere where Winnie was sure to find it after she left.

The flower vender looked up as she stopped by the stall.

'What'll it be, dear? Fancy bouquet? Or cheap and cheerful?'

'Cheap and cheerful.'

She'd forgotten how expensive London taxis were. The clicking taxi meter gave her a stressful forty minutes, cursing every red light, inching through atrocious traffic. Gazing at the choked streets, she remembered her dismay when she'd first arrived from Marbella, how oppressive England had seemed, how pale and sun-starved the inhabitants. Of course it hadn't helped that she'd been virtually ejected from her home, consigned to boarding school, driven from paradise by…that bitch.

Her gut twisted, memories flooding back: her mother, wildly dancing flamenco in their Spanish villa, or sobbing terrifyingly for hours. Bipolar, Olivia guessed now. Manic-depressive. Unbalanced. Whatever you wanted to call it. All Olivia knew was that somehow she always felt it was her fault, that if she were better, nicer, more whatever, her mother wouldn't be so sad.

The fatal overdose had come when Olivia was six.

Then, after the sadness, there followed glorious unregulated chaos. Olivia and her dad were more like best buddies than father and daughter, living the good life among Marbella's ex-pat community. Olivia was included in every late-night dinner, every all-night party, bedtimes were non-existent; meals were scrounged from the fridge or whatever you asked the maid to cook at no particular hour. No one fussed at her to do her homework. By the age of thirteen, school was pretty much optional. Dad had girlfriends, obviously, but nobody serious until SHE had come along.

What wiles had his nubile young mistress used to get his precocious teenage princess banished to boarding school in England? By Olivia's first holiday the interloper had moved in. The adored only child hadn't disguised her hostility and to her shock and chagrin found herself spending the next school break with her father's spinster aunt in London.

The stays with reclusive Great-aunt Winnie became more routine, the visits home rare. Not even glowing report cards and Olivia's entreaties could soften her father. He was too busy for distractions, he said, in the midst of a wild creative breakthrough, working on his latest sculpture. More likely the girlfriend was scheming to keep her away. When Graeme Wheeler died of a brain aneurism, his not inconsiderable estate was left in trust for sixteen-year-old Olivia with the proviso that his live-in slut could stay in the villa unless she married. And Winnie, last remaining relative, became Olivia's guardian.

Aunt Winnie... Frugal enough to make Winston Churchill proud, arguing over new shoes or a dress because the old ones were perfectly serviceable. Cutting mould from bread and using souring milk because throwing things out was a criminal waste. No wonder Olivia's stomach couldn't tolerate either now. Luckily she'd always had her allowance squirrelled away for luxuries she had to keep hidden.

She'd been a teenage horror then, spoilt, sullen and rebellious, but she could still feel the overwhelming heartbreak of her dad's sudden death. And then his will, insisting she let that cow of an interloper inhabit their family home indefinitely. She had never set foot in Spain again.

Glory be! Olivia shot bolt upright. Salvation!

The Spanish villa, mostly forgotten all these years, was ironically the one bit of her inheritance still intact. Something none of her debtors would know about. Something – surely – out of reach of the IRS. The mistress had moved on and remarried. Property managers had been handling rentals until it had apparently got too rundown to attract tenants and they'd started sending emails asking for further instructions. She'd always meant to take one last visit before selling, see if there were any valuable or sentimental relics of times past she might like to keep. But there'd simply never been time.

Wreck or not, she thought as the taxi drove through the wrought iron gates of the nursing home, it must have some value. Could she move there? No, she decided. Even if she was able to afford a flight, what would she do? Camp in an empty house, devoid of furniture? Would hardly add to the market appeal. She pictured a sleeping bag and sandwich wrappers. Ugh.

Another thought hit her as the taxi followed the driveway through rambling gardens, past a man-made lake with swans to an ivy-coloured Victorian building. What if squatters had moved in?

Her momentary elation had well and truly faded by the time she paid the extortionate fare. Reluctantly she pushed open the heavy door, anticipating sickening odours: urine, old people, boiled fish. She headed towards two women dressed in khaki scrubs at a semi-circular reception desk. A board listed Activities for Today: Piano Sing-A-Long, Bingo, Chair Aerobics, Bus trip to Regent's Park Zoo. Not exactly *One Flew Over the Cuckoo's Nest.*

'All about greed, isn't it?' one of the attendants was saying. 'That's what controls the world today. Those developers—' She noticed Olivia. 'Can I help you?'

'Winifred Powell?'

'Hairdressers. Second floor.'

Great-aunt Winnie was in a wheelchair under the dryer, giant rollers secured to her thinning scalp. Her posture was as upright as ever, eyes a faded periwinkle.

'Hello, Doris,' she greeted Olivia imperiously. 'Fancy you booking on this cruise.' She patted the rollers in her damp white hair. 'Remember, I saw the captain first.'

Well, this was new. The Aunt Winnie she knew was intimidating, sharp of mind and tongue, all spit and vinegar, elbow grease, crochet hooks wielded like deadly weapons, smelling of ghastly home-made remedies, mothballs and lavender sachets. Olivia could easily have imagined her in a triage tent among the trenches, barking orders at army surgeons in a starched white apron, but never in a cocktail dress batting eyes at cruise ship captains.

Olivia bent to kiss her cheek, pushing the bouquet into crepey freckled hands. 'I'm Livvy, Aunt Winnie. Graeme's child.'

'Graeme?' The old lady turned up her hearing aid. 'That rascal. Has he been expelled again?'

Batty as any underground cave system. Now what? She was oddly let down, disappointed even. Aunt Winnie wasn't much but she was Olivia's only relative, the one link left to her father. And what was the point of visiting someone who'd no idea who you were?

Then again it wasn't like she had any other pressing engagements.

The buxom Jamaican hairdresser gave Olivia a conspiratorial wink.

'Let's get those rollers out now, shall we?' She raised the dryer hood and began unwrapping curls. 'There, now don't you look pretty, my darling.'

Winnie stared at Olivia in the mirror. 'Can Doris come to my birthday party?'

'Of course,' the woman said in her rich melodious tones, spraying the blue-rinsed head as if attacking a hornets' nest. 'Doris is welcome. Be sure you invite her to lunch.'

That settled it.

'It's Olivia actually.' Olivia coughed. 'Mind if I take her out of here? If you're done?'

'No problem.' The hairdresser smiled. 'There's a visitor's room on the ground floor.'

In the day room Aunt Winnie proved a dab hand at gin rummy, while making rude comments about the other residents. 'Watch him, Doris,' she said as an elderly man hobbled by. 'Randy bugger.'

A silver-haired woman in a pink dressing-gown tugged Olivia's sleeve. 'Have you seen my moccasin?' She was a tiny wrinkled china doll. 'Mummy's taking me home today and I can't leave until I find it.'

'It's on your foot, you daft old bat,' Aunt Winnie said, acerbic as ever but with visible glee. 'And your mama's run off with the milkman so toddle off and leave us be.'

Olivia discovered she was surprisingly entertained. She won a tube of Smarties at bingo, took part in a lusty sing-a-long, lunched on roast chicken followed by baked apples and felt her jangled nerves loosen as volunteers from a nearby beauty college lovingly massaged her hands. There were only a couple of queasy moments. Once when the nurse arrived to take her great-aunt's blood pressure and once when Winnie asked her to escort her to the bathroom (luckily, a nurse dealt with that too). Silly to be so squeamish but both times she took the excuse to bolt into the ladies' room and wash her hands, staring with recriminating gaze at her selfish loathsome reflection.

It was easy to forget and ignore an old lady when you lived the high life on the other side of the Atlantic, imagine her somehow pickled in amber, preserved in time and daily routine exactly as remembered. Quite something else to be present and realise exactly how many devastating neglectful years had passed.

All too soon it was two o'clock. The ATM in the lobby devoured both her credit cards with nary a belch nor an apology. After her relaxed morning, it was a rude awakening.

Even the bus was an unfamiliar ordeal. People grumbled behind her in the queue, travel cards in hand, as the driver rejected Olivia's ten pound note and hesitant, 'One please.' He nodded at a sign, 'Buy ticket before boarding', sending her back through the pushing crowd, onto the pavement. When she finally managed to reboard and squeeze into a space that was standing room only, she was red-faced and flummoxed, staggering into someone's bony knees as the bus bumped down the street.

God, it sucked being poor. The baby on its mother's lap had a runny nose. Someone not far away was coughing. Germ central! She hated touching the overhead strap, the back of the seats. She hadn't realised how money cushioned her from minor unpleasantness: wet umbrellas, scruffy youths pressed against her, kids stepping on her feet.

But the indignities were only just beginning.

'We don't usually handle your line of work. If only you were a telemarketer.' The girl in the employment agency sighed. 'OK, what was your last salary?'

Foreseeing problems, Olivia omitted the last two years' mega-bonuses but still the girl stopped tapping. 'I couldn't... Why on earth would you leave?'

Olivia rolled her eyes, knowing it was hopeless. 'Oh, the usual. Swindler boss. Grand larceny. Personal vendettas. Death threats. I'm good with figures, does that help?'

Then on to the City, her watch showing three-fifteen. Probably she should have gone there first but turned out there was no rush, every worst fear justified. Those connections in the Square Mile who deigned to see her only wanted to satisfy their curiosity. How could Mandrake imagine he'd get away with it? Hadn't she had even an inkling? Where did she think he was hiding out? She sensed there were only two explanations for her demise. Crooked? Or stupid?

And then the feigned regret. Hard times. This economy, you know. (*And Mandrake's caper hasn't made it any better.*) It didn't need saying.

'My dear girl,' a one-time mentor, her first employer after university, summed it up, 'the word is out on you. Doom and destruction to anyone who takes you on. Jeffrey Winton's a powerful man. Besides – four billion dollars in missing funds? After MC Capital, you'll be lucky if anyone trusts you to serve the coffee.'

She was crossing the lobby of the imposing financial building when she saw a brash young city hotshot with slick hair, tailored suit, pinstripe shirt. Smirking in recognition, he pointed two fingers and cocked thumb, aimed an imaginary pistol, flicked to shoot and continued his merry way to the elevators.

Olivia felt herself blanch, whirled, and collided with a person exiting by the revolving doors, sending his iPhone spinning into the street. He picked it up then gawped. 'Bugger me! If it isn't the infamous Wheeler-Dealer!'

To think she and Andrew Mapleton had once been colleagues, starting their careers on the same day, if never exactly best of friends. The beefy blond rugby-playing upper-class twit had compensated for a deficit of brains with a surplus of arrogance and aristocratic connections. Now flushed and jowly, padded with fat instead of muscle, he'd retained the smugness and grating lordly drawl.

Olivia grimaced, heart still thudding. The young stockbroker type had disappeared. Was he trying to be funny? Was it a threat? He obviously knew who she was. What did it mean?

'Bugger you? Rather not, darling.' The automatic response was comfortingly familiar. Andrew had propositioned her at least three times a day, usually much more crudely. But that had been normal in a misogynist system that still considered women an intrusive novelty.

He chortled, looking down his nose as if humouring an uppity peasant. 'Same old Spanish Flea. What brings you back to the old hunting grounds?' He glanced back at the entrance. 'Not too popular, I imagine, after that balls-up in New York.'

'Are you kidding? They're beating down my door. Unfortunately, it's to throttle me, not offer me a job.' Dumb nickname. She'd always wondered if Andrew actually meant the aphrodisiac, Spanish Fly, but far be it from her to help him out. City guys had a strange sense of humour. That twerp earlier probably thought he was cool, blowing the smoke off and holstering his finger gun.

'Almost karmic, yah?' Andrew rocked back on his heels, hands in trouser pockets. 'Mandrake giving you the shaft like that.'

Olivia rolled her eyes. That again. 'Yeah, well for your sake, buddy-boy, you'd better hope that new age stuff's all hogwash. You're hardly an angel.'

She was turning to go when Andrew put out an arm. 'Buy you a drink? I'm down forty mill today. Market's screwier than an Essex whore. I say balls to it all. Let's get jolly well slaughtered.'

Olivia was in a self-destructive mood, as bar followed bar, followed by nightclub, then another nightclub. The evening became a blur as Andrew ordered drink after drink. Pounding down Mahiki's lethal Treasure Chest cocktails, enduring Andrew's dismal dancing, slapping his hands away as she sat on his knee, watching gobs of sweat drip from his forehead and nose.

Finally they took a taxi back to Beth's, Andrew insisting on walking her to the door, like the gentleman he never was and never would be.

'Gotta splash my boots,' he slurred coarsely as Olivia tried locating the lock with her key. 'What about coffee? I'm waishted. Might not find my way back. Don' worry, not trying to ride the baloney pony. The old one-eyed trouser snake's dead to the world. Couldn't get it up even if you begged.'

He always had had a way with words.

Olivia lurched into the kitchen to switch on the kettle. When she carried in mugs, Andrew was flopped on the sofa.

'How about a small pick-me-up?' He patted the space beside him. 'Got brandy?'

His arm caught her and pulled her into his lap. She jerked away, struggling out of reach, rubbing her cheek where he'd tried to kiss her mouth and missed. 'Why don't you pick yourself up and get lost. I'm off to bed. Alone.'

In the bathroom she sat slumped on the toilet for a long, long time, trying to summon the energy to rise. Somehow she made it to her bedroom, toppling onto the duvet.

'Olivia. Out. Now!' Beth tugged her arm violently. Olivia realised she was being towed down the stairs, unsteadily reaching for the wall to stop herself toppling. She'd never seen her friend so furious.

Andrew was where she'd left him, snoring on the couch, shirt half-buttoned, looking hopelessly debauched. Jessie stood in the living room doorway, holding her teddy.

'She wanted to watch her Bob the Builder DVD,' Beth hissed. 'And we find...this!'

Granted, mouth hanging slackly open, reeking of sweat, cigars, peach liqueur and brandy, Andrew was no oil painting. Blearily

Olivia checked to make sure his flies were closed, family jewels packed out of sight.

And then she saw it. A rolled up twenty. White powder lines on the glass-top table.

'You and that piece of trash brought coke into my house?' Beth squeaked with rage. 'You exposed my four-year-old daughter to that filth?' Her voice choked. 'Pack your bags, Livvy. I want you and this sleazebag gone this instant or I'm calling the police!'

Chapter Seven

'This one is Perseus.' Rosie studied her guidebook. 'And the snake-haired head's Medusa. She used to turn people to stone with a single glance.'

'And he killed her for it.' Anya circled the towering bronze figure. 'Typical man. Can't handle strong women.'

They were on the Avenida del Mar, the palm-fringed walkway stretching from Marbella's old town to the ocean, joining the cosmopolitan crowd admiring the Dalí sculptures, posing against the fountains and seeking refreshment in its delightful pavement cafés. It had taken some effort to drag Anya from the wreckage of another orgiastic breakfast but after four days spent solely in the resort, Rosie was obstinate about seeing the sights.

Colourful in skimpy summer dresses, they wandered barelegged through the Parque Alameda, shaded by banana trees taller than houses. In Plaza de los Naranjos they paused to breathe in the heavenly fragrance of orange blossom and sample the Tinto de Verano. Anya wolf-whistled at two motorcycle cops, zipping past in their mirrored sunglasses and sexy uniforms.

How enchanting it all was, Rosie thought. The ancient churches, narrow alleys and time-worn stone steps. Funky shops selling religious ornaments and all kinds of trinkets.

'Handbags? Watches? What you like? I do good deal. Lovely lady.'

Rosie grinned, waving away the Lookie Lookie man, one of the street vendors from Senegal. Who needed a fake Rolex when she could afford the real thing now? Unbelievable. All those nights, lying awake, fretting about money. Over. Just like that. Not that she didn't still feel intimidated by these ultra-chic boutiques and restaurants. But if they thought her a peasant, so what? She could only think of Julia Roberts in *Pretty Woman*.

Mistake. B-I-G mistake.

'OK,' Anya spoke from under her eye mask, as a manicurist massaged her limply outstretched fingers, 'you're rich, you're gorgeous – don't argue – you can have any man. Any man at all. Who'd it be? And don't choose Charlie,' she added quickly, 'or I might seriously puke.'

'Charlie who?' Rosie gave a fake yawn, ensconced in a vibrating massage chair. 'Mmm, hard to decide. Patrick Dempsey might do. Or Ryan Gosling. Yikes!' She jerked her foot, a dab of polish smearing her big toe. 'Sorry, that tickled,' she told the woman holding the brush. 'Why? What's your biggest fantasy – money no object?'

'Easy. I'd be a mysteriously enigmatic rock star – have my own "House of Anya" like Lady Gaga and travel the globe first class with piles of ultra-fit oiled-up male groupies.'

'But what about your Greek God?'

'Yeah, right, think I'd give up the world on a platter to play housie with Mr Macho? Hardly.'

Rosie grinned, sure the 'treat 'em mean' façade was all an act. She'd seen the way Anya mooned over her boyfriend, Darius. 'You're loopy about the guy, admit it. Three months already – has to be love!'

Anya made a face. 'I'm not a bleeding-heart romantic like someone else I know. If Darius messed me about,' she gave her friend a look from over the hand dryer, 'he'd better check both ways crossing the road, I can tell you. Wouldn't be feeding him choccy biscuits, that's for darned sure.'

'Wasn't all Charlie's fault.' Rosie rushed to continue, seeing Anya slapping her forehead. 'No, straight up, I'd let myself go. I'd put on weight, was always tired and—'

'Will you stop!' Anya ordered, raising her palm. 'You're a disgrace to your sex.'

'Well we have to be civil anyway. He's my kids' dad.' Still talking, Rosie approached the reception, but the manager waved away her Visa.

'Sorry, I can't accept this.'

'Oh, but the sign says…' Dismayed, Rosie eyed her new platinum card.

The man smiled. 'Your friend's already paid.'

'What?' Rosie whirled and gaped at Anya.

'When you went to the loo.' Anya smirked triumphantly. 'Gotcha. Can't let you treat me like a kept woman, can I?'

And nothing Rosie could say would change her mind.

Their next outing wasn't so successful. Rosie's revenge – surprise treat to Marbella's finest hairstylists didn't work out as planned. Nor did the 'easy stroll to Puerto Banus'. When the footsore pair arrived at the harbour, hours later, they were exhausted, Anya's mood foul.

'Truthfully, Anya,' Rosie reassured her for the fifth time as they limped towards the masts of the marina, 'your hair looks fabulous. Edgy, modern and extremely sexy.'

Anya stooped to check in the wing mirror of a parked Lamborghini. 'Yeah, well, maybe I liked it better before that moron hacked at it with his sodding shears. Obviously they gave the only decent stylist to the person footing the bill.'

Rosie jerked as if she'd been slapped. She walked to the water's edge feigning interest in a shoal of fat black fish swimming near the surface.

It had all been so divine. The plush surroundings, colourful flower arrangements, flutes of chilled champagne. Never mind that it had cost… well, so much that Rosie's hand had trembled as she signed the receipt. She was thrilled with the way her new flattering layers and subtle golden highlights framed her small oval face. But it was Anya who'd insisted on dramatically chopping off her waist-length dark brown waves for a short elfin style – regretting her daring before the first few curls had hit the floor. Still, was that reason enough to make Rosie feel bad? When all she'd done since they got here was try to please her friend.

A tanned arm came round her neck. 'Sorry, babes,' Anya apologised, pecking her cheek. 'I'm roasting and my feet hurt like hell.' She patted her shorn head. 'I'll get used to the hair. Edgy and sexy, you say?'

They felt better after a cool drink and set off to wander the marina, admiring the flash cars and extravagant yachts.

'Wish we could see inside them.' Anya peered through padlocked gates. 'Perhaps you could buy one, Rosie?'

'Totally out of my league.' Rosie drooled over the shiny wooden deck, dizzying mast and polished brass handrails of the largest yacht she'd ever seen. 'You'd have to be filthy rich.'

'Yeah, too bad you only won a lousy million.' Anya dug her with an elbow. 'Gutted for you, babes.'

They stood aside to let a man in a loose-fitting Hawaiian shirt and chinos pass between them. Hazel eyes met Rosie's, their disarming crinkles softening strong rugged features and a short close-cropped haircut. She grinned back, a blush staining her cheeks. The red and purple print looked familiar. She was sure she remembered seeing someone with a shirt like that just this morning, talking to the desk clerk in the hotel lobby.

A fellow guest? Or just a small world?

The next dock gate was unlocked. A young guy was standing beside a board that read 'Live the dream' with photos of laughing couples sipping cocktails with friends. He was immaculate in a crisp short-sleeved beige shirt and matching ultra-pressed shorts.

'Excuse me, señoritas, I am Carlos.' The swarthy young Spaniard removed his sunglasses, flashing impossibly white teeth. 'We are having a small party on board my yacht.' He pointed to the enormous motor cruiser behind him. 'It would give me great pleasure if you could join us.'

'Uh, sorry, but I'm afraid—' Rosie began, remembering how she'd thrown up on her one and only ever boat trip.

'Love to.' Before she could protest, Anya had taken hold of her elbow and propelled her forward.

In the main salon a heavily made-up woman thrust a glass of fruit punch into their hands and escorted them to a long buffet table laden with luxurious nibbles. Another wearing an identical frilly blouse was playing hostess, smile as fake as her perma-tan. A pull-down cinema screen was prominent at one end of the room and few of the bemused guests, mostly couples in beachwear, seemed to know each other.

'Peculiar sort of party,' Rosie mused as she sipped her drink. 'Hope the punch's not drugged. What if they're planning to kidnap us all? Sell us into the sex trade?'

Anya snorted derisively. 'Wouldn't get much for this lot. Where's Carlos? Thought he said this boat was his?'

'Nipped back outside as soon as he got us in here.'

'And I suggest we all do the same.' The words were delivered close to her ear in a deep Scottish burr.

Rosie whirled and nearly bumped into an expanse of brightly coloured cotton. Strong hands steadied her. It was the guy from the dock. Slightly over medium height, he looked muscular and outdoorsy, nose broken, age approaching forty and mental health – his next words showed – very much in question.

'Come on, Jane,' he urged, firm fingers gripping Rosie's arm. 'Kinney's been waiting half an hour. Did you forget?'

Anya's mouth dropped open in surprise.

'What?' Rosie tried tugging herself free. 'You must have the wrong—'

'Time?' He was far from handsome but his clear piercing eyes really were compelling, Rosie noticed, almond-shaped with enviously long lashes. Too bad they were wasted on what Luke would call a 'nutter'.

'No, I double-checked,' he said loudly. 'And you know how Kinney hates being stood up.' He bent his head, breath tickling Rosie's ear. 'Look, you and the other lass need to get out of here. *Now!*'

Engines were starting up. Carlos, beaming smugly, was now back inside, refilling his own glass of punch. Through the window Rosie could see crew unfastening lines from the mooring cleats.

'Welcome, welcome, welcome.' They heard one of the permatanned women say as the stranger bundled them down the slipway and onto the quay.

'What was all that bollocks?' Anya exclaimed as they watched the vessel chug backwards, churning up water. 'And who's this bleeding Kinney?'

'Uncle's sheepdog.' Their new acquaintance looked apologetic and amused. 'Alex MacDonald, local estate agent and interfering jackass at your service.' He handed them over a business card. 'Saw you there on the dock and it seemed a shame to let you fall for that scam.'

'What scam?' Rosie asked, puzzled. Her wrist was tingling. 'Who are they?'

'Timeshare merchants. Unscrupulous bunch. They get you on board, ply you with booze, and by the time you've sobered up, you're the proud owner of a shoddy apartment not worth the paper your contract's printed on.'

'Give us some credit.' Anya bristled. 'We're not that naive and we'd have had a free cruise. Besides aren't there cooling off periods, if you fall for that crap?'

'Not if ownership's less than three years.' The wind ruffled his light brown hair as he shoved his hands deep in his pockets. 'But if you're eager for a relentless sales pitch, bad canapés and a bunch of seasick drunks, they'll be sailing again tomorrow.'

'I think I'd jump overboard.' Rosie shuddered.

'I apologise if I acted out of turn.' The stranger checked his watch. 'I'd buy you both a drink to make up but I have to post signs on a villa we're listing today. Later perhaps? Where are you staying?'

So he hadn't spotted them in the lobby? That was odd. Rosie was sure she'd seen him glance over but perhaps he'd been looking at something behind them. His eyebrows elevated when Anya mentioned the resort.

'I've got some clients there. Ver-ry deluxe.'

'Yeah, well, some of us wouldn't consider a two-star fleapit.' Anya shot a mocking sidelong glance at Rosie as if afraid their digs had ruined her street-cred.

'It was a splurge,' Rosie said in weak defence. 'So what's this villa like?'

'Stupendous. Original features, wonderful layout, in a sought-after area.' He jangled his car keys, grinning at the clichés. 'A bit rundown, truthfully, but it's got some seriously stunning views. Up in the hills a way if you fancy a short drive.' He looked from one to the other. 'How about I shout you lunch after I'm finished? Shouldn't take long.'

'Yeah, never know,' Anya said, snottily. 'Rosie might be in the market for a holiday home.'

'Dilapidated caravan in Wales more like.' Rosie blushed to the roots of her hair, horrified by her friend.

What was the matter with the girl? Was she jealous? Trying to make out Rosie was a spoilt rich bitch? *Too good for a two-star fleapit indeed.* She'd picked the hotel as much for Anya as herself.

Or had she? Perhaps her friend would have been happier in a place more modest. She'd never actually asked.

She was horribly conscious suddenly of her pricey haircut, her designer glasses and the sundress straight from the resort's ultra-expensive boutique. Now it felt somehow wrong. Any other time she'd have been in old vest and cut-off jeans. Would she still be getting that same warm appraising look? Was there something about her now that said, to those in the know, 'money in the bank'?

She was about to make her excuses when Anya burst in. 'You're on,' she declared. 'We've missed the boat and anything's better than walking in this heat. Whisk us away, señor.'

Chapter Eight

At least the spider seemed to like her accommodation, spinning her complicated web across the ceiling. Olivia watched morosely from atop the foul smoke-scented bedspread, workout gear still damp from the morning's run. She considered a shower but the thought of the cramped ugly bathroom changed her mind.

Jesus, these cut-price hotels knew how to pack them in. A horrible cell of a room containing a narrow bed, peeling laminate nightstand and dirty fringed lamp. No TV, no hairdryer, miniscule shower, whose spray drenched the disgusting brown-stained toilet – probably the only cleaning it received. Just off Tottenham Court Road, it was a high-rise cement block, clearly a haven for impoverished and desperate immigrants. Yet the cheapskates gouged the unwary £7.50 for a lousy Continental breakfast with stale white rolls and undrinkable orange squash – highway robbery!

No mini-bar here. Olivia longed for a slug of vodka, tequila, even – ugh – Jägermeister, but she hadn't touched alcohol since she'd checked into this seedy pit, a way station for those on their way to or coming back from hell. Booze, obviously, was too dangerous a crutch in her current situation – even without the scene at Beth's or her mother's tragic precedent.

At least there was one cure that didn't involve expense. To numb her despair, she was pushing herself to run twice a day, skirting around the scaffolding that encumbered the multitude of bookshops, weaving between shoppers on busy Oxford Street and cruising past towering Centre Point with its private clubs and prestigious tenants.

Was it safe? Muggers? Nutters? Druggies? Bring 'em on. She hardly cared any more. So bloody what if crazies were still posting death threats on Twitter, targeting her almost as much as Mandrake because her social profile – and broken engagement – made for an interesting angle. So bloody what if Brad's father had put a hit on her – a notion normally too bonkers to seriously consider, straight from a bad TV show. She had to get out, would go insane locked in this unhygienic hellhole, afraid to breathe fresh air or even the cocktail of traffic fumes that passed for it in Central London.

Moodily she scratched the red welts on her ankles, courtesy of whatever wildlife lived in the carpet. Complaints had been met with stony indifference. Alternative accommodation had proved too expensive or even grimmer.

Laptop open on her thighs, Olivia selected her entire stack of unread emails, saved one, and hit delete on the rest. With warped satisfaction she continued erasing folders, contacts, unanswered messages from friends, business memos. Only when finished it occurred to her the Feds might question this impulse if they ever came seeking evidence. Oh well, too late now. Let them find her first. Even jail – white-collar jail, of course – might be an improvement.

She'd thought she was so smart. Had it all together. She should have known better. That eternal embittered teenager that still resided somewhere inside her psyche should never have permitted her guard to drop. Hadn't she always known things could go from triumph and accolades to ashes and terror in hours… minutes… seconds even?

That was how quickly the murderer could strike, the car bomb explode, or an unannounced aneurysm call down death. Hadn't she learned as a kid that even the happiest of times turned to hell eventually? If reminders were needed, she'd travelled past the 9/11 Memorial often enough to drive home that message. And hadn't she always admired Mandrake's coldly surgical machinations, the dispassionate way he cast aside his charm and bonhomie to make decisions with the mighty dollar as the only meaningful goal? All the clues for approaching catastrophe were there if she'd only cared to look.

She was left with one email to answer. The real estate agents in Marbella. She clicked on Skype and made a phone call.

A woman answered and Olivia introduced herself.

'Ah yes,' she said in fluent but accented English, 'you spoke to my husband earlier in the week, no? We have placed your villa on the market only today.'

'It's ready then?' A glimmer of hope.

'Well it would do better perhaps with a coat of paint but as you requested a quick sale...'

'How long do you think it'll take?'

'Well, my dear, properties aren't selling as well as a few years earlier but I assure you we will do our best.'

Do their best, maybe, Olivia thanked her and clicked off, *but the way her cash was dwindling, if they couldn't follow that up with a sale and soon...* Suddenly, even from the thirteenth floor, the streets below didn't seem so far away.

She walked to the window and peered down at the seething mass of humanity. They were all out there, pushers, pimps, prostitutes and the punters they preyed on, and yet those seedy undercurrents seemed honest commerce compared with the financial sharks and ruthless manipulations that she knew ruled the world. And yet – she'd been good at the game. Good at spotting areas of vulnerability, good at finding the loophole of advantage or the corporation ripe for plundering. She'd shed her share of blood, metaphorically at least, perhaps even sent people jobless on to these same streets although it was with a press of a button or a phone call, nothing one had to witness first-hand.

The sad thing was she missed it. Missed being in the thick of things. Missed being one of the players instead of a pawn.

Beth was right. Olivia Wheeler was no minnow waiting to be swallowed alive. Give her half a chance, a decent grubstake, and she'd fight her way back up one of these days. People would choke on those nasty comments, apologise to her face. In the meantime she still had a few survival skills.

⚜ ⚜ ⚜

'Gold's taken rather a tumble recently.' The hollow-cheeked man in the pawn shop eyed her sapphire-studded designer bracelet, Brad's last birthday gift. 'I'll give you...'

He named a sum so paltry, Olivia's hands itched to grab his grimy collar and shake him until his metal fillings rattled. 'I could get five times that much on eBay.'

She'd said as much at the consignment shop, getting rid of most of her designer gear for a price so low it wasn't even laughable. Twenty pounds for a four hundred dollar blouse. Fifty for a cocktail dress. But she needed to eat and cocktail parties didn't seem in her immediate future.

'Yeah? Go for it.'

She haggled, but the final amount was still criminal. No wonder the poor got poorer. Everyone kicking them while they were down.

She gave the bracelet a last wistful look. 'I'll come back for it. Soon as I find employment.'

'What they all say,' the man said lugubriously, putting it behind the till. 'Nice bit of workmanship there though.' He nodded at her watch. 'Might be worth a bob or two.'

Olivia glanced at the filigreed gold on her wrist, the delicate face, the jewelled surround. 'No, it was my mother's. It's not for sale.'

A hefty-looking wild-haired fellow in a ripe-smelling army greatcoat stopped Olivia a few minutes later.

'*Big Issue*?' He held out a newspaper. 'Written by the homeless for the homeless.'

At least she still had a bed. That put it in perspective. What was his story, she wondered, as she handed over two pound coins. Victim of divorce? Drugs? Drop-out?

Brad's father had always been disparaging about the homeless. 'You're only subsidising their addictions. After all, twelve million wetbacks can find work without problems.'

Well, fortunately, she wasn't that far down yet. What was that well-worn line she'd used, when people commented on her luck? It wasn't the cards life dealt you; it was the way you played them. Now she could practically hear Life cackling, *'See what you can do with these, sucker.'*

She left the magazine, unread, on the Northern line tube. She'd been scouring the internet and evening papers for alternative accommodation and today she finally struck…well, if not gold, silver or brass, at least a very tarnished pewter. A rundown studio in the area they called the Harringay Ladder. Not much more than a bedsit really with a microwave, two-ring electric burner, toilet and a teeny-weeny shower, only marginally cleaner than the one at the hotel. First thing she'd do was invest in a gallon of bleach.

The furnishings were dingy, the eight-unit building smelled of curry, and she imagined cockroaches scuttling the minute the key turned in the lock. Even while she was agreeing, a part of her refused to believe it had come to this. But it was cheap enough and she had the place to herself. She told herself things were looking up. No, they truly were. Don't think about her great apartment so close to Central Park, don't think about the fabulous ensuite bathroom, the jetted tub, the oversized two-person steam shower with its deluxe needle massage heads, the walk-in closet nearly as big as this tiny room. Don't think about five-star restaurants, luxury hotels and mindless shopping sprees. Bloody sign the lease and get on with it.

Anything to get out of that nauseating no-tell hotel. She wouldn't have to listen to her neighbours, a pair of Japanese students, scream abuse at each other or pull the bedclothes over her head to muffle the sound of rapturous lovemaking from the couple on the other side. One more night of that and they might find her lying in wait with a sharpened steak knife.

She handed over a chunk of the money she'd just acquired to her new landlord – or building manager, it wasn't clear. He towered over her, like a Not-So-Incredible Hulk, food stains on his giant paunch, belt straining to hold up his button missing, semi-unzipped trousers. She turned her face away to avoid the rank odour of his breath.

'Need anything, just give me a shout,' he wheezed, counting the notes with fat sausage fingers. 'I'm just across the hall.' Nicotine-teeth leered as piggy eyes traversed her body with flesh-creeping implications. For just a flicker she recoiled and reconsidered.

Forget it. She gave herself a mental shake. There was nothing else out there. For every decent room in a shared flat, dozens lined up to do the song and dance interview; for every revolting bedsit she'd rushed to see, someone else had snapped it up. Here at least she wouldn't be lining up for showers nor put up with someone else's plates cluttering the sink.

Only temporary, she assured herself. Only until the villa sold. It was an address to put on résumés while she searched for work. And not all that far from the nursing home. Hopefully she could slip her rent in the mail slot and never have to see her loathsome landlord again.

Give him a shout? Not for fire or flood.

'Doris!' Great-aunt Winnie exclaimed, as Olivia walked into the visitor's room. 'Where have you been, you naughty imp?'

On an impulse, returning from Helmshott Manor, Olivia noticed a familiar clock tower and jumped off the bus at Crouch End. She'd always liked the area, the trendy boutiques and restaurants, the vibrant atmosphere.

She idled away an hour drifting in and out of shops but it wasn't nearly as much fun with no money to spend. On a side street, she passed a cheap and cheerful café called Hellas that, according to the menu pasted on the window, served everything from an all-day breakfast through to moussaka, kebabs, pizza and burgers.

Underneath the menu was a card. 'Help Wanted'.

Inside, posters of Keffalonia depicted a startling blue ocean and whitewashed churches. Serving the few occupied tables was a young punkish-looking girl with unnaturally black hair, tattoos and a stud in her eyebrow.

'Where's the manager?' Olivia asked.

A flat and a job in one day? Could she be that, uh…lucky? She shuddered, thinking of the nature of the flat, the nature of the job.

Only temporary.

'You mean the owner?' The girl turned, yelling, 'Oy boss. Some lady 'ere after yer.'

A man glanced up from his books, swarthy complexioned with coarse masculine features and bullish curls pulled back in a pony-tail. Coal black eyes studied Olivia as she walked across. He leaned back in the chair, oozing testosterone, white shirt opened to display a heavy gold chain, small gold loop in his ear.

'Hi, I'm…' She hesitated. Olivia sounded too posh and she wanted anonymity, didn't she? 'Livvy. You need a waitress?'

'Well, hello Livvy.' White teeth flashed a grin as he indicated a chair. 'I'm Darius.'

Chapter nine

The white stuccoed villa was worth the trip for the views alone; its low-pitched terracotta roof floating above Marbella's wooded hills. Sighing happily, Anya settled on the terrace with the bottle of Rioja Alex had bought, next to the free-form swimming pool, while the other two measured the dusty sprawling rooms and threw open shutters to let in the light.

'Could use some TLC all right.' Alex scrawled dimensions on his notepad. 'Fresh coat of paint would help a lot.'

'I love it exactly the way it is.' Rosie ran her hand over peeling paintwork. 'Makes it look old, historic.' There were so many great architectural details. Pillars. Arches. Just like a film set. 'And that fish sculpture looks so real, leaping out of the swimming pool.' The bronze piece was massive, four feet long at least. 'I swear I've seen it before. Déjà vu all over again.'

'You probably have.' Alex nodded. 'It's been featured in books and postcards. They even sell copies of the thing on key rings. The place was built by a rather talented sculptor. Not Dalí, exactly, but still very successful in his day. Being sold by his daughter now.'

In the study a gargantuan built-in desk unit, shelves to ceiling, dominated an entire wall. Alex scratched his head, baffled. 'This has to go. It's riddled with woodworm, but how? Can't take an axe to it without damaging the wall.' Idly he tugged at a drawer. 'Probably swollen shut. No, wait, something's caught.'

He slid his hand into the gap, wrestling with the recalcitrant object and extricated, with difficulty, an envelope.

'What is it?' Excitedly Rosie peered round his arm. 'Treasure map? Last will and testament?'

'Aren't you the romantic?' He laughed and showed her a line drawing of a chubby-faced baby. 'Nope. Sketches mostly. Scraps of paper. Notes. Former owner's I'd guess. Looks pretty random but still he's been dead some years. Might mean something to his daughter.'

They went to join Anya. Rosie breathed in the scent of tropical vegetation, enthralled by the garden's lush beauty. A hawk described slow circles in the air above as Alex pointed out landmarks along the coast and the distant town below. A gentle breeze rustled the pines and fluttered through the apricot hibiscus, caressing her neck. A strange lethargy overcame her, as she felt herself almost drowsing in the sun.

'...from the Hebrides originally,' Alex was telling Anya, his lilting Highland brogue soft and sexy, like molten caramel. 'Off the West coast of Scotland. My parents and I lived with my uncle when I was a young lad. Here.' He handed them a small card each. 'He just sent me these. Said he's started letting out the old crofter's cottage. If you hear of anyone needing a place to get away...'

The card showed a quaint low building with a lavender door against a backdrop of mountains and sea.

'Cute.' Anya turned it over.

'Aye, it's a beautiful place. Though I thought I'd die of boredom in my teens. Dreamed of running off to sea, looking for adventure.'

Rosie yawned. 'I used to pretend I was adopted. Couldn't wait for my real parents to track me down.'

Anya refilled her glass, shirt tied under her voluptuous breasts and shorts unzipped to catch maximum rays. 'I was Peter Pan.' She tilted her face to the sun. 'Broke my leg jumping out of a tree. Always wanted to be a boy.'

'Not any more though?' Alex's eyes creased with amusement.

'Hell no!' Anya tossed her head, thrusting out her chest and they all laughed.

On the way back, Alex stopped for lunch as promised; fresh olives bursting with flavour, crusty bread and crunchy calamari, bowls of paella, rich with garlic and saffron. He seemed to know everyone, customers sitting at nearby tables, a guy drinking at the bar, the waiters pausing to banter in Spanish as they carried ginormous platters across the cobbled courtyard.

'I'm surprised they're still serving. It's already three-thirty.' Anya glanced at her watch.

'We lead civilised hours.' Alex winked. 'Besides no one eats dinner here until ten.'

As they feasted, he entertained them with stories of the Spanish bureaucracy and the barmy ex-pats.

'They call it the Costa del Crime.' He poured them all wine. 'Ever since the Great Train Robbery back in the sixties Marbella's attracted the underworld and gangsters on the run. Never know who you'll bump into in the supermarket.'

'Is it dangerous then?' Rosie remembered her mother sneering whenever Spain was mentioned, Marbella in particular. Common, she'd always said. All those naff package tours.

'It's got its seedy side – massage parlours, strip joints. But it's incredibly vital and exciting too with some of the best bars in Spain and nightlife second to none. Celebrity-spotting's a local sport.' He crumbled a chunk of bread. 'I'm out of the party loop these days but Sinatra's still a favourite hangout. And you haven't had pizza until you try Picasso's.'

'I can't believe we've been eating in the resort every night,' Anya told Rosie, conveniently forgetting she was the one who hadn't wanted to leave. 'I could so easily live here.'

'Not me,' Rosie said. 'Don't get me wrong, it's beautiful and the boys would adore the beach.' She felt a pang, missing them sharply. 'But they'd never want to leave their friends. Not to mention their dad would throw a fit.'

'You're married then?' Alex sounded surprised.

'Divorced.' Perhaps it was the good time she was having and the wine relaxing her but the word didn't summon the usual ache.

'Except he's round her place all the time,' Anya supplied.

Rosie flinched. 'To see his sons, yes. He's a marvellous dad.'

'Oh sure, father of the year.' Anya turned big shining eyes to Alex, pouting sexily. 'My guess is our Rosie's still a touch in love with him.'

'I am not.' Why was Anya saying these things? To a virtual stranger? 'He's engaged for pity's sake.'

'Like that makes a difference,' Anya muttered, bending for her fallen napkin.

Heat surged up in Rosie's throat, choking her words. Lowering her head, humiliated, she reached for the bill but Alex got there first. 'I'll sort this.'

Squashed and silent in the back of Alex's convertible, Rosie was still disproportionately hurt as Anya laughed and sparkled up at their driver. Of course why shouldn't Anya flirt? She wasn't engaged to Darius, and Alex was just the kind of manly man she'd go for. But implying that she, Rosie was still in love with Charlie! It was so needless. Anya, with her sultry beauty, was so incredibly sexy that no guy in his right mind would look at wallflower Rosie in her presence.

As if sensing her confusion, Alex caught Rosie's hand as he helped her scramble out. 'Thanks for all your help up there.' His arresting eyes held hers. 'Listen, Rosie, I know tomorrow's your last day but how'd you like to spend it in Morocco? I'm picking up some rugs and I'd love to show you around. We could catch the early ferry to Tangier, shop in the Kasbah, take a camel ride?' He turned to Anya. 'You too, of course, Anya. What do you both say?'

Anya stared at Alex's hand still, Rosie realised, linked in her own. The look her friend gave said it all.

It wasn't just the cocktails at the swim-up bar that were cool that late afternoon.

The chilliness followed them into their air-conditioned suite. How magnificent it was – two huge bedrooms with enormous-sized beds, and bathrooms crammed with lavish toiletries, a marble bar and gigantic flat screen TV in the ornate sitting room. But filled with suffocating silence, it actually felt almost cramped.

Showered and changed, Anya returned to the living area, boldly exotic with gelled hair in a strapless dress that matched her blood-red lipstick.

'Ready?' she asked. Her dark shadowed eyes glowed like the large obsidian beads around her neck.

'When you are.' It was the most they'd spoken since Alex had roared away. Rosie sat primly on the leather sofa, uncomfortable with her Chloe aqua-marine cotton-blend dress, which, even with tanned legs seemed too short and too bright.

'About tomorrow.' Anya drew a deep breath. 'I'm not into this Tangiers thing. At all. In fact I'm amazed you'd even consider it.'

'Why not?' Defiantly Rosie straightened her bare shoulders, willing herself not to instantly crumble. 'I've always dreamed of seeing Morocco. Shopping in the Kasbah. How cool would that be?'

'Cool? Die of heat, more like.' Anya snorted. 'And I suppose I'm to be the gooseberry while you two make goo-goo eyes?'

Rosie startled. 'No. Of course—'

'Besides I've been thinking about this whole timeshare bandit thing. What if it was a scam? A set-up?' Her friend continued, relentless now. 'With him and Carlos?'

'Like how?' Rosie's head swam with puzzlement. 'One ushering us on board, the other whisking us off? Rather elaborate, don't you think?'

'Well, it is the "Costa del Crime" according to your thug.' Anya picked up a light shawl and wrapped it around her shoulders. 'Might not be surprising it's you he's targeted. He could be a conman, a gigolo or even a murderer for all we know.'

'Gigolo, conman *and* murderer?' Rosie's laugh tried to disguise her hurt. 'And what was all that twaddle about me being in love with Charlie? Why tell him that? After all—' She stopped abruptly.

'After all you've done for me?' Anya folded her arms, head cocked challengingly.

'I'd never say that!' Rosie was shocked and affronted. She'd wanted to remind Anya how many times she'd nagged Rosie to forget her ex and show some interest in other men. But it was so hard. Charlie had swept her off her feet, stormed past her shyness. And yes, there was something about Alex's easy-going presence that also made her feel it was OK just to be herself, no awkwardness, no effort. But she was loath to expose this fragile glimmer to Anya's worldly scorn.

'Bleeding well hope not,' Anya retorted. 'Look, Rosie, I just don't want you getting hurt. You're stinking rich now. And we were talking about your win when he passed us. I mean, Christ, he could even have followed us from the hotel. I'm totally sure I saw someone wearing a shirt like that in the lobby this morning. Might have been lurking around on the hunt for wealthy victims. Possibly in cahoots with the staff.'

'And of course no one would fancy me without the money.' Rosie sounded bitter.

'Don't be a doughnut.' Anya tutted and gave her a one-arm hug. 'You're gorgeous, Rosie. Intelligent. Sweet. But you're not exactly street-smart. And he's a typical estate agent, isn't he – a bit too glib, a bit too smooth-talking, just like Charlie. I'd be worried sick if you take off for an Islamic country with a total stranger. Not to mention it's our last day and I really, really want to enjoy it with you. Just the two of us.'

She paused, perhaps sensing Rosie weakening. 'Up to you, babes, but I think you should cancel. If you want I'll call him?' She drew out his business card from her bag. 'Well?'

Rosie stared out the window, brooding, as the plane circled above Gatwick airport. She was having flashbacks to last night, the sweltering nightclub, Anya flirting with three young Spaniards, giving them the full throat-stroking, hair-fiddling, breast-thrusting routine. While Rosie, bored, ignored, sat fending off the advances of spotty British lads desperate to get laid.

She'd whiled away the miserable hours thinking about Tangiers and Alex. Conjuring fantasies in which they haggled for trinkets in the souk or strolled about the Sultan's fountain-filled palace courtyards. Her disappointment was crushing. If only she'd had the good grace to suggest at least a farewell drink instead of garbling some abysmal excuse and instantly hanging up.

Of course she wouldn't have dreamed of dragging Anya on a day trip against her will. Nor was Rosie the type to dump her mate the instant a man appeared on the scene. But would it have been so terrible for her friend to have endured Tangiers? For Rosie's sake? In London and for most of this holiday she'd uncomplainingly followed her friend's lead. Would it have hurt her to do something important for Rosie, just once? Without reacting as if asked to sacrifice a kidney?

After all, Rosie had paid for the whole blooming holiday. Flights, hotel, hairdressers, clothes, meals, margaritas at the airport…

Stop it. Rosie.

She pulled herself up short.

No. It wasn't about the money, it truly wasn't. More about Rosie being too feeble to assert herself, always giving way to keep everyone happy. It was herself she was angry with. Most likely Anya *had* just been protective and genuinely nervous. Morocco might freak out many people. She'd always thought Anya adventurous but you never really knew someone until you travelled together.

But was this what it was going to be like? Looking at nice people with suspicion in case they wanted something from you? No, she'd never be like that, she vowed. So what if Alex had happened to be in the hotel lobby? That didn't make him a stalker. It was just typical of Anya's ever-persistent cynicism to think the worst.

And what about Anya's comments about Charlie? Jealousy? Or mere thoughtlessness? Perhaps Anya had even been scared that Rosie and Alex would hook up and she'd be dumped until it was time to go home. For all her surface toughness Anya was more vulnerable than she cared to let on.

Well, she needn't have worried. The last thing Rosie could imagine was a casual fling. She'd hadn't had much confidence with boyfriends before Charlie and certainly none since. In fact – and she was deeply ashamed of this – the last time she'd had sex was only shortly after Charlie had left, when he'd shown up tipsy one night after a big argument with The Witch...

The idea of being left alone with Alex. Or any man. Him perhaps trying to kiss her...or more...was terrifying. Far scarier than whatever other evils Anya's imagination conjured up.

Sadly it seemed, new clothes and a fancy haircut couldn't magically erase a lifetime of insecurities.

She braced herself as the wheels descended in preparation for landing.

Anya reached over and took her hand. 'Brilliant holiday, Rosie. Thanks, you're a real star.'

'No, thank you,' Rosie said, automatically. 'For coming with me.'

She meant it. Of course she did. But from now on, she realised, she'd better watch her step. A million pounds clearly came with an escort of unwelcome complications...

Chapter Ten

'Here it is. The heart attack special.' Olivia clattered a brimming plate on the plastic tablecloth. 'Moussaka, chips, fried tomatoes, sausages. Can one man really eat all that?' Teasing, she added, 'And since I'm looking at enough cholesterol to kill a grizzly bear, perhaps you wouldn't mind signing this liability release?'

She flapped her pen and order pad under the nose that had been stuck in a laptop three lunchtimes now in a row. Long fingers stopped tapping his keyboard and the customer cocked his head in amused scrutiny. He had a thin scholarly face with unkempt wavy hair, round wire-rimmed glasses and the mouth of a revolutionary poet. Not a student as that abysmal green sweater and his wiry frame first implied but her own age or older.

'Abnormally high metabolism,' he remarked mildly, rubbing the stubble on his narrow chin. 'Watch me and weep. And by the way, new girl,' soulful brown eyes glinted under sooty lashes, 'my cholesterol's fine but old Darius might just have a coronary himself if he hears you scaring off customers.'

Olivia snorted. 'Given the lousy coffee,' she glanced at the pungent brew she'd delivered earlier, 'I'd say their loyalty's beyond reproach.'

The doorbell clanged as a group of people walked in, shedding coats and dripping umbrellas, adding to the warm fog steaming the windows. The sky outside was a mass of thunder clouds. So much for sunny June. She thought of Brad playing tennis or strolling along his father's private golf course.

'Hey, Marcus.' Someone leaned over Olivia's customer and helped himself to a chip, a tall broad-shouldered someone with a heart-shaped face and a wicked smile that made her knees go weak. She took in thick luscious black hair, strong brows as dark as his leather jacket, a small sexy beard and blue eyes that skewered with one glance. The man was a sex God.

'Zac, what's up?' said Marcus.

His friend pushed the empty chair back with his foot. Sliding in, the newcomer took a few more chips, pulling Marcus's plate towards him. 'Thought I'd catch you here. Best place in the world for a hangover.'

'Help yourself, why don't you,' Marcus said, dead-pan.

'Ta me old mucker, I will.'

'Hi.' Of its own accord, Olivia's voice dropped two octaves. 'Can I get you anything?' It came out sultry and hopelessly suggestive – almost blaring the subtext, 'Coffee, tea or me?' as her hip unconsciously cocked in a provocative pelvis-displaying stance.

The corners twitched on Marcus's long expressive mouth as if this was a familiar, oft-repeated scenario.

Irritated, Olivia straightened, pulled out her pad and yawned, looking away, tapping her foot in mimed impatience. Last thing she needed was to add to some guy's already inflated ego.

Looking up, the newcomer's rakish grin suggested it was business as usual for him. She hoped he couldn't see her heart pounding under her Café Hellas white blouse. She scowled, thinking of Brad. Anyway she was off men. Lousy, untrustworthy pricks. OK, she could admire this one as one might admire…uh, a gorgeous prancing stallion, say…but that didn't mean she wanted to approach and get kicked or bitten.

Zac dipped another chip in ketchup and nibbled the end. 'Not bad.' He quirked an eyebrow at Olivia and she wasn't sure he was talking about the food. 'I'll have a cup of undrinkable coffee and a stale BLT with wilted lettuce and a hair in the middle.' He watched her scribbling. 'Now you say I can't possibly serve you that,' he coached. 'And I reply, why not, you did yesterday, boom, boom.'

'Customer's always right,' Olivia drawled. 'You want a hair, I'm sure we can oblige. Boom, boom.' She weaved between tables, with a slight Marilyn Monroe wiggle, sticking the note on the hatch. Irma, the tattooed young waitress, gazed dreamily in Zac's direction, black-lipsticked mouth gone slack.

'Put me out of my misery,' Olivia begged, peering from behind Irma's shoulder. 'Tell me he's gay – please.'

'Sorry.' Irma gave a sigh and a small shake. 'He ain't. Brings girls here all the time. I know he's like really old, thirty or summat, but he's like one killer dude.'

The 'killer dude' was the only highlight in the next few hours of another exhausting day. Olivia had never waitressed, had never needed a paper round or a part-time job in a store for pocket money. By mid-afternoon her whole body ached in sympathy with her swollen feet and the smell of cooking oil seemed permanently lodged in her clothes and hair.

Worse, she felt incompetent. Slapping meals on tables wasn't exactly rocket science, no lives were at stake, no futures on the line, but having always aced everything she tackled, it was frustrating to have Darius chivvy her for being slow while Irma waltzed by, balancing five plates on her skinny arms.

From seven in the morning to nine at night, the comfort food and moderate prices of Café Hellas attracted a mixed clientele typical of Crouch End: yuppie couples, families with kids, yummy mummies. It had grown trendier of late, ever since a proudly displayed review had labelled it 'a popular hangout for locals in the know'.

Still Olivia's job search had failed to turn up any better prospects. It was staggering how fierce the competition for miserly salaries and a life of drudgery. And she was inevitably over or underqualified. Not to mention the problem of references.

A high-pitched giggle drew her attention to a quartet of the preppy type once nicknamed 'Sloane Rangers', who'd seated themselves in her section, all sporting quilted green vests more suited for a shooting weekend on a country estate than slumming it in London. A blonde with a jaunty ponytail flicked a paper pellet at her companion. Olivia saw an unmistakeable ski-jump nose and swerved, changing direction to clear another table.

Of all the gin joints…! Sara Goswell was the sister of one of Olivia's early boyfriends, a baronet. The girl had been a royal snob, disapproving of her brother 'stepping out' with someone of such low breeding.

Sweat trickled under Olivia's armpits. Dare she tell Darius she was ill and hide in the loo? Sara probably never looked at wait staff but she'd only have to give one upward glance to recognise Olivia. Would the humiliations never end?

She ducked her head away as she walked past with an armful of plates, ignoring Sara's call. 'Waitress! I swear they get worse every day. Deaf or dense, yah?' And then. 'You actually like this dive?' Clearly Olivia had gone unrecognised.

There was a bit of chit-chat and then Sara's posh decibels again, booming across the restaurant with aristocratic disregard for fellow diners. 'It was on TV last night. Late-night show with her fiancé – Brad Winton, that fabulously good-looking, stupendously wealthy New Yorker? Well, he was explaining how she's vanished. Did a disappearing act a few days after the news broke. Clothes gone from their flat. Bank account cleared out. Hasn't been in touch with a single one of her friends. Sounds jolly suspicious, yah?'

Olivia felt her legs go rubbery. She could barely take the plates into the kitchen. Irma walked in, looking puzzled, as she stood at the sink gulping water. 'Uh, ah, I don't feel too good.' It was the best she could come up with. 'I need a bit of a break. Can you cover for me?'

Before Irma could even nod agreement, she'd wobbled out the back door. She was a fugitive on the run. Oh how she wished she had a coat collar to pull up, a trilby hat to pull down.

Slipping into the coffee shop opposite, an espresso bar offering Italian lattes, French pastries and free wireless, she googled her own name on her new UK phone.

Reference after reference jumped up, an overnight mushrooming since the interview with Brad. The interview itself, replayed on YouTube, Brad veering between righteous resentment and good-guy concern, the host's feigned sympathy and smirks to camera. There were articles from today's US newspapers, photos of her at society functions – including one leaving the CRAWL benefit. And speculation. The devastating disgrace and loss of fortune had led her to suicide. No, she was hiding out in Alaska under an assumed name.

Or yet another theory. She and Rupert had been in cahoots, Wheeler's colleagues claiming 'a special bond between the financial whiz kid and his pretty young employee'. She'd left the country to join Mandrake. They were shacked up somewhere, enjoying their billions.

There were even a few pithy sound bites from old Pop Winton, calling her 'a mercenary gold-digger', and an ancient photo of her father with one of his life-sized sculptures that was really dredging the bottom of the barrel.

It was all wild speculation and meaningless hype. Her heart thumped as she scanned hurriedly through. Not one solid claim she was a serious suspect or wanted by the police. But Brad's comments had escalated the press storm she'd left behind into a veritable witch-hunt. Typical media bullshit, creating a tsunami out of a mild spring breeze. Running off, it seemed, was as good as an admission of guilt. Although she hadn't exactly been lying low. Her passport had been scanned by immigration, after all. She'd signed on at employment agencies for God's sake, gone trawling through the City asking for work, and been out drinking and night-clubbing with Andrew. Yet she couldn't see anything online that linked her yet to London.

She sat at the coffee shop, watching the café door until the ghastly foursome had left. In the end though she had to go back. What choice was there?

⚜ ⚜ ⚜

'Oy! Livvy.' Darius called her over in one of the lulls. He sat at a table, the week's accounts spread in front of him.

'You look like someone worked you over with a wet tea towel.' He scratched his head with his pen, dark eyes penetrating. 'Still think this job's a doddle?'

She had said that, hadn't she? Claimed she'd worked in diners all over the Midwest rather than risk rejection. Too bad every time Darius looked her way she was spilling something, dropping something or delivering the wrong order. But damned if she would let him fire her.

'Four-year-old could handle this.' She flapped the menu with fake bravado. 'You got the right idea, boss. Keep it simple. Fried egg. White toast. None of this "Would you like those eggs scrambled, poached, sunny side up, over-easy, over-hard with wheat, rye, sourdough, bagel, muffin or biscuits" they mess with in the States.'

Walking past, Irma rolled her kohl-rimmed eyes in disbelief.

Darius grunted. 'Oh yeah? Well maybe I should hire that four-year-old. Kid wouldn't sod off for half an hour when we're at our busiest. Or spout off to good customers about cholesterol and heart attacks.'

Hell fires. He'd heard her. Or, no, she'd seen him and Marcus share a joke at the cash register. Probably tattle-tailed, the scumbag. Bloody, untrustworthy, men. Try to add a little levity to a mind-numbingly boring job and it came back to bite you.

Only temporary, she reminded herself. Only temporary. After Sara Goswell's arrival she was definitely going to up the job search.

'And hurry it up, will ya?' he urged. 'This might not be America, maybe the punters say tom-ah-to instead of tom-ay-to, but they still get hacked off if their lunch is cold.'

'Sure thing, boss.' She dipped a curtsey and Darius grinned. He was an OK type, quite sexy in his macho Mediterranean way if you didn't mind a heavy hand with the aftershave.

'Bloody bills.' Darius's attention was back on his work. 'I've added the things umpteen times and I still can't make 'em tally.'

Olivia's eyes automatically went to the ledger, reading the figures upside down.

She stabbed her finger on the page. 'There's your problem. This column should be 436 not 532.'

'No way.' He reached for the calculator. 'Or...maybe... Yeah, but, how...' Darius's puzzled expression changed to delight as the café door swung open and a bronzed girl dashed in from the rain, exposed shoulders scorched red under a strappy top, radiating sun and coconut tanning oil.

'Thanks, Rosie!' she yelled back at a black taxi visible through the open door. 'See you back at the house.'

Darius stood up and she ran into his arms, grinning ear to ear.

'Looking great, angel,' he said, admiring. 'All brown and beautiful.' He rubbed the top of her head. 'And your hair, wow, radical!' He put on a menacing frown. 'Here, what's all this then about last-minute holidays to Spain?'

'Rosie paid. You'll never guess. I wasn't supposed to tell anyone but...' They both noticed Olivia at the same time as she edged away.

'Let's move on out of here. Girls can close up, can't you girls?' Darius tipped his papers into a briefcase, wrapping his arm around the newcomer. 'Got some catching up to do, innit.' He smacked his girlfriend's bottom, giving it a sexy pinch as they left.

At closing time, Olivia went to put out the garbage and found Irma, smoking a cigarette.

'You're dead funny, you know,' the younger girl said cheerfully, stubbing out the end under her thick-soled Doc Martens. 'I nearly wet myself when you told Darius that crap about easy-over and what-not. Bloody obvious you've never done this before.'

They walked back into the building together.

'Never fancied America,' Irma continued on as they removed coats from pegs. 'I'd be scared to live there. All those guns. You see so many murders on the telly, don't you?'

Olivia shuddered, remembering how many internet comments had threatened her demise. But that was just spouting off, wasn't it?

'Isn't there crime in every country?' she said, more to reassure herself than placate Irma. 'Half of Kansas doesn't bother locking their doors. Anyway, my great-aunt's house, a mile from here, had more bolts than a bank vault. She might have been a tiny bit touched in the head though.'

And if my luck doesn't change soon, I'm going to take after her.

'Yeah, London's got its share, I 'spose,' Irma said, with gloomy unreassuring relish. 'Loads of muggings round here and there was a bloke knifed in Archway last week. You gotta be careful walking around at night.'

'I was never scared in New York,' Olivia mused. 'Whatever time it was.' Not until the hate messages anyway. 'The energy's just so amazing – most exciting city in the world.'

Saying that she realised how much she missed it. Would she be able to go back one day? Should she have toughed it out?

'I'm meeting some mates at the pub,' Irma informed her. 'Fancy a drink?'

'Not tonight.' Even if she could afford to buy a round, socialising, answering personal questions, held no appeal, especially with this latest development. Better just to stay home. Some unwary soul in her building had left their internet access unsecured. She was making full use of it every night, following the hunt for Mandrake, pushing her Spanish estate agents for a quick sale, killing time with inane YouTube videos and yes, maybe she had taken a quick glance at the markets every now and then. It was galling to see that the stocks she'd picked out before she'd moved everything to Mandrake's fund were weathering this latest storm.

''Nother time then.' Irma locked the door. 'See ya.'

Olivia had a strange feeling the second she entered her building, stomach muscles tightening inexplicably. Perhaps it was Irma's talk of 'murders on the telly'. When she saw her front door was open a crack, her heart jumped, hammering in her ribcage like a rabbit in its burrow. She held her breath. Was someone in there? Should she run? Call the police?

She'd visions of dragging back a reluctant constable only to discover some foolishly simple explanation. Wouldn't be the first time a door hadn't properly closed behind her or been blown open by the wind.

Moving quietly, she gave the wood a light push.

She saw the man right away. Surprise was followed by sharp anger. She had few valuables left but those remaining, including her laptop, were precious and the landlord's hand rested guiltily on the top drawer of her small dresser.

'How dare you?' She was so incensed that her voice shook. 'How did you get in? You've no right.'

He took a step towards her, holding up a ring full of keys as explanation. 'Sorry, love.' His yellow chip-toothed smile was shifty and conciliatory. 'Didn't mean to startle you. Last tenant told me the latch to that window's a bit dodgy and I haven't been able to get to it until today.' He patted the screwdriver emerging from his cardigan pocket, two high spots of colour lighting up his puffy cheeks. 'Month or two ago, not far from here, a young lady was attacked by a man in her room – crawled right through her window while she was asleep. Not to worry though, like I said I'm right across the hall. You hear anything strange, just yell.' Heavy drooping eyelids curtained something avid in his gaze. 'I don't sleep much anyway.'

Olivia felt chilled, struck again by his bulk. OK he was a fat slob, she doubted he could move fast, but he was a snoop, double her size and weight. Plus he had keys to the apartments. She made a mental note to buy a heavy-duty padlock.

'Don't worry about me,' she said icily. 'My father's a cop and I've been shooting a gun since I was six. Got my first 38 special when I turned fourteen,' she patted her handbag, 'and I sleep with it under my pillow. So,' her smile was a glittering threat, 'don't be surprising me like that. I'd hate an innocent man to get hurt.'

He rasped a speculative hand over his chin. ''Course you're joking,' he smirked. 'Or I'd have to evict you. Can't have illegal handguns on the premises.'

'Who said it's illegal?' She tapped her watch. 'My dad should be off duty in a couple of hours if you care to ask him. I'm sure he'll be interested in why you're snooping about here.'

'Don't get shirty, girl. Just trying to be helpful. Anyway I'll be off, got supper on the stove.'

She slammed the door, pushing a chair under the handle as his heavy footsteps receded. God, he was repulsive. And full of bull. She went to the window to confirm what she'd checked that first night, nervous about the possibility of intruders. It was impossible to open, the latch story pure fabrication. The window was painted shut.

Chapter Eleven

Sunday morning Rosie waited at the bus stop, rain lashing furiously against her saturated umbrella. A sane person would have called a cab, she chided herself, belting her fashionable but flimsy, short navy mac tighter round her shivering body, but it had never been an option in the past and it seemed a shame to waste a perfectly good bus pass.

Besides, she was in no hurry to reach her destination.

Splash!

As she moved forward to check round the bend, blissfully unaware of the puddle by the kerb, a Range Rover raced through it.

She was soaked from highlighted head to her mud-spattered almond-toed ankle boots fresh from one of Marbella's designer boutiques. So much for clothes giving you confidence.

And confidence she should have in bucketloads right now. All her debts were repaid, she'd money to last a lifetime, she was glowing from her week in the sun and Charlie would bring the boys back later tonight.

So why wasn't she over the moon high-fiving with the stars?

She was absolutely drenched to the skin – and freezing. But there, miraculously, was a black London cab, yellow light ablaze. She ran out in the road, raising her hand. Agent Million would understand her splashing out – bad pun included. Especially since she was off to a family lunch party, where her mother lay in wait ready to explode.

Walking into home sweet home last night, she saw the red light blinking on the answering machine and knew instantly she'd been rumbled.

The messages were all in the same sharp, demanding tone.

'Rose, where are you? It's Saskia's birthday Sunday and I wanted to talk about what you might bring.'

Click.

'Rose, it's Maxine... (rustle rustle)...Rose? Why aren't you answering me? Are you there?' Long pause. Did she think Rosie was standing over it, fielding calls?

Click.

'Rose, I'm getting seriously annoyed. Could you *please* call me back? Saskia will be devastated if you miss her birthday lunch.'

Beeeep. Click.

Uh oh, she was in trouble. Her mother would be all stressed about getting everything perfect for her granddaughter's birthday and she clearly hadn't expected to find Rosie missing in action.

Suitcase dripping on the taxi floor, Rosie's damp skin prickled with foreboding. Her mother had a fairly unpredictable temper but today there was good reason to be annoyed. She really ought to have shared her good news the second Agent Million left. Or at least admitted she was off abroad. But often their calls were weeks apart and so Rosie had hoped, naively, she might get away with it. In all the excitement she'd forgotten her niece's birthday.

If her brother, Paul, was the apple of his mum's eye, then his youngest curly-haired daughter must be the delectable toffee coating and, she, Rosie, the troublesome worm.

Listlessly she drew a smiley face on the steamed-up window. Why did she feel such gut-wrenching guilt? If there'd been an emergency Maxine or Charlie could have called Rosie's mobile. Her mum had that thing about them costing the earth, but it wasn't like she was short of cash. Maxine's first husband, Paul's dad, had passed on when Paul was eight, leaving his widow with a nice insurance payout. In contrast dying was about the only thing her second husband,

Rosie's dad, had done right judging by the way his widow refused to speak his name.

In her darkest moments, Rosie couldn't help but wonder if her mother hadn't driven them both to an early grave.

Maxine Butterworth opened the door to her semi-detached home almost before Rosie pressed the bell. 'There you are. Finally. No boys?' She peered over her half-crescent bifocals as if Tim and Luke might be lined up single file behind her daughter in some Diversity-inspired dance routine. 'You look like something the cat dragged in.'

Great start. Rosie forced a cheerful smile. 'The cat was a Range Rover, it splashed rather than dragged and the boys are with Charlie half-term.'

'Half-term?' Maxine ushered her daughter inside, a pop-up book on fairies in one hand, a questioning expression on her plucked and shaped brows. For being in her mid-sixties she was surprisingly attractive and dauntingly energetic. 'I'd have thought...' She stopped, squinting accusingly. 'You're very brown. You are aware sun beds cause melanomas, aren't you?'

'No, I...I mean yes. I mean, sorry I...' Balls. Two seconds in and Rosie was tongue-tied and apologising.

A small beribboned whirlwind rushed to grab her knees. 'What've you brought me, Auntie Rosie?'

'In that plastic bag, sweetie.' Rosie bent to hug the little girl, uncomfortably aware of her mother's scrutiny. 'The parcel with the tigers on it.'

When she straightened, Paul and Dee had emerged to greet her. Paul's second wife was seven years his junior, three years older than Rosie. Dressed in cerise mohair sweater and white skinny jeans, Easter's pink streaks had been replaced by a platinum bob. Dee was a hairdresser and liked to experiment.

'What's happened to you then?' Her purple talons fingered Rosie's new cut as they entered the living room. 'Great highlights – that's quite a makeover. And I love those fake Versace boots.'

'Thanks.' Rosie looked down, uneasily. 'Hope the water stains come out.' She glanced around, sensing something missing. 'Didn't Saskia invite friends?'

'We had the proper party yesterday,' Maxine said dismissively. 'This is solely for family. But Saskia disliked her Cinderella cake. She's into fairies these days so she's asked me to copy one of these onto a lemon sponge.' She flapped the book in her hand.

So. Not just one cake then but two. Remembering her mother's no-nonsense attitude towards birthday celebrations when Rosie was small, she couldn't help but marvel at the power of grandchildren. Or was it only granddaughters? Her sons rarely merited this attention.

She sat down, pulling off the boots to rub her ice-cold toes and Dee picked one up.

'Bloody hell, I think they actually are Versace.' She circled Rosie like a shark as if wondering which part to nibble first. 'And that skirt's Ralph Lauren. What have you done? Robbed a bank?'

'Whatever, she's here now.' Paul took off his glasses and wiped them on his shirt, inadvertently exposing flabby white flesh. 'Can we please eat? I'm dying of starvation.'

'Don't fret, pudding-pie.' Dee cast a disparaging glance at her husband's belly. 'It's ready to dish up. Well?' She focused back on Rosie.

'Are all these presents for me?' Saskia had emptied the plastic bag on the floor.

'For everybody.' Rosie's cheeks reddened under their watchful eyes. 'I was in Spain. I won some money.'

'What?' Now she'd got everyone's attention.

'How much?' Dee.

'And you didn't tell us?' Maxine.

'Not the online poker again?' Paul's heavy attempt at humour.

'Here, Mum, this is for you.' Rosie handed over a package, hoping to distract them. 'And Dee and Paul. And this is for Kylie. Is she about?' Even though she could be difficult at times Rosie was actually very fond of her terminally cool, thin-verging-on-anorexic teenage niece.

'At the pictures.' Maxine unwrapped an intricate lace tablecloth. 'Hmm. Nice enough, I daresay, but hardly practical, is it?'

Helplessly Rosie glanced across at Dee but a crisis had arisen and she'd dropped her new t-shirt so she could rush to Saskia who was in tears. The gypsy doll with ruby-red dress, mantilla and real jet-black hair had been flung onto the floor.

'I hate dolls!' Saskia shrieked at a decibel pitch that could shatter crystal. 'I want fairies!'

'Maybe it's a fairy flamenco dancer.' Rosie tried placating her. 'We could make her wings.'

Paul shook his head with battle-weary resignation. 'Don't bother. When she gets in a state like this it's like a hurricane, you've just got to wait for it to blow itself out.' He pulled on his reading glasses to peer at the 'I heart Marbella' mug she'd handed him. 'Mug, eh? Very useful.' He laid it on the coffee table. 'Shall we move into the dining room?'

He looked longingly through the wall arch at a table set for a formal dinner, best china, immaculately folded cloth napkins and far more cutlery than anyone could possibly need for a single meal. Maxine's quest for perfection knew no bounds.

'One of those scratch cards?' Dee held Saskia by the arm as she strained to kick the hated doll. 'Girl in the salon won two hundred on those.'

'No – Premium Bonds.' Rosie looked at her mum. She had the sense of impending doom, something like Mary Queen of Scots might have felt before the executioner finally let fall the axe.

'And you blew it all on a holiday.' Maxine was noticeably disgusted. 'Just what I'd expect. No thought of saving for a rainy day. Well, if you can't make your mortgage next month, don't come poking me for a loan.'

Poking me for a loan? A lump rose in Rosie's throat. When had she ever asked her mum for money?

'You still didn't say how much?' Dee's eyes gleamed avidly. 'I saw those boots in a mag. Five hundred at least.'

'You wasted five hundred pounds on footwear?' Maxine was shocked.

Rosie picked up the doll, and smoothed down her mantilla headdress, a slight smile playing about her lips. She was strangely distanced from the hysterics she knew would come. For once in the history of her family, she held the advantage – however brief, however explosive the repercussions.

'Could you all hold on there a sec?'

Going outside she retrieved her suitcase from behind the wheelie-bin and rolled it forward into her mother's lounge.

'You're not…' Maxine blanched and for one terrible moment Rosie was in total tune with her thoughts.

'No, Mum, I'm not moving back in,' she managed to choke out, feeling her mother's rejection all over again. 'I just, well, I bought everyone a few extra small gifts.' She couldn't look Maxine in the eye, she'd seen enough and the truth was crucifying. Instead she laid the suitcase flat on the shagpile and unzipped it. 'The mug was just a joke, Paul. And Dee, I know you'd never ever wear that Me Encanta España t-shirt – so, here…'

She began handing out the presents, but it was a muted shadow of her happy imaginings.

Out came the iPad for Paul, the perfume, jewellery and clothes for Dee and Maxine, all chosen with such care. And finally, the fairy doll with its gossamer wings and sparkly silver hair. 'For you, darling Saskia.' Rosie handed it to her niece. 'I knew you liked fairies. I like fairies. You can still keep the other doll. They could be sisters maybe?'

The tears instantly stopped. This alone was worth the effort.

A constant chatterer, Dee clasped a Juicy Couture patterned tank to her pointy breasts, for once rendered speechless.

'I won the big prize, a million pounds.' Rosie stared up at three blank uncomprehending faces. 'And frankly, Mum, I'm not too worried about rainy days. The weather looks just fine from here.'

She was back home by early evening, Paul and Dee's effusions ringing like tinnitus in her ears, counterbalanced by her mother's tight-lipped response. 'Full of secrets. I'll never understand you, Rose.'

Couldn't the woman simply be glad for her? But no, when Rosie had given her a hug and said, 'Anything you want, Mum, I'll buy it for you,' her mother's body felt like rigor mortis had set in.

'Fortunately I've all I need, thank you. The tablecloth was quite enough.'

'Come on, Mum,' Rosie had pleaded. 'You must want something? Car? Conservatory? New house?'

'Why would I want a conservatory?' she hissed. 'I'd have all the neighbours complaining for starters. As for a new house, well it was good enough when you were growing up.'

For a second they both stared into each other's eyes, hostility meeting hurt, before Maxine turned and glared at the gifts scattered on the table. Her gaze fell on the mug she'd given Paul, lips twisting in disgust.

'Splashing money around. On rubbish. You're your father's daughter all right.'

'What are you saying? Dad liked to spend?' Rosie knew so little about her dad. Apart from his death in a car crash, the most Maxine would say was that he was the biggest mistake she'd ever made, subject closed. Which only made Rosie wonder if she hadn't been the second biggest.

'Forget it!' Maxine snapped, clearly sorry she'd spoken.

'No, tell me.' For once Rosie asserted herself. 'How am I like him? I've a right to know.'

'I beg your pardon? You might be a millionairess now, but this is still *my* home, young lady, and I will not have you disrespecting me like that. Now come along, Saskia. Time to cut that cake.'

And with that she flounced off. Leaving Rosie intrigued. Maxine was cross, yes, but there was something else, something Rosie couldn't put her finger on until after she'd arrived back at her own house emotionally exhausted, and reflected on it over a large glass of Chablis.

She'd seemed so shocked. Affronted, yes. Maxine was an interior designer; Rosie had known she'd hate those tacky souvenirs. Still was that any reason to act as if someone had slapped her? As if Rosie winning a fortune was a personal insult.

And that look in her eyes? When she'd mentioned Rosie's dad?

If it wasn't ridiculous she'd almost swear her mother was terrified.

But of what? And why?

Chapter Twelve

'. . . and slice of baklava.' Olivia scrawled a note on her pad. 'OK. Be back in a jiffy.' She had a new appreciation of waitresses, she decided. Never again would she sit in restaurants drumming her nails at the slow service or return her plate because the china was chipped. Or if she did – because even a hairline crack could hold billions of bacteria – she'd be super-nice about it.

Of course she might never trust a restaurant again since seeing their secrets; spying a mouse scuttle behind the oven and the chef dusting off a dropped chicken kebab and replacing it on its bed of rice.

Shc sauntered over to the teenagers who'd just walked in, intentionally avoiding the corner where a certain occupant attempted to catch her attention. Tattle-tale. Trying to get her in trouble with Darius when she needed this job so badly.

She and loyal little Irma had been giving Marcus a dish of revenge literally served cold the last few days, slopping his coffee into its saucer, letting his food congeal on the counter but today Irma was visiting the dentist and Olivia knew she'd be forced to serve him eventually.

'Now there and what would you like?' She gave the newcomers her biggest smile, noticing she'd acquired an Irish brogue – as if she were play-acting a waitress named Livvy just for fun.

'Some service would be nice,' said a familiar voice. 'Maybe even a coffee. If it's not too much trouble.'

She didn't turn her head. 'Hold up,' she said, irritably. 'I'll be with you in a minute.'

'Oh excellent,' Marcus said, dryly. 'I was beginning to feel invisible.'

Olivia swivelled. He was just behind her, bouncing slightly in his old converse sneakers, a coiled spring of suppressed energy wearing another disreputable sweater and well-worn jeans that the Salvation Army would surely have rejected.

'Oh?' She arched her eyebrow. 'You mean people are starting to see through you?'

'Table in the corner?' Marcus jerked a thumb in that direction. 'Or did we switch to self-service?'

'I'll get to it. Now where were we?' She returned to the teenagers as she saw Darius glance her way. 'Oh yes, your order.'

The doorbell rang, two people entered, and Olivia froze. Sara Goswell again with another girl who looked vaguely familiar. Damn. Olivia had thought, given Sara's snobby attitude, she'd be saved a return. Instead the girls made their way to a table, shucking off coats. Olivia saw their heads draw together, saw them cast a surreptitious peek in her direction, then giggle.

The penny dropped with the clang of falling hopes. Someone had recognised her. On the last visit? On another? She couldn't trust herself to serve that table. The merest hint of a sneer from Sara would find her wearing a plate of moussaka.

She saw Darius heading her way with a thunderous frown and leaned in to the teenage couple. 'Would you like some suggestions?'

The boy looked up, truculent; his face blotched with acne pimples. 'No we'd like you to piss off and give us time to think.'

'Sorry,' the girl apologised, digging him sharply in the ribs. Moving away, Olivia heard them fighting. 'So bloody rude,' the girl scolded. The boy swore.

'Having a problem today?' Darius blocked her path.

'Nope. Everything's good.'

'That's funny, because I've customers starving to death while you faff about over here. Corner table? I had to take the order myself. Now get your bum in gear and serve it to him. I'm surprised he hasn't pissed off to Starbucks by now.'

'Never happen, mate.' Unnoticed, someone had arrived behind them. Olivia turned to see the sexy dude called Zac grinning broadly. 'Old Marcus wouldn't be seen dead in that den of sin.' He was wearing his leather biker jacket, swinging a full-face helmet. 'Thinks the Yanks are an evil imperialist power. Corrupting the world with fast food and filthy dollars.'

Explained a lot, Olivia reflected moodily as Darius pulled Zac to one side for a private discussion. Marcus, the grumpy treacherous troublemaker had it in for her, splitting on her to Darius because he was under the misapprehension she was American.

Grabbing his laden plate of mezze, she headed towards the despised corner, keeping her head high and dignity intact until her foot hit a pool of spilled water and shot from under her.

Everything went flying. Fava beans, calamari, olives, aubergine salad and meatballs sailed briefly into orbit before landing, mostly on Olivia who was flat on her back. The clatter of cutlery stopped in abrupt astonished silence. Someone gasped, someone laughed and then the room got loud again.

A hand reached down to pull her to her feet. A few fava beans slid down Marcus's shoulder as his surprisingly strong grip hauled her upright.

'You OK?' He wiped off his glasses, unaware that a piece of bell pepper sat in his soft brown curls.

Olivia bit her lip, mortified, a lump rising on the back of her head. 'Fantastic. Never better.' Her ruined clothes looked like a Jackson Pollock canvas, splattered with tomato sauce. Diners grumbled as they dipped napkins in water glasses to attack stains.

Darius gave a slow hand clap. 'Nice going, you didn't wanna work today, you just had to say summat. Better go home and clean yourself up.'

Then as if things weren't bad enough, she heard a fake roof-raising shriek and the voice she dreaded.

'Olivia Wheeler. It *is* you, isn't it?'

Idiot! Incompetent! Olivia swore as she gingerly soaped the grease from her tender scalp. Humiliating herself in front of everyone. Getting sent home. She cursed Marcus too, knowing it wasn't his fault yet certain he couldn't have enjoyed it more if he'd masterminded the event.

She slumped on her bed in a towel, feeling useless and depressed. With it came old unwelcome feelings of shame and remorse.

If only she hadn't chattered innocently to her mother about how she and Dad had met the babysitter at the Alameda, all of them eating ice cream.

If only she'd come straight home from school that afternoon instead of having a sleepover at a friend's house.

If only someone had realised that her mother's cheerfulness was an act or had found her stockpile of pills.

If only her mother hadn't been left alone, no ladies arriving for cocktails, no Dad or Olivia when she needed them most.

If only Olivia had done something, anything to prevent it happening.

Statistics whirled through her head, facts gleaned in a futile attempt to assuage the sickening guilt. More deaths occur worldwide from suicide than from accidents, murders and war combined. Twice as many women as men attempt suicide but four times as many men succeed in killing themselves. Most suicides have had had at least one psychiatric illness: depression, alcohol abuse, bipolar disorder. It was a myth that those who talk about it don't do it.

Had Olivia's mother talked about it? Everyone knew she had her blue spells, days she stayed in bed. 'What an old lazybones I am,' she'd say when Olivia found her napping. 'A touch too much fun last night, darling.' But she was brilliant too, unpredictable, zany and fun. Nobody else's mum whisked them off to Paris for some mother-daughter time; jumped into swimming pools fully-dressed; or walked into town barefoot because they hated the confinement of shoes.

Enough! Olivia didn't want to remember. The shock of coming home to find that figure lying on her bed, apparently asleep.

The sick whirling feeling as the ambulance arrived, the paramedics working in vain. The sorrow, the anger, the horror of it all.

She put on jeans and sweater and pulled out her iPhone, scanning her emails. Mostly spam, very few from known contacts and she'd no desire to open those. Her spirits lifted as she saw a message from the estate agents handling the villa sale asking her to call. An offer already?

'Not yet, I'm afraid,' the person on the phone apologised, the Skype call half-way decent for once. 'We've priced it low but things just aren't moving. No, but Señor MacDonald found some papers, of your father's we believe, forgotten in a desk. He asked me to contact you. In case it was something of value.'

'And was it? Valuable?' Olivia crossed her fingers, slender body tense in anticipation. How odd if her father should reach a helping hand from beyond the grave. She remembered the gigantic desk well. She used to lurk under it, pretending to be a spy. It would be just like her dad to hide money or bond certificates in its cavernous depths.

'Alas, no, I do not think so.' There was the trace of a Castilian lisp in the warm voice. 'But I am no expert and who can tell what a daughter might cherish or admirers of her father's work find interesting. It appears mostly inconsequential. Scribbles and sketches and what looked like part of a letter.'

'A letter?' Olivia sat bolt upright. 'What does it say?'

'We did not read it,' the woman said with admirable delicacy. 'But if you give me your address, I will be pleased to send it out in the post today.'

Chapter Thirteen

When Rosie met her first boyfriend, she was sixteen and deeply unhappy at home. Jed, The Jerk, as she'd later describe him, was nineteen with a flat. Both had left school early, both were unemployed, immature and in a bad place. Him with drugs, her with Maxine.

Even as a small child Rosie had fathomed that her relationship with her mum differed from her friends. She didn't read Rosie bedtime stories or play games with her. She seldom cuddled her or stuck her drawings on the fridge.

Rosie had tried, God knew. Doing funny things to make her mother laugh. Smothering her in affection in the hopes of getting some in return. Working at her lessons so Maxine would boast about her achievements the way she did her son's. To no avail. Her mother would unwind Rosie's hands from her neck, stash the report cards away without comment and fail to crack a smile at Rosie's made-up Michael Jackson dance. At best Rosie felt unnoticed, at worst the Cinderella stepchild, tolerated but never doted on like her older brother. And when the teenage years hit, Rosie decided she'd had enough.

Maxine around then was a contrast of characteristics – strict but neglectful, work-obsessed but with little patience for her youngest child. Always the perfectionist, not a cushion out of place or a crumb on the carpet, yet there was never a home-cooked meal on the table. And she was scolding – if not outright berating – her daughter virtually daily.

So when Rosie started dating The Jerk, it wasn't so much that he was cute (rather gangly with a gargantuan Adam's apple) or that he'd got great prospects (a dope-dealing loser) but with him she found much-needed affection (at first), and the fact that he owned a flat (a squat) and wanted her to shack up with him was at least a chance of escape.

How *great*, she'd imagined, not to have her mother harping on about cleaning up after herself, tidying her bedroom, not marking the walls with posters. How *fantastic* to have no curfew when she wanted to stay out late. How *brilliant* to be able to leave towels on the floor, water in the bath, plates in the sink. Not to be criticised for her music, her make-up, clothes, attitude.

When all the arguments came to a head one night, Rosie jammed a few clothes into a holdall and caught a bus to her boyfriend's. Freedom! OK, she rapidly realised it was the pits living with a dishonest unfaithful junkie but nine months passed before she contacted Maxine, pride interfering each time her fingers reached for the phone. Thinking about it after, and especially once she'd had her own children, it'd been a completely selfish thing to do to someone and her mother must have been worried sick.

Or was she?

No police or welfare officer ever turned up searching for Rosie. Had Maxine really been *that* bothered?

When Rosie did eventually call, Maxine had listened calmly, asked her to come over, brought out the good china and Fortnum & Mason fruit cake but there was no great reconciliation on the doorstep, no falling weeping into arms. Instead all that remained of their lousy relationship was polite indifference. No bickering or bullying anymore, but no caring either. It was like she'd washed her hands of Rosie. They spoke like strangers. Any love, however dysfunctional, that existed between them had gone forever and Rosie was never forgiven and certainly not invited back to live in the family house.

⚜ ⚜ ⚜

'Bums!'

Looking out of the window, a dismayed Rosie saw Valerie sitting in Charlie's car. Understandable perhaps. It would have added another twenty minutes to their five-hour journey from Cornwall to drop her off in Highgate. Yet it was still a huge shock. So far Rosie had managed to avoid any contact with the woman who'd lured away her husband. Charlie, sensitive to her pain (or his fiancée's shame), had always carried out the swap-over alone.

'Bye, Aunty Val. Hiya, Mum.' Luke tumbled out of the car first. He raced up the stairs, never knowing how that casual 'Aunty Val' stung. Charlie walked up carrying Luke's bag and Tim followed dragging his along the ground, garments spilling out as he walked.

'Let me help, sweetheart.' Rosie flashed a curious glance at the passenger as she picked up Tim's clothes littering the short path.

Valerie's head was turned away, long dark hair behind one ear, revealing a few inches of cheek. A very ordinary cheek. No witchy wart or burlesque blusher. Still it was a cheek that Charlie had presumably smothered with steamy fervent kisses (unless he'd skipped past it in his rush to more tantalising parts of her anatomy) while his dopey unsuspecting wife was bathing his kids and his dinner drying to a crisp in the oven.

It was maybe illogical to feel such resentment towards this usurper when it was Charlie who'd betrayed her trust. But seeing her in the flesh, hearing her children treat her like a favourite aunty, the normally mild Rosie realised the only hatchet she wanted to bury was in her rival's neck.

Charlie stood back, hands in pockets, as the boys racketed up the stairs. 'Great suntan, Rosie. How was your holiday?'

'Good, thanks. Yours?' She felt like a gaudy butterfly suddenly, in the bright colourful dress she'd put on after indulging in a deliciously scented bubble bath on return from Maxine's. In Marbella its hemline had seemed modest enough but now she was conscious of exposed knees, legs and feet unusually bare.

'Oh you know Cornwall. Smashing in the sunshine, rubbish in the rain. Not Val's cup of tea at all.'

'Oh?' She noticed the pinched lips and the slight implied criticism of Val – a first. Charlie loved Cornwall, would live there if work allowed.

He rubbed his hands together, cheerfully. 'Good news is Val got promoted and the showroom's doing better. We've expanded our used car section, that's where the money is these days. Here,' he pulled out a cheque from his wallet, 'this month and last's. You're the best, Rosie. Lot of wives would have been nagging about it no end.'

She took it with slow reluctant fingers. Wasn't that always the way? When she was desperate the money wasn't there. Now she didn't need it, he was rolling in wealth.

'Thanks. They're talking about redundancies at the school.' She could hardly bear looking at him, simply wanting him and his floozy both gone.

'They are?' He seemed concerned. 'But you're safe, aren't you?'

His blue eyes roamed over her, noting all the changes. He was wondering what – or perhaps who – was responsible for the new hairstyle, the updated wardrobe, the impromptu trip to Spain. She knew the way his brain worked. Just like she knew he loved roasted beetroot but not pickled, craved capers on his pizza, fainted when he had his blood drawn. Everything about him was so familiar and yet it was alien too, all claimed by that woman waiting in the car.

'So,' she could tell he was as curious about her presumed lover as she was about his girlfriend, 'package deal was it?'

'Not exactly.' Rosie bent to pluck a weed from one of the flowerpots, faking nonchalance as she tried hiding her trembling hands. 'Look, you're going to find out soon enough.' She braced herself. This was it then. Time to begin the speech, the one that she'd rehearsed ever since Agent Million had come a-calling. 'So I may as well just say it. Something amazing happened—'

'Yeah, I guessed that much. What's his name?' Did she detect a trace of jealousy in his rueful grin? 'Better be good enough for you, that's all. Is he loaded, I hope?'

'No but I am.' His interruption had thrown off the second half of the sentence, delivered so eloquently to her reflection only twenty minutes before. 'Something amazing happened…' she repeated, forcing herself to meet his gaze. 'Not with a man…although I might have…it's not like it's any of your business anymore.' Now she was getting side-tracked and coming across a mite bitter, the last thing she'd wanted. 'The Premium Bonds,' she added swiftly. 'I won. A cool million.' She paused and added, 'Pounds,' although it was obviously extraneous. What other currency could it be? A million yen? A million rupees?

His expression was priceless. The flash of surprise. An instant for the cogs to turn. His laugh was loud and genuine. She half-expected Valerie to lower her window to better eavesdrop. For a brief moment she was on a high.

Charlie took a step back, shaking his head.

'Good one, Rosie. Very funny. Don't worry, I get it. You're a hundred percent right. None of my business.'

He was still chuckling as he walked back to the car. Dope. Well, he'd find out soon enough.

Short while later her sons, in pyjamas, were wolfing down macaroni cheese at the kitchen table. She managed to extricate a few details about the holiday. It sounded pretty miserable. Lousy weather, boring country walks, fishing in the rain with nary a bite.

'Aunty Val hated it,' Tim said. 'They had a fight. Told Daddy she'd never go back.'

Her heart skipped with illicit pleasure. That probably thrilled Charlie's parents – not! Besides pissing him off.

'There must have been some good parts,' she probed as they ate their supper. 'Come on. You were with Gran and Grandpa. And Cornwall's a beautiful place.'

'We visited one cool beach,' Luke ventured as he put his dish in the sink. 'Where we started to build a dam.'

'But we couldn't stay because Aunty Val kept moaning about being cold,' Tim finished.

'Daddy lent her his jacket,' Luke volunteered. 'But she was still freezing.'

A vision arose like an erupting boil. The dark-haired girl with teeth chattering. Charlie tenderly lacing his jacket around her shoulders, pulling her to him, kissing her nose, warming her up.

She swallowed. Everything inside tensed as the old emotions of hurt, jealousy and anger rose up again. 'But other than that you all got on OK? Who cooked?'

'Gran mostly but Aunty Val made a yummy cottage pie.' Luke rubbed his tummy. 'With loads of thick luscious gravy.'

'Not as good as yours though.' Tim looked up at Rosie with eyes just like her own. Sugared the vinegar somewhat. He was shyer and more sensitive than his confident, impulsive brother, more in tune with his mother's churning emotions.

She gave him a grateful smile. 'As long as you both ate it.' She ruffled their heads.

And they were all that mattered. Her two chickadees. Home to the roost. She followed their weary legs up the stairs. No longer babies – too heavy to carry, too cool to be kissed, but not too young to need her more than they'd ever admit. These two rascals were her priority now.

How she loved them with every inch of her exploding heart.

The same heart that thudded as she tucked them both into bed, turned out the lights and blew them a silent unseen kiss.

And the same disobedient heart that obstinately, unwisely, insisted on yearning after her ex.

Chapter Fourteen

Still no sign of the envelope from Spain containing this mystery letter. She should have asked the estate agent to read it over the phone. What could it be? One of those her dad had sworn to send weekly to her boarding school? He'd penned only a few, full of amusing inappropriate gossip and soon-to-be-broken promises for the summer holidays. But there was no saying this letter was for Olivia. And what if it had gone permanently missing, the mail being what it was? As she cleared plates and took orders, Olivia was tormented by curiosity.

Yes, she'd gone back to the café the next day. Sneers or not, she was no rabbit to be so easily scared away.

Darius swaggered over, smirking as he slapped a tabloid in front of her. 'You made the papers, girl. Eggs over-easy, my arse.'

Olivia bent her head to see a grainy photo, probably captured with someone's cell phone, of herself sprawling on the floor, fava beans in her hair, and mouth agape in surprise. Her face whitened as she scanned the text.

*FROM FINANCIAL F***K-UP TO FLYING FRY-UP!*

Another spectacular slip-up for Olivia Wheeler, 33, former employee and victim of charismatic crook, Rupert Mandrake, who stole over $5 billion from his wealthy hedge fund clients. Once a society favourite and rising star of the financial world, Wheeler is reduced to waiting tables in a Crouch End café after allegedly losing job, personal fortune and New York's most eligible bachelor to her fraudulent boss's infamous scam. As former colleagues languish in jail *and the international manhunt continues for Mandrake, sources tell us Wheeler has been wheedling her old City employers for work with even less success than her waitressing skills. Or is she – as internet rumours have suggested this week – laying low, waiting for the heat to subside, before she joins her lover? Too bad she won't spill the beans and reveal where Mandrake stashed that loot!*

Irma had come over, craning her neck to read the article. She finished the paragraph and stared up with shocked panda eyes.

Olivia grasped the edge of the table with white knuckle fury. Damn Sara Goswell. And damn this malicious rag with its gossipy innuendo. Instantly the packed room seemed full of mocking, avid faces. How many of them had read the story? How long before other spiteful busybodies or gloating enemies showed up like gawkers at a plane wreck?

She whirled on Darius. 'Who the hell took that photo?'

Involuntarily he stepped backwards, caustic amusement on his swarthy face. 'Could 'a been anyone, couldn't it?' He rubbed his hand over his square jaw. 'Now I got a business to run and unless you got a line on that dough they're on about, you've customers to serve.'

He stuck his thumbs in his belt loop and grinned broadly.

'Not that a little street theatre ain't good for business.' He winked at the nearest table. 'Flat on your back one day. Criminal mastermind the next.' His audience chuckled. 'Maybe I can make a poster for the window. What'cha think, Livvy?'

A red mist descended over Olivia's vision. Blinded with rage, she hurled the nearest coffee cup with all her might. It missed Darius's ear by inches, crashing against the wall.

She'd just time to register his shocked expression and his bellow 'mad bitch' before she flung open the door, shouldered past an astonished Marcus and stormed out, 'open' sign flapping with the force of her exit.

Then she was in the street again, adrenaline subsiding, feeling heartsick and betrayed, not least by her own emotional outburst.

Olivia Wheeler just didn't do emotional. In her world she'd always had to hide any hint of vulnerability behind a hard-nosed façade. Successful women didn't succumb to hysterics and breakdowns. And if people called her a ball-breaking bitch, well she could handle a few jealous insults.

Now she hardly recognised herself. She'd lost it with Shipton, she'd lost it with Brad, and hell, she'd really lost it in there. Getting fired wasn't as troubling as the sense of everything she knew and believed about herself – her strengths, her weaknesses – evaporating into a void. Which left – what? Who?

The nursing home was busy, staff changing sheets, attendants taking yellow bin bags filled with who knew what to who knew where. No one paid Olivia any attention as she walked to Winnie's room.

'Don't just stand there like a lemon, girl.' Winnie, fully-dressed and sitting on her bed, beckoned her forward. 'Help me with this darn contraption.'

Her great-aunt might look frail but she'd the grip of a latched-on pit bull as she rested her weight on Olivia's shoulder, determinedly edging thin legs in crinkled support stockings and fluffy slippers into the confines of a Zimmer frame.

She transferred her grip to the metal handle, back straightening, legs wobbling. Was Olivia strong enough to hold Winnie up if she lost her balance? She craned her neck to look for assistance but the corridor, Grand Central Station moments ago, was deserted.

'Shouldn't you wait for a wheelchair?'

'Nonsense, child. I'll not be kept prisoner in my own room.'

'OK then.' Olivia hadn't the energy to argue. 'Here we go.'

Their progress was achingly slow. They were near the door when a nurse came in.

'Oh no you don't, babes.' She took charge, steering Winnie back onto the bed. 'You wait here until Dr Harden makes his rounds. He wants to see you.'

'Well, I don't want to see him!' Winnie snapped moodily. 'Dr Blood.'

The nurse smiled indulgently and began wrapping a nylon cuff above the old lady's painfully bony elbow. With a shock Olivia realised why she looked familiar. It was Darius's girlfriend, the one who'd visited the café all tanned from her holiday. Small world – too small. But her aunt's carer didn't recognise her – why should she? She'd had eyes only for her boyfriend.

'Don't mind me.' She began pumping a black rubber bulb and staring at the blood pressure gauge.

'Go on then.' Winnie jutted her chin at a folded up newspaper. 'Read out the crossword.'

Olivia let her hair fall forward hiding her face as the nurse put the stethoscope in her ears and placed the disc on Winnie's chest. She started to read, throat feeling instantly hoarse. Of all the rotten coincidences.

'Speak up, girl. Don't mumble,' Winnie grouched. The nurse cast over a sympathetic glance, the last thing Olivia wanted. She spoke louder, enunciating as if at an elocution lesson.

'Two across. Four letters. Stylish sounding bird.'

'Chic!' Winnie fired back, fast as a game show contestant.

'All done.' The nurse packed her things. 'Oh look, the PAT dogs have arrived.'

Two cute black Labradors stuck their noses through the door, tails wagging. Winnie sat up straighter.

'Get them out of here. Filthy curs!' She waved them off. 'Shoo, shoo.'

'Someone's having a bad day,' the nurse said calmly as she left.

Her and me both, Olivia thought. She fished on the ground for her handbag, ready to make her escape.

Winnie flopped back on the pillows, irritable.

'I honestly don't know why you stay with him, Karen,' she declared, watery eyes accusing. 'He's never been any good. Have you no pride?'

Karen? That was her mother's name. Olivia eased herself back into the chair, bag in lap.

'You mean Gray?' she guessed cautiously. 'He loves me, Winnie.'

'Darn funny way of showing it.' The old lady spluttered and started a coughing fit so hard Olivia was afraid she'd choke. 'What will happen when people find out?' she gasped, when she could breathe again. 'He could be thrown in jail, not to mention the scandal, the lives he's ruined. And those poor girls.'

What poor girls? Olivia leaned forward. Was she still talking about her dad? And if so, where did jail come into it? Her babysitter had been a college student, eighteen at least. Had there been younger ones? Minors?

'What girls?' she asked softly. But her aunt pressed her lips obstinately together and right on cue the doctor walked in and Winnie was on a different tack, berating him.

It was still light, not quite eight, before Olivia made her way back to her apartment. She'd sat in the library for hours, using their computers, eating a blueberry muffin crumb by crumb and checking out help wanted ads. She had to watch her pennies now. There weren't many of them left.

She hesitated when she saw the policeman standing on the front doorstep. More bad news. There were seven other flats in the building but she sensed immediately he was waiting for her. A London 'Bobby', he wore the absurd helmet American tourists loved, looking up as she approached.

'Miss Wheeler?'

The landlord was behind him. She saw his bulk in the shadows of the hall.

'Yes?' Why so nervous? She'd done nothing wrong. Was he here to tell her Mandrake had been arrested? That she was needed at the trial?

'Afraid there's been a break-in. Mr Rathbone here called us when he noticed your lock smashed. I'd like you to take a quick look around and tell me if anything's missing.'

Olivia pushed past the lurking landlord. Splintered wood showed where the door had been forced open, her few possessions wildly scattered.

'Probably pressed buttons until someone buzzed them in. Works every time.' The policeman was behind her.

'I didn't hear a thing,' the landlord growled. 'I had the radio on loud. Bloody vandals. Area's gone to the dogs.'

'Know what they were looking for?' The young policeman's tone said it all. Drugs. What else would people hope to find in a dump like this?

'Nope.'

A thought struck Olivia. Crossing the room, she pulled a book from the shabby chest of drawers and shook out its pages. Gone.

'I had four hundred quid in there,' she said grimly, setting her mouth to stop her lip quivering. Not daring to hope, she pulled open the drawer in the kitchen where she'd put her mother's watch when its flimsy clasp had finally given way. Empty, save for a spoon and fork. She ran her hand down the back to make sure.

'Bad luck. If you'd like to fill in a report, come to the station tomorrow.' He raised his helmet and scratched his forehead. 'Not much chance of catching them though. This sort of thing's usually young people. Addicts looking for whatever they can lay their hands on. Money preferable.'

Money. She recalled the nasty implications pasted all over that tabloid. That same newspaper landed on the hall mat every morning. Coincidence? Could someone actually believe she'd got billions stashed away? She caught the landlord's sly glance and suspicion flared. She had a strange urge to fall on him like a shrieking she-devil until he confessed.

'Too late to get that door fixed tonight,' the policeman was saying. 'Have you somewhere you can stay?'

Rathbone curled his upper lip in what was meant to be a smile. 'I can keep an eye on the young lady. I'll sleep with my door open. In case she's worried about intruders.'

As if. She'd never sleep a wink with Rathbone out there. Spying on her. Never feel safe sleeping here again. Probably she was being paranoid but still... 'No need,' she lied. 'I've got friends nearby.'

Oh, if only that were true.

Chapter Fifteen

'Don't forget, twelve-fifteen meeting.' Pauline Dawkins stuck her head around the Orange classroom door.

'Got a feeling this won't be good.' Carol, the teacher Rosie was assigned to this term, walked with Rosie to the ICT suite, spilling folders from her overloaded arms.

They passed the toilets and Rosie nipped in. Gemma emerged from a stall, sighing. 'I dreamed about him last night.'

'Simon?' Automatically Rosie checked for feet under doors. She was the sole confidante Gemma had trusted with her secret just as Gemma was the only staff member Rosie had told about her win. 'Was it erotic?'

'How could it not be?' Gemma's eyes glazed over. 'We were together giving a standing ovation to a mono-cycling poodle. The poodle dropped to a bow and Simon placed his hand ever so lightly against my back. His fingers nearly burnt my skin.'

Rosie laughed as she tugged a hand towel from the machine. 'That's erotic? A mono-cycling poodle and Simon Cowell's hot little hands?'

'Guess you had to be there.' Gemma giggled as they emerged into the hall. 'What a fantastic top. Love that turquoise. Where did you get it?'

'Just some Spanish market.' Rosie cringed, not wanting to admit how expensive it had been. Gemma's eclectic wardrobe, like Rosie's until a few weeks ago, came mostly from charity shops.

They were the last to arrive. Academic staff, TAs, one-to-one support workers, nursery nurses, even old Mick, the Premises Officer, crowded the horseshoe of tables, shuffling, coughing and whispering. The tension was palpable.

'Thank you for coming.' Miss Kirby, the Head Teacher, leaned her weight on the table. 'I realise many of you are worried and by calling you here today I hope to put a stop to rumours. I'm asking you, however, to keep this information confidential.'

She stared down at her notes, face solemn.

'As you're aware, the government drastically reduced the education budget this year. In these bleak times I'm afraid our Governors have no option but to merge classrooms, cut some staff back to part time, let others go.' She waited for the murmurs to quiet. 'Letters will be mailed tonight with more details. If anyone's considered moving on, now's an excellent time to take advantage of the redundancy package.'

Eventually the volley of questions died down. The Head nodded to Pauline who left the room and returned quickly, hands behind her back.

'On a far happier note.' Miss Kirby closed her file, looking relieved. 'Pauline, dear, would you do the honours?'

Swelling in importance, Pauline flourished her concealed booty, a champagne bottle and giant card adorned with balloons and streamers. Carol fetched glasses as people perked up like wagging-tailed puppies anticipating treats.

'A wee bird's told us some very exciting news. And well, all of us here at Avondale Infants would like to say *congratulations.* Well done!' Card under her arm, Pauline started clapping, the noise rising in crescendo as everyone joined in. Someone slapped Rosie on the back. To her horror they were all staring at her, nodding and grinning.

'Speech! Speech!' Carol cheered.

'Um, er, th-thank you,' Rosie stuttered. She saw Gemma, face buried in hands, looking incredibly guilty. 'But…um…well done for what?'

'For what, she says?' Pauline rolled her eyes causing a ripple of laughter. 'Scooping the jackpot of course. Three cheers for Rosie. Hip Hip…'

'I didn't mean to,' Gemma explained anxiously. 'Pauline asked about your holiday and I accidentally gave the game away.'

Rosie was still reeling from the overwhelming flood of attention, everyone asking about her plans.

'Not a clue,' she kept saying. 'Haven't had time to decide.'

One of the nursery nurses scribbled a number. 'My husband's a financial advisor. He'd love to help.'

'Well, I…thanks.'

She wasn't the only one. Someone's son was an estate agent, another's brother managed a bank, two husbands and one wife were mortgage consultants. The unwelcome fuss continued until a quarrel erupted in the playground and reluctantly everyone dispersed.

A strange sensation, being the hot topic of the year. Shyly Rosie kept her head down as she walked from lesson to lesson, feeling as if spotlights shone on her every move.

It was almost quitting time when Carol, sounding oddly apologetic, asked her to make twenty copies of a word search puzzle.

Rosie headed to the new all-singing-all-dancing-but-impossible-to-actually-use photocopier. After a confusing few minutes pressing buttons, receiving A3 instead of A4, landscape instead of portrait, the machine ground to a juddering halt, amber light flashing.

'…least we've one definite.' Pauline's voice sounded in the next corridor. 'Who'd stick around here after winning a million quid?'

Rosie shrunk back as the photocopier started up again, sheet after sheet spewing out. Terrified they'd investigate, she yanked the plug from its socket.

'But Rosie loves it here.' That was Gemma. 'She might want to stay.'

'Then she'd be downright selfish,' Pauline said, crisp, no-nonsense. 'We all have families to feed. And Gemma, my love, according to HR, if it isn't her, it's you.'

'We'll be sorry to lose you, Rosie,' Miss Kirby said, brow furrowed. 'The children love you but I can't deny it's a relief. I hate to cast out anyone in this terrible economy.'

Silly sentimental tears threatened to spoil Rosie's brave nod, but it was her or Gemma. She stood to leave just as the bursar scurried in, pushing up her bifocals.

'There's a reporter lurking around asking questions about Rosie. We sent him packing but he's outside the main gates.'

'You'd better slip out the Harlow Road exit, Rosie.' Miss Kirby grimaced. 'Don't worry about working out your notice. We can handle things.'

Achingly sad, Rosie hustled out the back entrance. She loved Avondale Infants. The school had saved her sanity in so many ways and she couldn't even leave through the front gate.

Meanwhile Charlie had the boys for the weekend. No reason to rush home. She felt strangely adrift.

She pulled out her mobile. 'I'm sneaking out the school. Press is snooping around. Someone's blown the whistle.' It sounded bizarre.

'You what?' Anya giggled.

'And I resigned. Fancy a drink?'

'I'm seeing Darius later. Meet you at his place? Six o'clock?'

Someone seized her arm from behind. 'You're her, aren't you?' A wild-eyed older woman had imprisoned her elbow, strong fingers biting painfully into the flesh. Rosie jerked back and tried to pull away but the grip intensified.

'Let go. You're hurting!' She was scared suddenly.

'Please! You've got to help me.' Her assailant looked quite mad.

'Mum, stop it.' One of the dinner ladies trotted towards them as fast as her great weight would allow. 'Leave her alone.'

'They're taking our house.' The woman rushed on double-speed, tears streaming down her cheeks. 'It's only twenty thousand but they're about to evict us.'

Her daughter reached them both, panting and purple.

'I'm so very sorry.' Gently she removed her mother's grip, finger by finger. 'She's not herself. Come on, Mum. Let's get you a nice cuppa.'

Words floated back, wailing on the wind.

'But she's got all that money. Why *can't* she help?'

'Twenty thousand pounds! To a total stranger?' Rosie held the phone away from her ear as Anya's screech threatened to burst her eardrums. Well, of course with Rosie not clicking off her horrified friend had overheard almost everything. 'Oh my days! Are you out of your mind? We need a proper talk. I'll see you at Darius's. And for bleeding hell's sake, I don't care how many begging, snot-nosed orphans you pass on the way home, don't hand out so much as a postage stamp.'

Darius was wearing stonewashed denims, pointed boots and an untucked mint-green shirt with a wide seventies collar. He smelled of aftershave, earthy and virile.

'Anya told me the news.' He gave her a rib-cracking squeeze. 'Bloody brilliant.'

'Unbelievable, yes.' She could hardly blame Anya for taking her lover into her confidence but still… What part of top secret did her friends not get?

'Beer? Wine? Something stronger? This needs celebrating, girl.' His living room was remarkably neat, the furniture masculine, décor sparse.

'Anything but ouzo.' She smiled, settling on the sofa. 'How's business?'

'Just fired a psycho waitress,' he called from the kitchen.

'Oh, why's that?'

He reappeared, wrestling with a corkscrew. 'Attacked me, mad bitch.' The cork gave way with a pop. 'Found out she was a crook.'

'Yikes! Better off without her then.' Rosie accepted the Chardonnay.

'Cheers.' Joining her on the sofa Darius clinked her glass with his beer bottle. 'So what'cha going to do with all that dosh?'

'I'm still acclimatising. I resigned today.'

'Well, no need to work now, eh?' He draped one arm casually over the cushions.

'I suppose.' Rosie stared glumly into her glass.

'Cheer up, sunshine. You should be out there having fun, girl.' Darius shifted his bulk closer. So lightly she could have imagined it, his fingers brushed her hair. 'Hey, you need a friend for a good time, just call me. I've a *million* ideas.'

She was all of a sudden aware of his heavy thighs inches from her own, his arm behind her neck as his big grinning face closed in. She felt paralysed, a startled rabbit to his King Cobra, as thick lips swooped, breath hot.

Was it possible, she thought, even as she choked and tried to push him away. She shoved the glass between them and wriggled to the far end of the sofa, sliding away from his reach. *Anya's boyfriend – Anya's doting boyfriend – was making a pass.*

Then she was on her feet, flustered. Darius was grinning, looking pleased with himself.

'That the time?' Rosie gulped her wine. 'I really should get going.'

A key sounded in the door. Darius jumped up to give Anya a big smacking kiss on the mouth.

'Good seeing you too.' Anya punched him playfully. 'Sorry I'm late, Rosie. He keeping you entertained?'

'Oh yeah.' She fumbled for her handbag. 'He's been great. But, um...I've got to run. I've, ah, remembered...I have...this...this thing.'

She couldn't get out quick enough. Anya's astonished protests ringing in her ears.

Taking the outdoor steps two at a time, Rosie landed with such force that the heel snapped off one of her ridiculously expensive boots and sent her flying, head first. She landed, not face down into the pavement as expected, but into a pair of strong arms.

'Don't tell me, it's raining gorgeous blondes.' The stranger laughed.

He set her upright and began, oddly, patting down her back.

'What are you doing?' Even in her current distress, Rosie was affected by that swashbuckler smile. He looked like a gorgeous leather-jacketed pirate, a thin beard adorning his chin.

'Looking for wings.' He stepped onto the road shouting up at the window. 'Hello up there. Anyone missing an angel?'

'Shhh, quiet.' Rosie flapped her hands at the lunatic, terrified Darius or Anya would peer down to see what the commotion was.

'Name's Zac.' He thrust out his hand.

God, he was a heartthrob. Rosie wasn't sure she'd ever seen a man so handsome.

'I'm Rosie.' She started to hobble, hopelessly lopsided, past a big scarlet Harley, two helmets hanging on its back.

'Here, let me give you a ride.' Zac picked up one of the helmets, offering it to her. 'One more good deed and I'll have filled my quota for the day.'

'You don't need to. Honest.'

'I'd like to. *Honest.*' He was mocking her. 'Where to? Dinner?'

'I can't, sorry. I've two growing sons to feed.' Not a lie. She did have to feed them. Just not tonight.

'And hubbie?' Zac picked up her ring finger, so vulnerably naked. Rosie blushed, torn between attraction and terror. She felt about fourteen, an inexperienced virgin.

'No hubbie,' he stated. 'Tomorrow then? My psychic powers tell me you've a craving for...' His face screwed with stagey concentration, fingers to temple. 'I'm getting Oriental. Not Thai. Vietnamese? Wait – *Nasi Goreng.*' Leaning casually against his bike, he smiled at Rosie's round-eyed surprise. 'I'm guessing you could murder some Malaysian.'

'That's so...weird. I totally adore Malaysian food.'

Then they were flying through the streets, her arms tight against his waist, her face pressed against his back to shelter from the wind. It was heaven.

Outside her house, he scrawled her number on his hand. 'Got a favourite restaurant?'

'You tell me,' she challenged. 'Mr Psychic.'

'I've a better idea.' He gave a wicked grin. 'I'll show you mine.' He revved his engine to a throaty roar. 'And then later, darling, you can show me yours.'

Chapter Sixteen

Olivia was jumpy as a feral cat – or her namesake fox – alone on the train. It was past midnight, all the night owls and partygoers emptied out.

She sat next to the pole as the train rattled and shook through a tunnel. She was still in her grease-scented Café Hellas white blouse, her daypack stuffed with a few hastily gathered possessions. For the first time in her adult life, until Darius paid the wages he owed, her entire fortune totalled less than twenty pounds. That missing four hundred represented her most desperate act yet – selling her Apple Airbook. The money had offered options. Now she had none.

The train stopped and a loud gang of teenagers staggered on board, laughing and shoving each other roughly, smelling of booze. A wave of nervousness made her pull her small rucksack to her belly, feeling hideously vulnerable against their exuberant testosterone, locked in a tin can with no place to run.

She got out at the next stop. She hadn't dared go to Beth's. That left Andrew's flat in the trendy East End, where they'd briefly stopped so he could change out of his city suit. Suppressing her unhelpful pride, she'd found the place easily enough, pressing the buzzer for a long time before accepting he wasn't home. She sat down at a bench, experimented with stretching out, using her pack as a pillow. It would be a miserable night but could she do it? Would she dare close her eyes, even for a short nap? A policeman strolled past, gave her a look and she stood up, heading down the street again.

There was a crash of thunder and the heavens opened.

Running, bag over head, she finally discovered shelter – an independent cinema showing an all-night Horror Movie Marathon.

And what a night it was. Chainsaws, slashing razors, zombie cannibals. The dark dingy interior was mostly empty. She could see the silhouettes of heads; two couples making out, a few isolated souls she suspected sought shelter like Olivia herself. Two rows ahead a woman in a wool cap, a jacket and multiple ill-fitting coats sat next to a bundle of plastic bags.

Her ears were still ringing with the sounds of terrified screams when she staggered out into the dawn. Her brief snatches of sleep had been filled with dreams of grisly carnage, echoing the images on-screen. She never wanted to watch anything rated beyond PG again.

But at least light was filtering into the sky, the shadows leaching into a washed-out grey. She walked like an automaton, hardly noticing her throbbing feet or the passing miles. She was cold, so cold. She could well have been the sole survivor in a post-apocalyptic city, the once grandiose brick buildings oddly hushed, their shops depressing with metal barricades and 'cheques cashed' signs. When hours later she turned a corner and arrived at Café Hellas she was almost surprised.

Closed. Olivia checked her watch and slumped to sit on the stone pavement, leaning against the window. Darius wouldn't open up until seven. She felt braver in the light of day. She could return to her ravaged flat, shower and change into clean clothes rather than enter the café looking a disaster. And if that landlord bothered her? She reached into the front of her bag and transferred a small object into her pocket. Not exactly a 38 special but it did provide some reassurance.

She still didn't like the idea of returning to the flat. What if Rathbone asked her to pay for the damaged lock? So not going to happen. And her rent…how would she cover that? What Darius owed her wouldn't buy food for long. London was amazingly expensive – no dollar menus, no free coffee refill. At least one of the perks of Café Hellas had been eating for free.

She shivered, feeling again that strange sense of identity slipping away. Olivia Wheeler – the old Olivia – had welcomed challenges, thrived as easily in the fickle shoals of Manhattan society as in the plots and intrigues of the financial world, making million dollar decisions. Nothing had intimidated or scared her off.

That Olivia would have commanded her landlord to fix her lock double-quick, sending him slinking from her anger. That Olivia would have scoffed at some trivial bad press or Darius's scorn. She could easily have imagined that Olivia, thrown into chaos, using luck and ingenuity to spring back on her feet, reinventing herself as financial advisor to a dowager duchess perhaps. *Or lady-in-waiting to the Queen,* she mocked herself, *with digs in Buckingham Palace.*

Only she was an illusion, that over-confident superhuman bitch. Never actually existed. And now she, Livvy, as everyone called her here, was flailing in a nightmare. Funny, she'd always believed she had more gumption.

She didn't know when she became aware of the feeling someone was watching her, the warning tingle of her scalp. Casually, too casually, she stood up, began walking, slower at first, then faster. She heard footsteps coming up behind her at a rate that suggested someone meant to close the gap. Hairs stood up under her collar as Irma's stories of stabbings and muggings flooded back. She steeled herself not to look. As she increased her speed, the sound behind her accelerated in an eerie echo. The yell as she began to run only spurred her on.

Olivia forgot her blisters, her weary legs. She cut across the road, round a corner, crossed the next road and on, feet pounding the pavement. There was a second shout. She sensed rather than saw the pursuit fade out, the person drop back to a walk, breathless most likely, hoping for an easier victim.

Her heart was pounding, sweat pooling on her body as she allowed herself to slow. She'd paid no attention to direction in her headlong flight and the streets were unfamiliar, deserted. She reached into her pocket again and unwrapped the plastic from the top of a small cylinder before choosing a road more or less at random.

A memory nudged her tired mind. Driving down the Strand in a sleek black limo beside her parents. A liveried doorman had welcomed them into the Savoy Hotel, a bellman ushering them up to their glittering suite. They'd gone to see *Guys and Dolls* at the National Theatre, A rare treat. They hardly ever went with Daddy on his London business trips but this had been a special occasion – her fifth birthday. Not the last time she'd stayed at the Savoy but certainly the most magical.

She clenched her fists, rebelling against her current state. Never, she vowed, would she feel this friendless and helpless again. She'd rebuild her life, bigger, better, and this time no one would be able to topple her from her dreams. She'd learned her lesson. Put not your trust in any man. Nor all your money in a single fund.

Passing a small park she heard scuffling noises, a muffled howl. Two skinheads were kicking something in the bushes. She heard the thud of leather as heavy boots lashed into a bundle curled foetal-position on the earth.

'Leave him sodding alone! I'm calling the cops right now.' Her words rang out of their own volition. The yobs turned to stare. Olivia fished for her mobile but her trembling hands came up empty. Where, when, had she lost it?

One last kick, then the youths moved fast, bounding forward across the sparse grass, not running away but to block her escape. One was slight, acne-spotted under his shaven skull, the other bulky and menacing. Olivia backed away, cursing her mouth, wishing she'd done kickboxing instead of yoga. She wasn't brave. Hated pain.

'I said get lost!' She spat it out, defiant. 'Cops are on their way.'

The larger one snatched her daypack in one swift movement, pulling it from her arms. He turned it upside down, found nothing but clothing and tossed it away like so much trash.

'Are they now? Well, too late for you, bitch,' the shorter one sneered, pushing in close with his skinny frame. His scowling eyebrow was pierced with a ring. She swung her purse, catching him on the ear.

He slapped Olivia across the face, a backhander that made her head ring. Rough hands had grabbed her, pulling her into the bushes. She grasped a jacket, struggling, jerked her knee up but it glanced harmlessly on a thigh instead of her intended target. Her fingers clawed, seeking eyes but she was pulled backward by her hair. Fire blazed across her scalp as filthy fingers clamped over her mouth and nose. Then she was on the ground, head slamming into dirt with the force of a hammer blow.

Olivia struggled to breathe, tried to bite, scream, hit wildly with head, arms, feet, elbows, but a heavy weight held her pinioned and a stinging slap rocked her head back into the ground, lip splitting from the force. She heard her blouse rip as, frantic, she tried to get her hand into her pocket. Her fingertips barely touched the thing she was looking for when, with a jolt, her jeans were pulled over her hips, the object pulled out of reach.

Before she knew it, the skinny male was on his knees, fumbling with his zipper, and then falling backwards with an odd grunt. The brute holding her down turned his head, swore and lumbered to his feet. She heard the crack of a stout tree branch rebounding off his upturned arm and saw the fallen attacker clambering back to his feet.

But at least they weren't paying attention to her. Olivia rolled to one side, swallowed her bile, and staggered upright. Regaining her wits and her jeans, she found the canister, aimed straight-armed and pressed the button.

She started coughing right away, tears streaming from her eyes, as a few particles of burning spray drifted back to her. But the wind was blowing away from her and the effect on the fighting men was dramatic. They reeled and stumbled, hands over their eyes. Two staggered off, choking, banging into trees in their sightless flight.

She turned to the third man. He was on his knees, head almost kissing the ground, upper body spasming as he retched. She might have felt triumphant if she hadn't seen familiar tousled hair instead of bald tattooed flesh. Filled with guilt, she dropped beside him.

'Blink.' She put her hand on his shoulder. 'So your eyes'll water. Whatever you do, don't rub them.'

A ragged tramp-like figure hobbled painfully over, forehead bleeding, face pinched and white.

'Get my bag,' Olivia ordered. 'There's a water bottle.'

She saw his head shake. 'I think maybe no help,' he said in a strong foreign accent.

The coughing man raised his head, tears still streaming down his cheeks, one of which was cut and bleeding. Later there would certainly be a stupendous bruise.

Her suspicion was confirmed.

It was Mr Tattle-tail himself.

Marcus.

Chapter Seventeen

'Now these babies are pure sex.' Anya flourished a pair of towering scarlet stilettos. 'Mag-nif-i-co.'

'Far too Moulin Rouge.' Obediently Rosie reached out anyway. 'I'll never be able to walk.'

'Get your dreamy hunk to lend a manly shoulder.' Anya swivelled on a Jimmy Choo heel.

Rosie wrapped the flimsy impractical straps around her ankle. Those six inches would put her virtually eye to eye with Charlie. She could imagine his jaw-dropping surprise. He'd long ago stopped seeing her as anything but a mother and an unglamorous one at that.

'Why'd you rush off last night?' Anya twisted her foot admiringly. 'Thought we'd all have dinner.'

'And be a big green gooseberry?' How could she tell Anya that her wonderfully loyal Greek boyfriend wasn't all he seemed? She stood, wobbling. The absurdly high sandals flattered her tanned legs but did she dare walk?

'Never. Not with me and Darius. Listen,' head down, Anya seemed engrossed in unfastening the zipper, 'I was out of order in Spain. It's just...well, I've always paid my own way. I felt like a leech you shelling out for the hotel, hair, everything. And then that Alex drooling over you...' She looked shame-faced. 'Guess I'll have to get used to our new glamour puss hogging the limelight.'

Rosie was touched.

'No, it was my fault. I went a bit mad, obviously. Flashing my money like Lady Muck. And we'd have been out of our minds going to Tangiers with a total stranger. I'm glad you had some sense.'

'Yeah but who wants to be sensible?' Anya tossed back her hair, relieved. 'So me old mate, let's find you some super sexy undies and a rocking dress to go with those killer heels, then turn you loose. Who cares if they're,' she picked up the box and whistled, 'four hundred and ninety-seven pounds. Blood-de-hell!'

Fifty hours of work at her old salary. Rosie's stomach flipped as the reality of what they were about to do swamped her. 'I can't.' She panicked. 'I'm not ready for this. I haven't slept with anyone since I met Charlie. And high heels and sexy dresses – that's not me. I don't know a good wine from a bottle of plonk. I've nothing to talk about except the kids. He'll be bored witless.'

'Crap.' Anya shoved Rosie and shoes towards the till. 'He flipped over you, didn't he? Remember, you're hot and you're loaded.'

Scenting a sale, the bored shop assistant moved towards her.

'Only interesting thing I've done is win a million pounds,' Rosie rambled feverishly. 'And that doesn't go far these days. Just about buy a nice three-bedroom house, the estate agent said.'

'You're moving then?' Anya stopped pushing, horrified. 'Leaving us?'

'No. Just someone from work's husband called me this morning. On the off chance I was looking, that's all.'

Anya laughed, mirthlessly. 'I'd bloody move. It is Grotsville after all. Shoddy old houses.'

'I love my house. Shoddy or not.' A blush started to rise up Rosie's neck. She extracted a folded cheque from her purse. 'Please, please, Anya, don't take offence but this is for you. For your roof. You've been an absolute Godsend through my hard times.' Tears sprang to her eyes. 'I'd never have survived without you.'

Anya was backing away, shaking her head.

'You're hopeless, you. What did I just tell you? I don't want your money.'

Rosie grimaced, face stubborn. 'Then do it for me. How can I splash out when every time it rains my best friend is catching drips in a bucket? I'll only find someone else to give it to otherwise. You know me, Anya. I'll be miserable if I can't at least share some of my good fortune. You'll be doing me a favour, honestly, you will.'

'What's this I hear about you winning the lottery?' The wizened old man who lived opposite accosted Rosie as she approached her doorstep laden with her brand new purchases. 'Heard you've gone doolally with foreign holidays, face lifts, liposuction and the like.' He struggled with his wheeled shopping cart. 'Help me pull this up the steps, can you, ducks? Overdone the tinned dog food.'

'Wow, you look stunning!' Zac rose as the maître d' escorted a tottering Rosie through the exquisite South-East Asian décor. 'Give us a twirl.'

Rosie, in her new taffeta cocktail dress, obliged, blushing. Flower-shaped floating candles lit the booth with romantic light, both delightful and familiar. This had been one of Charlie's favourite haunts when they first met, his dealership only a mile away. But as Anya said, 'So what? He doesn't own Highgate Village. Or the restaurant either.'

'It's the clothes,' she demurred, scanning the room for potential spies. 'Everyone looks good wearing Marc Jacobs.'

'That a fact?' Zac teased, handing her chilled white wine. 'My granny's birthday's coming up. I planned on getting her the usual bath salts and moustache wax but if you say so...'

As dinner progressed, Rosie found herself falling more and more under his spell. Before she knew it her lips were well and truly loosened.

'According to local gossip, you're looking at thousands of pounds worth of liposuction and plastic surgery.'

She explained her encounter with the neighbour.

'And I can barely see the scars.' Zac scrutinised her, amused. He was wearing a collarless charcoal shirt with dark jeans, black hair and tanned complexion looking more dashing and piratical than ever. 'Congratulations, Miz Frankenstein. Job well done. But thousands of pounds. You must be loaded.'

'Wait. Back up,' Zac interrupted, righting himself after he'd mimed falling off his chair. 'She called herself Agent Million? Was she wearing a mask and black leather?'

She hadn't meant to tell him. Honest, she hadn't. But after all it was her only exciting event in years. And the night had passed with the mad whirling rush of a midnight funfair. She *liked* Zac.

'Sounds paranoid,' he said, when Rosie explained Agent Million's cautions about secrecy. 'Does she think everyone's out to con you? Utter rubbish and – did I mention? – you are *so* paying this bill.'

He was a great listener, Rosie discovered, sympathising as she relayed her sadness about resigning ('You did the right thing, definitely'); the shock of Darius's uninvited kiss ('the dog!'); responding in just the right way to the good, the bad and the funny.

By dessert, she realised, appalled, three hours had passed and she'd done all the talking.

'So anyway—' Both started speaking.

'Jinx!' Rosie said automatically.

'Jinx?' Zac looked puzzled.

She groaned, hands over face. 'Nothing. My sons yell out jinx if they both say the same thing at the same time. Then they're not allowed to speak until someone frees them.'

'Frees them from who?'

'Big old jinx God in the sky I guess. You're meant to repeat their names three times. But they can't ask you. They just have to look at you meaningfully and start grunting.'

Zac furrowed his brow, lowered his head and grunted so loudly the person in the booth behind him turned to look. Oh well, she'd asked for it.

'Zac, Zac, Zac,' she muttered, feeling daft. 'OK you're free.'

Despite his earlier joke, he paid the bill. 'You can get the next one, promise.' He slid his arm through hers. 'I'll take you home.'

'Sure you're OK driving?' Her heart leapt at the thought of next time. 'We got through lots of wine.'

'You mean you did.' He grinned, as they stepped outside.

'And I've been talking all evening,' she apologised. 'Boring you rigid, no doubt.'

'Boring? There's episodes of *EastEnders* with less drama. No, truth is, I find you extremely…' He paused, looking devilish. '…nice.'

'Nice?' Rosie protested, the wine and attention making her flirtatious and unusually bold. 'Not magnetic? Mysterious? Irresistible?'

Zac tilted his head, considering. 'Sorry, think I have to stick with….' he grasped her hand, kissing her knuckles, '…nice…' He kissed the back of her wrist. 'Nice…'

Rosie shuddered, forgetting to breathe as his lips moved up, tickling the delicate flesh on her inner elbow. 'Nice,' he whispered, sounding husky, delectably seductive.

Mesmerised, Rosie stared, as if her outstretched arm belonged to someone else.

'Rosie?'

She jerked down her arm, still blazing from Zac's kisses.

Charlie stared, incredulous and a little rumpled. Clearly a few beers to the good – or bad.

'What are you doing here?'

'Might ask you the same.' Rosie gathered her wits as Zac put a steadying arm around her waist. This man had cheated on her. Divorced her. If she had sex in the middle of the high street it was still none of his business. 'Where's Tim and Luke?'

'Home asleep.' He took in her cleavage, the short hem that showed off her legs. No doubt attributing the changes to the man at her side. She slid her arm around Zac's waist and was rewarded when Charlie flinched. 'One of my mates had a birthday bash.' He seemed distracted. 'I popped by for a quick one.'

'You left them alone with Val?' She didn't mean it to come out the way it sounded.

'Only for an hour or so,' he said, edgily, staring hard at Zac. 'And who's this?'

'Zac,' she said. 'Meet Charlie.' She didn't feel nearly as cool as she'd hoped. Wasn't this her big fantasy? Zac was a great substitute for Colin Farrell. But somehow the slight confusion in Charlie's face and her hammering heart robbed her triumph of much of its sweetness.

'Pleasure.' Zac held out his hand.

'Charlie Dixon.' Ignoring Zac's gesture, Charlie casually lit a cigarette. 'The husband.'

'Ex,' Rosie responded smartly. 'But good seeing you. Say hi to your fiancée.' All of a sudden she was angry. Let Charlie feel bad. He was heading back to Val's bed. And to her sons. While she…

She turned to Zac. 'Your place or mine?'

Grinning he handed her a helmet. She hitched up her taffeta dress and clung to him as they zoomed away.

Leaving Charlie in the dust. Served him right.

'Rosie?'

'Yeah.' Rosie yawned as she clutched the phone. Who'd call at this ungodly hour?

'Do me a favour, will you?' The voice was female. 'Look out your window. But be discreet.'

Obediently, she stumbled to pull back the curtains and peeked out. A mass of bodies jostled in the street below. Someone looking up shouted. Cameras clicked. Shocked, she picked up the phone again.

'What the… What's going on?'

'This morning's *Sphere*. What were you thinking?'

'I don't understand.' Awake now, fear rose in Rosie's throat.

Outside she could hear voices yelling. 'Rosie. Rosie. What's it like winning a million? Rosie, tell us about the bloke who… Rosie, when are you moving from Grotsville?'

'*My Premium Bond Nightmare,*' Agent Million declaimed, paper rustling. '*Winning a million has jinxed my life,' says Rosie Dixon (33). 'My mother's being hateful, the cold unfeeling cow. My neighbours in Grotsville bitch behind my back, my best friend's boyfriend turned into some hideous lothario and made the world's most pathetic pass, and I lost my job thanks to a Simon Cowell obsessed co-worker. Everyone's turned against me. What good are Marc Jacobs, liposuction and plastic surgery if at the end of the day my husband's still in the clutches of a ravenous harpy and my twin sons without a dad? I've been shocked at the greed, ingratitude and viciousness of people.*'

'I didn't say that.' Rosie was stunned. 'It's all lies.'

'Oh, it gets better. Continued inside over two glorious pages. Who did you talk to?'

'This guy…' Rosie's stomach dropped as she realised she'd been duped. Had he been waiting for her outside Darius's flat? But how had he known? 'He didn't say he was a journalist. He's twisted everything.'

'Well, he's done a real hatchet job.' Agent Million sounded frustrated. 'So you didn't call your ex-husband's fiancée a ravenous harpy? Or your mother a cold unfeeling cow?'

'No, I'd never…well maybe, but…' Her hand flew to her throat. 'Oh Christ, they'll never speak to me again. What am I to do?' She sidled to the window again. The yelling continued unabated.

'There's *hundreds* of them out there.'

'The media love this sort of shit. Someone new to crucify. Get packed, quick as you can. I'm sending round a car.'

Chapter Eighteen

The view from the roof was dizzying. Below Olivia's feet, London life continued with the muffled buzz of traffic, the sound of salsa music filtering from an open window, birds twittering. Olivia, bruised, battered, with a stabbing pain in her ribs from yesterday's brawl and a tender throbbing bump on her head watched as Marcus climbed out the window, then leaned back in to pick up a tray of espresso coffee, boiled eggs and crusty bread.

He placed it on a small bistro table in the centre of the tiny patio he'd created on the level area outside his bedroom windows. There were planters with flowers in them and two metal chairs, all in a space not much larger than an area rug. Behind his glasses his eyes still looked red and bloodshot, much like Olivia's had been after her weeks-long drinking and crying binge.

She'd had to drive his car last night, crunching gears on the unfamiliar stick shift and going the wrong way round a roundabout while Marcus, gasping and coughing, flinched at their erratic progress. They'd argued over their destination, he pushing for her to see a doctor, Olivia repulsed by the thought of fussing and expense. Anyway she'd won that battle, one of the benefits of accidentally incapacitating your opponent.

On the pavement, when she'd turned to leave he'd grabbed her sleeve, not noticing her wince.

'No, you don't. What if I have a delayed reaction, pass out unconscious or choke on my own vomit? You owe it to me to stick around. At least for the next few hours.'

And then he'd led her inside, helped her wash the cuts and bruises on her face and hands, given her aspirin and clothes to sleep in and showed her to a spare bedroom. She'd never been so happy to crawl under the duvet, crawl being about all she could do in the shape she was in.

'OK, I have to ask.' Marcus propped himself against a chimney stack, one ripped jean leg dangling over the roof edge as Olivia, clad in borrowed t-shirt and boxers, tried to find a comfortable sitting position, the very movement causing another excruciating stab. 'Mace? How? Got any other illegal weapons I should know about?'

'If I had don't you think I'd have used them?' Olivia lifted the ice pack she was dabbing on her swollen lip. 'It was only pepper spray. They sell it everywhere in the States.'

She shuddered, remembering the disgusting hands pinning her down, her futile struggles, the filthy smell of her attackers. It was the sense of helplessness that had scared her most, the terror of being powerless, only too aware of the horrors to come.

Gingerly she pushed back the hair that had fallen over her black eye. 'So where are your tights and cape? I thought it was only superheroes that prowled the streets at night looking for violent crimes.'

Marcus shook his dark curls. 'You're changing the subject. How did you get it past customs? I'm surprised you're not sitting in a terrorist cell.' He watched her lift the last spoonful of egg to her lips, nibbling with extreme care. 'Don't like the bread?'

'Gluten free.'

'Figures.'

And what did he mean by that snide remark? Irritated, she tore off a tiny corner with her teeth. It tasted great. She spread a little butter on the next chunk.

'The canister was in my checked bag, OK? Must have forgotten to mention it. Your turn. It's a big bloody coincidence, don't you think, showing up like that, just when I'm being attacked?'

'Not so much. I followed you from the café. I did call out to you but you took off as if all the demons of hell were on your heels.'

Oh. So that's who'd yelled. She could have saved herself a headlong flight and a near-rape if only she hadn't been so freaked out.

Marcus tossed a mobile phone in her lap. 'Here. You dropped this as you were exiting Café Hellas yesterday, trampling innocent children in your hasty departure. Darius gave me your address but you weren't there. Heard about the break-in. Even met your landlord, lovely chap.' He grimaced with distaste. 'Anyway I didn't like the look of him so I thought I'd hand it back in at the café when it opened. In case you came back for it.'

One mystery solved. Angry as she'd been she wouldn't have noticed the small clatter as it fell to the floor.

She turned the iPhone over, examining it from all angles. 'Awful early in the morning to be stalking the streets, wasn't it?'

'Could say the same to you,' he countered. 'I'm an early riser, even when I'm not researching for a documentary. There are some people I can only be sure of finding in the wee hours before morning. What's your excuse?'

'Long story.' She gave him an abbreviated version of the night's events.

'And here I thought you were just another druggie.' He leaned back with a cynical smile. 'Might have excused your terrible driving. And explained some of your more erratic plate dropping, coffee cup tossing behaviour.'

'If you'd heard Darius you'd have thrown something too.' Olivia's fists clenched. 'I'd like to strangle the sod who wrote that drivel. I can believe Sara Goswell sold me out but she can't string two sentences together.'

'Easy, killer.' Marcus stretched out and loosened her fingers. 'It's only a crap newspaper. So, now, what are your plans?'

'Plans?' Olivia snorted. 'Yeah, the ones I've made until now have worked *so* well.'

She rose to her feet, aware of imposing far too long. She didn't want to feel like an intruder, didn't want to feel any more obligated to her former adversary. 'Think I'll fetch my clothes from the dryer and get out of your hair. Here, let me clear this up.' She bent to gather dishes and yelped at a new flare of agony.

'What is it?' He was on his feet with one lithe bound.

'My side. Hurts like hell.' Olivia pulled her t-shirt up, stopping just below her bra and discovered a blue and yellow bruise the size of a grapefruit.

'Could be broken.' Gently his fingers traced a rib. 'What were you thinking of, climbing out of a window when you could be seriously injured?'

'What were you thinking of, suggesting it?' She pulled her t-shirt back down, feeling unusually rattled by his touch. 'Heck, it's nothing compared to the lump on my head.'

Next thing his fingers were in her hair. 'No arguments. Forget the dryer. I'm taking you to a doctor. Right now.'

'No insurance. And not eligible for national health. I'll be fine, honest.'

'Yeah, of course you will,' he stated, dryly. 'Silly me. Just like you were fine last night. Showing off your kung fu skills. And,' he grinned, mocking her, 'look how well that turned out.'

It was much to Olivia's annoyance that she ended up stuck in Marcus's doctor's waiting room, dressed in a pair of his jeans and a hoodie, as he tried to make her giggle by inventing ludicrous diseases for the other occupants. 'Foot and mouth,' he whispered, referring to a man with a bandaged foot. 'Or maybe Tolio? Ganglion?'

'You the husband? Want to come in?' the nurse asked him when she finally called Olivia's name.

'I'm her chaperone.' Marcus put down his copy of *Cosmopolitan*. 'But if you insist.' He leered stagily. 'Wouldn't mind seeing her naked.'

The nurse shot him a look. 'In that case better not,' she said, reprovingly, and with a protective arm ushered Olivia away.

When Olivia walked back out, she was clutching a prescription.

'Cracked rib. Give it time he says,' she informed Marcus. 'Not even worth taping, doesn't help seemingly.'

'Think you've got problems. Check this out.' He tapped the tabloid he'd been reading. 'Local lady won a million quid on the Premium Bonds and it's given her all kinds of massive headaches.'

'Can I see? Maybe she needs a good financial advisor.'

'Down, girl.' Marcus held the newspaper out of her reach. 'We've a few other things to sort out first.'

In short order they had her owed wages from Café Hellas and were back at her ransacked flat. Marcus's expression spoke volumes about the shabby surroundings.

'Come on then,' he said. 'Get your things.'

'What? I live here, remember?'

'Yes, well much as I'm sure you love this dive,' he glanced at the battered lock, 'and can't bear to leave your pervy landlord, it so happens I have a spare bedroom and a genuine job offer.' He gave a low bow. 'You would of course be doing me a great favour if you'd consider the position.'

Olivia gave him a suspicious look. 'What position? Missionary?'

'More like Man Friday.' His lips flickered with amusement. 'Or in your case Monday to Friday. We can call you assistant producer if you like. I'm working on a documentary and your experiences are right on the money – pun intended. Besides I could use a little organisation in my creative chaos. Average pay. Perks include scintillating wit, fascinating company and free room and board.'

Wow. It was so tempting. Anything to get out of this hellhole. But what was his angle? Marcus seemed like an honest sort, a bit too straight and righteous if anything, but as the saying went, 'If it seems too good to be true, it probably is.'

'But not, I hope,' she gave a mock curtsey, smiling sardonically, 'friends with benefits. Or any hanky-panky from the boss.'

He rolled his eyes. 'Heaven forbid. I believe my last relationship with a psycho has cured me of any of those notions for a while.'

That made two of them. She was still heart-sore about the end of her love affair with Brad. Men! How many times had they let her down? And here she was, about to trust another one.

'About our third flatmate though,' he started. 'I should tell you—'

There was a noise as the door opposite opened, followed by the sound of heavy footsteps ascending the stairs. One flight, two flights, then a knock and someone's voice answering. Olivia peeked out into the hall and up the stairwell. Rathbone was just entering someone's apartment. He'd left his own door cracked open.

Marcus's presence emboldened her. It rankled that he'd seen her as a victim when she was anything but.

'Tell me if he comes back,' she hissed at Marcus and was across the corridor before he could stop her.

Where would Rathbone have put it? Her heart was thumping, her palms clammy as she scanned the small room, a studio much like hers, with an unmade bed, a door leading to a kitchenette. It was as messy as she might have imagined. She saw a small box on a cheap tacky nightstand, pulled open the lid. Her watch was there, along with a familiar clip of bills. Quickly she snatched up the lot and dashed back across the hallway, just as she heard Marcus whistle and the sound of footsteps descending stairs.

A noise. Mr Rathbone filled the doorframe, an unpleasant expression on his fat face.

'You're back then,' he rasped, scratching at a spot on his skin. 'I s'pose you want me to get a new lock? It'll have to come out of your deposit. Unless you're gonna pay for it now?'

Marcus stared at Olivia, eyes asking a question. She couldn't look at Rathbone. She was flushed with exultation (she had her money and watch back), terror and an insane desire to giggle. Quickly she began throwing things in her case, feeling a surging panic at her reckless actions. What if he went back in his apartment and found everything gone? He'd know who took it. What would he do then?

'The lady has decided to leave this toilet bowl,' Marcus said to Rathbone. 'We'll be out of here in minutes and she won't be back, so you can stuff your lock and feel lucky she doesn't call the police or the board of health.'

Olivia looked up, then, gaining courage again from his calm presence. 'Where's my mail?'

'Mail? What mail?' Rathbone yawned, scratching his great belly through the missing buttons on his grubby shirt.

She frowned. 'There wasn't an envelope for me? From Spain?'

He bared rotten teeth in a nasty snarl. 'Just give me your new address. I'll send it on. And don't imagine for a bleeding minute, you're getting your deposit back.'

They were back in the three-storey Crouch End house, Olivia's things placed in the guest room. She began tackling the overlay of chaos, gathering plates and mugs from every room in the house, washing dishes in the sink as Marcus dried.

What the hell had happened to her envelope? she wondered. Was that low-life hanging on to it out of spite? Had it been thrown out with the junk mail? The exultation had vanished now. Granted she had the watch but there had only been five twenty pound notes in the money clip, the rest of it already gone. And any chance of Rathbone passing on her letter had vanished with her dumb, impulsive act. They could hardly give him Marcus's real address. Oh yes, living at blah blah blah. Come round any time you're looking for your things or feel the need to bash in a head or two.

Marcus seemed to read her mind. 'I could go back there in a couple of days, check the mail slots. He can't know you took that, not for sure. Unless he makes a habit of counting his ill-gotten loot every few minutes.' He mimed wringing his hands with Fagin-type greed.

'No, too risky. It's probably nothing important anyway.' She felt a pang as she said it. 'Scribbles and sketches, the woman called them.' But still, something of her father's. After all these years.

'And meanwhile I'm harbouring a criminal.' Marcus grinned to take the sting from his words. 'A break-in artist. Do not EVER do anything like that again while I'm around. It was gutsy but insane. Not to mention completely illegal. Thought I'd have a heart attack.'

Olivia refilled the sink, her eyes falling on the tabloid paper with its screaming headline: 'My Premium Bond Nightmare'. Hands dripping, not touching the print, she scanned the article. Hyped up hysterical dross, but entertaining enough when she wasn't the unfortunate subject.

Marcus wiped his hands on the towel. 'Can't believe everything you read in the papers. Especially that rag.'

Olivia's eyes fell on the byline.

'Zac Zawinsky.' She wrinkled her brow. 'Zac? That wouldn't by any chance be the Zac who comes in the café? Your buddy.'

Marcus took the newspaper and flipped it in the bin.

'Yep, same Zac.' He sounded too casual.

Olivia stared accusingly. 'And does he by any chance contribute to an anonymous gossip column? No, don't say. He wrote that lousy story about me, didn't he? And you knew it all the time. Why didn't you tell me? You must have had a bloody good laugh at my expense.' She was working up a head of steam now. 'Oh yeah, I can just see you both, sharing chips and sniggering about the lies you've fabricated. Well, you can stuff your bloody job. I don't need a pity party so you can assuage your guilt.'

'Calm down hotshot.' He put his hands on her arms as if afraid she'd start throwing cups. Fair enough, he'd seen her do it before. 'Think before you storm off. You've got what – two hundred pounds or so with the money Darius gave you? How far will that get you?'

They stared at each other and he let go of her. 'I had nothing to do with that article.' He sounded nearly sincere enough to be believed. 'Or any other crap Zac writes.'

'Yes, but you still hang out with the sod, don't you?' Olivia challenged. 'Never mind his hurtful lies and shaky moral compass. If you gave a fig about any of that, why are you even friends?'

'Hardly friends.' The words came from a dark-haired man, plastic Buddha keychain in one hand, motorbike helmet in the other.

Idly he pressed a button so that a white light flashed from the miniature head. He was tall, lean and handsome, his smile lazy and oh so dangerous.

The voice was a sexy purr.

'I'm his brother.'

Chapter Nineteen

'Sue the socks of them!' Rosie's brother raged when Agent Million arrived for a damage-control meeting the next day.

'You can try, Paul. But it will only give them more to write about,' the young woman disagreed. 'And no one cares if they do retract. Besides, Rosie must have told him those things, however distorted. She admits her memory is a blur.'

Rosie shrank into the overstuffed sofa, longing to disappear. She'd always taught her sons that if they'd nothing good to say about a person, not to say anything at all. But all the nice things she did remember saying, Zac had left out. How much she liked living in Forge Street. How she'd loved her job and missed her former colleagues. She'd poured out her heart with the same reckless generosity with which the manipulative reporter had refilled her wine glass.

Idiot!

She squirmed with shame recalling how close she'd come to sleeping with Zac. No wonder he'd sent her home. It was no gentlemanly regard for her inebriated condition. He'd planned to screw her a whole other way…

Ever since Agent Million's car had dropped Rosie at her brother's door, the driver lugging in her hastily filled holdalls, she'd been obsessively reliving the worst of her ordeal. In the restless hours between midnight and dawn, she soaked her pillow with tears as she thought of the tabloid's portrayal, and the world of hurt she'd inflicted on so many people.

Thank the Lord she'd resigned from Avondale Infants before she was sacked for shooting her mouth off about the redundancies. Bitching about being squeezed out. Revealing Gemma's secret.

What must she have thought, innocently opening up her Sunday rag to see '*I lost my job thanks to a Simon Cowell obsessed co-worker*'?

They all jumped when the doorbell rang, chimes echoing through the house.

'If that's reporters…?' Paul seethed.

'Already? How would they find us?' Rosie looked around wildly, as if prepared to duck behind the sofa, until Agent Million put a soothing arm on her hand.

Dee stood up, lips pursed, looking ready for war.

'Don't worry. I'll handle this.'

The sound of a muffled argument from the hall. Then a familiar voice – Anya's – raised in anger.

'I know she's there. Rosie! Rosie! Get out here!'

If she'd had any illusion that her friend had rushed over to support her, it would have vanished at the grim expression on Anya's face, her attempt at a hug met with stiff armed rigidity. Quickly she closed the door to the living room to block the sound of Anya's raging voice from the others.

'I got to know. What's all this sodding bollocks about Darius trying it on? Every bleeding person I see keeps asking if he was the "hideous lothario" and he says you're off your rocker. So – was it him or not?'

Rosie fell back, dismayed. 'Everything got distorted,' she faltered. 'It wasn't—'

'You mean it *was* him,' Anya cut her off, 'and you didn't say anything? Tell me exactly what happened. If he so much as groped a tit, I swear I'll disembowel him.'

'No, nothing like that,' Rosie said, horrified. She ended up downplaying the attempted kiss, torn between a desire to defend herself and not wanting to cause her friend pain. But without it, wilting and under fire, her encapsulated version of events sounded nebulous and trivial.

'So basically he suggested you might have some fun with your money.' Anya's face was scornful. 'And you took it to mean he was after a shag? What are you, five years old?'

'Maybe I was wrong to…' Rosie intended to add, 'go round there alone' but stopped mid-sentence, shockingly realising that Anya for all her bravado, didn't want to hear that Darius, her first ever steady boyfriend was a sleazebag. Didn't want to hear that he'd come onto another woman practically under her nose. It was actually easier to believe that her nouveau-riche friend had turned into a mud-slinging, publicity-seeking, liar.

Anya was glaring but there was fear behind those irate eyes and with sudden clarity Rosie saw that her friend had already chosen whose side she was on.

And besides why should she forgive Rosie? When Rosie couldn't forgive herself.

'…jump to conclusions,' she finished. At least one relationship in this sorry mess might be saved.

'Yeah maybe you were!' Anya snapped, but the wind had left her sails and Rosie couldn't help but notice the tension dissipate from her body. 'And maybe next time, you'll think twice before you call up the press.'

'It wasn't like that.'

'Sure, but then what'd I know? I'm just one of those *backbiting neighbours from Grotsville.*' She dug into her purse and waved a slip of paper. 'Keep your bloody money. I wouldn't take it now if the whole house caved in!'

And with that she ripped the cheque into minuscule pieces.

Toothbrush in mouth, Rosie stared at her white-faced, red-eyed reflection. Ugh. Even with the help of Dee's sleeping pill, it had been another bad night. Two weeks gone by and not a word from Anya, her attempts to call going unanswered. So much for the power of friendship.

She padded into the kitchen in a borrowed pair of pink pom-pom slippers and matching quilted housecoat to find her sister-in-law cooking breakfast.

'Sleep OK?' Dee cracked apart a couple of eggs.

'Not bad.' Rosie lied.

'Paul's put an extra mattress in the spare room for the boys. And another journalist came round but we sent him packing.'

'Not again.' Rosie's guilt wave intensified as she surveyed the feast of sausages, mushrooms, tomatoes sizzling away on the six-ringed range. 'This can't be for me?'

'Got to feed you up. No,' she waved away Rosie's attempt to help, 'you sit down, love. You still look like death warmed over.'

Rosie obeyed, sitting at the table. How kind and supportive Dee and Paul had been through what Dee called 'this hoo-ha'. Fending off reporters. Telling callers they had no idea where Rosie might be. No recriminations. No mention of Rosie betraying friends, family, workmates, with foolish wine-loosened gossip. And to a journalist, of all people.

Well, perhaps her sunny nature did make her too trusting, as Charlie had always said. It was still hard to believe that anyone, let alone funny, charming, handsome Zac, could be so mean, malicious and downright cruel. But how else could she have been misinterpreted so badly?

Thank Christ there were still people who stood by her. The ones who counted.

Even Charlie had come up trumps. Rosie had called on the day of her headlong flight to tell him where she was. He'd arrived a few hours later with Luke and Tim, striding in with a big grin and a ruffle of her new hairstyle.

'A million pounds on the Premium Bonds. Hah, hah. That's our Rosie – full of surprises. You got me all right. Let me think you were joking.'

'You saw the paper, I suppose?' She'd led him down the hallway, unable to meet his eyes. Showing praiseworthy tact, Dee took the boys into the kitchen with the offer of Coca-Cola.

'Ah, yes.' Charlie prowled the living room. 'So did the kids. Got to it first, unfortunately. I told them I'd never read such a load of tosh in my life.'

She dared to look up then and saw indignation mixed with his amusement.

'I suppose Valerie's livid?'

'About the ravenous harpy comment?' He laughed, much to her relief. 'Spitting nails. Took me an hour to convince her that our sweet Rosie would never spout all that ridiculous rubbish. Val's got a lot of good points but sense of humour isn't one of them. It was flipping obvious someone's done a hatchet job on you. I suppose that bloke I saw you with…'

'Was the journalist, yes,' she said, abashed. She blushed, twisting her hair through her fingers. 'After my story, not my body.'

'More fool him.' He patted her shoulder, then gave it a squeeze. 'Don't worry, Rosie, this'll all blow over. Couple of weeks' time it'll be old news. Forgotten. But I was thinking, why don't Val and I take the boys in case those reporters find you here? You won't have to worry about getting them to school and they'll be protected from the worst of it.'

Charlie had been right. Yes, reporters had flocked to her brother's door, trying for a quote and, failing that, turned to anyone they could find in 'Grotsville' or even Avondale Infants for a vitriolic rebuttal. There'd been jokes on breakfast and late-night TV about the 'Millionaire Miseryguts'. She wasn't particularly computer-savvy but Dee had suggested she kept away from the internet, tutting about trolls, thinking they could post any kind of viciousness and get away with it.

But it was only a million pounds after all and the Great British Public's attention span was short and fickle. Nearly all of it had died down.

All except the letters.

'Paul collected your post again last night.' Dee laid the full English breakfast down in front of Rosie.

'I suppose there were tons.' Rosie had been appalled by the deluge – some shockingly vitriolic, some anguished pleas for aid. Always soft-hearted, she'd found herself in tears, even sending cheques to the ones who touched her most. Yet more and more requests flooded in, terrible stories that kept her awake at night. All those people who'd lost their jobs. All those sick children. When Dee discovered her sobbing, inconsolable, over the photo of a toddler with leukaemia, she'd taken over the mailbag.

'Nothing I can't handle.' Dee sat down with her cup of tea. 'And certainly nothing you need to worry about. What time's Charlie bringing the boys back?'

'Around eleven. I'd better get dressed.'

'And put on some make-up!' Dee shouted after her. 'Show those sons of yours a happy face. If you can't manage a real smile, paint one on.'

'You know the old saying; friends come and go, but family's forever.' Dee scraped the leftovers into the bin as Rosie loaded the expensive German dishwasher, the two of them working side by side. 'Even your mum will chill eventually. She just needs to blow off steam first.'

She glanced at the kitchen clock. 'Talking of which, I'd better run. The salon owner's totally got it in for me. Jesus, I'd love to get out of there!'

'Can't you work somewhere else? You're so brilliant with hair.'

'My clients say I should open my own salon. Wouldn't even cost that much to set up but it's nigh on impossible securing loans these days.' Dee gave a heavy sigh. 'And then Kylie's after Paul to buy her a car and...' She stopped. 'But I shouldn't burden you with our petty problems. I expect you heard the yelling last night?'

'Yelling?' Rosie attempted a blank expression. It'd been hard to miss. Slamming doors, raised voices.

'*Well, if you'd get a bloody job...*' That was Dee.

'*At your age I was already contributing...*' Paul.

'*All my mates' parents give them...*'

'Honestly, don't ever be a stepmum.' Dee peeled off her rubber gloves. 'If you meet a man with kids, run like billy-o.'

'Don't worry, kids or no kids, I'm staying well away. My first return to the world of dating could hardly have been more of a disaster.' Rosie experienced a surge of sympathy for her sister-in-law, who she'd never truly appreciated up until now. 'What if I were to help? With the salon, I mean. I'm sure it'd be a great investment.'

'Oh Rosie,' Dee's face lit up as she hugged her, 'that'd be wonderful. I actually have a business plan drawn up. Hang on a sec, I'll go fetch it.'

Rosie smiled as her sister-in-law dashed up the stairs.

See, some good *could* come out of anything.

It was the best she'd felt for weeks.

'One of my mates got a proper good Mini for two hundred quid.' Kylie returned to her favourite subject that night as she picked in a disgusted way at Rosie's pasta bake. 'S'not like I'm asking for a bleeding Ferrari.'

'Watch your mouth, missy,' Paul retorted. 'And if it's the speed-freak who picked you up the other day, that thing's a danger to him and everyone else on the road.'

'You can leave the table if you want,' Rosie told the boys who were enthralled by their panda-eyed foul-mouthed cousin. Little Saskia hummed, oblivious, as she played with her fairies.

Luke and Tim rushed eagerly towards their shared room, new Xbox and the TV Paul had kindly donated. To Rosie, their absence had seemed a bitterly cruel punishment, despite talking daily on the phone...if rote replies of 'fine' and 'nothing much' could be classified as talking. Yet they'd shied away from her kisses, impatient to escape her attempted explanations for two weeks at Dad's and now this stay with Uncle Paul.

'They get it,' Charlie had soothed, sympathy large in those familiar blue eyes. 'They're more resilient, savvier than we give them credit.' And he was right, of course. Her heart had squeezed, realising he knew them all too well and clearly understood that Rosie wasn't quite ready to see her sons changing, growing up and slipping away. She dreaded them escaping into the teenage years, finding her a superfluous nuisance, the way Kylie felt about Dee.

That was what single people like Anya could never understand. Whatever Charlie had done, whatever he thought about her now or in the future, they would always be linked by their offspring, always have that in common.

'Why not see if Asda's recruiting?' Dee was suggesting to her stepdaughter. 'When I was younger than you I swept up at the local hairdressers every weekend.'

'There's petrol. Insurance. We've already paid for all of your lessons,' Paul chipped in.

'Waste of money,' Kylie shot back. 'If I never get to drive.'

An answer for everything, intimidated by nothing. Rosie was awash with admiration for her niece, wishing for a fraction of that courage.

'I'll buy Kylie a car,' she announced. 'It's her eighteenth soon, isn't it?'

Stunned silence. Dee and Paul spoke together.

'That's so kind, Rosie. Kylie, thank your aunt.' Paul.

'Oh no, it's far too generous. You're already helping me with the salon.' Dee.

'She's giving you a hair salon?' Kylie whirled on her stepmother. 'Oh so it's all right for you to suck up and take advantage but not me, yeah? *What a hypocrite.*'

There was a brief shocked silence. Paul recovered first.

'No one's taking advantage,' he pronounced sternly. 'We're talking two entirely different things. Dee will return every penny with interest. She's found a superb spot in the shopping centre, very reasonable rent—'

He stopped as Dee gave him a silencing frown.

'Actually,' she smiled brightly, 'I was thinking of that place for sale in the high street. It's a top location, sure to attract all the shoppers. The start-up costs are a teeny-weeny bit higher but buying in a depressed market makes masses more sense…'

Kylie gave a loud contemptuous snort but Paul pursed his lips with an approving nod.

'Smart thinking, ladies.' As if Rosie had had any input in this new development. 'Madness to expend energy building up a clientele only to have some greedy landlord triple the rent the minute you show profit.' He surged to his feet, full of revived vigour. 'Well, if you want to splash out on our terrible teen here,' he beamed at Rosie and laid a paternal hand on Kylie's shoulder until she jerked away in annoyance, 'who am I to stop you? Anyone fancy car shopping Saturday?'

Chapter Twenty

Olivia watched the autistic boy clutch the mane of a shaggy Shetland pony, face aglow with pride. She'd found the DVD in a stack of papers and was impressed by the deft unsentimental way Marcus let the events speak for themselves.

'Checking out Marcus's porn?' Zac was in the doorway, the laconic words making her jump. 'You won't find any. Might interfere with his right-on, politically correct, feminist principles.'

He flopped with casual insolence onto the sofa, tossing his leather jacket beside him. His soft cream shirt was open a couple of buttons and with his dark gypsy colouring and those sizzling blue eyes, he looked like he should be striding the moors in some historical drama, clad in riding breeches and brandishing a crop. Every time she saw him, be it wrapped in a towel coming out of the bathroom, or heading to his room with some giggling girl on his arm, she thought how unfair that those looks went with that lousy selfish personality. Or perhaps the lousy personality developed from the looks?

'What's your problem, Zac?' Olivia twisted her increasingly unkempt hair into a ponytail. 'Did big brother Marcus steal your favourite 'ickle teddy so now poor Zacky has to get back at the world?' She held up another DVD entitled 'Nature or Nurture: Genetics Unravelled'. 'Will this explain how someone decent and someone pure poison can come from the same parents?'

'Golly. *Decent?*' he mocked. 'How sexy. I hope no one ever calls me that. Bad boys are much more fun. And with Saint Marcus in the family, someone had to be the black sheep.'

He watched her sitting on the floor, shoving files into the bottom drawer of the filing cabinet. 'Although apparently he has no trouble getting you on your knees.'

Olivia studied him out of the corner of her eye. Both brothers shared high cheekbones, straight noses and sensuous mouths. Yet stringy, serious Marcus, scruffy as an unmade bed with his Harry Potter glasses wouldn't draw a second glance at a bus stop while Zac, a head taller, buffed from the gym was undoubtedly a heartbreaker.

And so blatantly trouble.

And yet...she could see why some women – loads probably – would find him irresistible. He was transparent. He offered a good time for a night or two. Nothing heavy. And no tears when it all finished.

Unless you were dumb enough to fall for him.

Love was bullshit anyway. Evaporated at the first hint of adversity. Or temptation, she decided, reluctantly remembering her father's infidelities. Men either couldn't keep it together or couldn't keep it in their pants.

'Truce?' Zac suggested. 'I don't suppose you'd believe me if I said I had nothing to do with that particular gossip column. Besides you were a lousy waitress. Although the café is far duller without you flinging food.'

'I almost got raped, you asshole.'

He had the gall to laugh. 'Hardly my fault.'

He disappeared into the kitchen and came back with two bottles of Corona, twisting off the caps. He handed one to Olivia and when she didn't take it, put it on the desk.

'Don't be fooled,' he said. 'Marcus is as bad as me. Worse. He's had the same mistress for years and no one else stands a chance. All kinds of hot women have tried to get his attention and been left discarded and broken by the wayside.'

A mistress? Really? She wouldn't give Zac the satisfaction of asking.

'Leaving you to pick up the pieces, no doubt.' She forgot her resolve to freeze him out.

Zac's cheek brushed hers, breath tickling her ear. 'Well, someone's got to give the poor girls the rogering they so desperately crave.'

Olivia swerved and shot out a fist to punch him. But Zac had already pulled away. Losing her balance she crashed backwards into the filing cabinet.

'Ow. Ow. Ow. You bastard!' She howled with pain, clutching her side.

Zac dropped beside her, looking appalled. 'I'm sorry, I—'

'Get away from me, you monster.' She swatted at him again but the effort only sent the tears further down her cheeks. 'Shit! My rib. It was getting better too.'

'Look, I didn't mean…' Zac's face was a study in guilt. 'I was just playing around. Can I get you something? Water? Nurofen?'

'You know how many people die from painkillers?' she gasped. 'I haven't touched the prescription Marcus filled.'

'Might be a good time to start. Where are they? In your handbag?' Uninvited, he rummaged through it, extricating the bottle. 'I had you down for a *Sex and the City* girl. Wild parties, one-night stands, ecstasy, cocaine.' His strong fingers wrested off the cap and tipped two pills into his palm. 'Open up, sweetheart.'

His face was inches away, his azure irises holding her hypnotised. She could count his lashes; see the vertical hairs at the start of the broad sweep of eyebrows. He pushed the pills into her fingers, raising them towards her mouth, handing her the Corona to wash them down.

'Good,' he said approvingly, helping her hobble to the sofa. 'Personally, I'd be popping that codeine like Smarties.' He propped her with a cushion and kissed her forehead. 'I am *so* not into suffering.'

'Not your own suffering certainly.' Marcus walked into the room, a brown paper bag in his hands. 'What have you done to my assistant?'

Zac stepped away from the sofa, gesturing with palms spread wide. 'She fainted, poor thing. Wilted while trying to make order from your chaos.'

Marcus put the grease-stained bag next to the prescription bottle. 'Perhaps some Chinese will revive her. Working lunch. We've things to discuss.'

'OK, the new documentary.' Marcus heaped mu shu chicken, sweet and sour prawns and beef and broccoli onto this plate. 'Provisionally titled – Million Dollar Question. Loosely stated, we're exploring the effects of poverty and wealth.' He pointed a chopstick at Olivia. 'You ought to like this.'

She shoved a piece of pineapple around her plate and grimaced. 'Oh, yeah, I'm sure I'm going to be ecstatic.'

'I've been doing a lot of research. Did you know at Stanford they've been studying the way money affects people's brains?'

'No. Do tell.' Zac took another swig of beer, having invited himself to eat with them.

'Wait,' Olivia said. 'I think I can guess.' She didn't know why but she took great pleasure in provoking Marcus, especially in front of Zac. 'It can't buy happiness but it will allow you to be miserable in comfort?'

'Hah, hah, very funny, my children. Actually they had some amazing results. Merely thinking about money made subjects less likely to help strangers in trouble. People given a dollar bill screen saver nearly always chose to work alone while those watching tropical fish opted for teamwork. And surprisingly, money actually worked as an anaesthetic. Handling cash helped volunteers feel less pain.'

'Doesn't surprise me,' Zac said. 'I always feel better with a few hundred quid in my greasy mitt.' His chopsticks captured a battered prawn and he held it out to Olivia. She let him pop it in her mouth.

'Yes,' she said, when she finished chewing, 'and of course there's those hedge fund managers who take home several hundred million dollars a year with bonuses. I guarantee they're feeling no pain.'

Marcus paused and studied her. 'Ah yes, the glorious hedge fund industry. You're still a supporter then, I take it. It's all fine and dandy, perfectly moral.'

Here it comes, Olivia thought. The disapproval. The implicit criticism of the world she'd so recently left. Sanctimonious prig.

She spread her hands. 'Oh, hell, what do I know about moral! But someone's got to buy all that impressionist art, don't they?'

Marcus looked at Zac. 'You see?'

Zac nodded, chewing. Something was going on here. But what?

'And when the global economy is in a massive recession and the leading hedge funds still make billions in profit, that seems OK to you too?' Marcus's voice was mild, enquiring. 'What about when George Soros breaks the Bank of England by short-selling ridiculous quantities of pounds or the schemes of some unscrupulous swindler like Bernard Madoff or your Rupert Mandrake turns the stock market upside down and puts the world in turmoil? It doesn't make you think the money men have a little too much power?'

'Look,' Olivia was feeling hot now, 'I'm not talking about crooks. I suffered from Mandrake as much as anyone.' She remembered Pa Winton, the devout Republican and his fist-thumping declarations. Frankly she'd abhorred his blustering politics. But there was something about Marcus that brought out the devil's advocate. 'All I'm saying is that the big decision-makers, the people who run the country deserve—'

'Deserve to take home over four hundred *million* a year?' Marcus laughed. 'And I suppose the CEOs who mismanage their companies into virtual bankruptcy and get saved by massive government bailouts *ought* to get multi-million-dollar bonuses?'

'Oh, I can see this is going to be fun.' Zac grinned.

'Not exactly.' Olivia turned on Zac. 'And don't you act all high and mighty. After what you did to that poor Rosie Dixon.'

Zac snorted. 'Poor, my arse. I did her a favour. You could tell she was just dying to tell those people what she thought of them, all those so-called friends who'd hurt her and spurned her but she'd never have the nerve. I just got it out there in the open.'

Olivia gaped. 'You really believe that?'

'As much as you believe the rubbish you're spouting.'

'OK, enlightening though this is,' Marcus took control again, 'let's get back to the point. Which is...what happens to people when they go through dramatic financial upheaval? When your average Joe suddenly acquires enormous wealth? Or the rich find themselves without the funds to buy a shoelace?'

Zac caught Olivia's dawning suspicions. 'Ah hah, the ulterior motive. I told you he was dangerous. You didn't think he hired you merely for your looks and filing skills, did you?'

'I hired you,' Marcus held her gaze, steady, sincere, 'because you're bright, because you and I have opposing viewpoints I suspect, and because I think I could use your help.'

'That's a first,' Zac observed. 'He's an egomaniac control freak. Likes to see his name on all the credits – producer, writer, director, interviewer, sound man, cinematographer, editor – did I miss anything?'

'Best boy? Gaffer? Key grip?' Olivia suggested, fighting between being flattered and the sensation she'd been lured into a complicated snare. *Marcus is as bad as me,* Zac had said. 'Craft services – do you buy your own lunchtime sandwiches?'

'Oh, you two are hilarious.' Marcus pushed his plate away. 'I will use crews occasionally. Especially for interviews. Tough to be asking questions and controlling sound and camera at the same time. But working solo, you don't have to deal with anyone else's bullshit.'

'Makes for a lonely Oscar night though.' Zac refilled their wine glasses. 'Not that Marcus would ever sell out and go Hollywood on us. Can you imagine his scrawny white body by an LA pool? Or that ratty old sweater mingling with all the posers in New York? Never happen, mate.'

'You make me sound xenophobic,' Marcus stated mildly, tossing them each a fortune cookie. 'So I love London, big deal. And what's wrong with this sweater?'

It was another disreputable garment that might have been knitted by a blind arthritic Chinese woman, Olivia thought, probably on a pair of oversized chopsticks.

He opened his briefcase and pulled out a sheaf of papers.

'Right, this is what we've got. There was a lottery winner in Somerset who used her windfall to get her private pilot's licence. Started a company chartering small planes.' He flipped the page. 'A retired businessman who put his life savings into developing his transvestite grandson's designer clothing line only to go bust two months later.'

'I read about him,' Olivia said. '*I helped him achieve his dream,*' she quoted. '*And now I'm working in a drycleaners at eighty-two.*'

The two brothers stared at her.

'Photographic memory,' she explained. 'Sort of a curse.'

'Would that I was cursed that way. When I've hours of footage to edit.' Marcus shook off his amazement. 'Well, obviously there's a bunch more. We'll have to weed through them. Take this list of homeless folk – here's a man who owned a nationwide construction company, had the country mansion, the pied-à-terre in London, collection of priceless vintage cars. Had a breakdown after his divorce, hit the bottle and lost the lot. Been on the streets last two years.'

'Most people are too dumb to feel sorry for.' Zac opened his fortune cookie and read, 'He who throws dirt is losing ground.' He laughed.

'What about the Premium Bond woman?' Olivia suggested, interested despite herself. 'Zac's Miseryguts Millionaire. Everyone hates her, thanks to "you-know-who". Talk about a witch-hunt. I'd forgotten how tacky the British press could be.'

'Now that hurts my feelings.' Zac pouted sorrowfully.

'Like you have any.'

'Stop. Stop.' Marcus pounded the table. 'You know you *do* have talent,' he told Zac. 'But you could be using it for good instead of adding to the morass of malicious pulp.'

'Most of us think a little "more ass" is a good thing, bro,' Zac punned. He winked chummily at Olivia. 'Marcus would love to see me in a war zone. Front lines. Penning luminous prose, ducking bullets, dandling wounded orphans. He can't wait to weep over my heroic early grave.'

Marcus snorted. 'Better than getting stabbed in an alley because you spilled the beans on some lunatic's sexual perversions.'

'Like dandling orphans, whatever that entails,' Olivia chipped in. 'Sounds totally sick.' She couldn't help it. A part of her was enjoying sparring with the two brothers, putting her mind on something other than her own problems. Perhaps this wouldn't be too bad after all.

'Called making a living,' Zac informed his brother. 'We can't all be bleeding-heart sentimentalists. Livvy understands, don't you, Liv? When her boss or someone like him finds a vulnerable company, rips it apart, do you think they're sobbing buckets over all the sad unemployed workers?'

'Back to Rosie Dixon. Good idea actually.' Marcus called order. 'She might well appreciate the chance to set the record straight.'

'If you can find her,' Zac said. 'She's in hiding. I'd go after that Agent Million personally. She sounds as sexy as hell.'

Olivia opened her fortune cookie and read. 'Do not mistake temptation for opportunity.' She crumpled the cookie into bits. Was she as callous as Zac implied? Business was business, yes, but the ruthless greed of Mandrake, her one-time hero, had devastated so many lives. In her frequent nightmares, men in tuxedos blew out their brains or shot at her. In other dreams, animal enclosures were thrown open, the bewildered creatures driven out to starve.

'Anything else, Livvy?' Marcus asked.

She wondered if her face had given her away. 'A heck of a lot of folks lost their shirts with Mandrake. Most far, far wealthier than me. Some of them angry enough to kill – or so they're threatening.' She managed to say it without sounding overly dramatic or a sympathy-seeker.

'Other side of the pond,' Marcus said decisively. 'We need intimate. Personal. And over here. So viewers can relate.' He put the papers back in their case.

'What did yours say?' Olivia pointed at Marcus's discarded slip of paper.

'Many a false step is made by standing still.' He took his plate to the sink. 'OK then. Livvy, your first job is to track down Rosie Dixon. And while we're at it, we might as well prepare for your interview. I'll give you a list of questions so—'

Olivia's stomach hit the floor, her newly swallowed food threatening to rebound.

'Interview? Questions? I thought you just said Mandrake's victims—'

'Um,' Zac said. 'I think I'll just…' He raised one finger, sentence unfinished and left the room.

Marcus scratched his head, frowning. 'I said the others' stories didn't interest me. Yours does. Well, of course I want to use you. What do you think this is all about?'

'No good, scheming, devious—' Olivia seethed, rolling over in the queen-sized bed.

Zac put a hushing finger on her lips. 'Enough. You're repeating yourself now. You've already said devious three times.'

'Double-dealing, conniving, calculating, controlling, manipulative—'

Zac kissed her shoulder, his hand carefully taking the weight off her damaged rib. 'It isn't as if I didn't warn you.'

'You *did not* warn me. Did you ever once say, Livvy, he wants to use your story? Livvy, you're being duped?' She stared at the top of his thick glossy hair. What was she doing here? A couple of drinks in the pub, a chance to vent, that was all she'd intended, and Zac had been waiting outside for her when she stormed out of the house. But the more she'd talked, the angrier she'd got and the angrier she'd got, the more her judgement had been impaired.

She just couldn't believe she'd been so taken in. Fallen for Marcus's knight in shining armour routine, melted when he'd bathed her cuts, swooned over his kindness at the doctor's, even worried – very slightly – that he might have a more personal reason for offering her shelter. When all the time he'd wanted…

'I'll bet he started planning the minute he realised who I was.'

'Very likely.' Zac nuzzled into her neck, his tongue finding the hollow in her throat.

Well, at least Zac was obvious. No smiling sharks hidden in these shallow waters. It was stupid to feel betrayed. Just as stupid as thinking that having sex with Zac would somehow put things right. Make her feel better.

Although, truth been told – she quivered under his expert touch – having sex with Zac was rather mind-blowing. Like nothing she'd experienced for quite some time. Just as the moves he was making now were stirring up an increasingly passionate desire for a third go-round. And no holding back on the sound effects, of course. If they kept that sod Marcus awake all night with their noisy passion, too bad for him.

Yes, Zac was exactly what the doctor *should* have ordered. A gorgeous sexy stud. So much better than codeine. Some fun for a change. His cheerful seduction was so obvious, might even be laughable if he wasn't completely ravishing and clearly entertaining himself with his own bad boy Errol Flynn imitation. Certainly she'd been giggling as he'd carried her up the stairs, head burrowed in his manly shoulder, but still able to peek at Marcus's face as they'd swept past him without a word.

Marcus hadn't looked in the least bit happy. Especially when Olivia tightened her grasp and kissed Zac full on the lips.

Oh yes. Petty it might be. And maybe she had been hasty and reckless in cutting through Zac's bullshit in the pub, grabbing him by the hand and suggesting he drag her off to bed.

But she did feel better after all.

Chapter Twenty-One

'You really think this necessary?' Smiling inwardly, Rosie surveyed the black wig in the mirror, swinging the two long braids. Pocahontas? Or sixties folk singer, given Dee's Dorothy Perkins crochet dress? 'I'm not exactly in the Witness Protection Programme.'

'No but I'd bet you could walk past a hundred paparazzi with no probs.' Kylie giggled as Rosie struck a pose. She handed over a pair of star-shaped pink-tinted sunglasses, showing more enthusiasm than Rosie had ever seen from the world-weary teenager. 'Here, these are proper cool.'

'They are?' Rosie was somewhat doubtful about fashion advice from a seventeen-year-old in Lurex micro-mini, cerise leggings and Ugg boots. She was sorry that she hadn't been more involved in her niece's life. Kylie's mother, Paul's first wife, had been...highly strung. A water-glass ring on her gleaming woodwork was a crime punishable by hysterics. As for her flimsy antiques and objets d'art, once Rosie's boisterous boys began crawling...

And then with Paul and Dee's active social life, scheduling visits had seemed virtually impossible. But perhaps all that would change?

'Ready?' Paul yelled up the stairs.

Chatting to Saskia and Kylie, it was a while before Rosie realised their destination.

'Not Charlie's showroom.' She clutched Dee's headrest, horrified. 'Can't we go somewhere else? Please.'

'Don't be silly, R.' Paul assumed the chivvying jolly tone he might use to send a weeping daughter to her first day of school. 'He insisted we drop by. And why shouldn't he treat you right – keeps the money in the family.'

Rosie's innards twisted with dreadful reluctance. It was one thing to dream about flaunting her new-found wealth in front of Charlie, another to actually do it, boldly showing up in his own sales lot as a buyer just like Valerie had done before her. Using their connection to wangle a great deal, when she decidedly didn't need any more favours or reason to feel indebted.

Worst of all, what if he decided this was all some elaborate ploy to see him? OK, so she *did* see him, quite often, between dropping the kids off and picking them up and, yes, he *had* been surprisingly understanding about her supposed slur on his fiancée's character. Still she didn't want him to imagine that, because of a bit of sympathy and, well, a million pound win, she, Rosie, fantasised she was 'back in with a chance'.

Even if Rosie did have a better sense of humour than his current girlfriend. It was crazy how often she returned to that throw-away comment. Hah hah, for all her glamour, Valerie couldn't get a joke. She wasn't funny. Or much fun either from the tiny amount the boys had said after their holiday. Good. But in all fairness she had to remember Charlie also said Valerie had her good points. Whatever those were. Rosie could think of two, stuffed into a padded Wonderbra.

As they pulled into the showroom car park, Charlie, booted and suited, left his glass office to greet them. Belatedly Rosie remembered the ridiculous wig and snatched it off, leaving half her hair squashed down, the rest sticking up unflatteringly.

'Paul, Dee, been too long.' Charlie shook hands with his former brother-in-law, kissed Dee on the cheek and then Rosie, grinning at her pink starry glasses. 'Cool shades.'

'Hello,' Rosie muttered but Charlie had turned his attention to Kylie. 'So Kylie, how's it hanging?' He held out a palm to be slapped but the teenager rolled her eyes and pretended not to notice.

'How you holding up?' He returned Rosie's subdued 'fine' with a squeeze. 'Boys get settled in, OK? All Tim's told me about is the seven hundred TV channels.'

'Only two hundred and ninety-three,' Paul jumped in. 'Some of them HD. Good to see you, mate,' he added, sweeping loose tendrils of grey hair over his bald spot.

'Luke loves the garden.' Rosie side-stepped Charlie's sheltering arm, flustered at this show of affection in front of her family. Her brother had badmouthed Charlie ever since his desertion. What must he think of her, permitting such intimacy?

Paul coughed and Charlie returned to business. 'So, young Kylie needs wheels, eh? I'm finishing with a client but Steve'll show you around.'

They were following Charlie's associate to the used car section when Dee grasped hold of Rosie's arm, fingers clutching temple.

'Splitting headache.' She winced. 'Is there anywhere we can sit and let them get on with it?'

'There's a waiting area inside.' Rosie was secretly relieved. She found it hideously disconcerting to see Paul so chummy with Charlie and the less she had to do with this car purchase the better. Bad enough to be hanging around on 'his turf', the discarded wife, where she'd once known and been friendly with all his employees.

The two women sat flicking through magazines while Saskia crayoned. Rosie, engrossed in an article, discovered Charlie at the door watching her.

'Everything all right?'

'We're letting them get on with it.' Dee smiled up at him. 'Paul takes hours making up his mind.'

'Then let's hope Kylie's quicker,' Charlie quipped.

'I need a poo poo,' Saskia piped up.

'Hold on, darling.' Dee took her small daughter's hand. 'Where's your ladies', Charlie?'

He pointed her in the right direction, and then sat down next to Rosie. 'I'm still pissed off with that journalist. What a complete wanker.'

'Sorry.' Rosie blushed.

'Always were too trusting, love.' There was an awkward pause as he realised his blunder. Embarrassed, he picked up her discarded magazine. 'Ah… "The Trials of Twins". We know all about that, don't we? Midnight drives with them squalling in their car seats, refusing to nod off.' He let it drop on the table. 'Those two treating you, OK?' He nodded towards the door.

'Oh they've been so sweet. I'm helping Dee buy a salon.' She didn't know why she blurted that out. Only that she'd always told Charlie everything and it was a hard habit to break.

His expression turned dubious. 'Does she have any experience running a business?'

'She's a good hairdresser. And she's not getting on with her boss.'

'Sounds like Dee. Never been the easiest person, eh?' Probably remembering Dee's meltdown over the half-thawed turkey that one excruciating Christmas. 'But is that a good idea? Mixing family and business. These things have a way of souring. If it doesn't work out, you'll be out of pocket and could ruin your relationship to boot.'

'Yes, well, until this all blew up I wouldn't have said we had much to ruin,' Rosie said, somewhat defensively. 'But she's been fantastic these last few weeks.'

'Shouldn't stick my nose in.' Charlie put his hands on his legs and pushed himself up. 'Just don't want to see you taken advantage of, Rosie. I still care for you.'

Taken advantage of? Blood rushed to her head. What right did he have to be so patronising? And *care for her* – it was a pretty weak consolation prize.

'They're family,' she said, heatedly. 'I can trust my own relatives even if *other people* have no problem lying and cheating.'

'Enough said.' Charlie looked hurt.

There was a strange silence. Slightly remorseful, she asked, 'How's Val?'

'Still not too pleased with you.' He grinned ruefully. 'No, she's great. Working all hours. Feel like I hardly see her some weeks.'

'Well, I suppose it's like that, being so high flying.' How strange. She couldn't actually be defending the vile horror, could she? It was just Charlie's proximity making her nervous.

They heard Dee's heels clicking towards them, Saskia chattering away.

'I'll check on Kylie.' Charlie headed for the door.

A short time later Rosie saw them all crossing the forecourt, Paul and the salesman jovial and companionable, Charlie face thunderous, Kylie traipsing moodily behind. How bizarre, Rosie mused idly, as they went to meet them. You'd think she'd be the most excited.

The salesman, Steve, beamed as he led everyone over to his desk. 'Right then, if we can just settle the paperwork.'

'You don't think you should talk this over with your sister?' Charlie's lips compressed in a disapproving line.

'We've already discussed everything,' Rosie cut in. *There, that put him in his place.*

'I'll stay out of it then.' Charlie's voice was curt. Had he argued with Paul over the salon loan? She should never have mentioned it.

His office door slammed. Rosie watched him through the glass, scowling at his monitor. If it'd been a cartoon, steam would have gushed from his ears.

'So then, did you require the paint protection aftercare pack?' Steve held out a pamphlet.

'Do we want the paint protection aftercare pack, darling?' Paul asked Dee.

'If it makes the paintwork last longer, why the devil not?' Dee smiled giddily back. Kylie slumped on one of the sofas, switched on her iPod and plugged in her earphones.

'I understand it's an extremely generous gift.' Steve turned his salesman charm on Rosie. 'So if I could just ask you to sign here…?'

Rosie glanced down as she scribbled her signature, her heart stopping. A spanking new BMW. Thirty-nine thousand pounds! Surely Kylie…

'It makes masses more sense this way.' Paul looked slightly embarrassed. 'Dee can have my old car and Kylie can have Dee's. Won't matter then if she gets a few scrapes.'

'Don't mind, do you, darling?' Dee rushed to hug Rosie. 'It's a once in a lifetime thing. We've never owned a new car before.'

'Neither have I,' Rosie wanted to croak, understanding Kylie's disgust. For all her 'Any old crap car will do' Kylie thought Dee's Playboy pink Fiesta was 'totally gross'.

She looked up to see Charlie staring at her through the glass wall, hands in trouser pockets, handsome face thoughtful.

'We'll drive back with Saskia,' Dee was saying, 'So we can swing past the post office, sort the tax. Kylie can take you both home, if that's OK? I insured her yesterday.'

'Fine,' Rosie said numbly.

'Rosie?' Charlie stuck his head through the door. 'Got a sec?'

His secretary looked up as Rosie entered. She was a stranger, the one who'd told Rosie about Charlie's affair long ago resigned, thank goodness

'Let's take a walk.' Charlie yanked his jacket from the peg. They'd barely gone ten yards when he exploded.

'I cannot believe it! Did those two spring it on you the way I think they did?'

'Well, uh, I…'

'Bloody knew it!' His face was puce. 'Ignore you for years, now all of a sudden they're your best mates. And by the way,' he mimicked Dee's simper, 'you couldn't buy me a car, darling, could you, and finance my hair salon, darling? What's next? Holiday in Honolulu? University fund for the girls?'

'They've been kind enough to put me up,' Rosie protested.

'Jesus, Rosie, for thirty-nine grand you could be in the penthouse of a five-star hotel. For a year. Don't you realise they're leeching you dry?'

'He's my brother. I don't mind, honest. He probably deserves a nice BMW if that's what he really wants.'

Probably – but still she felt sick. Why hadn't Paul told her his plans? Or Dee, who'd been astute enough to sort out Kylie's insurance. The salon *did* seem to be getting more expensive every time they sat down to estimate costs. And they *had* mentioned an exquisite Tuscan villa they'd seen somewhere that'd be perfect for a family holiday – 'just the thing to win over your mum'.

But Paul was her only sibling and she'd just won a million. Definitely she could afford to buy him a car and Dee for that matter, and perhaps she'd been thoughtless, not offering. It was the way they'd sprung it on her, making her feel conned. And worse, with her ex-husband as witness.

'It's you who deserves better,' Charlie said with surprising fervour. 'Better family, better friends and a much better husband than I turned out to be. I can't bear standing back, watching a bunch of freeloaders milk you like a Jersey cow.' He sighed, running his hands though his hair. 'How much have you spent so far?'

When she gave him a rough estimate, factoring in the holiday, salon deposit, car, cheques, presents, donations, etc., he whistled softly. 'A hundred and fifty grand round about? Already? And where's *your* new BMW, Rosie? What about that art course you used to dream about? Or buying yourself a nice house? This money is a golden opportunity. You don't want to fritter it away.'

'I'm not frittering anything. I'm setting up trust funds for the boys. And the financial team's giving me advice.' Well they would if she ever called them.

'Just make sure they're independent and check what they're charging for commission,' he advised.

There was a shriek. A woman was tearing across the car park towards them. 'Bitch! I recognise you. Ungrateful bitch.' Crimson nails slashed the air like talons and Charlie yanked Rosie back just before they raked her face. 'Millionaire Miseryguts!' she spat, breathless. 'Don't want that money, give it to me.' Her tight hard face screwed with fury as she tugged at Rosie's handbag. In the busy car park, heads were turning. An interested bystander started filming with his phone.

'Get out of here for God's sake, woman.' Charlie pushed her off with one hand, drawing Rosie into his protection with the other. 'Leave us alone. We'll call the police.'

The handbag broke. Coins, pens and Rosie's wallet spilled on the pavement. More were rushing towards them from the street outside, several running, others reaching for camera phones. 'Yeah. That's her.' Rosie heard.

'Shit!' Charlie swore and shoved her into his BMW. They headed out the car park, hardly slowing down to let the mob scatter.

'People are mad, eh?' Charlie handed his handkerchief to Rosie, patting her knee sympathetically as her gulping shudders slowed down. 'Look, Rosie, old girl.' He slipped unnoticed into the old endearment. 'You need to get away. You've given Paul and Dee enough. And you can't return to that wreck of a terrace in Grotsville.'

Rosie flinched at the easy way he repeated her now infamous slur on her old neighbourhood.

'What about Wales? Or Scotland? Bit of country air. And then when things die down…' He hesitated. 'I've got a mate bought into this plush gated estate not far from Val and me. Classy houses, all mod-cons, but then his company folded. He'd lease it to you tomorrow if you're interested, probably sell it to you too for a song. The kids will love it. Close to Horatio Barton, one of the best private schools in the country.'

How ironic. A few months back, this moment would have seemed a dream come true. A great house. A good safe area. Close to Charlie who might – just might – realise exactly what he'd lost. But despite the concern in her ex-husband's eyes, she was too shaken by the morning's events to feel any gratification. Refusing to cry, instead her inner turmoil made her snappy.

'We like our house. We have great friends, Tim, Luke and me. Are we supposed to abandon everything on your say-so? The way you abandoned us?'

Charlie looked momentarily thrown. 'OK, I deserve that. I hurt you, I know it.' He made a remorseful gesture. 'But I'm saying this for you now, not me. I only want to help.'

Rosie closed her eyes, head back on the seat, heart full of doubts. She'd never been able to stay mad with Charlie for long but still, another upheaval? And yet he was right. She couldn't bear to stay on at Paul and Dee's after today's events. Couldn't return to Forge Street.

'Schools break up soon for summer,' Charlie said, reading her mind.

A loud ringing filled the car, Charlie's Bluetooth speaker switching on. Rosie gasped as a familiar voice began to speak. Charlie indicated and executed a swift illegal U-turn.

'You bet it's serious.' His face was hard. 'His mother and I will be right there.'

'But why?' Dee whined, for what might have been the thirtieth time as she watched Rosie pack. 'The boys have only just got here and you're whisking them off again? It isn't fair. We had loads of plans. We were going to do so many lovely things together.' She sat on the bed, watching as Rosie opened drawers. 'This isn't about the car, is it? Because Paul really feels b—'

'Of course not.' Rosie focussed hard on selecting underwear, an all too easy task when she'd brought so little with her. 'It's just... that crazy woman. It was awful. I want to get away where no one knows about us...I mean...me._And...and...it'll be better for the boys. They've had a dreadful time at school. Getting teased about my terrible ungrateful attitude. Taunted. Bullied. Luke's been giving all his pocket money away and poor Tim...' She choked as she thought about it. 'I can't believe they never said anything.'

'But the whole summer... In Scotland. I could understand if it were that Tuscan villa.' Dee gave a weak attempt at a laugh. 'Better pack your sweaters!' She fingered one of Rosie's new purchases, a designer silk scarf. 'Oh well, Skye isn't that far. And we have to break in Paul's new car anyway. A short road trip will be just the thing. Although goodness knows how I'll bribe Kylie to—'

'No.' With horror Rosie envisaged the whole lot descending on her. 'Really, we'll be better on our own. Just the three of us.' She saw Dee's disbelieving stare and flushed up to her highlighted roots. 'It's just...' she was stammering now, trying to improvise, 'I want to make it up to them...the boys...have me all to themselves...less chance of being noticed or followed...you'd hate it anyway...and Charlie said...'

'Charlie!' Dee's face was livid as she spat out the name. 'That's it. He's behind this, isn't he? Trying to alienate you from us. Oh, don't think I haven't noticed him smarming up to you, making himself comfy in *our* home, whispering poison about us in the showroom. Not coincidence, is it, that you're rich as stink and immediately your lying, cheating ex-husband is your new best friend.' Her nose wrinkled as she put on a squeaky mocking voice. '*Wants you to move close to him. Wants to get you away from that nasty Dee and Paul.*'

She stood up abruptly, crossing her arms, sharp and no-nonsense. 'Well, let me tell you something, Rosie, my friend. Charlie Dixon only takes care of Charlie Dixon. And if you're looking for advice from the man who did the dirty on you, then you're acting like a gullible fool...'

Chapter Twenty-Two

'So right, where are we at?' Marcus twisted the chains of the swing. They'd the place to themselves, a rundown playground in a small dusty patch of green.

'Running though our lists of suspects – I mean interviewees,' Olivia quipped, rocking beside him. She was more confident now that her own interview was over. Yes, she'd felt a real plonker, admitting her foolishness, spilling her fears and details of her ordeal to the camera. But Marcus had talked her through it, his probing gentle and supportive. She thought she'd come out of it OK. And frankly her public image really couldn't get any worse.

She flipped a page of her spiral notebook, feeling like Sam Spade's secretary in some 1940s Humphrey Bogart movie, scrawling mysterious ciphers in shorthand. Why didn't Marcus own a voice recorder at least? After all he got to play with camera, microphones, lights, computer. She bet Zac used something cunning and sexy – a briefcase videocam or a ballpoint spy pen.

Zac had taken her dancing last night, feeding her cocktails, whirling her around until she was drunk, giddy and giggling. The breeze lifted her hair as dreamily she relived the sweaty hours that had followed, their bodies intertwined, her half-muffled cries of passion. She shouldn't like him so much. He was immature, irresponsible and morally dubious. Any sensible woman would run a mile but then she'd served a long enough sentence in that particular prison. It had been years since her whole life hadn't revolved around work.

Her mind ran over little images of his body with all the loving detail of an artist. His smile. His muscular arms. His amazing flat belly with that sexy line of hair leading to…

Oops. Marcus had stopped talking, expression slightly exasperated. Quickly she wiped the soppy smile from her lips and poised her pen.

'OK then.' The swing unwound to normal. 'We've still got a load of people to contact. And a shooting schedule to set up. I've some numbers, the others you'll have to track down. Then the homeless guys – I'd like to get them in the can before they go walkabout.'

'So do we hire a studio?' she asked. Marcus might be an energetic fidgety little devil, she thought, but he was also way too serious. Zac had suggested he went out with them last night but he'd just cast his eyes to the heavens and continued studying footage.

'No, the location tells half the story. That's why we interviewed you in the park, so people could see exactly where you were attacked. Talking heads are boring. Nowhere too noisy though or the mike has to compete. Indoors, we can use an overhead boom or a clip-on.'

He tilted his head to the sky, running it through mentally.

'Signed releases from everyone. Location too if we're filming on their property. That way they can't back out if they worry they've said too much. Or decide they look fat.' He made a face.

'And you never bother with a script? Is that normal?' Olivia used her arms to send the swing soaring again.

She was quite certain Marcus didn't approve of her fling with Zac. Was it the suddenness? Too damn predictable? But he was so deep into this project, he was mostly oblivious to the two of them giggling around him. Just yesterday she'd interrupted him in the midst of his editing, flipping a sheaf of papers under his nose until he looked up, blinking.

'I just found these stuffed in a box. Honest, Marcus, what the heck!'

She laid them out like a poker hand. 'Final notice. Late payment. Second request. And cheques. One for five hundred pounds and another for three hundred that's over six months old!'

'Can't you sort it out?' He had run his hands through his untidy hair. 'I'm rather busy right now.' And he was lost again in his task.

'Up now. We need to crack on.' Marcus pulled Olivia to her feet. 'I want to talk to some of those unfortunates who are out there flying a sign. You know, "Will work for latte", that sort of thing.'

Olivia rolled her eyes. 'Money for jam, you mean. Biggest scam ever. We had a baglady close to our Manhattan apartment who waved the same banner, rain or shine, for the entire two years I lived there. It said "Pregnant, please help" even though she was nudging sixty. I actually used to give her a few bucks until Brad pointed out she netted something like two hundred dollars a day. He used to say I should invest in some cardboard and a marker pen.'

Marcus dropped her hand. There was a nasty gleam in his eye.

'No!' Olivia pulled away, alarmed, but he was striding towards a rubbish bin. He pulled out a squashed up box, opening it flat. 'Great idea,' he said, scrawling huge words with a Sharpie felt tip. 'We'll give it a go.'

Olivia was still fuming as they sat in the pub.

'Oh come on, it wasn't that bad,' Marcus declared, sliding a glass of wine to her. 'Free money. Easy as pie, right?'

He'd virtually had to push her into the intersection. 'Think of it as an acting job. Or a religious experience. The Sadhus of India live off the charity of strangers.' At the last minute he took off his baseball cap and crammed it on her head.

'Goddamn you, Marcus,' she'd shouted back. And there she was. On the centre island between two lanes of traffic, waiting for the lights to turn red, waving a stupid piece of cardboard.

'Homeless', he'd written. 'Anything helps.'

She could see him across the road, filming her with his small handheld camera. She stuck out her tongue, hating him, wondering if he truly hated her. Why else, just when she began to feel comfortable, would he decide to humiliate her yet again? Well, she would show him.

She pasted a smile on her face, shoved the baseball cap as low as it would go, hoping to hide most of her face from the occupants in the cars. Reactions varied as they pulled up to the lights. Some stared openly. Others refused to acknowledge her, looking almost as mortified as she felt. Kids stuck up their middle fingers. Every now and then someone would roll down a window and she'd move forward, accept a coin – ten pence, fifty pence, even a couple of pounds – one flung with such force it had hit the top of her head. She was hot with shame, exposed, a red blush spreading up her neck. A couple of drivers tried to engage her in conversation before the light changed. One creep propositioned her. A woman told her to stop loafing around and 'find an effing job'. And all the time Marcus's camera whirred, unseen.

She tipped the coins on to the pub table and Marcus picked up the camera again, filming her as she counted them out. 'Enough for lunch?' he asked.

'If it is, I'm not treating you. I earned it.' She stared flintily at the lens.

'So, Olivia,' it was his interview voice, 'you were out there an hour? How much did we make? Tell me how it felt. Was it really – what was it you said – money for jam?'

Lunch arrived, Olivia's seething muted to a low undercurrent at the sight of good-smelling food. There was no point in sulking openly with Marcus. He simply didn't notice.

'You asked about script?' His glasses were sliding to the end of his nose and he pushed them back up again. 'Some filmmakers have it all mapped out in advance, never deviate from the storyboard. My approach is more organic. I know where I'm going and what questions I'm going to ask but I like to leave some wiggle room. Be open to spontaneity.'

'Oh yeah, I've seen how your spontaneity works. Wiggling is all well and good until I'm the one on the hook. Can I have some chips?'

'Help yourself. How's the shepherd's pie?'

'Great. Want to try?'

They traded plates. Probably the fish and French fries were cooked in trans-fats, likely doing awful things to her hitherto exemplary cholesterol but Olivia had well and truly loosened up on her stringent diet. No need to keep skinny for work and hard to be fussy when Marcus was filming someone digging pizza out of a trash can. So far there'd been no ill effects.

'How's the search for your pal, Rosie?' Marcus forked up mashed potato.

'Hardly my pal.' Olivia sprinkled malt vinegar liberally. 'And as of today I've drawn a blank. I went by her house yesterday. Absolutely deserted. There was one thing though…' She paused.

'Yeah?'

'She lives next door to Darius's girlfriend.' Olivia had felt goosebumps when she'd spotted the familiar figure get into her car. 'Saw her at the café once – the girlfriend, I mean. And she works as a nurse in my great-aunt's care home. London really is a freaking village. It occurred to me—'

'That she's probably the one who told Darius about Rosie's win? And maybe old Darius was the lech who made a pass? I'll look into it. Zac plays football with him. That might explain how he found out too.'

'You didn't ask?'

'He insists he can't reveal his sources. And if Darius did try it on – well, a million quid is a lot of temptation. Oops, sorry.' He'd eaten half her meal.

'Most men will cheat if they can do it without being caught.' Olivia handed back the fish and chips and watched him demolish that too. 'They hardly need a boatload of cash.'

'Rather cynical, are we?' Marcus reached in his back pocket for his wallet.

'Realistic.'

'I think people give plenty of clues to their basic nature if you pay attention. Problem comes with ignoring them or hoping they'll change.'

Was this a warning about Zac? Or was he thinking of himself, justifying those hearts Zac had said he'd broken? And who was this mistress? Someone married? A little delicate probing seemed in order.

'What about you? I've yet to see you on a date.'

'Taking a break. Last girlfriend threw a Thesaurus at me, screaming all I cared about were my blankety-blank-blank films. She had a way with words.'

'So,' Olivia scrutinised him, 'I guess you'd say that work is your mistress?'

'Hah. No. That's the sort of bollocks Zac would spout.'

She knew it. Somehow she just couldn't see him sneaking into a woman's bedroom while her husband was out.

'You look like you need your daily caffeine fix.' He took her arm companionably. 'Come on, I think the budget can stretch to a cappuccino.'

'I did have one good lead,' she said as they walked past the clock tower. 'I'm seeing Rosie's ex-husband this afternoon.'

Charlie Dixon was the very embodiment of a successful car dealer, charming, easy to look at, with an expensive suit and a friendly smile.

'Great little runabout, isn't it?' He leaned a hand on the door of the red convertible. 'Keyless go. Built-in nav system. Automatic roof. Works off the remote.' He pressed a button to demonstrate. 'Make it easy these days, don't they?'

The new car smell and gleaming paintwork was intoxicating. Olivia extricated herself reluctantly. She was wearing a short skirt, figuring it never hurt.

'Actually I'm here for my boss, Marcus Gilbert, the filmmaker. You're Charlie Dixon, aren't you? Used to be married to Rosie?'

His smile faded. 'Yes, but if you think you're—'

'Don't worry. Last thing we want is to harass her. It's absolutely disgusting the way she's been treated.'

He dropped the remote into his pocket. 'Come into the office.' He poured two paper cups of coffee from a machine and loosened his tie. 'So what's this about?'

'Rosie's had a hard deal. And Marcus and I think she'd benefit from appearing in his new documentary.' She sparkled up at him. 'But seems she's not at her old address.'

'Nor would you be. Press out for blood. Friends treating you like lepers. Besides,' he swivelled in his chair, 'that place is a dump. Never liked the kids living there and that school's a bloody disgrace. I've persuaded her to move.'

'Thought you were divorced?' Olivia's tawny eyes flirted with him over the coffee cup.

'Yeah, we are.' He clicked his pen, 'But someone's got to look out for her. Rosie would give away her last penny, she's that trusting. Her own brother dragged her here to buy him a brand new BMW.' He changed tack abruptly. 'What's the deal with this film then?'

'It'd be a chance to tell her side of things. Set the story straight.'

'Yeah, well that reporter screwed her over, right enough. Whole world against her. My kids getting picked on, fights at school. And her family's no big support. Mother's an arrant bitch. Rosie's bent over backwards to make her happy but all the money in the world couldn't buy my ex-monster-in-law a heart.'

Pure gold. Marcus would love this. 'What about her father?'

'Died when she was a toddler.' He shrugged, fair brows coming together. His eyes were a paler blue than Zac's, but equally arresting. He was a handsome man, Charlie Dixon. Too bad he'd turned out to be a cheater too.

'And Rosie's how old?'

'She was thirty-three in March.'

Five months younger than herself, Olivia thought. They could practically be twins.

Through the glass wall, she saw two people stroll around a shiny new mini, shadowed by another salesman. Charlie followed her glance. 'They won't buy,' he said. 'That type'll negotiate every last cent out of the deal and then drift away saying they'll think about it.'

The clock on the wall said five-fifty pm. Zac was taking her to the movies tonight. At least she knew exactly what she was getting with him. In some ways he was the most honest rogue she'd met.

She leaned forward. 'Do you have a number for Rosie? And perhaps her brother and mother?'

Marcus had mentioned it could take twenty or thirty hours of footage for a paltry sixty minutes of film.

'Could we interview you?' she asked. 'If we did it here? Might be great publicity.'

'I'd have to speak to Rosie first.' To his credit he didn't cave at this blatant bribe. 'Don't want anyone else getting hurt. You swear this will help her?'

'Absolutely.' Olivia flicked back her hair with a dazzling smile. 'We're not out to slam her, honest. Quite the reverse.' She handed over a card. 'If you talk, ask her to call Marcus Gilbert, however late. We could drop by to see her tomorrow morning.'

'You'll be lucky,' Charlie said. 'As you Yanks say, you're a day late and a dollar short.'

Half an hour later Olivia burst into the living room, startling Marcus and Zac. The brothers looked up, Zac freshly showered and changed, Marcus as shaggy and unkempt as the Shetland pony in his earlier documentary.

'We're buggered!' she announced dramatically. 'Our bird has flown.'

Chapter Twenty-Three

Rosie sat on the dry-stone wall, feet dangling above a grassy hill that sloped down to the small curve of golden beach. White crests smashed against a series of black jutting rocks protruding from the headland. The violence of the ocean perfectly suited her mood.

Yesterday's rain had left the air clean and fresh-scented with a tang of peat smoke from Tighban's tall chimney. Grey stone glinted silver between trees and overgrown bushes, turret reaching up into the dazzling sky. Two cannons poked from the crenellated parapets, one aimed at the mountain pass, the other at the glittering blue below. It was all very lovely but still she felt sick and grumpy.

Gullible fool, Dee had called her. And she was right. Gullible fool to fall for Zac. Gullible fool letting Paul and Dee con her into buying that car and funding the hair salon. Gullible fool for melting, weak-kneed, when Charlie Dixon showed the slightest concern. She had to be smarter. She had a million problems now and there was no one she could trust.

There was a shriek and a clash of sticks. Luke and Tim were sword-fighting, clambering over slabs of ancient granite, leaping with bloodcurdling yells onto the purple carpet of heather. In London she worried about Luke especially, with his tough inner-city friends. She'd caught him sneaking cigarettes, his 'girlfriends' continually phoned the house and she had a strong suspicion that one of his classmates was responsible for the graffiti that had appeared on a nearby vacant house.

Tim jumped from a rock, slashing at Luke's legs. The bruise on his eye had faded to a dull blue and yellow. Poor Tim – attacked by bullies, thanks to that wicked newspaper article. Charlie had been furious, berating the headmaster, scorning his self-justifying lecture about Tim's lack of tact in showing off the latest Game Boy to less fortunate children. Shaken as Rosie had been by that woman at the garage, it had been a relief to let Charlie take control. But now she was regretting that too.

Everything would be different after this holiday. The boys would be in a posh private school. They'd all be living in a spanking new house. Charlie had arranged the whole shebang down to packers and movers. Well, she couldn't go back to Dee and Paul's and the idea of returning to her old home, with Anya snubbing her and the neighbours hostile, was too depressing.

Instead they'd be living minutes from Charlie's doorstep. That knowledge – a dream come true before her financial win – now filled her with anxiety. Dee had suggested he might try to take the boys, could even go for maintenance. Could that happen?

If only he'd had this turnaround before she was rich. And what would Vile Val think of their close proximity? She had a sense from Charlie's comments that there was trouble in that particular paradise. Or was she reading too much into nothing? Every couple squabbled. Or if they didn't, someone wasn't getting their opinions taken into account.

She closed her book with a sigh. Could it be – cliché or not – that she'd actually been happier when she was poor? Stressed, yes, worried sick half the time, but Anya had always been there with a glass of wine and Gemma to have a laugh with at work.

She felt guilty even thinking it. Ungrateful bitch. Millionaire Miseryguts. Still she couldn't help feeling heart-sore and betrayed. Seemed like since the win nobody could see her, Rosie Dixon, for the pound symbols blurring their vision.

But not here. Not in Skye, this beautiful Scottish island. She had a whole new identity and Luke and Tim were forbidden, on threats of permanent grounding, to divulge her secret.

The air grew abnormally clear, an accumulation of dark clouds rapidly scudding their way. It had poured each of the three days since they'd arrived in the misty isle.

'Quick guys!' she yelled as the wind picked up. 'Inside!'

Shepherd's Brae was a squat traditional crofter's cottage beneath the hillock for which it was named. It had seemed like a God-sent solution when, haunted by Tim's battered face and the image of crimson talons reaching for her eyes, Rosie had stumbled across the card. She'd stared at the photo of a whitewashed building with a lavender door, remembering a warm Marbella breeze, a glittering swimming pool, and the friendly estate agent, Alex, handing her over the small rectangle. '*If you hear of anyone needing a place to get away...*'

Reality was less idyllic. They'd arrived at dark in a thunderstorm after driving around lost for hours on unlit roads without a single signpost. The spry little housekeeper, Etta had fussed over the drowned rats, gathered a raincoat and large metal key and popped into the passenger seat to guide them down the track to their home for the next eight weeks.

'I've stacked up peat for a fire.' Her accent was soft and lilting. 'And put on the heating. We haven't had a guest in a while and we'd no' much time to prepare. It may be a wee bit damp.'

Damp? Seeping, more like. Vaporised ice gripped Rosie's bones as she stepped into the small stone dwelling, mocked by a sadly inadequate bar heater. Could it possibly be colder inside than out? Two tiny bedrooms, claw foot tub with rusty plumbing and low-ceilinged living room belonged to another, harsher century. Whitewash flaked from thick walls onto hard slate floors. There was a musty old rug, two mismatched armchairs, a sagging sofa and a bookcase full of dusty Penguin paperbacks. Etta switched on the electric kettle, and then set to making a fire.

'Check this out, Mum.' Luke had pressed a small red button underneath a mottled lifelike trout pinned to a wooden plaque.

The chilled air was filled with a warbling rendition of 'Take Me to the River' with the fish flipping its mechanised tail and opening and shutting its toothy plastic mouth.

Maybe it was travel fatigue but after Luke pushed that button for the third time, Rosie was ready to grant its wish and sling it out the window.

'Aye, Donald's nephew brought that back from America,' Etta said, proudly. 'And here's the meter for the electric. You'll need plenty of coins now.'

As if on cue the lights went out.

That first night, sleepless, Rosie huddled, shivering, under two mildew-smelling feather downies. Her toes banged against a stone hot water bottle which had been placed at the foot of her bed. Wind and rain lashed the rattling windows as she cursed her mistake, thinking of her nice warm bed in Paul's centrally-heated home. Freezing, miserable, she mimicked the fish's sentiments. 'Take me to the river. Drown me now.'

Fortunately in daylight the cottage seemed quaint, idiosyncratic rather than depressing. Maybe it would be OK. It had to be. Anyway the scenery was stunning even if she had bundled up in a thick woollen sweater while the boys ran around in t-shirts and splashed in the frigid ocean.

Sanctuary. That was all she wanted. Away from Paul and Dee's grasping, Anya's enmity, her mother's hostility. Somewhere where no one knew her story. No angry faces judged her. No mob clamoured to tear her apart.

The rain had stopped pattering the window as quickly as it had begun. In the sudden silence hens clucked, sheep bleated and the boys argued over their Monopoly game. Rosie, reading on the lumpy sofa, felt sleepily content.

There was a tapping on the door. Through paisley curtains she recognised the tall spindly frame, white beard and bushy hair of

Donald, their ninety-three-year-old host, leaning on his crooked stick, the border collie, Kinney, by his side. He was puffing on his pipe and talking to someone, too low to be understood. She opened the door and froze in surprise.

The man holding a jug of frothing fresh milk was tanned and rugged with light brown hair and a familiar broken nose. The hair was longer but it was definitely him.

'We just finished the milking.' Donald waved his stick as Rosie gasped.

'Alex!'

'And so you know each other? Well, well, well.' The old man rubbed his gnarled hands together. 'We weren't expecting this rogue home for weeks yet but here he is early and just as well. You'll all have dinner with me tonight, Mrs Packard – or should we call you Della? No, no, I won't hear a refusal.'

Alex nudged him with an elbow, looking as uncomfortable as Rosie felt.

'Perhaps...?' He paused. 'Mrs Packard...has other plans?' He handed over the milk jug with a question in his gaze.

Oh, why did *he* have to turn up? Intruding on her peace and quiet? And worse, making her feel a right div about her pathetic alias. She'd liked him well enough in Spain but that had been the briefest encounter, what seemed a lifetime ago.

Why would fate be so cruel? Not only for having essentially stood him up but being caught in a gigantic fib as well.

They were all waiting for her answer.

'Call me Rosie,' she said, aware of Luke and Tim crowding the door behind her. 'It's my middle name.'

Luke snickered then yelped as she trod warningly on his toe. Another bad example for her kids, but what else could she do? Rosie Dixon was at best a nationwide joke, at worst reviled and despised, and she simply didn't feel like going into explanations. Nor did she want to accept Donald's dinner invitation but she'd always been hopeless at saying no.

Quick, she thought. *Come up with a good excuse.*

'Chicken was delicious,' Rosie said as Etta cleared away plates from the long antique oak table that could seat twelve or more guests. 'Thanks so much.'

'Ah well, Alex's the better cook,' the little woman admitted cheerfully, 'but I couldn't put him to work his first night home.'

The boys had been remarkably well-behaved, managing not to fidget when Donald bowed his head to say grace or giggle too loudly when he poured his cup of tea into the saucer and lifted the dish to his lips.

Now Luke stared round the grand ceremonial dining room, past the fire blazing in the giant hearth and clanking pipe radiators, his attention caught by the display on the wall.

'Can I see the swords?'

'Go ahead.' The old man stood up too, piercing eyes gleaming over his hawk's beak of a nose. His skin was pale and he looked thin and fragile as a peeled twig but he held himself erect.

Luke paused in front of a slender weapon with a velvet-lined metal basket to protect the bearer's hand.

'That one belonged to my ancestor, Angus Mor MacDonald. He fought with Bonny Prince Charlie and fled to France after the Culloden massacre.'

'Any relation to Flora MacDonald?' Rosie asked, scooping the last mouthful of gooseberry pie and ice cream.

'A distant cousin, maybe,' Alex said. She felt awkward with him. Compared to the easy conversation they'd had in Spain, there was too much uncomfortable silence. If it hadn't been for Donald's friendly chat, she'd have been tongue-tied the whole meal. She knew the stiffness was coming from her, she could feel it throughout her body. He couldn't have known she'd be here. It was some kind of ghastly coincidence.

Just like his showing up at the marina? After seeing her in the hotel?

Nor did it help that Donald was asking her – or rather Della Packard – a slew of difficult questions. Where did she live? What did she do? And where was Mr Packard? Every time she stumbled through an answer, she had to avoid Alex's eyes. She was a liar and he knew it. Either she was lying now or she'd been lying in Spain. Was it too much to hope he didn't remember whatever personal details she'd so recklessly shared?

'I'll just get rid of these.' Alex picked up the dessert plates and Rosie joined the boys in admiring the swords, shields, even a battle-axe, that hung between ancestral portraits and swathes of clan tartan. A youthful beardless Donald stared proudly from the last painting, dressed in regimental kilt. World War II, Rosie guessed.

Oh well, Rosie told herself, who cared what the dratted man thought. He had no villa to sell here, no reason to bother her for a minute beyond this infernal dinner.

Anya had been so right. Beware of charming strangers. Zac had taught her how dangerous that combination could be.

The innocent credulous Rosie was dead. She'd learned what poison rested in people's souls. Never again would she trust so easily. Even if she hadn't been badly burned, how would she know if it was plain old Rosie anyone liked, and not just her bank balance?

'People actually fought with these?' Luke was facing a gigantic long-handled claymore, far taller than he.

'Oh aye.' Donald nodded. 'That one was bloodied at Bannockburn, Prestonpans *and* Culloden Moor where many brave Scots were slaughtered. Still,' he brightened fractionally, 'it took a few English heads along the way.' He studied the blade mournfully. 'No doubt I'll be selling them all at Sotheby's one of these days. A crying shame.'

'Is it worth a lot?' Tim asked. 'Maybe we could buy it, Mum?'

'Tim!' Rosie admonished as Alex came back into the room. He leaned against the stone hearth, watching the goings on with veiled eyes.

'Not enough to keep the roof over our heads,' Donald said lugubriously. 'The house is falling down. Wet rot, dry rot and the chimney ready to tumble in the next stiff breeze. Oh yes, hundreds of years those swords have been in our family and the treacherous English will doubtless get them after all.'

'The house is fine,' Alex said, evidently irritated. 'I'll get after the chimney in the morning.'

Luke touched the sword tip. 'We're English.'

The old man laughed. 'Ah well, I'm not saying you're all bad now, wee laddie. Your mother's right bonnie for a Sassenach, is she no, Alex?'

There was a short sharp silence. Alex sighed. 'Yes, that she is.' He caught Rosie's eye without a smile. As if he'd been forced to say it. Well, in Marbella he'd seemed to find her attractive enough, she thought, with a mental toss of her hair. Or was that when he thought she and Anya were easy targets? Two young single women looking for fun in the sun?

Two wealthy young women who might want to purchase a villa?

'Did Prince Charlie ever come here?' Tim stared about the panelled room.

'Nah. This was built after the pardoned Jacobites returned from exile. The redcoats burned the old house down when they couldn't find Angus Mor. He was sore wounded in the battle but when word reached him the soldiers were coming, he slipped away, dragging his injured leg along the cliff path. He knew a cave, you see…'

'Have you ever seen it?' Luke sat up, enthralled.

'Oh yes. I used to climb down to it when I was a boy. And so did Alex here. They call it the rebel's cave.'

'It's nothing to see. Just a slit in the rock.' Alex glowered at the portrait of his Jacobite ancestor, looking tougher and far more dangerous than that genteel white-wigged individual.

'Aye and it'd have been a treacherous descent on that black winter night even with two good legs,' Donald continued with relish. 'And Angus hid in that miserable crack for ten days, feverish from his wound, with no' a bite to eat and only snow to quench his thirst. Well, well...' He stared at their enthralled faces. 'There now, I'm sure Alex would be happy to take you, mind.'

'Awesome!'

'Can we?'

'Oh, no really...'

Rosie and her sons spoke simultaneously. All eyes turned to Alex. He was poking the fire, his back to them.

'There's a great deal to do around here, Uncle. And weren't you just complaining about the dangerous state of the chimney and the terrible need of repairs?'

Rosie blushed fiercely. 'I wouldn't dream of putting you to the trouble,' she said, stiffly.

'Nonsense.' Donald slapped his nephew on his shoulder as he straightened. 'I'd take them myself if I wasn't an ancient cripple. Alex, lad, have you been away so long you've forgotten Highland hospitality? The chimney can wait. Sure, and hasn't it been lovely and calm, with only a wee bit wind? Don't you worry, Rosie, lass. He'd love showing you around.'

Maybe so. But not if I can avoid it, Rosie thought.

Chapter Twenty-Four

'Just like you see in James Bond.' Adjusting her cleavage, the blonde gave a collagen-boosted pout, every inch of her face worked on from the prominent cheekbones to the abnormally tight skin. 'World-class jewellers knew me by name. Beautiful boys hanging on my arm.' She gave a nostalgic sigh, stroking the miniature poodle on her lap. Seventy years if she was a day, Olivia guessed, crepey wrists and neck encircled in gold and diamonds. 'A real jet-setter, I was.'

Olivia made an assenting sound, hoping to draw the heavily made-up eyes from Marcus and the camera.

'Don't worry, you'll be edited out,' he'd promised. 'Just sit there and stop them fixating on the lens.'

Despite herself she was getting caught up in the project. It was almost cathartic to listen to these people, discover screw-ups so much grander than hers. Last night she'd felt positively regretful as Zac dragged her from the screen where Marcus was looking over yesterday's work. She'd been admiring the way he'd used pinpricks of light in the pupils to convey emotion. The man was a genius.

Good luck, bad luck – like the Zen story sometimes it was hard to tell which was which. Take this cheerful soul, ensconced in a caravan park – basically living in a trailer – happily admitting to squandering a prince's ransom on trips to Monte Carlo, gigolos and roulette. Then again nearly a third of multi-million lottery winners became bankrupt within a few years, naive about investments or the expenses that came with eighteen-bedroom mansions and twenty-acre trout lakes.

Once Olivia might have found her foolish beyond words but that was before she'd had her own small fortune stolen from under her work-obsessed nose. Despite constant calls to Spain and numerous viewings, the villa still hadn't sold, nor had the mysterious envelope shown up. Marcus had been back to Rathbone's twice to look.

And what was happening with her Manhattan apartment? She imagined bills piling on the doorstep, power switched off, and threatening letters from the bank. Was Brad sorting it out? She had no idea.

'Maybe we could all fly to Monte Carlo?' Olivia suggested, as they wrapped up the day's shooting. 'Show her throwing a few hands at the casinos.'

'Or maybe,' Marcus modified, 'we could take her down the Playboy Club. Use Zac as her escort. Let her have a spin on their wheel. What's happening with Rosie?'

'Nothing. Still missing,' Olivia admitted. 'The husband's being cagey. Says her mobile isn't working. I'm seeing the sister-in-law tomorrow.'

'We could drop her. Rosie. We've got plenty of contenders.'

'Yeah, maybe.' Now why did she find that so disappointing?

She was meeting Zac in a Soho bar after this. Probably she drank too much when she was with him. Zac wasn't a moderation kind of guy. Initially it was what she loved about him, despite occasional excruciating hangovers. He'd made her feel reckless, careening on a whirly fairground ride, laughing as life's problems blurred.

But out every single evening? It was getting a touch too predictable. Exhausting to have to be bright and witty for his countless friends. Boring even. She wondered if she could ever talk him into a quiet night at home. Snuggling on the sofa. Watching TV. Just enjoying each other's company.

'Ever considered going commercial?' she asked Marcus as they lugged equipment to the car. 'Full-length features. Romances. Comedy. Gotta be a lot more fun.'

'Oh yeah, tons,' Marcus said, dryly, slamming the trunk. 'Star tantrums, endless takes, studio bosses. Freak snowstorms throwing you over budget.'

'But you could have a box-office smash. Get an Oscar. Make your fortune.'

'Or the studio might send it straight to video,' he countered, tipping her – or technically his – baseball cap over her eyes. 'You've no control. Whereas even a novice documentary-maker has access to cable channels, internet, film festivals, distributors.' He squashed the tripod in beside the lights. 'There's some amazing work out there. One award-winning short can shake the world.'

Olivia made a derisive sound. 'Yeah, I'm sure the government's trembling as we speak.' She slid into the Toyota, putting her feet on the dashboard and applying mascara in the pull-down mirror. 'Besides, who watches them?'

'You're starting to sound like Zac. Larger audiences than you think. Anyway it's not all about the money.'

'Actually it is.' She grinned at him, unrepentant. 'This movie is definitely about the money.'

'Yeah, but it's not what *I'm* about.'

'Spoken like a true commie bastard,' she teased.

He laughed. 'Capitalist pig.'

'And proud of it, comrade.' She made a fist, punched the air like Che Guevara. Marcus was so passionate about his work, his idealism made him an easy target. Of course she related to his movie. Especially the tales of loss. But it just confirmed her experience. You made your own way in this world. And if you failed, it was all too easy to slip, hopeless and abandoned, between the cracks. You couldn't rely on love, friendship, even family. She'd seen it in the eyes of the homeless woman's that they'd interviewed yesterday. The terrible knowledge that nobody cared if she lived or died.

⚜ ⚜ ⚜

'Muffin?' Marcus offered, as Olivia paraded into the kitchen and snapped off a smart salute. No prizes for who'd sprinted round the block for breakfast stuff. If it wasn't for the only functioning adult in the house, they'd all be eating Coco Pops and drinking curdled milk.

Zac grinned, shirt unbuttoned, feet bare and hair still wet from the shower they'd shared. 'Never thought I'd fancy an Andrews Sister but, man, that uniform's turning me on.'

'Idiot. I'm Vera Lynn.' She did a twirl. Khaki army uniform, cloth buttons, rank badge on shoulder. She scratched at her arm. 'The material's itchy as hell and look,' she held out a hand, 'I'm trembling like a bag of jelly.'

'Told you,' Zac said. 'No good comes of volunteering. Think of those poor sods in the First World War. Marched off to be heroes and came back mustard gassed.'

'Wasn't my idea. The Home Manager heard me goofing about to some of my great-aunt's records and roped me into it.' Olivia donned her wig with the curled-under fringe, picked up her rucksack, checking song sheets, poster, laptop.

'Get Zac to go with you.' Marcus handed her a mug of tea. 'Moral support.'

'Sing to a bunch of wrinklies?' Zac shuddered comically. 'Take Marcus. He always did have a thing for *The Golden Girls*. He can bring his guitar.'

'You play?' Surprised, she turned to Marcus.

'So does Zac. As kids we even tried the boys' band thing. Zac thought with his looks and my talent… What?' She must have looked gobsmacked because he laughed. 'Did you think this was my entire life?'

'I had no idea.' She knew so little about him. Or Zac, she realised. She tried to imagine him, sitting on a bed somewhere, serenading her. It wouldn't come.

'Luckily we were rubbish. I'd have loathed stardom and Zac would have been even more unbearable. Forget the taxi.' Marcus picked up her bag of CDs. 'I'm heading that way anyway. Sorry I'll miss your command performance but I can drop you off if you're ready in five.'

In the morning room, two elderly men were playing chess, other residents occupied the wing-backed armchairs, dozing, knitting or chatting with visitors.

'Great old building, eh?' Marcus surveyed the landscaped lawns. 'Hard to believe we're in London.'

'Gray? Is that you?' The old lady perked up at their approach.

'No, this is Marcus.' Olivia had managed to persuade Marcus to carry some of her stuff in. 'He's my…' Uh, what? Boss? Landlord? Lover's brother? Friend?

'Heard a lot about you, Aunt Winnie.' Marcus gently squeezed a frail age-spotted hand.

'Sit.' She patted the chair next to her. 'You're making my neck ache. What's with the Beverly Sister getup?'

'Vera Lynn. It's the sing-a-long, remember? Hello Beryl, you lost something?'

'Moccasin,' the dishevelled woman wheezed, looking like a distraught marshmallow in her pink dressing-gown. 'I think Eve took it.'

A tiny old lady looked up from the magazine she was holding at arm's length. 'I did not! Cheek. You're the one always losing things.'

'What about under your bed? Hold on.' Olivia disappeared out through the double doors and returned with the missing item. 'There you go.'

'Oh thanks, dear.' Beryl's plump hands pressed hers in gratitude.

'And Eve,' Olivia took a pair of glasses from the table next to Winnie, 'how can you read the song sheets without these?'

'No wonder I couldn't see a blooming word.' Eve accepted them gratefully. 'Bonkers as well as blind.' She nodded approvingly at the wig. 'Nice hair, love.'

The door opened and two Labradors walked in with their owner. Olivia pushed Winnie's wheelchair towards the window. 'Here.' She handed Marcus a dog biscuit. 'My aunt hates dogs. Keep them away.'

He widened his eyes. 'You brought dog treats?'

Marcus was grinning when they headed for the social room.

'What?' Olivia scowled, warningly.

'Nothing, tough girl.' His smile broadened. 'But if you're not careful someone might think you've a heart.'

Olivia's cheeks reddened. 'Yeah, well, it's like a time warp here,' she said gruffly. 'Beryl's always losing her slippers, kicks them off when she naps. And Eve keeps forgetting her glasses. Same conversations too, round and round.' She stopped in front of a mirror to adjust her wig. 'But I love hearing their stories. Beryl used to be Borough Mayoress, the woman in pearls was once a lady-in-waiting to Queen Elizabeth, and Eve, the little one, is a war heroine. She was in the French Resistance. And now she's walking out with Elijah, who's pushing ninety. They're darling together. And half of them never get visitors. Families can't be bothered.'

And hadn't she – and even her dad – been just the same with Aunt Winnie? She was dismayed to find her voice catching.

Marcus gave her a strange look. He took hold of her upper arm, stopping her in her tracks. 'Are you crying?'

'Dog allergy.' She half-laughed as she wiped a tear.

Long fingers brushed the moisture from her wet cheek. They were very close, his expressive eyes boring into hers. Time seemed to stop. She could feel his warm breath, the heat from his body only inches away. His dark pupils held her, mesmerised. Almost unconsciously she tilted up her chin.

'Hey, Livvy, got yourself an entourage.' They sprang apart as a nurse sauntered past, gesturing at the residents shuffling towards them.

'Good.' Flustered and hot, Olivia gathered her wits. 'They can help me set up. Right, there you go, Marcus.' She took her props from his burdened arms, handing them to her new helpers. 'You've done enough. Follow the exit signs and you're back in the car park.'

'These my marching orders?' Marcus lingered, leaning his elbow on the wall. Perhaps it was the World War II theme, but something about his stance and maybe the brown leather jacket made her think of a fighter pilot saying goodbye to his girl on the eve of battle.

'You said you were busy,' Olivia reminded him, briskly. 'Besides you'll only make me nervous if you watch. I can catch the bus back. I'll see you tonight.'

'Actually you won't.' He straightened up, placing his hands in his back pockets. 'I'm going out directly after my meetings.'

'Oh?' She had no business to make that sound like a question.

'Just some old friends from college. Ordinary wage-earning stiffs hooking up for laughs and beers at someone's flat in Brixton. No one rich, hip, glittery or famous. Would hardly be your style. Or Zac's .'

It was as if he'd slapped her. She'd never heard Marcus be so casually cruel.

'No, sounds pretty dull.' Her lips were stiff. 'Have a good time then.'

He turned away, raising his fingers in a Victory salute. 'Knock 'em dead, Miss Lynn.'

'Rosie winning the Premium Bonds – imagine!' The sister-in-law 'call me Dee' fussed with teabags and milk, stylishly retro with her permed platinum hair, clinging Capris, boldly patterned blouse and pearly pink lipstick. She added a wafer biscuit to each saucer. 'And now you want to put her on the telly. Lucky girl.'

'Only if she'll agree.' Olivia accepted the cup.

'Not that she doesn't deserve it.' Dee batted caterpillar lashes. 'She's had such a struggle since her husband walked out. Although, hate to say it but she had let herself go. You know men. You have to make a little effort if you don't want them straying.'

Poor hapless creatures, Olivia thought. Victims of their own lower natures. It was as good an argument as any against marriage.

Unbidden her mind flashed to Marcus. Had they really nearly – kissed?

No, it had just been…a moment. A true nothing. Marcus would never make a play for his brother's girlfriend. And even if she wasn't involved with Zac, she didn't like Marcus *that* way.

And thank goodness. How complicated and tacky would that be? Being attracted to two brothers.

Anyway she was still mad at him about the glittery comment. Implying that she, Olivia, was a shallow flighty social climber. With difficulty she made herself concentrate again as Dee handed over a cup.

'She's in Scotland, I understand?'

'Yeah, just upped and left.' Dee's laugh sounded fake. 'We took her in after the press wrote those terrible things and then her ex, that Charlie Dixon, starts poisoning her against us. Although can't blame her for wanting a holiday.' She softened it hastily. 'Been through the mill, poor girl.'

As Dee waffled on, Olivia's mind wandered. After all, who could imagine any poor girl stuck with someone as lofty-minded and worthy as her landlord, boss, lover's brother? Unable to buy a new dress or shoes without feeling mercenary and frivolous. Like being with Aunt Winnie all over again. Hell, he'd probably expect his soulmate to shop at charity stores. Ugh!

And so what if she and Marcus had had a moment of connection? He'd cancelled that out with his snarky comment, making it clear exactly what he thought of her. Definitely no reason to feel embarrassed this morning, especially when he was acting normal as apple pie. As if he hadn't given it a second thought.

And why should he?

Nothing.

Had.

Happened.

It just highlighted how bad Olivia was with relationships, if something so meaningless could throw her for a loop. Last night she'd tossed and turned in bed until Zac, a sound sleeper, had woken and made love to her a second time.

'Mmm, nice.' Afterwards he'd pulled her into him, snuggling up like spoons. 'Did you know this is the longest time I've ever been monogamous?'

Olivia gritted her teeth, hot and irritable. What did he want – an award? It had only been a few weeks.

'How very flattering.' She turned over, creating distance between them. 'But then again I am living in your house which makes it just a tad difficult to bring girls home.' Some demon goaded her on. 'What are we doing here anyway? I mean, what exactly is…this?' Her gesture encompassed the bed, the rumpled sheets.

She knew but didn't care that it was a mistake as soon as the words left her mouth. You couldn't pin down men like Zac. Ask if they loved you. Yeah, but what if she did make it back to New York one day? Zac loved America and could work anywhere as a journalist. But she was kidding herself if she thought he'd cross the street for her, let alone the Atlantic.

He was eyeing her warily now. 'What brought this on? I thought we were having fun?'

'And so convenient. All you have to do is walk downstairs.' It came out sounding bitchy. Another wrong move. Was it guilt, shooting herself in the foot?

'Well, I can tell this night's going downhill,' Zac said conversationally, slipping out of bed. 'I'm heading out. Get a few drinks.' He slid into his jeans.

Immediately she felt remorseful. This was what she did when intimacy threatened. He'd told her he was being monogamous, something he didn't need to volunteer, and she'd tried to start a fight.

'Want company?' she asked meekly. Her watch said 2 a.m. Double guilt. Where was he going? To an all-night club? Or to find less cantankerous company?

'No.' He dropped a kiss on her forehead. 'You need your beauty sleep.'

She cursed herself the rest of the night.

'Pity we couldn't film in my new salon.' Dee pulled a compact from her handbag and reapplied lipstick. 'Remember, if you need hair and make-up done I'll give you a smashing rate.'

'Well, thanks,' Olivia stood up to go, 'but since it's so hard to find Rosie we might be dropping her segment.'

'Her mum lives round the corner. Let me give her a call.' Dee punched a number in her phone. 'Line's busy. You might as well go over there. I'll tell her you're on your way.'

'Oh? But I understood she and Rosie don't get on?'

Dee's perfectly arched eyebrows rose. 'Who said that? Maxine's not one of those gushy types but she's devoted to her family. Oh,' she looked disgusted, 'bloody Charlie, I suppose. After the way *he's* behaved, he's got a nerve.'

Two streets away, Olivia decided that, if anything, Charlie Dixon had been charitable about the woman he called his 'monster-in-law'. The well-dressed Maxine snatched open the door, lips pressed into a line so thin they practically disappeared into the pinched white face.

'Hi,' Olivia began brightly, extending her right hand, 'Olivia Wheeler. I work for Marcus Gilbert, the documentary filmmaker. We were hoping—'

Hostility flared in those gimlet eyes. 'Yes.' It was a vicious hiss. 'Dee warned me. I know who you are and what you're about. Million pounds got everyone crawling out the woodwork, hasn't it? Well you won't get to Rosie through me. Clear off my doorstep before I call the police.'

The slam that followed almost broke the frosted glass.

Chapter Twenty-Five

'It so happens I'll be in Glasgow next week,' Charlie said on the phone. 'Skye's not so far. I could rent a car and drive up.'

Rosie's heart sank. 'No, Charlie, please don't. The boys are… I just need…' She trailed off, looking out the window. 'A little space.'

'Oh well,' he said diplomatically. 'We don't have to talk about it now.'

'Ready?'

Rosie had done her best to put it off but Tim and Luke would no longer brook delay.

Alex led them out the back gate, striding in his work boots, well-worn short-sleeve shirt and even more well-worn jeans through the rough heathery pasture.

Oh, why had Donald ever suggested this outing? she thought. The twins had never had so much freedom, off adventuring without adults, either on their own or with Etta's children. Rosie was fine with her solitary walks. But given the idea of a mystery cave, it was all the boys could talk about. And then the humiliation of having to actually ask the man to take them after all.

Alex stopped to pat an elderly white carthorse. The beast looked massive to Rosie's townie eyes, although docile enough with his sagging back, tangled mane and hairy feet the size of soup tureens.

'Does he bite?' she asked nervously. She liked animals but horses were just so huge.

'Lochinvar? No, he's gentle as a lamb, aren't you old fellow? Retired now but he could pull a cart with the best of them, bringing in hay or peat.'

A light breeze blew hair into Rosie's face making her wish for a hat. Well, at least there'd be no midges – another secret people failed to mention when waxing lyrical about the beauty of the Highlands. Of course the tiny biting insects mainly came out in the evening but when the plague descended it was like plunging into a dark itching cloud. Squelched the romance of golden sunsets and Northern Lights as effectively as wet socks and blisters.

'I've been meaning to apologise,' Alex said abruptly. He picked up a stick, slashing at the grass.

'What for?' Why had she found him so easy to talk to in Marbella? Was it the sun then, the beach atmosphere, the presence of Anya that had allowed her to feel so bold? Or had she really changed so much? She felt as if that Rosie had been an innocent giggling child, compared to the burdens she carried now.

'The cottage.' He sounded gruff. 'I assumed Donald had done it up, that he wouldn't print cards if it wasn't ready to rent.' He gave her a sidelong glance. 'It's not exactly El Gran Palacio.'

She seized the opportunity to put him straight.

'It's OK. Gran Palacio was the first time I ever stayed somewhere so posh. Kind of a crazy blow-out splurge.'

'Oh?' He had strongly-defined eyebrows, now raised in question. The moss-coloured cotton shirt brought out the green in his hazel eyes, the hint of gold in his light brown hair suggesting Viking ancestry. She banished the image of him stepping off a longboat, craggy and bearded with a horned helmet.

'No, usually it's a campsite, eating baked beans. But, uh, we won some money. So we splashed out. Barmy, I know.' She hurried on. 'Anyway I love Shepherd's Brae.'

'You have eclectic tastes, Della.' There was amusement on those rough-hewn, not quite ugly, features. The resemblance to Donald was strong.

'Rosie,' she corrected. 'Yes, well, the cottage was the cheapest thing out there. And I have to watch my pennies since we'll be here for the whole summer.'

Alex gave a slight laugh. 'Cheap, is it? Don't let Donald know, he'll be doubling his prices. Still, I think we can make it more comfortable. And I'll give you coins for the meter. Can't believe the old skinflint installed it. Terrified of the lights getting left on.'

'Oh, you don't have to. I can afford it.' She said it without thinking.

His eyes were hooded. 'Didn't you say you were watching your pennies? Eight weeks is a fair few coins.'

Who takes such long holidays? she could imagine him wondering. *And the second one this year.*

Instead he said, 'Packard…you said you'd been married. Is that your maiden name?'

She was saved from further lies by Luke's shout. 'Mum. Over here. Quick!'

They'd found something. Tim was kneeling, Luke, holding him back.

'A snake. A live one.' Tim's eyes shone.

Alex reached them first. 'It's a slow worm,' he said, gently picking it up.

'Looks like a snake to me. With that forked tongue.' Rosie peeked warily over his arm.

'Legless lizard.' Alex let the shiny bronze-coloured creature slither across his fingers.' He pointed to the head. 'Snakes don't have eyelids.'

'Can we keep it?' Luke asked. 'We've our gerbil cage back home.'

'Wouldn't be happy.' Rosie refrained from pointing out that with luck the rusty old cage would have been disposed of by the removal men.

'They're an endangered species anyway.' Alex helped the boys conceal the reptile with bracken. 'Even their habitat's protected.'

Poor thing, she thought. Imagining itself safe to venture out and sunbathe. And then to find four galumphing humans on its doorstep.

Just like Rosie, thinking herself safe as Mrs Della Packard – until Alex showed up.

As they walked along the cliff top, Alex pointed out a golden eagle, gliding effortlessly on the thermal currents. A couple of islands, little more than grass-covered rocks, dotted the bay and across the shining water she saw the ragged outline of the Cuillin Mountains. Alex was telling the legend of a piper who walked into a fairy cave and never returned.

Charlie would love it out here, Rosie thought, and then remembered his offer to drive up. If only she didn't feel so conflicted about everything. They'd always talked about visiting Scotland but somehow it had never happened. Now she didn't know. He'd been so nice those last few meetings and the boys would be thrilled to see him.

Was it herself she didn't trust?

Between her brooding and Alex's nature commentary they'd reached the cliff top before she knew it. It was a beautiful walk. Less enthralling was the scramble down.

Rosie stared with horror at the drop. Was Alex out to kill them? *Gigolo, conman, murderer* after all? Not that he could possibly benefit from their deaths.

The boys argued and pleaded for a full five minutes before she'd allow them to risk their lives on that steep treacherous sheep track. Alex went first to guide them, making sure they kept a firm grip on the rope someone had fastened to the cliff face many years before, slowing their slide down the crumbling scree.

More than once, paralysed with fear, she was forced to take his strong hand to steady both body and nerves, only too aware of the crashing waves and unforgiving rocks below.

The cave was tall and narrow, about seven feet deep, hidden from searching eyes by a giant stone that had landed on the ledge before its mouth. As they sat catching their breath, Rosie's heart hammered as if she'd run a marathon. Luke pointed to a small white dot on the boulders below.

'What's that?'

Alex squinted, following his finger. 'Dead lamb,' he said matter of factly. 'The cliffs are dangerous. Get too close to the edge and it's likely to crumble away.'

It happened on the way back.

Rosie grasped a rock and it came away in her hand. Seeing her slip, Tim reached to help but he lost his footing. A strong hand clamped on Rosie's wrist, hoisting her back up and she took hold of the rope just in time to see Tim, astonished, topple off the path in a shower of stones and earth. She screamed.

Alex jumped forward, peering over.

'Don't move!' he yelled. 'I'm coming to get you. Luke, help your mother back up.'

Tim was alive then. Sobbing with terror, Rosie lay on her belly, anchored by Luke to the rope and risked a peek. She could see where a huge chunk of cliff, still covered with grass, had slid away. Ten feet down Tim was clutching the merest wisp of bush that had broken his fall.

Alex clambered down with simian agility, landing beside Tim. Rosie bit her lip as he helped her son to his feet. With agonising slowness, they made their laborious way back up, Alex pointing out handholds, hauling Tim in places.

At last Alex pushed Tim up on the grass, wriggling behind him. Both were sweating, Tim's arms and bare legs covered in scrapes and angry scratches. Rosie gripped her son as Alex rolled over on the soft turf, exhausted.

'You maniac!' Emotion made her voice hoarse. 'You could have got us all killed!' She gathered Tim to her, squeezing him tight. 'Are you OK, love?'

For once he suffered her embrace without pulling away. A glisten of moisture appeared in his eyes and he squeezed them shut.

'I want to call Dad,' he said.

Rosie managed to read two pages of her book this time, before her conscience prodded her again. She closed her eyes, feeling the sun against her skin, aware of the chickens clucking as they foraged nearby and the sweet scent of burning peat hanging in the air. Then she sighed. It was no use. 'Tim, Luke,' she said. 'We're going to the big house.'

They found Alex in the cowshed, his head in the flanks of a cow as he squirted milk into the tin bucket. Rosie hesitated in the doorway.

'We've come to apologise. And to thank you for saving Tim's life. Tim?'

'Yeah, thanks Alex.' Awkwardly Tim scuffed one foot against the other. The barn was shadowy, smelling of hay and cow manure with a channel cut into the floor just under three swishing tails. Rosie took a few steps forward.

'I shouldn't have blamed you. You didn't even want to take us.'

Alex shrugged, engrossed in his task.

She could hear Luke kicking a football outside. Tim seemed fascinated by the rhythmic gush of milk. 'My dad's great at milking cows,' he announced abruptly.

Rosie laughed. 'When has he ever—'

'Loads of times. In Cornwall.'

That shut her up. He could be right. There was a whole part of her sons' lives that was closed to her now, the part they shared with Charlie and Val. Friends she didn't know. Events she never heard about. Just as she hoped Charlie would never hear of their son's near brush with death.

Alex glanced over at them, hair flopping over his forehead, gaze penetrating.

'Want to try?' he offered.

'Yeah.' Tim rushed forward.

Alex relinquished his three-legged stool. 'Careful now. If you pull too hard, she'll kick.'

Rosie sat on a straw bale. Alex guided Tim's hands until incredibly milk was once more jetting into the frothing bucket, Tim beaming with pride. Kinney lay alert, eyes transfixed on her master's face. That panting devotion recalled how completely Rosie had lost herself with Charlie. How suffocated he must have felt. Such a surfeit of unquestioning smothering love. But then she'd married young. She'd seen him as her flawless hero. If she had it to do again, she'd be so different.

Alex pushed the stool towards the next stall.

'Your turn,' he said to Rosie.

'No way.' Hastily Rosie retreated from his outstretched hand. The cow's rear end was splattered with manure stains. If she didn't get kicked in the head, that filthy swishing tail would surely swat her in the face. She stepped backwards, almost into the deep channel of excrement. She was teetering on the point of disaster when Alex yanked her forward. Momentum threw her into his chest. She grabbed his shirt to steady herself, feeling her heart thump suddenly and then pulled away.

Alex grinned. 'That was close.'

There was a splash, a yell, and Luke appeared in the doorway. His formerly red Converse trainer and lower leg were covered in a coating of brownish-green slime.

'Mum,' he said. 'Did you know there's a hole full of cow poo here?'

And then Etta came into the yard, wiping her hands on her pinafore, dark hair escaping from its clasp. She looked frazzled as she hurried over.

'There's a young lady on the phone. Works for some film director and awful insistent. Says she was given this number for a Rosie Dixon.'

Chapter Twenty-Six

'Ladies and gentlemen, we've started our descent into Inverness.'

Olivia woke with her head in Marcus's lap. She jerked upright, smacking it on the drinks tray. Luckily Marcus was holding his coffee over the aisle.

'You always talk in your sleep?' he asked idly, flipping up the tray.

'Whatever I said, it's lies.' She peered out the window at the lake, embarrassed at finding her cheek resting on his thigh. 'Look, Loch Ness. Think we'll see the monster?'

She checked the phone as soon as they wheeled their carry-on bags through the airport. Zac hadn't called or texted. Why had she been so insistent they needed this interview? To annoy that bad-tempered hag of a mother? To satisfy Olivia's curiosity about another girl Zac had seduced into hopeless indiscretion and almost – he'd confessed – into bed?

It was not – definitely not – for a jolly old outing with Marcus. She glared at his back as he strode off in front of her, talking on his mobile. That was the last thing she needed with this silly schoolgirl angst he kept inspiring in her, one minute liking him, the next ready to storm off in a rage. They were two incompatible personalities, already forced into unusual proximity being housemates and him her boss. And, reluctantly, she couldn't help but admire his talent, which set up a whole other artificial connection. Like the way you swooned over your ski instructor's expertise, turning him into a little God as he arced down the slopes, only returning to earth in the bar when he revealed panda eyes and dwarf-like stature.

Knowing all the while that in the real world you wouldn't give him a second glance.

Still she'd made a bad move asking Zac where this was heading. Olivia hated seeming clingy. It was probably a good thing she'd skipped town. Rattle his complacency. Let him miss her. Wonder even. A little jealousy never hurt.

It was the sister-in-law who'd found the card and phone number in Rosie's abandoned room.

Rosie had sounded flustered. 'I-I don't know,' she whispered, muffled as if covering the mouthpiece with her hand. 'Being on…' she grew even harder to hear, 'telly. I'd be scared witless.'

This was the bitch that'd badmouthed half of London, this timid little thing? If Olivia had any doubts Zac had fabricated the whole story, they were gone. Inwardly she sighed, wishing her boyfriend had a touch more empathy and a lot less killer charm.

'Don't you owe it to your boys to set the record straight?' she coaxed. 'Their father told me they'd been bullied at school.'

'You spoke to Charlie?'

'Yes, and he told us you'd had a raw deal. We'd like to help.'

At the car hire counter, Marcus sorted out details while Olivia rummaged in her bag for a sadly inadequate sweater. They walked across the car park, the Enterprise agent, a pretty girl, laughing at a joke Marcus had made, Olivia trailing behind, dragging her case.

Seagulls wheeled and screeched above puddles, the air moist under threatening clouds. The breeze raised the curls back from Marcus's forehead as he paused, let Olivia catch up then took her luggage, towing it beside his own.

He was wearing a raggedy old parka and hiking boots, while all Olivia had brought was a stylish jean jacket and she was already frozen, her hands numb. Could anyone be more different from her – or Zac? So careless of his appearance. So careful of people's feelings. Award-winner or not, there was nothing flashy about Marcus's enthusiastic yet down-to-earth character. She and Zac liked life with a little more glitz. She probably *would* have hated that stupid get-together with his mates in Brixton, she told herself, some dingy flat with a bunch of nobodies talking over old times.

And yet… She couldn't quite forget that strangely intimate moment at the nursing home. Since then she'd been hyper-aware of him in an alarmingly physical way. His slim hips. His sexy fore-arms. And yes, occasionally, idly wondering about the maybe kiss that hadn't happened.

Stupid. Stupid. Stupid. Forget admiring the fit of his scruffy jeans. She absolutely could not – ever – be attracted to Marcus. It would be disaster. Lower than low. She was involved with his brother. She'd never get suckered into such a tangled mess.

And neither would Marcus. That 'non-incident' aside, she could sense him treating her with the cheerful impartiality of a scoutmas-ter with a troop of prepubescent boys. No more hints of sexual misconduct would come from him.

Damn, she'd stepped into a puddle. Left foot soaked and turn-ing to ice, she realised the one thing she should have packed was a pair of rubber Wellie boots.

'You've never smelled the tangle o' the isle,' Marcus sang, happily off-key. 'Did you know that tangle means seaweed?'

'Figures.' Olivia wrinkled her nose. 'Someone should give the poor sap a whiff of Dior.'

Another squall of rain spattered the windshield. Showers aside, the drive was spectacular. Glittering lochs and dense dark forests, barren mountains with silver threads of waterfalls plummeting down to the road, rocky shorelines with isolated cottages by the water. Even a double rainbow as they pulled on to the Skye car ferry, shunning the modern bridge.

The Mermaid Inn was set in an emerald valley between two brooding peaks of the Cuillin Mountains, its white walls and black gabled roof offering refuge to climbers and travellers for hundreds of years. Soaked from their dash to the door, Olivia and Marcus were shown to adjoining distinctly modern rooms.

Marcus checked out the en suite bathroom, squinting suspiciously at Olivia. 'So much for the budget. How much did you say this cost?'

She feigned wide-eyed innocence. 'Everywhere else was booked. And did I mention they have a world-class restaurant?'

'Interesting flavour.' Olivia swirled the amber liquid in her glass. 'Smoky.'

'Talisker.' Marcus sat so close to the fire his baggy sweater threatened to singe. 'Made on the island. Taste comes from peat water.'

Olivia stretched out her legs, felt her feet bump against Marcus's and pulled them back. The fire was mesmerising. Brilliant flames flickered around a molten landscape of cliffs, castles and black and orange chasms. She could feel her eyelids drooping.

'Tired?' Marcus missed nothing. 'We could make it an early night. We'll scout locations tomorrow. Get all our ducks in a row before we meet Ms Dixon.'

Olivia yawned. 'I never go to bed before midnight. It's just longer lying awake.'

'My mum says that nothing cures insomnia like realising it's time to get up.'

Olivia smiled. Only a man who loved his mother would wear those horrendous jumpers. Although this evening she'd broken down and borrowed a red and purple monstrosity for herself. 'What's she like?' she asked.

'Great. Lives outside Oxford with my dad.'

'Any sisters?'

'No. Mum gave birth to a boy after me but he died within a few days. Zac came along a year later. Spoiled rotten as you can imagine.' He grinned. 'He changed his name when he was fifteen; Ben wasn't exotic enough for him. Always been a pretentious bastard,' he added with a laugh. 'What about your family?'

The moment she dreaded. 'Mum died when I was very young. And then Dad had an aneurism when I was a teenager. He was in Spain. I was at school in England.'

Marcus said nothing, but his brown eyes were fixed on her face, fully listening. Music and laughter rose and fell from the adjoining bar. His silence compelled her to go on.

'I was angry with him for ages. For dumping me in boarding school then dying on me. Naturally I blamed his girlfriend.' Her laugh was hollow, humourless. 'Mutual loathing at first sight but Dad was the one who called the shots. God, he was fun. Made life exciting, adventurous. For years I refused to see that he was also extremely self-centred and selfish. It was always all about him.'

'Now it starts to make sense,' Marcus observed.

'What?'

'Look, Zac's my brother and for all I kid about him, he's a great guy – though don't ever tell him I said that. But he's lightweight. And you're…' He paused. 'Not.'

Was he right? Unbidden Olivia thought of Brad, another Peter Pan if ever there was one. Was she trying to recreate something she'd lost?

'Mum killed herself.' She stared bleakly into the fire. 'I don't think I totally appreciated her until she was gone. I was such a daddy's girl. Anyway one day she took a load of pills and that was it.'

Silence. Marcus squeezed her hand.

There was a blast of noise from the other bar as the door opened and a cloaked hooded hunchback staggered in, shedding water.

Olivia and Marcus turned, startled, as the newcomer underwent some interesting contortions to struggle out of a rain poncho. The sodden garment landed on the floor, followed by a hefty backpack. The slender figure tossed back soaking ropes of hair, wiping moisture from a shockingly familiar face.

Olivia choked, whisky flooding from her burning mouth and nose as the drink went down the wrong way. Marcus thumped her on the back as tears sprang to her eyes.

She was on the other side of the Atlantic. No one from her old life in Manhattan could possibly know she was in Skye.

And yet they'd tracked her down.

'Don't mind Livvy.' Marcus came back from his room with a towel and handed it and a glass of Talisker to the newcomer. 'She's been paranoid ever since those death threats. Can't get over the idea that some crazed killer is after her blood.'

'That's total rubbish. You took me by surprise, that's all.' Olivia defended herself. Lucy Shipton, the banker's niece she'd met at that fundraiser so many months before. Oh God.

'I told you I'd be in Scotland,' Lucy reminded her. 'I've just finished an incredible six weeks sailing around the islands recording dolphin communications. Been camping these past two days but now the whole field's flooded. Why would someone want to kill you?' Kneeling by the fireplace, she twisted her long golden hair between her fists and wrung water out onto the hearth.

'Sore losers?' Olivia suggested. 'Don't listen to Marcus. It's weeks since I…' Her voice trailed off.

Lucy frowned, looking up with concern. 'I don't blame you. Mandrake destroyed…I don't know how many…thousands of lives. It's possible there might be a sociopath or psychopath among them. So they let you leave the country?'

'Let me?' Olivia felt irritated but it was more by watching Marcus take in Lucy's ridiculous beauty than by the question. 'I'm still a British citizen. Well, dual nationality anyway.'

'What kind of boat?' Marcus tilted forward, elbows on knees.

'Sixteen metre ketch.' It was muffled under the towel as Lucy rubbed her head vigorously. Her face emerged, glowing. 'We hit some rough weather too. Heavy storms just off Scarba. Luckily I'm never seasick.'

No, but she was making Olivia queasy. Marcus was eyeing Lucy like a cream-whiskered cat, practically purring, as if young beautiful goddesses with legs up to their armpits didn't wash up at his feet every day.

'And who might *they* be anyway? Who'd stop me leaving the country?' Olivia was fed up, remembering the sly hints and unvoiced accusations that had followed the scandal. Suddenly they didn't seem so far in the past.

'Nothing.' Lucy backtracked. 'I just thought you might be a witness… Oh don't bother, I'm stronger than I look.' She dimpled at Marcus as he chivalrously carried the backpack over from where she'd shed it at the door. 'I've been packing this thing around for weeks.' She hauled it over to an armchair. 'Not interrupting, am I?'

'No. No,' Marcus said, too quickly for Olivia's liking.

Lucy's baby blue fleece steamed as it dried in front of the fire. She sat cross-legged on the rug, luxuriating in the warmth.

'Sorry. Didn't mean to put my foot in it,' she apologised. 'Uncle Bill and I both think you got a raw deal. So where do you think Mandrake is now?'

'Dead, I hope.'

'Oh well.' Lucy flashed a beguiling smile at Marcus and held out cold fingers. 'Hi, I'm Lucy. I'm guessing you're the boyfriend.'

'No.' Marcus and Olivia spoke in perfect hasty unison.

'Just mates.'

'He's my boss.'

Lucy looked from one to the other, her voluptuous mouth curving slightly. 'Isn't this country awesome?' She diplomatically changed the subject. 'I kinda wish I'd taken marine biology instead of psychology.'

'Lucy's still at university,' Olivia said, feeling like a slouch in her oversized sweater, but realising she had the perfect way to defuse a definite vibration in the air. 'Stanford, wasn't it? Aren't you brave to be taking off so young? When do you graduate?' Not that it had anything to do with her but honestly the girl was hardly more than a child. She managed to stop herself adding 'honey' and cooing like a mother to a five-year-old.

Rummaging in her backpack, Lucy found a hairbrush. She started brushing, smiling at Olivia.

'I'm twenty-six. Graduate student, didn't I say? Doing my PhD in Cognitive Psychology. I thought this would be a fun break but I loved it so much I'm thinking of changing my thesis and focussing on the language of dolphins.'

'I sailed around the Outer Hebrides once.' Marcus took off his glasses and rubbed them on his sweater. 'I was filming a BBC special about puffins. Mostly on St Kilda.' He leaned forward to shake hands. 'Marcus Gilbert.'

'Marcus Gilbert?' Lucy did a double-take. 'Not the…you didn't by any chance make that astounding documentary about autism?' She clapped in glee at his nod. 'We watched it in one of our classes. I had to run right out and find the others…'

'Not that many to find.' Marcus almost blushed with pleasure.

And just like that, Olivia was forgotten.

Thirty minutes later, Olivia was feeling ancient. Ancient, ignored and completely redundant.

Another wave of laughter came from the other bar and a fiddle broke into a spirited reel. She stood up. 'Think I'll check out the band. No, honestly.' She waved down Marcus's attempt to rise. 'Why don't you stay here with Lucy? After all,' she smiled sweetly, 'it's not every day you meet a bona fide fan.'

Once out of sight, however, she retreated to her room. Kicking off her shoes, she dialled Zac's mobile.

'Hello?' He sounded breathless. Suspiciously so.

In the background a girl giggled. 'Silly. Put that away. I'm waiting.'

So much for absence making the heart grow fonder.

'Classy, Zac,' she said. And hung up.

Chapter Twenty-Seven

The voice floated through the open door of the small village shop as Rosie stooped to pet the resident tortoiseshell cat.

'Aye, he'll be after thinking he's got his fortune made all right. You know that one, always an eye for an extra penny.'

Rosie smiled. Village life ran on trivial gossip. When Luke sneezed yesterday every person they met enquired after the 'wee lad's cold'. So different from the anonymity of London. Or at least the anonymity of London if you hadn't won a million quid.

About to enter, her smile evaporated as Morag Mackay's soft voice replied.

'She's a lovely girl. I was expecting the Cailleach herself from that newspaper piece. Sounded a miserable wretch indeed, all that money and nothing but complaints.'

Rosie froze, no longer noticing the cat purring around her ankles. She withdrew her shoe from the step and retreated a pace or two, praying no observers would catch her lurking.

'Not a bit of it,' Etta clucked. 'Alex was fretting she'd find the cottage dismal as a black-hearted sinner but no, she's fair in love with the place.'

'And isn't he staying around longer than we're used to. What's that about? I wonder. Is he not wanted back in Spain?' There was the chink of coins, the ding of an old-fashioned till.

'Ah well.' Etta sounded evasive. 'Donald's still poorly. And the lad's got plans, right enough. I think Tighban's threadbare carpets and leaking roof have had their day. I canna say more than that.'

Shocked, Rosie reeled away from the door.

How long had her secret been blown? The *Sphere* and ensuing fuss were weeks old now. Wasn't it just last night she'd been scarlet-faced, stumbling for plausible excuses as to why some film director had called for a Rosie Dixon?

Uh, well, Dixon was her maiden name. Um, yes, a job interview. She'd panicked momentarily trying to remember what she'd spilled to Alex about her work, her loathsome treacherous face blazing with guilt. All the sleepless night, she'd kicked herself for not turning down that persistent production girl, for becoming so flustered she'd agreed to an interview which when aired would broadcast her deception to all her new Skye friends.

She'd thought them honest country folk, like Etta's husband, scrabbling to make a living between fishing, farming their small croft and picking up odd labour jobs. And now it turned out they'd been deceiving her! Probably sniggering every time they bought her a round in the pub, insisted she save her pennies.

Errands forgotten, she pelted down the street, heedless of surprised glances from those pegging out washing or bringing in peat. Anger gave her feet wings.

Alex had taken Luke and Tim to the communal sheep park for the shearing. To think she'd started to let down her guard. Idiot. Allowing herself to be drawn in for drinks with Donald and Alex when the boys were talking to Charlie on the house phone, letting the boys go with Alex out on his fishing boat or help carry a pail of milk to the newly weaned calf tethered near the shore. She'd have accompanied them on this sheep shearing outing except that every conversation, every small exchange, was tainted by her fake identity. How could he be friends with someone who didn't exist?

Only now it seemed that Alex too was a fraud. 'Always an eye for an extra penny.' 'Got his fortune made.' Oh, yes, she could imagine the schemes that would fix up the crumbling old house. The sort that involved a certain Premium Bond winner and her scads of cash.

How would they have made the pitch? Were they planning to play on her sympathy or her romantic heart?

What an absolute sucker she was! Of course she was lonely. It was so long since she'd had a husband, boyfriend, lover – or even a male friend. Plus she missed Anya and Gemma desperately. And, yes, Charlie too, more fool her. He was in Glasgow now and it was all she could do not to phone him, take him up on his suggested visit. And Alex being an eligible male, with those sexy crinkles around the eyes, his rough-hewn charisma, was just the man to inspire a massive crush. Is that what they'd counted on?

The boys and Alex were play-wrestling as they returned towards the cottage, the two smaller figures launching themselves on their taller foe. Kinney danced around, barking at their heels. Alex had Luke in a headlock, Tim pinned by the waist. Tim wriggled free, throwing his arms around Alex's neck in a strangling grip as Alex, laughing, knuckled Luke on the top of his skull.

How dare he! A red mist blurred Rosie's vision. Conniving two-faced...snake.

'Hey, Mum!' Tim yelled when he saw her. 'You should have come. We helped dip the sheep in a tank. And after they cut off their wool they paint a mark so—'

Rosie barely heard. She marched up to the dishevelled laughing Alex who was holding off Luke's swinging arms with one hand on his head.

'Stay away from my children.' She was almost sobbing, from tearful anger and lack of breath. 'I know all about your sordid game.'

Alex straightened. 'Is that so? Boys, why don't you go up to the house? See if Etta will give you two of the scones she baked yesterday. Your mother and I would like a wee chat.'

'Don't bother. I don't want to talk to you.' But the boys were already haring off. Alex walked into the cottage and she had no choice but to follow.

They stood facing each other. If this were one of her romances, the thought flashed ridiculously through Rosie's anger, this was the moment of truth, when the stony-hearted but totally sexy hero would reveal the tormented passion that had sparked his cruel actions. 'You little fool,' he'd say, and sweep her into a crushing embrace. 'Don't you know I love you? That's why I've been acting like an arrogant prick.' Or words to that effect.

Only real life wasn't like that. Wasn't like that at all.

'Now,' Alex said, 'what's all this about?'

'You lied to me. All of you. You've known who I am all along. Let me make an ass of myself…' She stopped and added bitterly. 'I heard all about your plans.'

'And what plans are those?' He folded his arms. 'Seems to me you're in no position to cast stones, Rosie Dixon. We spent a whole afternoon together, did you think I wouldn't remember your name? Or that we don't get English newspapers in Marbella? I'd have kept your secret but the people in Skye read the tabloids too. And access the internet. And watch TV. It's an island, not an isolation bubble. But since you obviously didn't want fuss, they respected your wish.'

That took some of the wind from her sails. 'Yes, but… They were saying—'

'What exactly?'

When she'd finished, he shook his head.

'Etta was teasing. About Donald thinking he's got his fortune made.'

'Donald?' She hadn't heard a name. Just assumed it was Alex.

'Yes, getting the cottage rented for the whole summer. He's been pleased as punch, going on about it. And I had no idea you'd be here when I came back. How could I, *Mrs Della Packard*? But my uncle's been very sick, he was in hospital recently with pneumonia and at his age we weren't sure he'd make it out alive. As for me sticking around, the man's over ninety and so fragile another winter might finish him off. I'm his heir and only relative. I owe him a wee bit of time, don't you think?'

Rosie bit her lip, mortified.

'I'm sorry. It was just… So many awful things have happened. And when we were in Spain, Anya said…'

'Anya said what?' He was perched on the arm of the sofa, swinging a foot.

'That you could be a conman.' Or a murderer or gigolo. She thought it diplomatic to leave those out.

'And you think I'm after your money? To get a new roof and whatnot.'

His foot stopped swinging as he contemplated her. The longer he looked the more she wanted to squirm. She busied herself putting away the dishes that were draining on the sink. It was as if every suspicion, every uncharitable thought, was written in scarlet on her cheeks.

'Take it from me,' he said at last, 'any plans I have don't include you. Or your money. And if you think I'm here to romance it out of you,' he sounded faintly bitter, 'well, you might be jumping the gun there too.'

'Of course not,' she responded hastily. 'I didn't...' He must think the money had inflated her ego to Buzz Lightyear's universe and beyond. She dared a peek. He was gazing down at his hands, flexing his linked fingers, but his expression said his thoughts were miles away.

He looked up and met her eyes again, head-on. His expression was sombre when he spoke.

'I'm surprised Etta hasn't told you. I'm married.'

The boat had been a mistake. It was chilly in these ungodly dawn hours but Rosie's chest felt suffused with heat. She swallowed hard, willing herself not to vomit. With luck she'd die before this afternoon's dreaded interview. Shivering, she pulled Donald's oilskin tighter as Alex pulled on the oars.

She was still stunned by yesterday's revelations.

'Married?' she'd blurted. 'Since when?'

'Last fifteen years.' Alex had stood up and filled the electric kettle with water. He flicked the switch, annoyingly at home.

'But... In Marbella...You were flirting with me...us,' she corrected hastily.

He rummaged in a cupboard for teabags. 'Is it a crime to be friendly? I showed you a villa, we had lunch, big deal. I'm an estate agent. That's what I do.' His matter of fact tone said it all.

'*And* you invited us to Tangiers.' Rosie frantically cast her mind back. They hadn't held hands. Kissed. Anything.

'Since I'd spoilt your boat excursion and I had business there anyway.' He turned from his tea-making to look at her. 'Thought you'd enjoy...' Comprehension seemed to dawn. 'You didn't think I was asking you on a...'

'No!' Too vehement. ''Course not,' she emphasised. 'I never...well, I knew... Not that I...' She gathered her wits. 'I'm glad you're married. My life's complicated enough without...' She stopped.

'Without fending off unwanted suitors?' His smile was ironic. 'I can imagine. Friends, then?' He held out his hand to shake.

And somehow he'd manipulated that awkward exchange into this insane adventure.

The boat lurched. Rosie gripped the sides as Luke reached for another float and Alex pulled in a wicker creel.

As a gawky tongue-tied teenager, he'd told her, Alex had tumbled head over heels for Maria, a passionate dark-haired, dark-eyed Spanish beauty. They'd married as soon as she'd turned eighteen. They ran a business together.

How could she and Anya have got it so wrong?

But she could almost swear... Had she imagined that vibe then? The special quality she thought she'd read into his smiles in Spain?

She watched him extricate two lobsters, clip the tendon behind the claws and drop them on the growing pile. Rosie raised her feet from the poor creatures crawling in the bottom of the boat as Tim replaced the rotting bait.

'So, lobster tonight?' She feigned jolliness.

'Too expensive for us poor locals.' Alex's wind-burned lips crinkled into a grin. 'They fetch good money down South. But this youngster needs a bit more growing time.' The undersized juvenile splashed into the ocean.

A memory flashed. Her first fishing trip. Charlie had laughed, kissing Rosie when she cried at the sad sight of a trout with a hook in its mouth. He'd suggested eating it right away so its death wouldn't be in vain but they'd no matches or utensils. Finally Charlie pulled into a petrol station and used their microwave, Rosie standing between him and the cashier to block his view. The whole service station had stunk of fish.

The memory of that smell was too much. She dimly heard Luke yell, 'This one's got crabs in. Monsters!' as she leaned over the side and threw up.

'Should have said you were feeling seasick. I'd have cut it short.' Alex rubbed her back as she sat drooping on the jetty, clutching his whisky flask.

She managed a weak smile. 'And miss all the fun?'

'We're starving,' Luke and Tim chorused.

Alex laughed. 'Heartless brutes.' He added, with more truth than flattery, 'You look like death warmed over. You should maybe take a nap...'

When she stumbled into the bathroom after a fitful doze, a zombie from the 'Thriller' video stared back, hair wild, face ashen.

'You're to be filmed this afternoon,' she told it. 'Better plaster on the slap.' Had she even brought foundation? The idea of gussying herself up made her even more nauseous.

A rapping drew her downstairs, still in her red tartan pyjamas. At the door Alex held out a pail.

'Not lobster, maybe, but still good eating.'

In the water were Luke's 'monster' crabs, legs scuttling in futile motion. Foolish tears filled her eyes. Her emotions were all over the place these past two days. 'They're alive.'

Bemused, Alex stared at his present. 'Yes, well, they have to be. You drop them in boiling water. Kills them instantly.'

'I'm not a murderer.' Rosie snatched the bucket from him. 'They scream you know.' She shoved her bare feet into her mud-spattered walking boots, marching through the yard. 'I'm letting them go.'

'Steam escaping the shell.' Alex fell into step. 'They've been out of the sea a good while – probably won't survive.'

'I don't care.' Water slopped, soaking her brushed cotton legs. If he laughed, she might throw the bucket at him, crabs and all but instead he took it from her hands.

They passed a derelict wooden shack piled with drying nets and the splintered remains of a boat where the kids liked to play pirates. Alex stopped on the edge of a rocky inlet. The crabs landed on the seabed, motionless and inert. Soon smaller crabs moved in for the kill, claws outstretched, ready for a rampant act of crustacean cannibalism.

A large tanned hand entered the water, scaring the intruders, the current of its motion pushing at the lifeless forms. Like a miracle, an eyestalk twitched, then a leg. With a scuttling motion the big crabs came back to life, heading for freedom.

It was only when Alex exhaled that Rosie realised she'd forgotten to breathe. They were kneeling together, thigh to thigh, shoulder to shoulder, so close that her hair brushed his. She was suddenly very aware of her inappropriate clothing .

'You must think I'm terribly soppy.' She busied herself fastening undone buttons, as he rose, jeans damp from the wet rocks.

He pulled her up. 'You've a kind heart, Rosie.' His fingers gently wiped something from her cheek. 'Toothpaste,' he explained. 'And you're a good mother. Those lads adore you.'

'I do my best.' She bit her lip. 'But the divorce was hard on us. Especially Tim. I think he secretly hopes his dad will come back.'

'And might he?'

'He's getting married again.'

Again she thought of the new house waiting for them. It would be easier on the boys, no doubt, having Charlie close by. But what would it do to her?

Idly, Alex swung the now empty pail. 'I'm away to Spain tomorrow morning.'

'Oh?' Well, of course, he couldn't ignore his wife all summer.

'I'll be back Saturday though.' He scuffed his rubber boot, popping little bubbles in the yellow-brown bladderwrack. 'Thought you and the boys might come to the ceilidh – the dance – with me. Etta'll be bringing her kids. It's a—'

There was a crescendo of shouts and a loud urgent whistle. A car horn blared. Alex started to run.

'Something's wrong!'

Catching up, Rosie found him talking to Luke and two of the local crofters. 'Heifer's in the bog. Luke found it. Escaped the top field.'

'Anything I can do?' Rosie asked, cursing her tartan sleepwear. The crofters were giving her outfit funny looks.

'I'll need rope,' he said. 'Can you drive a Land Rover?'

'Er, probably.'

'Donald'll give you the keys. Tell him—'

'I know, top field.'

'That's right. Hurry now.'

Next minute the three men and Luke were striding up the hill.

Donald looked up in alarm as Rosie crashed through the kitchen door, chest heaving, her pyjama bottoms soaked.

'Cow...bog...Land Rover.'

Donald plucked his cap from the coat stand and hobbled to the key hook.

'You drive.' He tossed it at her. 'But I'm comin' wi' you.'

Minutes later they were bumping along a deeply rutted farm track, heavy tyres splashing and sliding in the thick mud.

'It's been a dreary summer right enough.' Just as Donald said it, the Land Rover dropped down a deep pothole, skidding sideways as the steering wheel whipped away from Rosie's grasp. Next moment both near-side tyres were down a ditch. They were stuck fast.

'What'll we do now?' Her frustrated hands punched the horn. 'The cow could die.'

'Dearie me,' Donald said, in massive under-reaction. His eyes shot to an object standing idle in the field, then to Rosie, a big smile creasing his deeply-etched wrinkles.

'Oh heck!' Rosie clapped her hand over her mouth.

'Way to go, Mum.' Luke skipped beside her.

'Keep away, Luke.' She looked down at him from her great height. 'I'm *really* not good at this. Where's Tim?'

'Dunno!' he shouted up. 'Haven't seen him!'

'You haven't?' She felt a twinge of alarm but the tractor was already chugging towards Alex. His jaw dropped open, a look of wonder on his face.

'What the—?'

'Land Rover's in a ditch!' she yelled above the roaring engine. 'How do I stop the ruddy thing?'

'Press down the clutch. Close the throttle and turn the key.'

'How's the heifer?' she asked as she shakily let him help her down.

'We managed to haul her out. But, hey,' his arm hugged her shoulder, 'I'm not saying anything about sledgehammers and cracking nuts, but you in your tartan jimjams, driving the tractor – now that was priceless.'

Chapter Twenty-Eight

How could you fall asleep healthy and wake up sick as a kennelled puppy with distemper? Olivia coughed through a scratchy sore throat as a rooster crowed outside. Her nose was running and, staggering to the bathroom, she found a pimple on her chin, a mini Vesuvius – red as the garish bedspread.

Brilliant. As if her ego wasn't sufficiently assaulted. Zac cheating on her. Marcus drooling over Lucy Shipton. Well, Zac could go take a run and jump and Marcus was welcome to make an ass of himself, but she was damned if she'd feel like an old hag next to two cooing lovebirds.

A hefty application of concealer took care of the pimple and reddening nose. She went to town on her make-up, running a smoky line across her top lid, applying a vibrant lipstick that was definitely over the top for a wilderness populated mostly by sheep. Hair messily fixed with a tortoiseshell clasp in an artless sexy style that took forever, she still felt rough as industrial grade sandpaper but when she looked in the mirror, a warrior princess stared back, worthy of any Viking longboat.

No saggy baggy sweater today but a purple cashmere V-neck that moulded to her figure and ankle-length pencil-heeled boots that added precious inches. Marcus needed protection, after all. Someone as right-on as Lucy, so morally principled, so loftily eco-minded, would totally bring out the worst in him, however sugary-nice. She could see them now in their green-built, solar-powered earth house with composting toilet and a vegetarian dog. Their children would wear hemp and organic sackcloth, eat only what was grown in the garden, and never encounter the horrors of plastic or microwaves. TV banned, of course, unless to watch one of Daddy's documentaries.

Oh well, this too would soon be over. Interview today. Tomorrow London. She'd no idea what she'd say to her two-faced, double-dealing lover. Kneeing him in the balls might not be the best solution, however tempting the prospect. It'd be awkward enough still living in the same house.

She smoothed her hands over black jeans that were a touch snugger since coming to England. Her hopes that Lucy was already on her merry way, tramping over the heather in her Merrell hiking boots or sitting by a campfire with a bowl of organic muesli, were dashed when she found her with Marcus in the breakfast room, deep in conversation over egg-stained plates.

'Hello sleepyhead.' Marcus stood to pull out a chair. 'What happened to you last night? We looked for you in the bar. No lattes but I ordered you a coffee. And the Eggs Benedict are pretty good.'

'Great.' She pretended not to notice his elevated brow as he took in the sweater and make-up. Yesterday she hadn't even bothered with mascara. 'I had an early night. Wanted to study my Rosie file and wasn't feeling well. Think I caught a cold.' She coughed to demonstrate.

'Too bad,' Lucy commiserated. 'The band was awesome, had everybody singing along and dancing until way past closing time. We didn't get to bed until after two, did we, Marcus?'

She laid a hand on his sleeve. The gesture and her proprietary tone suggested that there'd only been one bed and little sleeping involved. There was a distinct aura of all-night sex-fest about the two of them. Lucy's hair was unbrushed and she was wearing a thin white t-shirt and men's pyjama bottoms printed with cowboys. Freshly scrubbed, with not a hint of cosmetics, she looked angelic and insanely young.

Olivia unfolded her napkin, feeling over-made-up, wrongly dressed and glaringly unsubtle.

Marcus paused from spreading marmalade, took Lucy's fingers and kissed them with an affectionate grin. 'That late? It's rather a blur.' He turned business-like. 'Livvy, after breakfast, let's get together. We need to talk about the interview. Bring your notes.'

'Never leave home without them, *boss*,' she drawled, a heavy emphasis on the last word.

Marcus gave her an appraising look. 'That's the spirit.' He bit into his toast. 'I'm still famished. Someone pass the cornflakes, please?'

'So you had fun with the lovely Lucy?' Impractical boots discarded after she'd almost twisted her ankle three times, Olivia stooped to pick up another shell, this one a vivid orange. The beach was cold and coarse beneath her bare feet, not powdery white sand at all but more like crushed up shells and coral fragments.

'Who wouldn't?' Marcus was watching her beachcomb, carrying her offending footwear along with his. 'She's a beautiful girl. Very intelligent. And funny.'

Sorry she'd asked.

'Yes, a real babe.' Now she sounded childish. 'Too bad you can't stand Americans.'

'I like everyone.' Marcus gave her a quizzical look. 'Did Zac say that? He's such a wally at times. Just because I prefer roast beef to Big Macs…' His mobile rang and he glanced at the number. 'Talk of the devil. Hiya bro.' He listened. 'Yeah, she's here.'

Olivia backed away, gesturing furiously. She wasn't ready for that conversation yet. Couldn't handle lies. Excuses. Or worse a break-up. Not this morning anyway.

'Sorry, mate.' Marcus didn't miss a beat. 'Guess she must have stepped out.' He slid the phone back in his pocket. 'Like that, huh?' he said, unsurprised.

Olivia shrugged. Much as she despised sympathy, his casual attitude stung.

Frowning, he scrutinised her, using one finger to turn her face towards him.

'You had to expect it. You knew who he was, Livvy. I'm surprised it lasted this long.'

'Yeah, well. Could have let me ditch him first.' Seeking diversion from tedious man trouble, she emptied her day's loot beside a rocky tide pool, weeding through her finds. There were so many pretty shells, most of them small whirls of white, cream and yellow. Her fingers selected a perfect scallop, a tiny starfish and what looked like a unicorn horn. 'What on earth shall I do with these?'

'Glue them onto a cigar box?' Marcus pushed his hair from his eyes. He seemed truly relaxed, shoes and socks in hand, trouser legs rolled up as he splashed in the freezing surf. 'Or a lamp?'

She groaned. 'I'm not six, you know. Why create junk that's destined for the trash?'

'Were you like this in nursery school?' Marcus dug something out of the sand and crossed the rocks to join her. 'Declaring finger painting a waste of time?'

'No, but I fought their ludicrous insistence on clothes.' She grinned. 'Stripped naked at the slightest chance. OK,' she dropped the rejects to the ground, stifling her pang of regret, 'that's it. Not another shell. No matter how beautiful.' The bulging pockets of her three hundred dollar True Religion skinny jeans were already seriously deformed. And who knew when she'd be able to afford another decent pair?

Marcus stopped her with a hand. He had a musician's fingers, long and supple.

'Sure about that?'

The porcelain shell filled his palm, one side pink and curved like a lemon, the other creamy and flat with a corrugated aperture shaped like a smile. Marvelling, Olivia took it from him, admiring its glossy surface, the three brown spots perfectly spaced along the centre. She ran her fingers along its whorled ridges, succumbing to its beauty and strange tactile appeal.

'It's a cowrie shell,' Marcus said. 'Also called a groatic buckie.'

'Amazing.'

She went to hand it back but he refused. 'No, it's for you. Legend has it they're good luck.'

'Don't you want to give it to Lucy?' She was provoking him.

He laughed. 'Just take the thing. If you want it.'

She emptied a pocket and stuffed the shell inside. The sun disappeared behind darkening clouds. Within minutes the wind was kicking up spray and pushing at their clothes.

'Let's find some shelter!' Marcus yelled, walking backwards to be heard. They huddled under his old parka in the lee of a small cliff.

'Rosie's our last interview,' he said. 'I'd have loved to get hold of this Agent Million but her people are proving cagey. Pity. She must have some amazing stories.'

'I read that there's two Agent Millions. Arriving in secret to notify Premium Bond winners. Now that's a fun job.'

'Talking of jobs.' Marcus inched in closer, pulling his end of the coat. 'What is happening with that saga in the States? I mean with you, specifically.'

'Ask Lucy. She probably knows the latest gossip.'

He gave her a look. 'I've seen the internet blogs. What I'm wondering is why someone who earned a six-figure salary, with all the smarts to run her own show, is hiding out, working as a badly-paid go-fer.'

'Is that how you think of me?' She felt ridiculously hurt.

'God, no.' He realised his mistake. 'Wasn't meant like that. You've been…amazing. Your contribution's invaluable to this documentary. But we both know you're wasted here – I can't afford to pay a fraction of what you're worth and you had so much going for you with your career. It feels like you're running away instead of sorting things out and moving on. Look, let's go back to the hotel, before the tide cuts us off.'

'Before your delicious American slopes off, you mean,' she retorted, not caring if it was bitchy. 'Don't worry, she's already asked if we can give her a ride into Portree.'

⚜ ⚜ ⚜

Lucy was in the lounge, flipping through a magazine, oversized rucksack at her feet. She jumped up when she saw them.

'I was worried about you both. Thought you might have got blown to Uist in that crazy wind.' She fiddled with her rucksack strap, the picture of shy diffidence. 'Would it be awful to ask another favour? I'm such a huge fan, Marcus.' Again that delicate hand reached out to touch his arm, eyes beseeching under huge lashes. 'How terrible would it be if I stuck around and watched the shoot?'

Such an innocent gesture. Such a modest request. Why did it put Olivia's back up so?

Marcus smiled indulgently. 'I don't see why not.' He pulled Lucy into him and kissed the top of her head.

She was jealous, Olivia realised with a jolt. Stupidly, furiously jealous. She'd been so looking forward to this interview. Loved the way she and Marcus worked together as a smooth-running team. Now to have this interloper butt in… Batting those baby blue eyes. Spoiling their precious moments.

She could sense this special, surprisingly happy, episode drawing to an end. When this film was over, Marcus would have no need for an assistant. Olivia and Zac wouldn't be making up. He'd been starting to get on her nerves anyway. She'd have no excuse to stick around.

With a sickening lurch, she realised her dreadful mistake.

She was in love with the wrong brother.

It had been creeping up on her, every day, every minute they hung out together. She'd have known it earlier if she hadn't been distracted by Zac. She was so hopelessly attracted to this guy, his passion for his work, his intense poet's face, his wiry energetic body, even the way his mop of curls kept getting in his eyes and had to be brushed away.

There was a burst of music and Marcus reached for his cell phone. She watched his expression change as he listened, coming to full alert as he stepped away from Lucy.

'Yes, this is he. Oh, hello there.' He waggled his eyebrows excitedly at Olivia. 'You are?' She heard him say. 'You will? Superb. When?' He stopped abruptly, slumping. 'Oh, I was hoping to have it tied up…' A long pause while he listened. 'This afternoon? Tricky.' His eyes were glued to Olivia's face but she'd a feeling he wasn't seeing her, the cogs of his brain working overtime. 'Yes. Sure. OK.' He sounded excited again. 'Call you right back.'

He clicked off, seized Olivia and danced her around in a circle, before linking his arm in Lucy's and spinning her around. Lucy kicked up her heels, head snapping back as she roared with laughter. She seemingly found everything Marcus did just too wonderful for words. What man wouldn't be flattered?

'You won't believe it,' he wheezed when they finally stopped, gasping for breath. 'Agent Million's agreed to be interviewed.'

'Holy crap!' Olivia said, astounded, heart still pounding from the dance.

'Bad news is she's taking her grandmother on a month-long cruise. Leaving tomorrow. If I can't find someone to do it today then—'

'Me,' Olivia proclaimed, surprising them both. 'If you can get me a flight from Inverness and one of your students to run the camera. We've talked about it enough. I know the questions to ask.'

He hesitated, reluctant. 'But you'd miss Rosie. After all your efforts…'

'Yes, but this is important. Let me do it, Marcus. It's our only shot.'

'And I can stand in for Olivia. I'd love to help.' Lucy stepped forward; twirling her long golden curls around one finger, alight with enthusiasm. 'I did some video work in media studies as an undergrad. So hey,' she gave Marcus a sweet smile, 'use me as you will.'

'Settled then,' Marcus said, decisively. 'Lucy'll assist me with Rosie and you, Liv, will interview Agent Million. I'll call the airlines now and get my mate Dan to pick you up. He'll handle the camera and the technical side. This is all highly confidential. Agent Million insists on anonymity.'

He took his baseball cap and jammed it on Olivia's red hair. 'Thanks, pal. You're a real trooper. What are you waiting for? Run upstairs and pack. Oh and another thing.'

She paused, already on her way out the door.

'Don't let Zac get wind of this. His bloody mischief could wreck it all.'

Chapter Twenty-Nine

Rosie was washed, changed and dreading the ordeal ahead, when Etta showed up carrying a bucket and mop.

'Alex asked me to give the place a going over,' she explained. 'Don't you look smart now?'

Rosie glanced down at her jacket and white polo neck sweater. 'I'm off to Portree.' She'd made up her mind. She'd meet Marcus Gilbert and make her apologies. Her hands felt clammy imagining his anger, coming all this way for nothing. But could she go through her entire life doing things she didn't want to do for fear of disappointing people? With her nerves, she was bound to be useless anyway. Say the wrong thing or freeze on camera.

The short bird-like woman shooed off the boldest white chicken who seemed to think she'd the God-given right to strut in anytime the door was left ajar. 'Out with you, hen, or you'll be howtowdie stew tonight.'

Belatedly Rosie remembered her request.

'I'm afraid the boys will be bored. Could they hang out with your kids?'

'Surely. Why ever not?' Etta tutted as she gathered up the living room rug. 'I'll have Alex pick up another rug in Inverness. This one's a disgrace.'

Tim opened a bag of crisps, his uncombed hair sticking up like a cockatoo crest, his t-shirt ripped and stained with ketchup.

'Why can't we go with you? I want to buy a present for Dad.'

Taken aback, Rosie struggled for a response. She wasn't planning to spend much time with Marcus Gilbert but how would she explain the encounter to Tim? One glimpse of film equipment and he'd never be able to keep it secret. She couldn't face everyone knowing she'd lied about the interview too.

'I thought you wouldn't want to,' she said gently, screaming inside. She had the sense of being ganged up on. Was she being unfair in trying to keep Charlie away? Last night when they talked he'd announced his intention to see Loch Ness instead of returning home on Friday. Inverness was only a couple of hours from the Skye Bridge. Too close. He was moving in.

'I won't change my mind,' she'd told him.

'I know,' he said. 'But I miss you. All.' There was a little too long a pause between *you* and *all.* She couldn't help herself.

'And what does Val think about you gallivanting off without her?'

'Not much probably. She's annoyed by a lot I do these days.'

I know how she feels, she had wanted to say.

'Well, I don't want to go,' Luke declared now. 'It's boring. Walking around the shops.'

'Quite right,' Etta agreed. 'There's plenty time to buy a present, Tim. My lads have been after their dad to take them fly fishing with their new reels. You should go with them. I'll keep your mother company.'

'What?' Rosie squeaked, aghast.

'You don't think I'd let you drive to Portree by yourself, do you?' Etta was already taking off her apron. 'The cottage can wait. We'll have a bit of girl time, so we will.'

Rosie drove slowly, fretting over the complications her passenger presented. Far, far worse than bringing Tim.

'Do you have a lot of shopping to do in Portree?' she asked, hopefully.

'Not at all.' Etta pulled down the passenger mirror to apply a startling pink lipstick. 'I thought we might browse around and maybe get a spot of tea.'

She gripped the ceiling strap as Rosie slammed on the brakes. A shaggy Highland cow, horns as wide as her outstretched arms, blocked their way, peacefully chewing the cud. They shooed it out of the road. Driving was a hazardous business between cattle meandering down the highway and black-faced sheep bounding everywhere.

Etta fluffed her hair. They'd made a stop so she could change into her best dress. Now, on top of everything, Rosie fretted she'd be late for this interview she didn't plan on doing.

'And how was it you met Alex now?' Eyes bright with curiosity, Etta flipped the sunshield up. 'In Marbella, you said?'

'Yes, walking along the sea front. He rescued us from a time-share ordeal.' Rosie told the story, omitting the lunch and the tour of the villa, incidents that could, perhaps, be misconstrued.

'Aye, he's a kind heart. I've known him since he was a bairn. We went to the same school, although he was a few years below. A harum-scarum wee wretch. Set on breaking his neck if the schoolmaster didn't do it for him.'

'Troublemaker then?'

'Ran his poor his mother ragged, so he did. She's Donald's sister, you know. Alex's father was a dentist. They only moved down South when his mam's arthritis got bad.'

'And Donald never married?'

'No, the girl he loved drowned at sea. Alex is like a son to him. He was that disappointed when the lad decided to make his life in Spain. Though why would a young boy care about a crumbling ruin, riddled with debt?'

'But Tighban is so amazing. Luke and Tim love it.'

For all its grim stone exterior and castle-like turret, much of the interior was a higgledy-piggledy rabbit warren where generations had randomly added on as the fancy took them. The boys had spent a delightful rainy afternoon, searching its odd corridors and tucked away rooms for secret passages.

She could imagine the young Alex in these fields and crofts, playing hide-and-seek in the heather, riding his bike to the one-room school with all of twenty-three pupils. How could he possibly get bored of the panoramic beauty, the steep mountains sloping to the sea, the wild clouds scudding across the sky?

'Yes, if you like wet rot, damp and sparrows nesting in the attic rather than discos, beaches and beautiful señoritas,' Etta said dryly. 'Aye, he was a devil all right. He sent me postcards from Spain, talking about nightclubs and wild nights at the casinos. Many a time I felt like joining him there myself.'

'Suppose you can't blame him,' Rosie said doubtfully. Nightclubs and gambling – it was a side of Alex she hadn't guessed.

'And what about your man?' Etta's beady eyes met hers in the mirror. 'Tim was telling me that the both of you may be making another go of it.'

'Tim said that?' Her head jerked in appalled surprise.

'Said you'll be moving in with his dad after the holidays. Oh dear, was he wrong then?'

Rosie heart squeezed painfully. 'Into the neighbourhood. He must have misunderstood. Poor Tim.'

With guilt she thought of Charlie again. But they'd be home in another week and then he could see his sons as much as he wanted. She'd asked for a few more precious days without the tumult of emotions her ex-husband always evoked. That didn't make her a bad mother. Did it?

'Kids are born survivors.' Etta patted her arm reassuringly. 'Now what are you after in Portree? Because I'm afraid if it's not a souvenir pincushion or a stick of peppermint rock, you might find it sadly lacking.'

There was a festival going on in the town when they finally pulled into the car park. A group of girls in pastel kilts were dancing a nimble sword dance, one arm upraised, black-laced toes pointing.

Portree was charming as ever, white buildings overlooking the glassy harbour, mirrored water reflecting the surrounding hills. Rosie's anxiety grew as Etta led her in and out of galleries and gift shops, admiring pottery mugs and hand-knit sweaters, waiting while Rosie purchased postcards. She was supposed to meet the film crew at a hotel on Quay Street but all her excuses – a trip to the bank, a professed desire to linger and take photos – had failed to dislodge her companion. Twice she nearly confided the truth but her courage failed her.

'I can entertain myself, you know,' she suggested, imagining Marcus Gilbert checking his watch.

'Oh, I'm having a great time,' Etta reassured her. 'Shall we try the tea room?'

The hell with it. She was so late and she hadn't wanted to do the film anyway.

She glanced in the bow window at happy people chatting and eating.

'Love to.'

And with that, feeling like a traitor most foul, Rosie turned her back on the filmmaker and his persuasive but pushy assistant. When their food came, she'd make some excuse to nip to the loo, find a telephone and call Marcus Gilbert so he wouldn't phone Tighban again.

She came back to the table, red-faced, relieved to have reached his voicemail and avoided lengthy explanations. Never had a convict eaten his last supper with more agonising remorse than Rosie tucking into her cheese toasty, head down, flinching every time someone walked past. She'd always thought herself honest and reliable. Well, there went her high horse, galloping off with the last of her illusions.

Etta drained her cappuccino. 'Are we in a hurry to get back?' she asked.

Yes, thought Rosie. *Let's go. Now.* 'Well,' she said weakly. 'I suppose the boys—'

'Oh they'll be right as rain. I was thinking while I'm here, perhaps I'd get my hair done.'

Rosie could have banged her forehead on the Formica table. Why now? Why not two hours ago? The entire bloody camera crew must be cursing the spoilt rich bitch who'd callously stood them up.

She waited, limp from the day's stress, flicking through hair magazines as Etta chatted to the stylist. She thought back to the salon in Spain, how cute Anya had looked with her flirty wispy style.

But all her good intentions had gone awry. Anya had been so hostile when she'd torn up that cheque. Gemma hadn't called, probably thinking the worst of her. Paul and Dee – well, they seemed more miffed about her leaving than pleased about the car or the transfer of funds to Dee's account. She'd probably find that even the dinner lady's mother was the poorer for Rosie's interference. Maybe she'd have been better off in a nice retirement home instead of alone with bills to pay and no one to find her when she broke a leg.

Millionaire Miseryguts was right. She'd lost her old friends. She was lying again, this time by hiding her involvement in the film. And if she'd been tormented by insecurity before, she couldn't look at anyone now without wondering if they were being nice to her for herself or because they knew about the money. So lost in thought was she, she didn't even look up when the door opened.

A man stood in front of her. Harry Potter glasses and brown curly hair that skirted the top of his shapeless green jumper.

'I recognised you from the paper.' His voice was low and pleasant. 'This might sound mad but...aren't you Rosie Dixon?'

'But weren't you in Portree only yesterday?' Donald looked at her in astonishment. 'What is it now? You've found yourself a boyfriend?'

Rosie squirmed all the way to her curling toes. Of course Etta would have told him. A strange man accosting her in the hairdressers, even though Rosie had hurried Gilbert outside, agreed to reschedule just to get rid of him.

'No, nothing like that. Etta's brother's taking Luke and Tim fishing again and I need a dress for the ceilidh.'

Don't, please, let them think she'd had a romantic assignment. Wasn't life complicated enough without them all imagining who knew what?

Donald's blue-veined crooked hands packed his equally crooked pipe with tobacco, tufty white eyebrows rising. He lit a match, sucking slowly until smoke rose.

'A dress, is it? Well, if you're swithering about what to wear…'

Twenty minutes later Rosie was checking herself doubtfully in the hallway mirror.

'It isn't a little too…' she searched for a diplomatic word, '*formal?*'

'Not at all, not at all,' Donald repeated twice, with an approving glance. 'It's a ceilidh, isn't it? They'll all be wearing the kilt.'

Rosie turned, twisting her neck to view the back. Lime-green, the dress brushed the floor with the rustle of silk. Puffy sleeves ballooned to the elbow then narrowed to the buttoned wrist. The high-necked front was fussy with ruffles and buttons, the ensemble finished by a wide paprika sash ending in a voluminous bow. It was hideous – wasn't it?

'Aye, you're a bonny rose, all right.' Donald's hand trembled as he handed over a black velvet choker with an ivory cameo. 'Here, lass, this was my mother's.'

She felt a rush of pity for the lonely old man. His true love dying. Living in virtual poverty as his beloved home crumbled and decayed. Ignored by his playboy hellion nephew. She fastened the choker and sucked in her waist feeling the seams strain. She wouldn't dare eat a bite all night. But perhaps…? Yes, maybe…

Her hand held out the voluminous skirt as she dropped an experimental curtsey. In the dimly-lit hall, her reflection smiled graciously. OK, it was old-fashioned but it was also romantic, wasn't it? Straight from Jane Austen. Even if the colour did make her look bilious.

The skirt billowed as she swirled.

'You'll be the belle of the ball, right enough.' Donald's rheumy eyes shone with admiration. 'Young Alex will be lucky if the other lads allow him a dance.'

Well, if the old man didn't see anything wrong in his married nephew inviting her to this shindig, why should she? They were taking the boys after all, though heaven knew Luke and Tim wouldn't be seen in a 'skirt', tartan or not. Alex should have warned her the event was so grand but the bloody man seemed to have a knack for omitting pertinent information.

Dreamily she imagined a ballroom of colourful dresses, moving in courtly patterns, a man approaching for her hand. Too bad that hard as she worked to imagine a Scottish Mr Darcy in kilt and sporran, the only image her wretched brain would produce happened to have a broken nose and Charlie's dazzling smile…

Chapter Thirty

'We want a dark silhouette, see? So I close down the iris to F16, get all the light off you, then flood the backdrop so it blows out.' Dan, the cameraman, pushed his woollen beanie hat up and nodded towards the improvised white sheet. 'Marcus'll use the pitch shifter effect to change your voice. Your own ma won't recognise you, darling.'

'Actually my mum's the one person I'm not worried about,' the subject said in her light musical voice. She clipped the microphone to her navy blazer, shaking out glossy chestnut bobbed hair.

They were in the upstairs bedroom of a small terraced house, crowded with film equipment. Olivia sat on the narrow single bed, surveying their temporary studio. 'You live here?'

'Yeah. Place belongs to my sister.' Marcus's friend was bearded and fat. He was also forty if he was a day. 'Don't worry. She took the baby out and her old man doesn't get home until late. So what's the story here? On the lam are you?'

'Licensed to kill.' Agent Million winked conspiratorially. 'That's why we had you sign the Official Secrets Act.'

Olivia grinned. Maybe she *had* half-expected a lithe rubber-limbed martial artist in black leather catsuit. Not this pretty secretary-type who Dan was trying to impress by spouting off on diffusers, gels and catch lights.

She shuffled her notes remembering Marcus's instructions.

'Get Dan to bring extra stock. It's disastrous running out if something juicy comes up. Remember, we love stand-alone sound bites. Leading questions – no "Yes" or "No" answers. *So Agent M,*' he assumed a girlish falsetto, '*Ernie spits out the winner's name, then what?*'

'Chill,' she'd said. 'I got it.'

The interview with Rosie would be in the can by now, his part done. She didn't even want to imagine how he and Lucy might choose to celebrate.

The buzzing started just as they'd wrapped and kept going as Agent Million handed back the microphone.

'Impatient, aren't they?' Olivia glanced at Dan. 'You expecting anyone?'

'Maybe my sister forgot her key. Or,' he yawned, t-shirt rising up to expose a paper-white, mole-speckled belly, 'could be one of my mates.'

Olivia peered through the blinds. There was a Harley outside. She jumped back, heart hammering.

'It's Zac! What the hell's he doing here?' She was torn between running like the clappers or craning her neck for a better peek at the lover who'd cheated on her.

Methodically, Dan dismantled his set-up. 'Dunno. Looking for you? Thought the two of you were having a thing?'

'Not any more. And he can't know I'm here. It's secret.'

'He often stops by, evenings. Especially when you've been off working. Likes our local. New barmaid. Double D.'

Might have been good if someone had warned her. The buzzer kept sounding.

'What's going on?' Agent Million headed to the window but Olivia waved her back.

'There's a tabloid journalist outside.' She struggled to stay calm. 'Will he go away, Dan, if we don't answer? Oh crap, your sister's coming back and he's seen her. Is there another way out?'

'Back garden. No gate though. You'd have to hop a few fences to get into the alley.'

They all looked down at Olivia's heels.

'One time in weeks I wear them. What about you?' she asked Agent Million. 'You OK climbing fences?'

She shrugged. 'If my cover's blown, my job's over. I could probably jump a five foot hedge.'

'Dan, call out the window. Say you're coming down but let us sneak out the kitchen before you open up. And keep him talking. Thanks for everything. We're getting outa here.'

'I still pinch myself.' Agent Million squeezed lime into a bottle of Corona, glowing from their headlong flight. She'd been a good sport, clambering agilely over rickety fences, giggling when they dared to slow their headlong flight. 'Didn't think I stood a chance when they told me what the job was. I was so nervous. It was like watching those balls on the lottery.'

Olivia's attention kept straying to the door. The pub was untrendy, empty, smelling of stale beer. But even if Zac walked in, so what? There was no way he'd identify Agent Million in this setting.

Not that she looked forward to their first – and inevitably uncomfortable – encounter since her trip to Skye. The hurt remained, even if her original outrage had faded.

How could she judge, given her impossible, inconvenient feelings for his brother?

Still they'd had a narrow escape. If Zac discovered them filming in secret – well, she knew his radar for a salacious story. He'd never rest until he ferreted out the truth.

Luckily Agent Million bore no grudge for what might have been disaster. She was a kindred spirit, independent and sassy.

'Only my parents know,' she'd said on camera. 'My mates think I'm a bookkeeper. The secrecy protects me too. I can't influence who wins but there are lunatics out there.'

She'd definitely been worth the extra effort, full of insights and anecdotes. Marcus would be thrilled. She was surprised he hadn't called. Wasn't he as anxious to hear about this interview as she was for news of Rosie's?

Olivia held out a crisp packet to her new friend.

'You make Premium Bonds sound better than the stock market.'

'Well, they're safe. And one person I met won a million with only seventeen quid.'

'Seventeen pounds,' Olivia mused, swirling her martini. 'That's about my budget.'

'I checked you out on Google. Rupert Mandrake. That was a rough break.'

'I over-extended,' Olivia admitted. 'Even if Mandrake hadn't been crooked, I was taking ridiculous risks.'

'Checked out your Marcus too. Watched a few of his documentaries. Remarkable work.'

'Yeah, he's remarkable all right. But he's not *my* Marcus.'

'Sure about that?' Her companion, astute as she was, must have read her face.

'Positive.' Olivia managed a fake laugh. 'I left him with a stunning blonde who's convinced he's Francis Ford Coppola in the body of Brad Pitt. Believe me, my presence isn't missed.'

Plus he probably thought she was busy having make-up sex with Zac. What a mess!

She put her glass back on the bar and looked off into the corner. 'Pool table's empty. Do you play?'

'You were saying…' Olivia leaned on her cue, '…about Rosie?'

'Oh yes.' Looking serious, Agent Million lined up her third shot in a row. 'Off the record, she's one of those ones you worry about. We try hard to take them under our wing, give them financial and legal advice.' The ball smacked into a stripe, knocked it into a pocket. 'That much money overnight – it's stressful in ways most people can't imagine. I know, I know,' she walked around the table, scrutinising her next play, 'you'd love to suffer that sort of stress.'

'Better than losing my shirt.' Olivia chalked her stick as Agent Million sank another ball.

'That's the million dollar question, isn't it?' She missed her shot and made way for Olivia's turn. 'Which screws you up most? Like I said on camera, our winners who cope best carry on as normal or have a real passion to pursue.' She took a swig of beer. 'But some go completely off the rails.'

Olivia sighted down the cue, calculating angles.

'We had a few interviews with those.' The white ball ricocheted off the side into a solid and popped it neatly into a pocket.

'Oh, the guilt of being undeservedly, unexpectedly rich!' Her new friend laughed, rolling her eyes. 'One woman gave it all to the dog pound and then wondered why her relatives hated her. You can't win. Be generous and you're resented. Be careful and you're resented even more.' She watched Olivia make two difficult shots in a row. It was going to be a close game. 'Poor dears can't understand why they're depressed when they have everything they've ever dreamed of. It's maybe not the root of all evil, even puny compared to some lottery wins, but a million pounds can still bring out the worst in some. Like alcohol.' She looked at her empty bottle. 'Talking of which…another round?'

They were on their second game, teaming up against a couple of hopelessly outclassed young squaddies when Olivia's phone rang.

Marcus. *At last.*

She walked away from the loud groans of the army boys and cupped a hand over her ear.

'How'd it go?' They spoke at the same time, waited, and then spoke again simultaneously.

'You first.'

She gave a quick rundown.

The reception was terrible but even with his voice fading in and out, Marcus sounded energised and happy. 'Well done!' he yelled fervently. 'Here. Lu wants to talk to you.'

Lu? But there was no time to protest.

'You'll never guess,' Lucy shouted, gleefully. 'Uncle Bill says for you to call him. It's about some fantastically important job in Shipton's new hedge fund department.'

'What! You're kidding.' For a second she could hardly breathe. It felt as if all the wind had been knocked from her lungs. Back to New York. Vindicated. It was her dream. 'But what about Brad's father…I mean, Mr Winton, and his blacklist?'

'Shipton's Bank doesn't care about any old blacklist. You impressed the hell out of Uncle Bill. Marcus and I are thrilled for you.'

'Amazing. Let me talk to Marcus.' Ouch. That 'Marcus and I' hurt.

She retreated to the toilet corridor where it was quiet.

'I can't believe Shipton's offering me a job.' Even now she half-hoped he'd tell her she was indispensable. Beg her not to go.

'Yeah. Fantastic opportunity.' The line was whistling. It sounded like a mountain top in a howling gale. 'You've Lu to thank. She called him up, you know.'

Some of Olivia's elation dissipated. So much for her big impression.

'You think I should take it then? The film's not even finished.' She forced a joke. 'How will you manage without your menial go-fer?'

'Hey, I've got it, hotshot.' His voice was maddeningly cheerful. 'You go take Wall Street by storm. Besides Lucy's decided to spend a few weeks in London. She wants to watch me edit.'

I'll bet, Olivia thought viciously. She felt like flinging her phone into the wall.

A static crackle. Marcus said, 'Sorry, what? Just a sec.' Then the line came clear. 'There was a slight hitch with Rosie Dixon. Had to reschedule, so we changed flights. We're spending a night in Inverness. Lucy wants to see the battlefields of Culloden. She's big fan of the Outlander novels.'

Perhaps she was having a heart attack? Surely a few innocent sentences couldn't cause this absurdly disproportionate pain?

'OK. Bye.' She could barely stumble out the words.

Stunned she walked back. The TV over the bar was showing a handcuffed man stepping out of a black car, two heavy-set suits on either side. His tanned face was thinner, once dark hair bleached to brass, but there was no mistaking that insouciant smile.

'Turn the volume up!' she shouted.

It was that asshole, Mandrake.

Chapter Thirty-One

The cottage was far too quiet, the clock too loud in the empty air. Rosie sat, afraid to breathe in her imprisoning lime-green bodice. Etta had called to say Luke and Tim were staying for tea and they'd meet her and Alex at the dance.

Great. Instead of them going as a family, she'd be alone with the man, no boys' chatter to fill the awkward silences. She hadn't seen him since he'd flown in from Spain this morning. She didn't want to admit how often she'd looked towards the house, how uneventful, dull and grey the last few days had seemed. And now...

She was having second, third and fourth thoughts about taking dress advice from a half-blind old bachelor. What if Alex thought she was overdressed? An overdressed ruffled frump?

Another week before they returned to London. The magical interlude was almost over. She'd miss Skye badly but she doubted they'd ever be back. Life had a way of moving on. Alex would return to Spain. Back to his wife. She'd have enough on her plate dealing with Charlie and Val. Some things were better left as happy memories.

Tyres stopped, an engine died. Rosie opened the front door, heart rising at the sight of Alex. He was wearing a red cotton shirt, hair brushed and tamed. And...jeans?

'Are we still going?' she asked uncertainly. 'Where's your kilt?'

'Kilt? Must be still at the drycleaners.' He took her hand, twirling her. 'I've never seen my grandmother's ball gown look quite so...*wow*!'

'Donald said I looked bonny.' Now she was less sure than ever. 'It's horrendous, isn't it?'

'No.' He gave a wolfish grin. 'You look very bonny indeed. Your car or mine?'

'I'm good to drive.' Rosie fished out her keys.

'Yes I saw that with the tractor.' Alex chuckled and ducked her swatting arm.

'Back, back. A little more.'

Rosie eased the car into reverse and then stamped on the brake. What had possessed Alex to check on the bull? It was meant to be a two-second visit, Alex leaning over the gate to scratch its hairy rump, but her three-point turn in this narrow rutted track was rapidly turning into a multi-pointed star.

'A smidgen more.' Behind the vehicle Alex waved.

There was a crunching sound then a lurch.

Alex approached her window. 'Too far.'

'Don't tell me.' Rosie shut her eyes. 'A ditch?'

'Good to drive, did you say?' He had trouble keeping a straight face. 'Here, I can probably shift us,' he opened the driver door, 'if you'll give us a wee push.'

The engine roared, car stubbornly stuck as Rosie heaved, body practically horizontal from the effort. Her muscles bulged, feet slipping, and then with a final surge, the wheels spun, kicking up a shower of dirt. They grabbed. Held. The car lurched over the hump as Rosie stumbled forward.

When she wiped her face, her hand returned filthy. Mud plastered her dress. A family heirloom and she'd ruined it.

'Ye Gods!' Alex joined her.

'I'm…' She spat grit from her teeth, wordless. If he laughed she'd kill him.

But his mouth held a severe straight line as he held out his hand, taking the very tips of her fingers. 'Perhaps a shower?'

'Will they let me in?' Clean, in plain white blouse and denim skirt, Rosie felt horribly underdressed.

'I'll have a word. Aren't you a guest of the laird himself?'

Alex opened the door to the community hall. The dancing was in full swing. Sets of people linked arms, jeans, skirts, summer dresses, shorts, whirling in complicated patterns. Rosie noticed Etta and the children galloping in a dizzying circle. Not a kilt in sight except the band's bagpiper and two decrepit old men nursing a bottle of scotch.

Alex answered her glare with a rueful shrug. 'I didn't like to say it wasn't fancy dress.'

'You rat.' She snatched up a foamy beer glass, threatening to toss its contents.

Alex grasped her wrist. 'I've a lot to tell…'

But before he could continue, a voice boomed, '*And now if ye'll all take your partners for the Gay Gordons.*'

A brawny hand seized Rosie, dragging her into the throng.

Hours flew by. Rosie marched forwards, backwards, was swung round by a variety of locals, reeling and spinning, plucked from one hooked arm to another. She'd no clue what she was supposed to do but she was laughing too hard to worry.

When the band took a break, Alex led her to Etta's table.

'Did you have a good visit, then, Alex.' Etta moved up to make room. 'And how was Maria?'

'Well.' It was noncommittal. And so it might be with another woman sitting – however innocently – by his side. 'She sends everyone her love.'

Etta looked at her children, lying with their heads on the table, at Luke, droopy-eyed, and Tim, yawning. 'Think I'll get this weary lot off home. Don't worry, I'll keep them with me until midday.' She nudged Rosie with her elbow. 'In case you're after a *lie in.*'

Pain. Blinding pain.

Scenes flickered behind Rosie's leaden eyelids.

Someone wagering that the 'Sassenach' couldn't handle a 'wee dram' of Talisker.

Defending her English honour with whisky shots.

Doing a limbo dance.

More drams. Wee and not so wee.

A body crashing into their table, definitely trollied.

Going outside, cold air hitting her, massive dent in the rental car. Deciding mustn't drive…

Trollied herself.

Alex pointing to a man passed out in the bushes. 'Your taxi driver.'

Trudging home across fields, tripping on tree roots, being helped over stiles. Starry night, boggy ground, hanging onto Alex's arm. Had she been pontificating about Van Gogh? Singing Don McLean's '*Vincent*'?

Dear Lord.

Her fuddled memory dredged up a kiss. Soft lips. Hard stubble.

Her eyes snapped open.

The door to the bedroom creaked.

Alex walked through. Shirtless, barefoot and smiling, carrying a breakfast tray.

'Rosie.' Alex pulled her hands away from her throbbing head. She'd slept with a married man. She was a slut, an immoral tramp, no better, after all, than Charlie or the witch who'd snatched him away.

Worse. Being drunk was no excuse. No consolation for the unsuspecting wife.

How could she have pretended, even to herself, that all those warm fuzzy tingles were platonic? Had she – she couldn't bear the thought – at some horrible subconscious level been planning this all along?

'Nothing happened.' His voice became more insistent. 'I put you to bed. We were both bladdered.'

'No thanks to me though.'

'You've nothing to feel bad about. I told you last night, remember? I'm separated. My divorce will be final in a few weeks.'

'Oh, yes. You would say that.' The *weasel*! He'd known exactly what he was doing. Getting her drunk. She remembered feeling giddy and reckless, the hell with tomorrow. Well, she didn't feel that way now.

He had the gall to laugh as he put his arm around her bare shoulders. His lips touched her skin before she pushed him away.

'No.' She pulled the covers over her head, her words muffled. 'I don't know what to think any more. First you flirt with me. Then you say I imagined it because you're married. Now you're all but divorced. I can't trust a word you say. You're worse than any of them.'

His hand patted the bump, trying to figure out where her body parts were.

'You could ask Etta.' The words penetrated her cocoon. 'She knows. It's only Donald still in the dark. His health's been bad these last years and he was raised in the Wee Free church. I can hear him now: "*The devil rejoices when man divorces*".' She felt the bed shift as he stood up. 'Maria and I didn't want to disappoint him in a telephone call and I haven't been brave enough to tell him to his face.'

Her head emerged. 'You still could have told me.' She pulled the old-fashioned comforter up around her as she slid out of bed, picking up what clothes she could find. They seemed to be scattered all over the floor.

'I could have,' he sounded frustrated, 'but then you'd have thought I was after your blasted winnings. I could see the way the wind blew as soon as you showed up. You couldn't even look at me, let alone behave like a normal person. I tried to keep out of your way but… I didn't mean to fall in love with you. You drew me in.'

His eyes were pulling her now. She'd felt it too. Like North and South sides of a magnet. The electric charge sparking between them. The visceral attraction.

'Oh, so now you're in love with me.' *Be sane, Rosie.* She had to keep her head.

'Last night took me by surprise too. I hadn't realised I—'

'Was in with a chance,' she finished for him. She backed towards the bathroom, duvet trailing. 'Oh no, I'm sure you hadn't.'

'Goddammit woman, your money's been nothing but a headache. If you're not freezing me out, you're bolting. You're a nice person, Rosie, but—'

'Nice! Nice!' She thought of Zac and how easily he'd tricked her. 'Why don't you just say stupid and be done with it.'

'OK, stupid then.'

She saw the muscles tense in his jaw as she dove into the bathroom and slammed the door.

She dressed in a hurry, hearing a ringing phone through the wood. Of course his ruddy mobile would ring here when hers never had service. Etta probably, calling to see if their conspiracy had worked.

She could hear him through the door

'Yes. She's here. Shepherd's Brae.'

Then he was pounding on the wood, urgent enough that she snatched the door open. 'Rosie. It's for you.'

Etta's voice was agitated. 'Luke stumbled into a wasp's nest. He's had a bad reaction, very bad. We're off to hospital. I'll pick you up at the gate.'

Blind with panic, Rosie stared at Alex. 'Luke... Hospital... A wasp's nest...' She couldn't finish.

'It's over an hour away.' He was lacing his boots. 'I'll catch you up.'

'What? How?' She grabbed his shirt as he went for the door. 'The car's still at the pub.'

'Maria has a peanut allergy. She's left an EpiPen at the house. Go on now. I'll meet you on the road.'

Rosie jumped in the car as soon as Etta's battered old van screeched to a halt. Luke lay next to a scared-looking Tim. His face was swollen, his mouth grotesque, his eyes vanished into puffy flesh. He seemed to be choking, gasping for air. She couldn't tell if he was conscious.

She grabbed his hand then Tim's. 'You're going to be fine.' Her voice choked. 'Please, Etta, can't we go any faster?'

Hogging the road with breath-taking arrogance, Etta tore round tight bends, hammering gears, mouth set in a tense white line.

There was movement on the hillside ahead of them. Alex was thundering down the slope, the old horse Lochinvar lathered in sweat. He leapt off, dropping the halter rope, as Etta pulled over. 'He's in a bad way, Alex.'

His face was rigid as he looked at the motionless boy and withdrew a plastic tube from his pocket. 'This should buy us time. Etta, you take Lochinvar back. I'll drive.'

Tugging off the top, he jabbed it firmly into Luke's thigh.

'Charlie. It's me.' Rosie gave him a quick rundown. 'He's fine now but they want to monitor him overnight.'

'I'll be there within the hour.'

She jerked with surprise. 'How? Private jet?'

'I spent last night in Kyle of Lochalsh. Tim rang me, begged me to visit. It was to be a surprise. And thank Christ for that.'

They stood in the hospital corridor, breathing in the smell of bleach. Alex hunched his shoulders, hands in his pockets. 'I'll be off then. Your husband will be here soon.'

She started feeling wobbly again. 'He could have died, Alex.'

'Not your fault, lass.' He took a half-step towards her then stopped, looking away as he crossed his arms. Oh, how she wanted those arms – strong male arms – around her, a deep chest to bury her head into, but the memory of their fight was too fresh. Even if he had saved Tim's life. She felt ragged and raw. If he touched her she might fall apart completely.

'Wasn't it? I should have been with them. Not foisting them on Etta or getting paralytically drunk or—' She gestured helplessly. 'And Tim – he must have been so unhappy, asking Charlie to come.'

'Don't blame yourself.' Alex did touch her then, squeezing her hand. 'Things happen.'

The swing doors flew open and he stepped away as Charlie swept in.

'Rosie!' His face was taut with concern. 'How's Luke?' He pulled her into a tight embrace, head bowed over hers. His aftershave was comforting and familiar.

'Where is he?' He sounded hoarse. 'I want to see my son.'

'Through here.' She turned to introduce Alex, ready to praise him as the hero of the hour. But the doors had closed behind his retreating form.

'What do you mean you didn't book accommodation? It's the height of the tourist season.' Seeing the boys' eyes widen, Rosie tried to sound less shrill. 'Where did you think you were going to sleep?'

'Why not our cottage?' Tim asked innocently. He and Luke had been overjoyed to see their father, competing to relay their adventures in one mad rush. It was disconcerting to hear how often Alex's name came up in these garbled tales but her ex had merely listened with amused interest.

Rosie sighed, defeated. 'The nurse said I could sleepover with Luke. I suppose you and Tim…' She waved her hand.

'So long as you're sure.' Perched on the side of Luke's bed, arm around each son, Charlie's blue eyes shone with sincerity.

Sure? As ever with Charlie, was there a choice?

Rosie walked out of her bedroom, grimacing at the sight of her ex-husband curled up on the sofa. Granted Charlie was on his best behaviour, cracking jokes with the boys, buying groceries and cooking dinner, happily poring over Scrabble and Monopoly. He was diplomatic enough not to call Val in front of Rosie although she'd seen him outside with his mobile pressed to his ear.

Still it was disconcerting spending this time together, acting almost as if they were a family again. Already the people in the village were treating the four of them as one happy little unit.

Filled with conflicting emotions she found herself continually snapping at the man.

'You don't lock the door.' He'd noticed innocently the first morning they went out.

'No.' She practically bit his head off. 'It's called trust, Charlie. Honesty.'

She was one to talk.

And then the singing trout. 'I like it!' she'd snapped when he called it 'an abomination', jumping down his throat as if he'd mortally insulted her first-born child. Luckily Charlie only laughed. Afraid that if he took offence she'd shove him off to a hotel? But how could she when the boys were so thrilled with his presence?

She felt bad too about Alex but there was no opportunity to sort things out. Their one encounter had been excruciating, Charlie insisting they all troop to the big house to thank his son's saviour, Rosie blushing as she trailed behind.

A few days later the family were picnicking, sprawled on a woollen blanket on the hillside, when Rosie spotted Alex leading the now much larger calf from the field. He spotted them, raised a finger in greeting, just as Charlie leaned forward and popped a grape into her mouth.

'There's your wild Highlander,' he said, mussing her hair. 'Haven't seen much of him, have we?' Charlie never missed a trick. 'Aren't you going to say hello?'

She gestured to approaching storm clouds, stashing sandwich wrappers and Tupperware. 'That dark line is rain. In about eight seconds it's going to pour.'

The next morning Rosie pleaded a headache when Charlie, Luke and Tim set off for Dunvegan Castle, a thirteenth-century edifice still inhabited by the original clan. It was their last day. Charlie had changed his flight to accompany them home.

If ever there was a time to beard Alex in his den, this was it.

A rental car was parked in Donald's driveway. Rosie hung back, not wanting to impose when they had company. But what if they stayed for hours? Some impulse made her ring the bell instead of letting herself in the kitchen door.

Etta opened it, a look of surprise – and something else – on her face.

'Rosie! Not seen you in ages.' She cast a look beyond Rosie. 'Charlie and the boys not with you?'

How swiftly they'd been lumped together. These past few days everyone they'd spoken to had marvelled at her sons' resemblance to their father, complimented Rosie on her 'fine tall husband'. It simply wasn't worth the energy and embarrassment to explain.

'Not right now. Is Alex here?'

Etta hesitated. 'He's with a visitor.'

Donald poked his head out.

'Is that you, lass?' he said, warmly. 'Come in. We're all having tea.'

He ushered her into the seldom-used formal drawing room furnished by a MacDonald who'd spent several years in India. Its heavy curtains were pulled back, light streaming onto the zebra hide lying on the couch back, leopard's skin pinned to the wall and old wooden gramophone with a trumpet speaker and hand-cranked turntable.

A woman sat on one of the faded sofas, china teapot and plate of shortbread on her shapely knees. She was as exotic as the room, beautiful, dark-eyed with lush raven locks. At her side Alex paused, cup frozen on the way to his lips.

'Maria, this is Rosie who's renting the cottage.' Donald squeezed Rosie's fingers, guiding her forwards. 'Rosie, this is Maria. Alex's wife.'

Chapter Thirty-Two

In her modern glass and chrome office, Olivia stared down at the anthill below. The traffic was at a standstill, jaywalkers weaving between cars. She could imagine the anxious passengers in those miniature yellow cabs, crazed by the lack of progress. All those frantic people going nowhere fast.

She returned to her high-tech swivel chair, tapped a key to brighten the computer screen. Soon she was lost in the intricacies of her work, her eyes only occasionally drifting to a pink curved shell on her otherwise sterile desk.

Agent Million had been right. Returning to America *was* the only move. After seeing Mandrake's arrest, Olivia had confided the whole story over Mexican food.

'So why bail?' the young woman asked bluntly. 'You did nothing wrong.'

'No one else thought that way. I guess it was all too much. The shock. Guilt.'

'Sod all that. You didn't know your boss was a cheating toe rag.' She tapped her nails on the table. 'About your apartment – most lenders avoid the hassle of repossession. I bet you a dime to a dozen your mortgage company would've worked with you on payments.'

'I didn't have a dime, remember? I couldn't get a job.'

'Well, you've got one now. Call them the minute you get back. It can take months before they start proceedings. Listen, most brilliant successes have had spectacular crashes. This is an amazing opportunity. Get to New York and tell that fat banker why he'd be completely mad not to hire you for three times the money he's offering.'

'And what if he's only considering me because his niece has the hots for Marcus?'

'So what? Oh, I get it. So there *is* something between you and Mr Filmmaker. Have you—'

'No.' Olivia drained her margarita. 'He doesn't think of me like that. Plus his brother and I – well, we're kind of sex buddies.'

'Complicated,' Agent Million mused. 'So you're shagging his brother, he's no clue you fancy him, and some young whippersnapper has just snared him. But there's this outrageous job offer in New York...' She laughed, feigning a swipe to Olivia's head. 'What's stopping you, you dope? You wouldn't see me for dust.'

She'd taken literally the advice to make haste, flying out the following day, first-class ticket and cash advance organised by Shipton. That was six months ago. She blushed to think of her hastily scrawled notes to Zac and Marcus. How ungrateful she must have seemed, not waiting to say goodbye in person. But her emotions were too turbulent. It had been hard enough to bid farewell to Aunt Winnie. The big tough businesswoman was afraid she might cry.

When she had summoned the nerve to call, almost six weeks later, Lucy answered the house phone, explaining Marcus and Zac were out. Three times she'd tried Marcus's cell phone but ended up clicking off, like some adolescent schoolgirl, at the sound of his message.

William Shipton's massive head and shoulders appeared in the door.

'Not interrupting, am I?'

'No, I'm good. Come in.'

He was carrying a jiffy bag. 'Excellent. Have to say we're thrilled with your progress. Keep it up.' He glanced at the envelope. 'A messenger left this in the lobby. Thought I'd bring it since I was heading this way.'

'Thanks, Bill.' Olivia was touched. Rupert Mandrake would no sooner have delivered a package to an employee as offer to drop off their dry-cleaning. Her heart flipped as she recognised Marcus's handwriting.

When she ripped open the staples a DVD in a leather case fell onto the desk. There was also a brown envelope and a note.

'*Livvy. Hi. Here it is – finally! Channel 4 are raving about it – and even I'm quite chuffed, thanks to your amazingly hard graft and razor-sharp contributions. Re the enclosed – seemingly the post code was wrong and it's been halfway around the British Isles – our wonderful Royal Mail. How's life in the Big Apple?*

M x'

That was it? x?

There was a buzz and her PA's voice came over the intercom.

'You wanted me to remind you – you're meeting Brad at one?'

She checked her phone. 'Bugger it! Got to run.'

They sat around the long polished oak table, the realtor between her and Brad, buyers on the other side, taking it in turns to scrawl signatures.

'Congratulations,' the closing agent said as she shook hands with the buyers. 'You now own a house in the Hamptons.'

Brad caught up with Olivia at the elevator.

'Hey. Wait up.' His hand grasped the metal edge and he joined her inside, tanned and golden as ever.

'You look great,' he said, eyes sweeping from her coiffed locks (Maurice had gone into hysterics at the state of her neglected hair), to her unbuttoned Alexander Wang trench coat and three-inch Manolo Blahnik boots, with a lingering look at the cleavage of her smart office shirt. 'How do you feel about this?'

Their sweet seaside cottage. 'Not as upset as I thought. You?'

'We didn't need that place anyway. Not with the guest house at Mom's and Pop's. Hey, the whole town's buzzing about you. Everyone's thrilled about your new success.'

'Oh? Would that be the same everyone who shunned me when I was down?'

'We all make mistakes.' He leaned in to kiss her lips. 'What time do you want dinner tonight?'

She sighed. Yes, she had let Brad back into her life. For two months now. She'd needed to contact him anyway to arrange the sale. And he'd refused to discuss it unless she met him for coffee.

'I was a jerk,' he'd said on that first 'date' in Starbucks. Handsome and lean in green polo shirt and chinos, he'd given her that repentant little boy look. 'Can you ever forgive me?'

'Make a difference if I don't?'

Burnished hairs shone on his tennis player arms. 'We all totally overreacted, I know.'

'Maybe a tad,' she said dryly. 'Your father threatened to kill me.'

'Oh that.' He laughed, showing perfect white teeth. 'He got over it. Not his first or even his biggest loss. But still, leaving the country like that and no word for months? You could have been dead for all I knew.'

Or cared? Olivia wondered. But he sounded sincere.

'Are you back in the condo?' he asked.

'Yes. It's the strangest thing. I imagined the doormat littered with foreclosure and eviction notices but the bank says everything's cool.'

'I've been staying there, paying the bills.' He fiddled with his sweetener packet, looking self-conscious. 'I know how much that apartment means to you. I kept imagining you walking back in one day.'

Coffee had led to dinner and then more dinners. Amazingly Brad was eager to pick up where they'd so abruptly left off. He loved her, he said. And if she couldn't quite bring herself to jump back into bed with him, she wondered if perhaps she'd underestimated him. Although she intended to keep well away from his parents.

It was so ironic. All her dreams materialising – the job, the money, Brad. She'd even hooked up with long-neglected friends, determined not to repeat the same mistakes. Set hours, weekends free. No staying up all night meeting with financial analysts on opposite ends of the earth. And then – wouldn't you know it – when she didn't need it, the Spanish villa had sold. Wasn't that always the way?

When she returned to the office, contract and cheque in her handbag, the envelope Shipton had brought up was still on her desk. She picked it up, heart thudding as she ripped open the top and scanned the paperclipped note.

'*There are some personal things here I didn't like to read. I hope they mean something to you. Warmest regards, Maria.*'

Scraps of paper landed on the desk, random jottings, rough sketches of what she recognised as her father's metal creations, and two pages ripped from a cheap spiral notebook.

She saw paragraphs started, heavily scored out, and begun again. Her brow furrowed as she deciphered the weak straggly handwriting, so different from her father's usual robust scrawl.

'*My darling girl,*' one segment read. '*Your old man is a coward. I should have told you this years ago. But even now I'm scared t—*' Then a lot of underscored lines.

Reading rapidly now, she scanned down, eyes widening with growing disbelief. In blotchy semi-coherence the letter stumbled on. At the end of the second page it terminated abruptly in mid-sentence. She tipped up the envelope looking for the rest.

Nothing. The most vital information of all was missing.

No wonder he'd never mailed it. How could he do such a thing? And never tell her? Their whole relationship based on a lie.

Had her mother known?

Mandrake had only stolen money.

Her father had stolen souls.

Agitated, she prowled the carpet threatening to wear a groove in its plush nap. Ancient history. And yet it wasn't, was it? But what could she do about it? Did she truly want to stir up a maelstrom of past grievances and bitter hurts, lay open the wounds her father had inflicted so heedlessly? Might her interference do more harm than good?

Perhaps, but she had to know.

What to do? She needed an accomplice. Someone unafraid to dig in the dirt or ruffle a few feathers.

She buzzed her secretary again.

'Can you get me this number?' She reeled it off. 'The name's Zac Gilbert.'

But when her phone rang at two a.m. with an international collect call, the voice on the other end was Irish and female.

'Miss Wheeler? Next of kin to Winifred Powell? It's Bernadette O'Donnell from Helmshott Manor. I'm sorry for the bad news but she's taken a sudden turn for the worse, not expected to last the night. We need to know what arrangements should be made.'

Olivia's mind was still reeling the next day. In her five-fifteen yoga class she toppled over in Vrksasana, the tree pose. Then her boot stuck in a grate just outside the bank building, soy triple shot latte cascading over her fawn suede skirt, as she entertained passers-by with her struggles to break free.

She made her first ever late arrival for a meeting with a hastily sponged wet spot marring her usually flawless appearance and a head so full she could hardly take in a word of the discussions.

She sent her assistant to buy a couple of skirts and was just fastening up the zipper of the selected garment when Shipton called for her.

'New client for you,' he announced gruffly. 'Founder of Anderson's Nuts and Bolts. Made parts for planes in World War II, expanded to European plants in the fifties and became a major supplier in the aerospace programme.'

He pushed a folder across the desk.

'Then in 2005,' he continued, 'when the company stock was hopelessly undervalued, some slick young whiz kid does a hostile takeover. Retires our guy as CEO, carves up the company and sells it off, bit by bit. Understandably, Anderson's fairly sour about hedge funds but he's decided to dine with the devil. Got all those grand and great-grand kids to think about. He may be in his nineties but he's sharp as a tack.'

'Can't wait to meet him.' If only it were true. Since her return the merry-go-round no longer seemed a dizzying, thrilling game, her investors mere numbers on a spreadsheet. She knew all too well the devastation a single blunder might cause.

'Excellent.' Shipton rubbed his palms. 'I'm lunching with my niece today. Must remember to thank her for sending you my way.'

'Lucy?' Olivia blinked. 'She's not in England?'

'No.' He stood up, brushed at his suit trousers. 'Back to Stanford I'm happy to say. Boyfriend situation didn't work out.'

'You look happy.' Olivia's secretary sounded surprised.

'Yes, I am.' For the first time since she returned to America, she realised. 'When Mr Anderson arrives, send him right in. Thanks.'

She wanted to tell the wealthy old codger to find something better for his billions. Live it up while he could, blow his money on round-the-world cruises or Vegas strippers, squander a bunch on his great-grandkids and, since stuffing it under his mattress would probably leave him with his nose rubbing the ceiling, stick the rest in gold or treasury bonds.

But William Shipton had been good to her and she couldn't betray his trust.

It'd be hard enough explaining why she was leaving. Why she was willing to throw away everything she'd wished, hoped and prayed for since starting as the most junior of juniors in her first City of London trading job. Why no amount of money was lure enough to keep her in a life that no longer fitted.

In her office she picked up the cowrie shell, her talisman of good luck. Her fingers stroked the strange ridges, travelled over its sleek polished surface with the three oddly symmetrical brown spots. She was transported back to a beach in Scotland with the wind howling around her and Marcus's fingers brushing hers as he handed over the shell.

'Just two more things,' she spoke into the intercom. 'As soon as I'm done with Mr Anderson, I need an urgent meeting with Mr Shipton. Then book me on the first flight to Heathrow.'

Chapter Thirty-Three

Rosie pressed the remote and groaned as the pleated blind came to a grinding halt halfway up the window. No amount of button jabbing would convince it to budge and there was no dangling string to tug it the rest of the way.

Was it only five and a half months ago, she'd thought it was the cat's whiskers, watching fascinated as the mechanised blinds smoothly raised and lowered themselves from across the room? What a hick, she must have seemed, marvelling as Charlie proudly showed her round the brand new house, glittering with marble, polished stone, shiny German appliances and gas log fireplaces. 'Developers are practically desperate,' he'd said. 'You'd be mad not to buy when your lease ends.'

Probably he was right. She'd never lived anywhere so fancy. And it was certainly peaceful in this gated estate, listening to the gentle snip of secateurs as next door's gardener pruned their purple hydrangeas.

Any minute the cleaners would arrive. A neighbour had recommended the sweetest Tibetan couple who communicated mainly with bows and smiles. Unnecessary, actually, because, jobless, she had all day to wipe down sparkly surfaces but Charlie insisted everyone had help around here.

'How much are you giving them?' Stopping by one day, he watched her fold notes into a brown envelope.

'They send it all back to Nepal,' she said, writing their names. 'Their family are all refugees, poor things.'

He picked up an open Sotheby's catalogue. 'Not buying them antique furniture as well?'

'It's only the occasional twenty.' She blushed as she snatched the brochure and slipped it into a drawer. The perils of internet browsing. One minute idly curious, the next frenziedly flapping a number in a burst of bidding insanity. Her gut knotted, imagining what Charlie would think of the 'secret purchase' lurking in the deepest corner of her walk-in wardrobe. She hadn't a clue what to do with it.

'Watch out, Rosie girl,' he'd warned, straightening a painting on his way out. 'If they start expecting tips from all their clients, you won't be popular.'

Well, he had a point. Across Sunnydale's sweeping lawns, it was hard enough getting to know her neighbours, who were heavily preoccupied with high-powered careers or 'good works'. She caught her reflection in the hallway mirror, pale-cream Merino wool cardigan and smart skirt and sighed, thinking of the women she'd invited to tea. The talk would be polite, but formal, everyone dressed to the nines. So different from herself and Anya who'd let themselves into each other's houses, pop the kettle on, flop down beside the other on the sofa without word or explanation.

It all seemed so long ago and far away.

She was so lonely. Useless. It had struck her hard last night at the preview of the dreaded documentary. The boys were out with Charlie, Paul and Dee 'busy' and so, friendless, she'd had to summon all her nerve to travel to Soho and walk in alone.

'Enjoy!' that nice Marcus Gilbert had said as he handed her a glass of champagne and escorted her to a seat.

Enjoy? Perhaps if she'd had someone there to giggle with, to reassure her she wasn't as bad as she feared. Instead, squashed between media types, she'd scrunched down every time her gigantic wind-blown nonsense-spouting self filled the screen.

And, worse, seeing Scotland made her heart ache, remembering that brief burst of happiness. Not a word from Alex since she'd seen him with his wife. Stupid Rosie – duped again.

She couldn't leave the cinema fast enough, imagining her family's reactions. Paul would be offended that she'd mentioned his car purchase and Dee was already miffed about Rosie moving to the suburbs and letting 'that Charlie Dixon get his feet under the table'. She heard an approaching car and wandered over to the floor-to-ceiling French windows, which filled the sitting room with light, even in miserable January. Charlie's car was pulling up next to her own gleaming BMW, an even fancier model than her brother's.

A key turned and the boys thundered upstairs, shedding uniform caps and jackets. Charlie followed, filling the room with his big cheerful presence. 'They wanted to change. Any tea on the go?' He helped himself to some from the lukewarm pot, leaning against the granite counter that looked into the living room. 'We're off bowling. Fancy joining us?'

'I've visitors coming.' She hesitated. 'Isn't Valerie going?'

She could actually say her name now and not feel consumed with jealousy. Moving forward, Rosie.

He shook his head. 'She's up the West End – shopping.'

'Even so. What'd she think?'

He emptied the cup in the sink. 'It's only bowling, my sweet,' he joked. 'Not a dirty weekend in Amsterdam.'

He was around so much these days. Helping with homework. Stopping by to unplug the sink. Once he'd got so absorbed in a film he'd forgotten the time and had to bolt out, running back to the woman he'd chosen over them.

Luke and Tim came into the kitchen then, arguing.

'iPads are so the coolest,' Luke insisted. 'The school wouldn't give them to us otherwise.'

'Yeah, but the Galaxy's got a better display and more storage,' Tim argued. 'And my friends all hate Apple.'

When had her children turned into such consumers? Was it their age or their shockingly expensive private school with its elite rugby team, trips to Egypt, winter skiing in Verbier. They mixed in circles where a million pounds was an annual income, not a one-off jackpot, and the future dukes, earls and tycoons' sons owned every gadget known to man. And though she didn't *always* give in to her sons' elevated expectations, she was staggered by the amount of electronic devices cluttering their bedrooms.

Charlie read her mind. 'We're raising a couple of princes here,' he said, aiming a mock cuff at Luke's ear. 'When I was your age, I walked barefoot to school, carrying nothing but a stale crust.'

'When was that?' Tim quipped. 'When dinosaurs ruled the earth?'

'Ouch!' Charlie clutched his chest. 'Come on, let's be off. Your mum's got visitors. Anyone special?' His eyes flirted naughtily. 'Should I be jealous?'

'I think you gave up that right a long time ago!' she snapped.

Not so far forward as she'd hoped.

He called again two days later. Rosie, happily attired in Levi's and an old favourite shirt, was sawing a knife around the rim of a pastry dish when her mobile rang.

'Hey, it's Charlie. What are you doing?'

'Making an apple pie. What's up?'

'Something big.' He sounded odd, she thought. 'Could I come over for dinner? Haven't had home-made apple pie for ages and I want to ask you a question.'

It was almost surreal, Charlie at the table head, carving the chicken, dishing out mashed potatoes. Afterwards he carried out plates, loaded the dishwasher, in no hurry to leave even after the boys had gone to bed.

'Val's at her sister's.' He uncorked a second bottle of wine. 'Spending the night.'

'Oh? Trouble in paradise?' My, she sounded waspish. Moving had brought her physically closer to Val but it hadn't made them friends.

'Sit down.' He handed her a glass and patted the sofa beside him. 'We need to talk.'

'Oh?' She sat.

'About us. *You and me, Rosie.*'

He was nervous, Rosie realised, for all his smiles.

Blood pounded in her ears. 'There is no us.'

'Here's the thing.' Gently he brushed aside a lock of hair that was obscuring her face. 'Val and I have been at each other's throats for months. You could say things really came to a head when I went to Scotland.'

'Oh?' Rosie's ribcage seemed paralysed. She could hardly breathe.

'We had a huge row today. It's definitely over.'

'Oh?' She sounded like a backing singer. She sucked in air, inadvertently inhaling his heady aftershave. It was so Charlie, that scent. For months after he'd left, she'd find her nostrils twitching if she smelled it on a stranger, fighting a bloodhound urge to follow the trail.

'Rosie Dixon,' he raised her hand to his lips, 'would you give me a second chance? I know what you're thinking,' he forestalled her comment. 'It's not the money. I've been going crazy for ages now, realising I made a colossal mistake. I need you Rosie. I'll never find anyone as decent and giving and good-hearted. And the boys need their father. When Luke got stung… Well, let's just say I was scared back to my senses.'

He took both her hands and turned her towards him, his blue eyes shiny with emotion. 'I'm asking – will you marry me? Of course I don't deserve you, but it would be you, me and our sons. I'll sign a prenuptial if you like. We'd be a family again.'

He pulled her into his shoulder. That strong safe shoulder where she'd leaned her head so many times. Shifting position, he kissed the top of her head, then let his lips slide lower. Unbidden, unwelcome, Val's face floated into her mind.

'Wait!' She pushed him away, jerking to her feet. 'It's not that easy. I'm…'

What? Gobsmacked? Flabbergasted? It was the fulfilment of all her dreams and yet she wasn't ready for it.

'Of course.' He leaned back, his blue gaze mesmerizing. 'Take your time. I know you weren't expecting this.'

No, but she'd prayed for it, hadn't she? A thousand times. And maybe if she'd dared to hope, she'd have seen it coming, the amount of time he was spending around here. There were even occasions recently, when he stepped in to take control, when she'd felt almost usurped. After all she'd had to make decisions without him for years. But there was no denying when he walked into a room, everything seemed brighter, funnier, more exciting as if someone had turned on the lights. And Tim and Luke would be ecstatic, having him around so much.

Charlie wasn't perfect. He could be kind or selfish, charming or manipulative. But she was hardly Miss Goody Two Shoes, was she? Besides her other sins, she'd fallen into bed with Alex, a married man. Cheating was cheating – isn't that what she'd told Charlie back when she owned the higher ground? Alcohol was no excuse. There was no such thing as 'Only sex, it didn't mean anything'.

Let's face it, she'd always loved Charlie. And he'd loved her too – long before she had the money. Wasn't this exactly what she'd always said? That they were meant to be together and destiny had made a terrible mistake in wrenching them apart?

How anxious he looked, watching her. So vulnerable.

She reached her decision. 'Yes.'

It took a moment to sink in. His face lit up like the twins at their first airshow when the fighter jets blasted by overhead.

'Yes? You mean it?' He whooped as he grasped her by the waist.

'I said yes, didn't I?' Flustered, she pulled away. 'But don't tell the boys yet. Or anyone. I need time to sort it through.' She stood up and walked towards the door. 'It's late and I'm tired. Go home, Charlie.'

She switched off the downstairs lights and set the burglar alarm. The walk up the sweeping staircase and through the bedroom seemed miles on weary legs. Tiredly, she pulled out pyjamas and turned on the bath taps, throwing in expensive salts. The water welcomed her like a fragrant hug.

What had she done? She soaped her legs, wondering. Why wasn't she as exhilarated as Charlie about it all? She didn't owe anything to Val, even though perversely she felt pity for her rival, instead of victorious. It was all so messy. So much hurt. Alex, too, strayed into her mind. But no. She'd always be grateful to him for saving Luke's life – and Tim's on the cliff – but the rest of that interlude was best forgotten. She ducked under the water to banish the image of Maria, his Spanish beauty, turning towards her with that unsuspecting smile.

She had one last thing to do and then she need never torture herself again with the antics of fickle Scotsmen. It was time for Rosie to grow up, face the truth. Life was tough, painful even. And she didn't want to go through it alone.

She was cleaning her teeth, clad in her tartan pyjamas, when the doorbell rang.

Rosie stopped brushing, foam around her lips. Almost midnight. Nobody visited this late. Not Charlie back surely?

The bell rang again. She padded across the cold tiled floor, back through the bedroom and tiptoed down the stairs.

Her heart thudded. She opened the door a crack. Then jerked it wide.

It was her mother.

Chapter Thirty-Four

Zac whistled as he surveyed the lights strung along the inky-dark Thames. He was as dashing and piratical as ever in pointed alligator cowboy boots, tight-fitting black trousers and an indigo blue shirt that brought out his gypsy colouring.

'The Savoy, huh? Did you rob a bank this time?'

'Just one last taste of the good life before the grim reality of being jobless again.' Hairdryer in hand, Olivia looked with satisfaction around the elegantly appointed suite. 'Clapton got it right. Nobody loves you when you're down and out.'

'Not so sure about that.' Zac had his head in the mini-fridge. 'Seems like you won a few hearts. Before you trampled them to dust.' He poured himself a bourbon and ginger.

'You can talk.' She turned her head upside down and blasted it with hot air. 'Bringing home a girl the second I left for Scotland.'

He frowned, swirling his glass. 'I had a dinner party. The "girl" had her husband with her.'

'Oops.' She flushed with shame. She'd never even asked him. 'Sorry.'

He grinned raffishly. 'Just my luck. The one time I get ditched I'm actually innocent.'

Olivia picked up her comb. 'I guess I owe you at least a cocktail. Do they still allow jeans in the American Bar?'

'Sweetheart, after what I've found out, I'm holding out for dinner. In the Grill.' Zac bounced on the king-sized bed. 'Cool.' He lay back, hands behind his head. 'Wanna test it out?'

'I'll take a rain check. Come on.' Eagerness dispelled some of her fatigue from the flight. 'Spill.'

'OK.' Zac produced an iPad mini and opened its leather case. 'Your dad's second marriage took place in London, right?'

'That's what the letter said.'

Zac tapped the screen, reading his notes. 'And he met Miss X at his friend's art exhibition so that gave me a starting date. I checked the registries – nothing relevant for our Graeme Wheeler. But then genius that I am I noticed the wedding of a Graham, spelt with an "H". It was about the right time and place so I checked further.'

'Here, move over.' Olivia clambered beside him trying to look over his shoulder. He held the tablet up.

'Uh uh, no cheating.' He continued from memory, holding it out of reach. 'I found a couple of folk in the old neighbourhood who'd been friends with Graham with an "H". It was a long time back but they'd made an impression. A delightful couple, they said. Newly-weds. Lovey-dovey. That's why it hit her so hard when he ran off. They remembered she had a little boy and he was an artist. One of them even dug up a photo, from a street party. It was your dad all right. A charmer they said.'

'I bet!' Olivia tasted bitterness in her mouth. Her own father. A two-timing double-dealing sleazeball! Fuelled by nervous energy, Olivia took Zac's empty glass to the mini-bar and made them both a vodka and tonic.

'Well, get this. The new Mrs Wheeler gave birth to a child four months after the marriage. Five months after you were born.'

'So that's it.' Olivia handed Zac the glass. 'She was pregnant.'

Zac nodded thanks. 'Why else risk a bigamous marriage? But whatever, old Wheeler was a ballsy son of a gun. He'd been married six years to your mother and they were also living in London then, barely ten miles away. I looked them up too. Seems like your mum had the money, supporting Graeme's attempts to break into the art scene, paintings rather than sculpture at that stage. Shortly after Wife No. 1, Wife No. 2 gets knocked up too.'

'Must have been a shock.' Olivia was rummaging in her case now, pulling out garments and hanging them up. She found a black dress and started stripping off her sweater.

'They moved to Spain just after you were born.' Zac watched her pull the dress on and wriggle out of her jeans. 'You probably know that piece. That's when he switched to sculpture and started dividing his time between London and Spain. Almost a year after their wedding, Mrs Wheeler No. 2 filed for annulment claiming that the marriage was never valid.'

'So you know who they are then? This woman. And my…' she couldn't say the word, '…her child.'

'Yep.' Zac closed his eyes, pretended to snooze. Crossing the room, dress still unzipped, Olivia hit him with a pillow.

'Tell me. What are their names? Where do they live? Did you talk to them?'

He warded off her blows, grinning. 'I'm scared to. It's too good. You won't believe it.'

'Why not?' She turned her back so that he could zip her up. 'Are they royalty? I've always felt a strange kinship to Wills and Harry.'

Zac sighed and stood up, hands in pockets, pacing the room.

'One of our paper's most popular features,' he said conversationally, 'was on coincidence. A man struck by lightning seven times. Separated twins who ended up leading virtually identical lives, including the names of their kids and spouses. Amazing reunions like the brother and sister separated and put in different orphanages as toddlers who discovered at seventy-six, they'd been living in the same street for forty years. Makes you wonder, doesn't it?'

'If you're about to tell me you're my brother,' Olivia said dryly, fastening the ankle straps of her high heels, 'I'm going to need years of therapy.' If she was taking Zac to the Savoy Grill – and there was no question he'd earned his dinner – she'd better dress the part.

'Darling, if we were siblings,' Zac said languidly, 'at least one member of our dysfunctional family would be crushed. Still you can't explain some of the madly bizarre experiences out there.

What about that Titanic woman who ended up on about three sinking ships?'

'Violet Jessop.' Olivia avoided voicing the questions that really interested her. *Who would be crushed? Why?* 'An Irish stewardess who worked for the White Star line. She was on board the Olympic when it collided with a British warship in 1911 and then survived the sinking of both the Titanic and her sister ship Britannic. As much bad luck as coincidence I'd say. And she still carried on working for them.'

'Surprised they didn't pay her to stay on shore.'

'Talking about survivors.' Olivia was caught up despite herself. 'Three ships were lost in the Menai Strait off the coast of Wales. The first in the 1600s, the second in the 1700s and the last in the 1800s. And each time there was only one survivor – a man named Hugh Williams.'

'Yeah, right, whatever. So we've established ridiculous coincidences do occur.' Zac looked over her shoulder as she applied make-up. 'So you'll believe that I'm not making this up, no matter how far-fetched?'

Olivia picked up her perfume bottle. 'Talk fast. If you don't want to walk into the restaurant smelling of Eternity.'

'I got to say I didn't care for the second Mrs Wheeler.' He stepped back, enjoying her torment. 'Offered to have me thrown in jail – I'm not sure what grounds. But here,' he tapped the iPad screen again, 'is a photo of her daughter.'

Olivia stared, hand frozen in the act of applying lipstick.

'No!'

'Yes.' Zac smirked. 'Look familiar?'

'No…' She took the screen from his hand and scrutinised it. 'I can't believe it…' It was a whisper.

'Believe it, baby. By the way, did you happen to watch Marcus's documentary?'

'I've been busy,' Olivia growled, tensely. 'What about it?' She was still stunned by his revelation.

'Shame.' Zac strolled to peer out the window again. 'Seems the least you could do after leaving him to that big-lipped praying mantis.'

'Leaving him?' Olivia protested hotly. 'There was so much mutual drooling I thought I'd throw up.'

'Oh, but there's all kinds of ways of coping with troublesome feelings. And Marcus has always been a noble idiot.' He flashed her that handsome smile. 'Here, I'll email you my findings on your dad. But you have to promise to check this out.' Walking to his bag, he pulled out a small clear case and waggled it in his fingers. 'I brought you a copy. Trust me, you really, *really* want to watch it.'

Chapter Thirty-Five

'Mum!' Rosie said in shock. Why was she here? Her mind skittered over possible calamities.

'I need to speak to you.' Maxine's mouth was set in a grim line, eyes anxious, body stiff.

'But it's almost midnight.' Shivering, Rosie stood aside to let her in. 'Couldn't it wait until morning?'

She'd travelled several yards before she realised Maxine wasn't following.

'Ask me.' Her mother's voice was so quiet Rosie was unsure she'd heard right.

'What? Come on in, Mum. If we're to talk, at least let's sit down.'

'You've always wanted to know.' Maxine was immobile, frozen. It crossed Rosie's mind that maybe she was having some sort of funny turn.

'Isn't it a little late to be playing twenty questions?' She kept her voice gentle.

'Have it your way then.' Maxine stalked past into the kitchen, head high and sat herself on a bar stool at the granite centre island. 'You've been pestering me for years,' she added harshly. 'Wondering about the past. So go ahead. Ask me.'

What an incredible sense of timing the woman had. The encounter with Charlie had been exhausting enough for one day. Every fibre of Rosie's body yearned for her mattress.

'OK.' She yawned, her mind a blank. Besides the obvious – *why don't you go home and let me sleep* – all the myriad things she'd wanted to discuss with her mother seemed to have evaporated. She poured milk into a saucepan, ignited the gas burner and ladled in spoonfuls of chocolate. There *was* a question, she realised. She'd never had the nerve to ask before.

'Why do you hate me so much?' She kept her voice even, focussed on stirring the saucepan.

'Hate you?' her mother said, bewildered. 'Why would you say that?'

Rosie raised her eyes, sighing. 'Come on, Mum, you can barely stand being around me. It's always been Paul the marvellous, Paul the Perfect, and now Paul's "tremendous wife" and Paul's "wonderful" kids. You couldn't give a monkey's about the twins and me. Don't know why we even bother pretending anymore.'

There. It was out in the open. Rosie felt a surge of relief as if a heavy burden had been lifted. Why hadn't she confronted her years ago?

'Is that what you think?' Her mother looked smaller somehow.

'Are you denying it?'

'Yes…no… I don't know.' Maxine followed her through to the drawing room. Her shoulders were stooped, face grey. 'I've tried being a good mother.' It sounded unusually weak.

'Yes, well, don't worry,' Rosie said robustly, putting a mug on the gleaming cherry coffee table. 'Not as if you locked me in a cupboard or beat me with wire coat hangers.'

'I did love you.' Too late to be convincing. 'But things were never easy, were they, between us?'

Quite the understatement, but Rosie let it go. 'So what did you come to talk about?' She tucked her chilled feet under her, cradling her cup.

Maxine turned haunted eyes on her daughter.

'Your father.'

Rosie sat upright holding her mug, her mother staring at her, twisting her fingers together.

'You want to hear about him, don't you?' Maxine's voice was sharp.

'You know I do. But why now?'

Maxine's eyes shifted uneasily. 'People have been coming round. Asking about him. I think one of them was that journalist hack you spoke to.'

'But why?' It was more surreal by the second. 'What did you tell him?'

'Nothing. I won't speak to strangers about private matters.'

''Course you won't, Mum. Considering you can't even speak to your own daughter about them.' Rosie bit back the retort, even more mystified. Why would Zac still be sniffing around? It'd been months since she'd won the Premium Bonds. In newspaper terms that was like trying to reanimate a week-old corpse.

'Go ahead.' A small humourless smile creased Maxine's lips. 'Before I change my mind.'

'Well I…it's just you've never told me anything about Dad. Not even the tiny details. Like…' She racked her brains for all she'd wanted to know. 'Was he musical?'

'Tone deaf.'

'Was he sporty?'

'He loathed football, cricket, all ball games. And sailing. Used to get terribly seasick. But he hiked and jogged. Kept himself in shape.'

'Did he cook?'

'Not well. He over-boiled an egg once. It shot right out of the saucepan.'

Rosie smiled at the image. 'Did he like reading? Speak languages? Watch films? Could he paint?'

A shadow ran across Maxine's face. 'He was a sculptor. And he spoke Spanish like a native.'

Bull's-eye. 'Did he…?' There were so many questions. Scrambling for their place in the queue. 'How did you meet?'

'Oh Rose.' Maxine paused a few beats, gazed at the ceiling and began to narrate, as if relating a bedtime story.

'We ran into each other, literally. At an art exhibit. I backed away from a painting and crashed into him. My fault, but he apologised. He took me to coffee, made me laugh like I hadn't since Paul's father died. We fell madly in love.' Her usual brisk tones were dreamy, maddeningly slow. 'He was funny, spontaneous, full of the joys of life. He didn't care that I was a widow with a young son. He adored kids. Said it added to my appeal.' She gave a twisted laugh at some inside joke.

'What did he look like?' Rosie prompted softly. It was hard to imagine her mother young and in love, and even harder to believe she was finally getting answers. 'Do I take after him?'

Maxine picked at a dried up food stain where Luke had spilled spaghetti sauce on the sofa arm. 'You have his eyes. Not the colour but the shape. And your laugh. It so reminded me…' She gave herself a small shake and resumed her story.

'Anyhow, within months I got pregnant with you and we married. Just the two of us and little Paul, with two witnesses he dragged off the street. My parents refused to attend, thought he was a no-good loafer, after my money. My first husband had left me reasonably off. But did I care?' She shook her head, focussed on the fabric beneath her fingers. 'I loved him, plain and simple. My business made enough to keep us both but he was proud, ambitious. Anyway he always had a studio. He'd spend the night there a lot when he was painting, he'd get so wrapped up in his art. Oh everything was fine until…until Marbella.'

'Marbella?' Rosie echoed.

Maxine shivered and tightened her coat around her. 'He'd lived in Spain before, was always going on about it. Graham swore no other place gave him so much inspiration – the light, the culture, the ocean. He wanted us to move there but I had my business to run and Paul's grandparents were devoted to him. And then you were born. Oh he was over the moon, we both were.' Her eyes glistened. 'He chose your name. "Look at those rosy little cheeks," he said. "Let's name her Rose."' She sniffed. 'I wanted to call you Saskia.'

'Well at least you got your Saskia later.' Rosie could have kicked herself for interrupting but her mother scarcely noticed.

'Well, it wasn't easy. There's me, working from home with ringing phones and clients, you squalling your lungs out, Paul a rowdy young scoundrel. Too much reality for Gray. He started to spend more and more days at his studio staying away from our chaos, I suspected. Then some Spanish friends asked him to caretake their villa in Marbella while they were on a year's sabbatical. At least that was his story. He'd have the peace and quiet to focus on sculpture – he'd changed mediums by then – work intensely during the week and be home for long weekends. And then once he was famous... Oh, it was all pie in the sky but I agreed. You could tell he thrived out there. And when he came home we'd be so happy. Passionate.' She said the word as if it left a bad taste.

As the story continued, Rosie sat motionless, cocoa forgotten, worried even a tiny fidget might break the spell and her mother would never open up again.

'You were nearly six months old when I decided to surprise him. He hadn't been home for weeks and I missed him. I packed Paul off to his grandparents and caught a last-minute charter flight. I kept imagining how thrilled he'd be to see me.'

Rosie felt a strange compassion for Maxine who looked crumpled, her face suddenly older. She could guess where the story was going. A man alone in Spain. Handsome. Successful. A free spirit besides.

'The first thing I saw from the taxi was a swimming pool and a red-haired toddler crawling after a Persian kitten inches from the edge. Yellow cotton dungarees. My heart stopped.' Maxine put her hand to her chest as if reliving the moment. 'I was terrified she'd fall in. Indignant at her parents' negligence. Some feckless ex-pat friend of Gray's, I imagined. Or perhaps the maid's daughter. I grabbed you and the luggage, hurried to get to her before disaster struck. Then the patio door opened.'

Rosie could see the scene. A young Maxine cradling one child, hastening to save the other.

'The mother appeared. A hippy chick with messy red hair. She pulled the kid back, then flopped on a lounger in her cropped shorts and minuscule vest and lit a cigarette.'

Rosie saw Maxine's knuckles go white, so tightly were her hands clenched.

'Well! I opened the gates, thinking I'd need to have words with Gray about hiring a better class of help. But then he arrived.' She swallowed hard. 'Naked apart from a towel round his waist. He started to kiss her neck and my world fell apart.'

'Oh God.'

Maxine continued grimly. 'The girl saw me first. She pushed Gray off, raised a hand with a big smile.'

'How *horrible*. He had a girlfriend.' Rosie understood only too well her mother's shock and grief. Hadn't she gone through the same thing with Charlie?

Maxine pulled away from Rosie's touch. 'Oh yes,' she hissed. 'He had a girlfriend true enough. *Me*.'

Her anger grew at Rosie's bewildered expression. 'That little scrubber was his wife. You were his bastard. And our marriage was a sham. No wonder he was always so private, wouldn't talk about his family life. He told his wife he spent all that time in London for business, meeting with patrons, visiting his aunt. God, her face when she saw me. There was quite a scene. She'd a temper to match that hair.'

'But what did you do?' Rosie was stunned, barely able to take it in. None of her fantasies about her father had encompassed a story like this. A bigamist?

'After the shouting?' Maxine crossed her arms tightly. 'I had the marriage annulled. Reverted our surnames back to Paul's father's, destroyed every photo, paper, ticket stub that connected me to him. I could have had him jailed – I suppose so could she – but the thought of a public trial and my parents knowing. It would have been better if he'd died.'

'Wait! Wait?' Rosie held up her hand, silencing whatever her mother was about to say. 'What do you mean – "better if he'd died"? You're saying...' this was the most unreal part of all, '...he's still *alive*?'

Rosie snuggled into the duvet, grateful that Tim and Luke were old enough to take themselves off to school. What a night. Maxine had stayed until three, refusing Rosie's offer of the guest bedroom. All Rosie's peace of mind had gone with her, the story she'd told looping over and over in her brain like an annoying pop jingle. Was it true? Had Rosie dreamed it all?

Her heart ached as she reflected on her mother's story. How different things could have been. If her father hadn't been a philanderer. If her mother hadn't been betrayed. If she'd been raised in the heart of a happy family, secure and confident in her parents' love, perhaps she wouldn't have been so unsure of herself and lacking in confidence.

In her mother's story she'd caught a glimpse of another Maxine entirely. Trusting, impulsive, affectionate, instead of bitter, cynical and cold. And her father. That dashing, fun, artistic man who'd adored her, even for so brief a time.

That was the part hardest to forgive. Anger stung as she slid out of bed, walked across the heated floor of the master bathroom and switched on the shower. Now she understood the way her mother had reacted to her all these years. Clearly she'd been an unwelcome reminder of a past Maxine wanted to forget. But could Rosie excuse the rest of her behaviour?

To think that when she was going through her tough teenage years, being berated by her mum every day, she might have had a dad to turn to. That when things were at their worst, he'd actually been alive. If she'd known that, would she have been in such a rush to throw herself into the arms of the first man to show her a little love?

And now it was too late. Her mother had robbed her of that chance. To learn of his existence only to discover he'd gone. It felt like losing him all over again.

Maxine had hesitated as she left, hands clutching her handbag. She looked a decade older than the woman at Saskia's birthday party.

'I wanted you to hear it from me, not someone else. Just remember, Rose, they took everything from us. You don't owe them a thing.'

'Rosie.' The name – or perhaps the force with which Rosie said it – surprised both of them.

'What?' Her mother looked confused.

'Everyone calls me Rosie now. I prefer it.'

Maxine had blinked. 'Yes, well…' It took her a second to gather her thoughts. 'As I said, we've had our ups and downs. But I only want the best for you, Rose… Rosie. I always have.'

The shower ran forgotten as Rosie brushed her hair, so vigorously her roots throbbed with pain. So much to digest. Charlie's declaration of love. Maxine's confession. Her father's crime. She'd barely got a wink of sleep last night. She needed to speak to someone. Talk it through. But with whom?

When it came right down to it, there was only one possible candidate.

Chapter Thirty-Six

'And no bleeding wonder the country's in the bleeding toilet. All these immigrants living off our hard-earned taxes...'

Olivia closed the partition between her and the taxi driver's racist rant, switching on her laptop. The DVD player sprang into action again. Was it the fourth or fifth viewing since Zac's astounding announcement?

Last night she'd had to watch the whole thing multiple times, just to make sure. Hallelujah! She wasn't in it! All those hours of humiliating footage, rehashing the Mandrake debacle, showing her homeless on the street, with a cardboard sign begging for coins... He'd used none of it. What was that about? Hadn't it been part of the deal, the whole reason for taking her in?

What had prompted him to spare her feelings after all? Kindness? Or something else?

She liked the song Marcus had chosen for the opening credits, a new Glaswegian band just beginning to get noticed. If she hadn't run off to New York, she'd have been involved in it all – music selection, the editing which she'd really been looking forward to, just the sort of detail work she'd relish. She could remember, almost second by second, everything they'd filmed.

Instead... She winced, imagining Lucy's pointy chin resting on Marcus's shoulder, oohing and aahing over a particular shot. Or worse, taking over. Long nimble fingers tapping away, coming up with genius cuts while Marcus stood watching, admiring and aroused.

Olivia forced back the surge of jealousy. She couldn't blame Lucy Shipton for being beautiful and available when she, Olivia, was tied up with Zac. And she'd been nice enough – or clever enough – to get her rival back to the Big Apple – dangling a piece of bait that Olivia had pounced on as if it were an Olympic gold medal. No, Olivia's disastrous decisions were all her own.

But it hadn't worked out for Marcus and Lucy. Their short fling had quickly run its course, according to Zac. She was back at Stanford. Which left Marcus alone, unattached, and probably still furious at Olivia's rude unceremonious exit.

She jumped ahead to the Rosie interview, mesmerised yet again. Her half-sister. Younger by mere months. She couldn't see any resemblance. Rosie was talking, the sound on low, blonde hair windswept as she struggled to keep it out of her round shy face. She kept staring away as if wishing a mini tornado would spirit her off, away from Lucy and the camera. If Olivia had been there, she'd have struck up a rapport, put her at ease.

If Olivia had been there... Interviewing the little sister she didn't know she had... The synchronicity of it boggled the mind. Even Olivia's computer-like brain couldn't fathom the odds.

If she were superstitious, if she didn't think all that stuff baloney, she'd say it was destiny. As if Mandrake was supposed to steal that money, Olivia meant to flee to London, Rosie fated to win the Premium Bonds, and Zac to expose them both just so the two sisters could meet. Rubbish of course. Yet so often they must have been within spitting distance of each other. Perhaps even in the same place at the same time. Her best friend worked at Winnie's nursing home for Christ's sake.

Then again – the taxi turned left onto the Archway Road – destiny would have been better served if someone – her dad, her mum, that cow Maxine – had just bothered to introduce them. Had they not thought it important? Or had they intentionally kept the sisters apart?

She shut the laptop as her name rolled on the closing credits. It was generous of Marcus to acknowledge her contribution. But did that mean he'd forgiven her for disappearing without a word of warning? Did she dare call him to find out? Olivia was anything but a coward but suddenly she was terrified to do this one tiny thing. And why?

Because it mattered. Whether Marcus would be thrilled to see her, indifferent, or tell her in no uncertain terms to stay away. It mattered more than anything else in her career-driven, money-obsessed history. It was the reason she'd found herself so often staring out the window of her high-rise Manhattan office, seeing his face, his smile. It was the reason her renewed success had felt empty, why Brad's attempts at reconciliation had been doomed to failure.

Rosie now – that was another story. Olivia was determined to find her half-sister. The mother's strange reaction made sense now. She must have flipped when she found a red-haired Wheeler standing on her doorstep. Olivia almost laughed. It was so insanely cosmic. Zac was fretting for permission to write the story. But she had to talk to Rosie first. Did she have a clue about Olivia or her father? She guessed not, recalling their few conversations.

The ex, Charlie, would know where she was. She'd get in touch with him this afternoon. But first there was poor Aunt Winnie to deal with. She couldn't believe she hadn't been there at the end. That while she was flying over the ocean, her aunt was gasping her last breath. They'd spoken only last week, however jumbled the conversation.

She'd keep a ring maybe to remember her by. Her few pieces of costume jewellery – well, perhaps the nurses would like them.

But wait. What was she thinking? Winnie was Rosie's great-aunt as well. Any trinkets belonged, by rights, as much to her as to Olivia. Even if they'd never known of each other's existence.

Again the sense of regret. If only they'd found out before Olivia had left London. Rosie would have had an aunt and Winnie might have had a visitor for the last remaining days of her life. Instead of a worthless niece who'd abandoned her for the second and final time.

The taxi had come to a stop now, the road to Helmshott Manor blocked by a monstrous traffic jam. She heard distant shouting.

She opened the partition again.

'What's going on?'

'It's that nursing home, innit,' the cab driver replied. 'The one what they're closing down for that new estate to be built. There's been all kinds marching about with banners. Not hear about it then?'

'I've been out the country.' Was that what that Home Manager, Bernadette, had tried to tell her when the line went dead?

'Yeah well they've been writing to the papers. Getting celebrities involved. Not that it'll help unless they come up with some real dosh. Money's only thing that talks, don't it?'

'Jesus,' Olivia said. 'Sounds like a madhouse. I'll walk from here.'

She could see the banners now, a small group of people walking with placards. She could just make out the chant.

'They won't...

They won't...

They won't destroy our home...

They won't...

They won't...'

Great. Adjusting the shoulder strap of her laptop case, she marched into the fray.

Rosie rang Anya's doorbell, oddly sad as she glanced over at her former abode. Life had been simpler there, short on cash but not short on happiness. She pressed the button for the fourth time, feeling a frisson of nerves. What if Anya was in there, peeking through a curtain, and refused to answer? Or slammed the door in Rosie's face? Or even opened an upstairs window and chucked down a bucket of water? As the chimes faded, she told herself she'd risk anything to build bridges with her old mate. She'd been a coward for far too long.

A face popped over the hedge. 'You looking for Anya, love? She's at work.'

⚜ ⚜ ⚜

'They won't...

They won't...

They won't destroy our home...'

Rosie wove her way through the throng of people marching in baby steps in a circle, waving their 'Stop the Closure' placards. A bulldozer was parked menacingly in front of the Manor's gates. And in its path, padlocked to heavy chains wrapped through the wrought iron was a solitary pugnacious figure.

Anya.

Whatever Rosie expected, it wasn't this. Seeing her best mate helpless, vulnerable and defiant as any suffragette, broke her heart. She dashed towards her. 'Anya! God in heaven, what's going on?'

Her friend rolled her eyes. 'Three guesses.'

'They're closing down your nursing home? I never knew.'

'What, you don't watch the news no more?' Anya scowled. 'Locked away in your ivory tower?'

'You know us princesses.' Rosie smiled feebly, disguising her alarm at her friend's predicament. 'We lead sheltered lives.' She touched the cold hard links wound around Anya's narrow waist, appalled by their weight and thickness and the huge forbidding padlock. 'Anya, I'm so sorry. For not being around. And for everything else.'

Anya shrugged. 'So you should be. Blabbermouth bitch.' But there was the merest glint of humour in her eyes and from the way she said it Rosie knew she'd been forgiven.

'So what's all this about?' She nodded at Anya's shackles.

'I'm not moving until they take that sodding machine away.'

Rosie glanced across at the bulldozer again, its heavy caterpillar tyres caked in mud. Even with no one in the cabin, it appeared threatening, powerful teeth ready to chew up anything in its path.

She felt genuinely terrified for her friend.

'Look, Anya...' She had to make her see this was folly. 'I know it's all awfully sad but—'

'Awfully sad?' Anya twisted round, wincing. 'It's a bloody disgrace. Some of our residents won't live through a move. It'll kill them. This place has been their home for decades. I *won't* let it happen.' She set her chin determinedly, tears in her eyes.

'It's a tragedy, I know.' Rosie soothed, stroking her hair. 'But I don't want to see you get hurt. Someone back there said the police have been called. Please Anya. This is so dangerous. You could end up in a lot of trouble.'

'So what should I do then?' Anya shook off her touch. 'Sit passively by and let people do whatever they like, whatever the consequences. You might let everyone walk all over you, Rosie, but there's times when you need to stand and fight.'

Rosie flinched, Anya's words hitting home. It was true. She'd always been a peacemaker, attempting to keep everyone happy, even at her own expense. And where had it taken her? Into a life she didn't want. On the outs with everyone except her children.

And Charlie...

She cast helplessly for another topic. 'Well, apart from that, how's things?'

'If you mean that wanker Darius, it finished months back,' Anya said, gruffly. 'Caught him at it with some slag. Tossed all the crap he kept at my place into the street. Except these.' She jangled the handcuffs. 'I wrote to you, you know. A couple of times.'

'Oh. I didn't get anything.' Could Dee have thrown them out along with the other begging letters?

Rosie stood beside her friend, giving her sips from her water bottle and feeding her half a Kit-Kat as Anya relayed the history of the Stop the Closure campaign. 'We've had kids setting up Facebook sites, grandparents gathering petitions, others writing to papers, tweeting like mad, lobbying MPs. Nothing budges them.'

Eventually Rosie could hold back no longer. She had to tell Anya about Maxine's bombshell.

'All those years, she let me believe he was dead,' she concluded. 'She kept my father from me. Stopped us ever having a relationship.'

'Perhaps she was trying to protect you. What he did was horrible.'

'I know, but to keep it secret? Didn't I have the right to judge him for myself?'

Anya shrugged. 'I always thought your mum was weird. So you've got a half-sister?'

'Yes, but who knows where. Maxine wouldn't say. She clammed up and left as abruptly as she arrived.'

'Perhaps that journalist knows,' Anya observed. 'If he got her nervous.'

Rosie made a face. 'Like I ever want to see *him* again. So tell me about Darius…'

Anya briefly filled her in on the break-up and Rosie in turn told her about Scotland and Alex.

'Charlie's convinced Alex planned to scam me somehow. Heard about the money. Lured me to a remote island to woo me for my cash. Says the wife was probably in on it too.' She kept her voice light but the very idea hurt like a burning skewer.

'Sounds even more far-fetched than my gigolo/conman/murderer theory.' Anya chuckled. 'So was it fantastic?'

'Was what fantastic?'

'You know.' She twitched her eyebrows twice. 'The sex.'

Rosie instantly coloured. 'We didn't get that far. Luckily. But I really liked him. Until his wife showed up…'

'Oh dear.'

'The worst thing is I thought we were friends. He saved Luke's life.' And two monster crabs, she thought, although you really had to be there. 'Yet he didn't even bother dropping by to see us off. If that's not a guilty conscience, what is?'

Anya shook her head. 'Bloody men. Talking of which, how is Charlie the charmer?'

'That's another shocker. He's actually asked…' She was interrupted as one of the protestors gave a shout.

'Look out, lads!' he yelled. 'Bobbies have arrived.'

The circle cheered, raising their signs higher.

'The cops,' Anya said, eyes blazing. 'You'd better get going.'

Rosie watched the line of uniformed police push through the sea of onlookers. She was filled with a sudden fierce resolve.

'No way. If they're going to arrest you, they'll have to arrest me too.' She snatched up a placard from the nearest marcher and climbed on the bulldozer, scrabbling up as high as her shaky legs would manage. Terror and exhilaration rushed through her as she started chanting along with the others. 'They won't, they won't, they won't destroy...'

The policeman took a threatening step forward just as a small commotion erupted in the rear. From her perch above the surrounding heads, Rosie spotted a TV van arrive, people stepping out. The cavalry! They couldn't arrest her now without it making the evening news. If she could just hold on. They were coming towards them... They were...

They paused in front of Anya. The TV interviewer adjusted her hair and checked her make-up, as the crew set up their equipment. Some people were approaching at a slow pace through the gardens, a woman, an elderly couple very close together, and – she blinked – two men, one of whom was the filmmaker Marcus, the other – she couldn't believe her eyes, the journalist, Zac.

'Are you coming willingly or do I have to climb up there?' the policeman threatened. He looked about nineteen, gangly, with acne and a bulging Adam's apple.

The TV news crew were ready now. The interviewer, a slim brunette with flowing locks, tottered in front of the camera in her high heels. Rosie saw her nod once towards the demonstration, her lips moving, but she couldn't hear the words. And here was Rosie out of it all. But this time she wasn't content to wait on the sidelines.

'I'll be back,' she told the constable as she slid down the other side of the bulldozer and ran past Charlie, heading for the side gate. 'Save my place.'

'And so,' the reporter was facing the camera as Rosie pelted up, 'in a last-ditch effort... Blast it! Cut!' Her face creased with annoyance as Rosie reached her, catching her arm.

'I need to say something...' Blindly, her outstretched hand closed on the microphone.

The brunette tugged but Rosie's grasp was firm. 'Please let go, madam. You're interrupting our work. She pulled hard, talking to her cameraman. 'Let's go over that last bit again.'

'No!' Rosie jerked back, her fingers tight on the microphone the way they'd gripped the bulldozer only minutes before. 'I want to talk.' Dimly she was aware of Marcus and that tosser Zac staring at her in astonishment. 'I'm Rosie Dixon,' she panted. 'The Millionaire Miseryguts Premium Bond winner. You people were stalking me for weeks hoping for an interview. Well, now I'm going to give you one. Like it or not!'

The brunette looked at Zac for confirmation of Rosie's identity, made a decision and gathered herself together. 'Fine.' She relented. 'But let me do an intro.' She fluffed her hair, arranged her jacket and started speaking to the camera.

'In a surprising turn of events, Rosie Dixon, the Premium Bond winner who some were calling Millionaire Miseryguts is with us at the demonstration today. Rosie, I believe you've something to say?'

She thrust the microphone in Rosie's face. Rosie's cheeks flamed, all her shyness flooding back as her mind went utterly blank.

'Ah…um…' she croaked, heat running up the back of her neck, causing her to sweat under her hair. She couldn't swallow. Her mouth was dry, her throat constricted. She felt her head swim, ready to faint under the pressure of all those watching eyes. And then she caught sight of her. A russet-haired woman standing between Zac and Marcus. She smiled and gave Rosie an encouraging thumbs-up.

Rosie gulped, summoning up her courage and started again.

'Yes, I most certainly do.' She stared at the glowing red light that showed filming was in progress. 'I'm outraged by the inhumanity, greed, ignorance…'

Rosie had to scrabble up onto the bulldozer again for the TV crew's benefit. They also filmed Anya, still handcuffed, arguing with a bearded police sergeant. And then the elderly couple who, strangely, were linked by handcuffs.

She beamed with triumph. Marcus had slapped her on the back when she'd finished her speech. For once she'd made her voice heard and it felt great.

More people were arriving all the time, some to gawk, others to join the protest or sign the petition. News travelled fast on the internet. There were already multiple videos on YouTube.

The girl who'd given the thumbs-up came over to stare at Rosie high above her.

'Hi,' she called up.

'Hi,' Rosie called back down.

'Great job, back there. I'm Olivia Wheeler.' She paused as if waiting for her name to strike a bell. 'I set up your interview with Marcus. In Scotland.'

'Oh yes, Livvy. Of course. Hello.' She grinned. 'Thanks for the thumbs-up.'

'My pleasure. You were awesome. We should talk, you and I.' She gave a lopsided smile. 'When you're not so tied up.'

'Um, OK.' Rosie shifted position, clutching a pipe as someone banged against her. She wasn't alone now up here. Several other protestors had climbed up and her perch was getting crowded.

'Rose Dixon? You're needed by the front gates.' A man wearing a fluorescent-yellow tabard looked up at her. 'The developers and council representatives have arrived. They've asked for you. As a spokesperson for the protestors.'

'But,' she hesitated, 'surely Anya…' It'd been a wild impulse that had sent her hurtling towards the TV cameras, forgetting her fears in the flames of a righteous cause. This wasn't timid Rosie, jilted wife, mother-of-two, discussing the woes of new-found wealth. This was life and death. But could she do it again? Confronted by angry developers and smug councillors defending their decision?

'It's you they want,' the man repeated. 'Go on, love. Give 'em hell.'

Chapter Thirty-Eight

'Damnit, I totally choked.' Olivia cursed, watching the determined figure marching towards the news cameras again. All those great speeches she'd been composing since she read the letter and she hadn't been able to summon a word. 'What could I say? Hi, there, sis. Did you know your father was a bigamist, already married to my mum when he wed yours and – oops apologies – that makes him a dick and you his bastard child?'

'Maybe a bit blunt.' Marcus grinned as he packed up his camera again. 'Three words would do it. I'm your sister.'

'Yeah and when she calls for a straitjacket?'

Her heart was still flip-flopping a bit when she looked at Marcus, struck by a strange shyness. There'd been little time for anything but stilted greetings, what with filming Eve and Eli's emergence from the bathroom, recording a short pithy interview, and then getting a text to say the TV crew from London Live had arrived. Turned out that Zac had some strange influence over Jenny Juniper, the famously married female presenter. Sex? Blackmail? Sometimes it was better not to know

And then Rosie, appearing like a genie without warning, had wrestled away the microphone and made her impassioned appeal.

Astonished, curious, Olivia had watched with growing admiration as the stuttering nervous girl gained courage and clarity. Her own flesh and blood, less than twenty feet away.

'Brilliant! This could be huge.' Zac pulled back Olivia's red hair, whispering in her ear as Rosie was hustled back to the bulldozer to be filmed on high like some flag-waving heroine of the French

Revolution. 'Two long-lost sisters find each other while battling to save nursing home. The media will be on it like wasps at a picnic. Get in there and talk to her. And remember, I get the print exclusive.'

Olivia saw Marcus watching and extricated herself. 'It's hardly the moment. She doesn't even know.'

'It's the perfect moment.' Zac had given her a tiny push. 'Deadlines, kid. Climb on that bulldozer, throw your arms around her and let Marcus take snaps.' Poor Marcus, staring from one sister to the other as Zac filled him in. Olivia wondered if she'd looked half as stunned when she'd discovered the truth.

But those moments of hesitation had blown her chance. And now Rosie was lost in the centre of a knot of tall men, the television camera aimed at her.

'Come on,' Marcus said. 'We're not going to let her take the heat alone.'

'I don't think we got an invitation, bro,' Zac remarked as they hastened after him.

Marcus snorted derisively. 'And your point is…?'

'It's my understanding Ms Dixon here is just a media-hungry attention seeker.' A balding councillor was addressing Jenny Juniper as Olivia, Marcus and Zac walked over. 'Like most of this…' he gestured at the demonstrators, '…rabble, she has no knowledge of the facts and absolutely no connection with this situation.'

'Rosie?' Jenny thrust the microphone at her.

'Well…' Rosie looked shaky and intimidated among these powerful men. 'Er, my best friend Anya has worked at Helmshott for years. And, well, er, I used to live around here…'

'And her great-aunt, Winifred Powell, spent her final days here,' Olivia piped up. '*Our* great-aunt in fact. She's as much right as anyone to speak up.'

She saw Rosie's jolt of astonishment, her eyes widen to two grape-like orbs.

'Is that so?' Jenny Juniper turned to Olivia. 'And you are?'

'Olivia Wheeler. Rosie's sister.' She saw Rosie's face whiten even further, consternation, doubt and disbelief flickering across her expressive features. Olivia hoped she wouldn't faint.

Marcus stepped in. 'This rabble, as you call them, are concerned citizens. Wondering how this project got rushed through so quickly with minimal publicity or public participation.'

'That's outrageous,' Watkins, the burly red-faced developer, spluttered. 'We went through an extremely stringent and costly review process. The residents will all be re-homed and this insane nonsense is only causing them unnecessary stress.'

'And what if they don't wish to be re-homed?' Rosie's colour flooded back, cheeks stained burgundy as she found her courage again. 'You're ripping old people from their beds. Throwing them out of the place they love.'

Of all times Olivia's phone interrupted the moment. She stepped away, about to switch it off and then noticed the caller ID. A quick conversation and once again Olivia moved into the spotlight.

'Gentlemen,' she announced loudly, feeling like Prime Minister Chamberlain holding up a white paper with Hitler's promised peace, 'I've a way out of this unfortunate situation. I represent an overseas investor who's authorised an extremely generous offer for the Manor. Disgusted by the way society treats its old people, Mr Anderson intends to run Helmshott as a non-profit. We can save all this embarrassment, negative press, political repercussions.' She raised her phone. 'Shall I tell him we have a deal?'

There was a long silence. Then Watkins shook his head.

'Absolutely not,' he said and turned on his heel.

'I had no idea she existed,' Olivia told Jenny Juniper. Cued in by Zac, the TV journalist was interviewing them in Helmshott Manor's common room. 'Or anything about her mother. Not until I got the letter.' She turned to Rosie. 'But it's weird. Ever since I read…' She saw Zac shaking his head in a 'don't go there' gesture. 'Well, since I first heard of you,' she amended, 'I felt connected in some way.'

'And, Rosie, what do you make of it all?' Jenny asked.

'I'm flabbergasted.' Rosie's eyes glistened. 'My mother didn't tell me until yesterday. And that it should be Olivia – it's fantastic.' She grasped Olivia's hand. 'I've always wanted a sister.'

'And there you have it.' Jenny Juniper turned to camera. 'A skirmish with developers turns into a startling discovery for two very courageous women.' She winked at Zac as Rosie and Olivia engulfed each other in a huge bear hug. 'Cut.'

Chapter Thirty-Nine

Rosie parked right outside the school gates, sliding her BMW neatly in as a Bentley pulled away. After a sleepless night, the events of the past few days whirling around her head, it was a miracle she could drive. One more incident, however minor, and her overloaded brain might explode.

'Told you we wouldn't be late,' she declared brightly.

'Don't care if we are,' Tim said gloomily.

'What do you mean?' She stared. He fiddled with the seat belt, not moving. 'I thought you loved it here.'

'Well we don't,' said Luke.

'Not more fighting?' A chill ran through her as she studied the well-mannered pupils emerging from their terribly smart cars in their equally smart uniforms.

Tim shook his head. 'We've no friends. Everyone's so posh.'

'It's always hard settling into new schools,' she said gently. 'Nobody knows each other.'

'But that's the thing, they do here.' Luke reached for his schoolbag. 'Most of them went to the same posh primary.'

'And had the same posh nannies. They say we're common,' Tim chimed in. 'They make fun of the way we talk.'

'And they say football's only fit for yobbos,' Luke added. '*Gentlemen* play rugby.'

'Want me to have a word with your teachers?' Rosie was dying inside.

The withering look both boys exchanged answered that suggestion.

'That'd make it worse,' Luke scoffed.

'Then they'd *really* think we were sad,' Tim explained.

'Oh,' Rosie said. The exhilarating tide of power she'd experienced yesterday had swept back out, leaving her beached in self-recrimination. She was useless. Money or no money, she couldn't save the care home. She couldn't protect her sons. She couldn't – wouldn't – give them back their father.

She looked at their downcast eyes, their drooping mouths, Tim's hand reluctantly playing with the door handle, but what choice was there?

'I'm sorry, kids, but you're just going to have to tough it out. It'll get better. I promise.'

With a heavy heart she watched them trudge away. Wondering as always if she was doing the right thing. Well, nothing she could do about it this morning. She checked the clock on the dashboard. Right now she had to be somewhere.

A few protestors were marching desultorily outside with a lone policeman watching them. The uproar was over, eyes downcast. Everyone seemed defeated.

The gates of Helmshott Manor were wide open. No Anya chained to them in brave resistance. She'd withstood the police threats of arrest, Rosie's pleas that she'd die of cold if she stayed there all night, even the summoning of a man with a bolt cutter. It wasn't until the Irish Home Manager had persuaded her the residents needed her help, their departure postponed for the following day, that she'd unlocked the handcuffs.

Rosie felt a lump in her throat, remembering how Anya had unfolded her cramped legs and marched stiffly to the Manor door without a word.

By the heavy equipment two men in hard hats conferred, staring up at the ivy-covered building as they planned their attack, the boss of the demolition crew in grimy donkey jacket, the Project Manager in a smart Crombie coat brandishing a clipboard.

Rosie found Olivia, Marcus and Zac by the main front door, chatting to Bernadette and Anya. Olivia gave her a huge hug. Her sister. They'd talked for ages yesterday when the fuss had died down. The media had lapped up the story of the Premium Bond winner discovering her suddenly impoverished, hitherto unknown, sister. They'd shown Jenny's interview on breakfast TV today, two talk show hosts wanted them as guests and Zac's feature had been syndicated worldwide. All well and good but it wouldn't save Helmshott once those heavy machines started tearing into brick.

'What's everyone doing?' Rosie asked Olivia.

'Waiting for ambulances.' Olivia nodded towards the white vehicles pulling up in the driveway. 'There they are now.'

'Ambulances?' Rosie felt a jolt of alarm. 'Has something happened?'

'Not yet,' Anya said bitterly. 'But there's residents here in their nineties, even a woman who's a hundred and one. They've survived two world wars, seen out three monarchs but they can't get a break from the f...' she caught Bernadette's warning glance, '...frigging money men.'

'Come on, Anya.' Bernadette steered her towards the door. 'We need to get the wheelchairs rolling.'

A beaten-up old mini overtook the ambulances and came to a screeching halt beside them. To Olivia's astonishment Beth emerged. Her former childhood friend had shed her social worker gear for a baggy t-shirt, tracksuit bottoms, and – of all things – a spade.

'Olivia!' Beth carried the garden tool like a flag. 'Thought I might find you here. Hi, you must be Rosie.' She pumped her hand. 'Beth, Olivia's best friend from yonks back. I saw you on TV. Good speech. And you...' She gave the startled Olivia a giant squeeze. 'Way to go, girl. I'm *so* proud of you.'

'Well...uh...thanks.' Olivia seemed at a loss. 'I'm not. We lost.' She nodded at the implement in Beth's hand. 'What's that for? Not planning to assault someone, are you?'

Beth scowled at the men in hard hats. 'I wish. I couldn't sleep for thinking of the diggers destroying all this beautiful landscaping.

There are inner-city gardens who can barely afford dandelions. Thought I might save a few plants for them.'

'Go for it,' Olivia suggested, gloomily.

The first wheelchair was being brought out, the woman clutching her shawl to her chest, shivering in the bright cold winter sun. Rosie blinked back tears. Marcus filmed the scene, his expression grim. Even Zac seemed unusually sombre.

'Think I'll give your friend a hand,' Rosie said gruffly to Olivia, unable to witness any more sadness.

She found Beth tackling a small rhododendron, face pink from exertion.

'Anything I can do?' Rosie asked.

'If you can just support it with the spade, love,' Beth said, her sturdy legs apart. 'I'll pull.'

They heaved and tugged. Just as the roots began to yield, something wriggled through the grass. Rosie leapt back. Beth gave a high-pitched squeal.

'What is it?' She clutched her hand to her breast, as Rosie bent down to investigate. 'An adder?'

Rosie stared at the head emerging to stare at her. It blinked and a memory jolted through her like a rush of adrenaline.

'I think...yes... God, I'm almost sure it's a slow worm.' She exhaled.

Her mind worked feverishly, remembering that conversation with Alex among the heather. Quickly she bent down, gently scooped up the snake-like creature and handed it to Beth. 'Whatever you do, don't let it go.'

Beth's mouth opened in astonishment as the small reptile started to wind around her wrist.

Then Rosie was pelting back to the Manor door, waving at the orderlies pushing the wheelchairs down the ramp.

'Stop! Everyone back inside. No one's going anywhere!'

Chapter Forty

'Ms Dixon's quite right. There's a whole nest of them there.' The Wildlife Liaison Officer came back to the small anxious group, dirt on his knees from crawling in the shrubbery.

Olivia stared down into the hastily procured shoe box. 'So that means…' She crossed her fingers.

'Demolition needs to be halted.' He beckoned the Project Manager to him. 'We're putting a Stop-Work Order on this place until they can be safely relocated.'

The manager gave a heavy sigh, tucking his pen under the clipboard clasp. 'Yeah? And how long will that take?'

Everyone held their breath.

'They're hibernating right now. Once they start emerging, usually May at the earliest, the site can be surveyed again. Then we can begin catching them.'

'Must be tricky,' Olivia said. The Officer eyed her appreciatively, taking in her slim figure, vibrant hair.

'Time consuming anyway,' he agreed. 'Nice hot day, you lay down roofing felt and corrugated iron. When the slow worms come to sunbathe – they like the heat, you see – they're captured and moved to another location. Then the developer does a destructive search.'

'Which means?' Rosie asked.

'Using a machine to turn over and strip their habitat looking for their homes. Then they submit detailed reports – numbers found, action taken – to the local planning authority and wait for permission to resume work.'

The Project Manager removed his hard hat. 'Boss'll have a fit,' he said mournfully. 'This'll delay us best part of a year. A while back they found Great Crested Newts on one of our sites. Put us behind six months and cost hundreds of thousands.' He sucked at his teeth. 'I don't want to be the one telling Crawford.'

Around him faces lit with jubilation. On the entry porch Bernadette wiped her eyes with her sleeve cuff.

'Then let me,' Olivia said decisively. 'In person would be best. Let's take the Harley, Zac. Quicker than battling traffic. Rosie and Anya, I'll meet you at the Town Hall after I'm through with Crawford. If I can't negotiate a deal out of this situation, I'll eat his bowler hat.'

'No orders for me?' Marcus was packing up his camera, amused by the way she'd taken command.

Zac tossed her a helmet, revving up his motorbike.

Olivia's pulse quickened. 'Yeah, go with Rosie. I want you to film those petty bureaucrats' reaction when they discover Helmshott Manor is saved.'

She threw her leg over the back of the saddle, adrenaline fizzing through her veins, heart racing as the bike roared. It was the battle ahead, she told herself, that had her so pumped up.

This was what she lived for. The game was in progress, the stakes were high and she held a winning hand. Poor reptile-beleaguered Crawford wouldn't stand a chance.

'Fan-bleeding-tastic,' Anya said coarsely, standing up and clinking a spoon against a glass to get people's attention. 'Rosie was amazing. Arguing with the council. Would you believe those numpties were insisting the residents had to be moved anyway, said the wheels were in motion. And then when Olivia burst in, waving the contract...'

She raised her glass. 'Here's to the sisters!' she toasted. 'A force to be reckoned with.'

They were celebrating in the main social room of Helmshott Manor, bulldozers and empty ambulances long departed. Bernadette had brought out some wine, the kitchen had conjured up snacks and staff members had hung up balloons. Between the pensioners, care staff, die-hard protestors, the room was packed.

Everyone cheered. Rosie dropped a curtsey.

Olivia grinned and toasted again. 'To Helmshott Manor and our billionaire benefactor – Mr Anderson and his love of nuts and bolts.'

Zac drew her aside as the chatter resumed.

'So? Proud of yourself?'

'For once,' she said, grinning. 'It feels good to be on the side of the angels. You?'

'Not bad. Two-page feature in the *Sunday Times* mag.' He swaggered.

'And you didn't have to go to a war zone,' Olivia joked. 'Or dandle orphans.'

Zac shuddered extravagantly. 'Dirty little tikes.' His gaze followed Olivia's as she glanced over to where Marcus was chatting to some residents.

'Talked to him yet?'

'Sure, tons of times,' Olivia said gruffly, turning her back on the group.

'You know what I mean.' Zac's sizzling blue eyes sparkled.

'And say what?' she snapped.

Zac wound a strand of red hair around his finger, a confirmed flirt even when he was being serious. 'Come on. I've seen the way the two of you can't stop looking at each other. There was a reason that Lucy girl didn't stand a chance. And not just because she was so beautiful, perfect and squeaky-clean.'

'Yes, well, there's an excellent reason I don't stand a chance either.' She tugged her hair from his grasp. 'And I'm looking at it. What self-respecting man would want his brother's discards?'

Zac tilted his head. 'For the record it was you who dumped me. And if the two of you have any brains at all, you won't let a minor fling get in the way of true love.'

Olivia's ego winced. 'Minor?' She knew her objection ludicrous even without Zac's laughter.

He gave her an exuberant hug. 'Darling, I swear at times you're just like me.'

'Jesus, Mary, I hope not.' The mild remark came from behind Olivia, sending her spinning around. Zac slid diplomatically away.

'Marcus.' Faced with him, one on one, her voice sounded high and squeaky, her mouth issuing a stream of chatter. 'Isn't it fantastic? Bernadette said most of the staff are dying to come back, her phone's been ringing off the hook, and Anderson wants to set up a charitable trust for Helmshott Manor and have me head up the organisation to run it. I know there's going to be a huge amount of details to sort out and I've loads to learn, but—'

Marcus held up a hand, his brow furrowed under its halo of messy curls. 'Wait. Isn't that a lot to take on? With a full-on career making squillions in New York?'

'New York's over-rated.' She traced the rim of her glass with a finger, looking at him through lowered lashes. 'And I'm tired of the money game. Figured I might give London another chance.' She looked away, embarrassed. 'After all I've got family here now.'

He turned her chin. 'Is that the only reason?' The intensity in those dark poetic eyes made her breath catch. He leaned towards her. They were only inches apart now, their bodies moving closer.

'Er, forgive me interrupting.' A voice broke them apart. It was Rosie, fidgeting, as she stepped from one foot to the other. 'But I have to leave now.'

'So soon?' Olivia said as Marcus's arm slid around her, pulling her back against him. She let herself lean into his support, feeling a thrill of happiness in all the places they connected. 'Anything wrong?'

'No.' Rosie smiled and kissed her cheek. 'Everything's just perfect. Have to see a man about a sword, that's all.'

And with that she was off.

Chapter Forty-One

'There we are, Headmaster. Timothy and Luke Dixon. They have their things.' The form teacher ushered them inside the Head's office then backed away and closed the door.

'I apologise for disturbing your classics class, lads, but your mother has some bad news for you.' The Head of Horatio Barton School nodded at a concerned-looking Rosie.

'Your aunt passed away this morning,' she told the boys gravely.

'Dee?' Tim said horrified.

'No,' Rosie replied hastily. 'Dee's fine. It's Aunty Kinney. Very sudden. Now come along then. Taxi's waiting. Thanks so much Mr Penger-Wallace. I'll be in touch.'

'Aunty Kinney?' Luke asked as they trotted down the corridor.

'Kinney's died?' If anything Tim sounded even more dismayed.

'No. Nobody died. No dog. No aunt.' Rosie felt a twinge of the old guilt for scaring them. 'It was a story. Thought you might fancy a few days off.'

'But where are we going?' Luke asked as they followed her through the quadrangle and out the gate.

'Scotland.' She pointed to the brown package peeking out of the open taxi window. 'We've an urgent delivery to make.'

'And what exactly is this?' Alex grasped Tighban's heavy oak door, body blocking the entrance. He frowned at the object Rosie presented, holding each end like a knight offering homage to his liege. She couldn't decide if she should kneel or curtsey.

Her hands trembled as he made no effort to take it. Well, Etta had said he was a proud man. She'd known he'd be difficult. Part of her had expected – hoped – he'd be back in Spain. The other part...

Why had she been so impelled to make the journey North without delay? Was it just that she'd been living with a deadly weapon in her cupboard for months and she wanted no more loose ends gathering dust?

She jutted her chin stubbornly, Luke and Tim behind her. 'What does it look like? Eighteenth-century, red velvet-lined Basket Hilt sword from the Isle of Skye, carried at Culloden. Auctioned at Sotheby's a couple of months ago. And before you say anything, it's not for you. It's for Donald.'

He quirked his well-shaped brows at that. 'Is that so? Well then, you'd better come in.' He stood aside to let them pass, tough and masculine in jeans and an old fisherman's sweater, well-worn patches on the elbows. There was a foot of snow on the ground and Rosie shivered in anticipation of bone-chilling damp. Surprisingly, the interior was actually toasty-warm. And was that fresh paint on the walls?

'Hi guys.' Alex's attitude was noticeably friendlier to the boys than to Rosie, who hesitated in the hall clutching the sword in its scabbard. Luke returned his high five but Tim barely muttered a return greeting, eyes downcast with embarrassment.

Poor Tim. Snatched unexpectedly out of school, it was only when they were on the train, concrete jungle giving way to endless fields, that he'd confessed.

'When you were in hospital with Luke...Alex visited us...at the cottage. And I made up a story.' He glanced out the window, face puce. 'I said you and Dad couldn't come to the door because you were both asleep in bed...together.' His head bowed as he held back tears 'And that you were getting married again. I'm so, so sorry, Mum.'

Rosie had almost choked. 'Oh that's nothing.' She'd punched him lightly on the shoulder. 'Quite imaginative. But I thought you liked Alex?'

Perhaps a child's intuition, she thought, spotting a rogue where adults were fooled.

'I did,' Tim acknowledged. 'But Dad said... He told me...'

'Oh yes, she could just imagine what Charlie Dixon had said. Her voice was gentle. 'Are you very upset that your dad and I aren't getting back together?'

'No, it's OK.' He seemed relieved at her reaction. 'It was weird at first, the divorce and everything, but I'm cool with it now.' Then he'd brightened as Luke returned from the refreshments carriage, arms laden with crisps, sweets and bottles of Coke, and the subject was dropped.

Well at least she and Charlie hadn't completely screwed up their children. Apparently they had the resilience and confidence to cope with their parents' mistakes. Or perhaps the cracks just hadn't shown up yet. Either way there was no way they were going back to that snobby stuck-up school.

Alex held his hand out and Rosie handed over the sword. He drew the blade from the scabbard, examining the steel. She'd expected more of a reaction. A refusal even. Lots of 'no, no, you shouldn't have' from Alex – or from Donald if Alex had been in Spain. And 'oh, but I insist' from herself. She'd imagined Etta rushing out to hug her. It was all a bit...anti-climactic.

'Where's Donald?' She noticed a brand new radiator. What was going on?

'Etta's taken him to the dentist.' He sheathed the sword again. 'Follow me.'

'And how's your wife?' She felt bolder addressing his muscular back.

'My ex?' He didn't turn around but instead opened the door to the dining hall and ushered her through. 'Fine, I'm sure. We haven't spoken since she brought the papers to sign but kind of you to ask.' Brrr – perhaps it *was* chilly, after all. 'And how's Charlie?'

'Great. We haven't spoken since I told him to where to stick his marriage proposal.'

She might have added more but the words died as she looked across at the display wall. Alex strolled over to the swords, pausing in front of one.

'Angus Mor's eighteenth-century Basket Hilt sword.' He nodded his head towards it. 'Red velvet lining. And, yes, carried at Culloden, blah blah blah.' He held up the sword in his hand. 'So I ask you again – what's this?'

'I feel such a wally,' Rosie groaned, sitting at that old antique oak table, head in hands. The boys had run off to see the shore and Shepherd's Brae just as Etta's car pulled up.

'Och away with you,' Donald comforted, patting her shoulder with his wrinkled hands. 'It was a very kind thought. And lucky for us. We were afraid we wouldn't see you again. Is that not right, Etta?'

'Aye and some people grumping around like a bear with a sore head.' Etta pushed a cup of tea in front of Rosie. 'And not man enough to pick up the phone and make a call.' She cast a dark glance at Alex, sitting hunched over. Rosie thought she heard him mutter, '*Haud yer wheesht, ye auld biddy*' but it could have been something else entirely.

She was still trying to get over her mistake. 'Of course there must be hundreds of Basket Hilt swords out there. But this one came from Skye. And you were so worried you'd be forced to sell it.'

Donald stroked his white beard, guiltily. 'I may have been exaggerating a wee bit. With himself,' he jerked his head at Alex,' always after me with the improvements. But ye're no telling me you got on the plane with that?'

'No, we took the train.' Rosie sneaked a peak at Alex again. All she could see was the top of his light brown hair. He hadn't said a word since the others arrived, apart from that one low growl. His legs were crossed at the knees and he seemed to be fascinated by his slowly circling boot. 'I see you've been doing up the place,' she added.

'That would be Alex,' Etta said, sounding proud. 'He's after turning it into a grand hotel. I told you he's an excellent cook, didn't I? And Donald's moving into Shepherd's Brae. He's taken a fancy to the cottage now it's all poshed up. Oh, you've missed a lot. We're to be in a film too, would you believe?'

'A film?'

'Yes, a romance about the Bonnie Prince.' Donald stuffed his pipe with tobacco and set a light to it. 'They're paying a pretty penny for the use of the house. And hiring the swords and artefacts besides. I'm sure they'll be happy to have another.' He waggled his beard at Rosie's sword.

Alex stood up, so abruptly they all stared at him.

'I'd like a word with Rosie if you don't mind.'

Before they could respond he'd taken Rosie's wrist and led her back in the hall.

'So you're not getting back with Charlie?' he demanded, his gaze stormy as a winter sea.

'No. I-I never was,' Rosie stuttered ungrammatically. 'Tim was making up stories. So you're really divorced?'

He brushed that off. 'I told you I was.'

'Yes, well, you also told me—'

Before she could finish the sentence she was rudely interrupted by his mouth swooping down on hers. He pulled her to him in a rough passionate kiss that left her breathless when she was finally released.

'But she was here. Maria.' She managed to gasp the words.

'With the final divorce papers and the sale of the business. We decided to tell Donald together. No misunderstandings.' He still had hold of her arm and Rosie was sure those strong fingers would leave bruises. She didn't care. She was flustered and elated all at once.

'She's a fine woman but we changed over the years. We wanted different things.'

'Oh.' Rosie dropped her head, shy under his scorching gaze. 'And what did you want?'

'I wanted to live here, back in Tighban,' he told her seriously. 'I wanted a family to know the land where I was born, to have it in their soul like I have it in my soul. And I wanted a sweet loving honest woman just like you, Rosie, from the moment I laid eyes on you.' He held her at arm's length, his gaze raking her face. 'The question is what do you want?'

What did she want? Her heart skipped. So many things. She wanted the man before her. Wanted him like she'd never wanted anything before. She wanted her sons to have the freedom again that they'd enjoyed that summer and to grow up with a decent sense of values, away from priggish snobs and taunting bullies. She wanted them all to have a normal life, where one's worth wasn't defined by the class of people they socialised with, the size of their house or the health of their bank account.

And, she thought stubbornly, she wanted...

'I want you to take the sword. Because I am *so not* carrying it all the way back to England.'

Alex laughed. 'The boys would adore it though. You're certain you want rid of it?'

'I do,' she said, aware that her words sounded uncomfortably like wedding vows.

He picked up her hand and kissed the knuckles. 'I'll only accept it on one condition.' Gently he traced her thumb with his lips, sending tingles through her entire body. 'That you and Luke and Tim come with it. I've fallen in love with you, Rosie. I want to marry you. It's a lot to ask, I know, uprooting your family, moving to the other end of the country to live in a crumbling ruin with a scruffy old sod like me, but do you think there's any possible way we could make a go of this?'

Rosie snuggled into his chest as his strong arms engulfed her. Oh, she knew it wasn't that straightforward. There'd be problems ahead – Charlie and custody for one thing. He'd been offered the Glasgow dealership in the past. Would he consider moving North?

Could they figure something out between school breaks and long weekends? She had all this money now. Surely that was good for something. But whatever else destiny had in store, she knew one thing.

She wasn't going to walk away from love. Somehow she would make it work.

'Now *that,*' she tilted her head to find his lips again, 'is the million dollar question.'

Epilogue

In a small village in the Yorkshire Dales, Agent Million's car slid to a halt outside a row of shops.

She checked her hair in the mirror, reading the numbers on the doors, as Ozzy Osbourne spoke once more.

'You have reached your destination.'

Authors note and contact details

A note from Pam and Lorraine (aka Ellie Campbell)

Thank you for taking the time to read Million Dollar Question. If you enjoyed it, please consider telling a friend or posting a short review. Word of mouth is an author's best friend and very much appreciated!

Want to be the first person we contact about free books or new releases? Sign up for our very occasional and valuable newsletter at http://eepurl.com/UDHbT. (We promise not to share your email with anyone or clutter your inbox.)

We love any chance to hear from or connect with readers. Here's how to get in touch:

Email: **chicklitsisters@gmail.com**
Blog: **www.chicklitsisters.com**
Facebook: **https://www.facebook.com/EllieCampbellbooks**
Twitter: **https://twitter.com/ecampbellbooks**
Amazon Author Page: **http://www.amazon.com/Ellie-Campbell/e/B0034OURJ8**

Biography

About the Author

Yes, it's true. Ellie Campbell is not one person but two. We are Scottish sisters, Pam Burks and Lorraine Campbell, who have managed to collaborate now on five novels without ending our friendship or killing each other. (Of course the fact one lives in England, the other in the USA makes a handy buffer for any rare artistic disagreements.) The youngest of four sisters, we spent much of our childhood pretending to be other people – usually cowboys or pirates – so perhaps writing together comes naturally. Plus we mostly love the same things – stories, laughter, friends, family, animals and travel. We've lived in Inverness, Edinburgh, Southern England and London and for years one of us was always travelling or living abroad, be it France, Australia, Thailand, Borneo, Colombia, Guatemala... Nowadays you can find Pam settled just outside London with husband, family and a dog, while Lorraine is in wild and wonderful Boulder, Colorado, with her husband, horses, cats, dog and chickens.

How to Survive Your Sisters

"A wonderfully warm and witty debut novel about family secrets and sibling rivalry"

The four MacLeod sisters are no strangers to sisterly rivalry and with one of them about to be married, there are bound to be fireworks. Perfectionist Natalie wants the 'wedding of the year'. Harassed mother, Milly, just wishes her bridesmaid's dress wasn't the size of a tent. Career-obsessed Avril secretly moons over a married man and world traveller, Hazel, the youngest, yearns to be taken seriously.

Forced together for the first time in years, and with an unexpected guest stirring up old resentments, squabbles are inevitable. But when tragedy strikes things really fly apart – as some shocking skeletons emerge rattling from the crowded MacLeod closet…

When Good Friends Go Bad

The four schoolfriends – tomboy Jen, snobby Georgina, hippy Meg and gentle Rowan – were inseparable until a childish prank tore them apart. In their twenties, an attempted reunion only widened the gap. Rowan failed to appear. Meg behaved outrageously and – sharpest cut of all – Jen discovered just how deeply Georgina had betrayed her. So now, a mother herself, in the midst of divorce, the last thing Jen needs is a call from Meg. Or is it? Will Meg's strange mission to track down the missing Rowan re-open old wounds, heal the rift – or throw Jen back into the arms of her never-forgotten first love? As their quest stirs up buried secrets and forbidden passion, Jen, Meg and Georgina will be tested on love, loyalty, and friendship, discover the truth about Rowan – and awake a danger that threatens them all.

Looking for La La

Bored stay at home mother, Cathy, finds her predictable routine upturned as she investigates a lipstick-covered love postcard sent to husband, Declan. Who is this mysterious La La? Could Declan really be having an affair? And – wait – is Cathy actually being stalked?

With all her friends hiding secrets, a sexy admirer igniting long-forgotten sparks, and the stress of organising the school's Save The Toilets dance, soon it's not only Cathy's marriage that's in jeopardy. Add in the scheming antics of Declan's new assistant and a possible murderer on the scene and the stage is set for a dangerous showdown and some very unsettling, even deadly, revelations…

To Catch a Creeper

Cathy is riding high in her brand-new job at a (surprisingly bitchy) top London advertising agency working with best friend Rosa. But when Rosa's pregnancy goes amiss and enemies sabotage her new career, she finds herself leading a chaotic double life of lies and deception, hiding a shameful secret from all, especially husband Declan who appears in the throes of a nervous breakdown. Meanwhile she's agreed to unmask the notorious Crouch End Creeper, a burglar terrorizing their neighbourhood. Little does she know that her meddling, assisted by fellow mothers (the Wednesday Once Weeklies) and the Neighbourhood Watch, will lead their dangerous opponent to murder. And that it's not only the tall elegant transvestite who is placing herself at risk...

Looking for La La: Excerpt

Chapter One

Not a sound is heard as it lands silently on the mat. No drum rolls, crashing thunder, shafts of light. The walls don't start crumbling, the ground doesn't vibrate with terrifying tremors and a yawning fissure fails to zigzag across the kitchen floor and separate my husband from his breakfast marmalade.

In short, I've no clue as to the impact it'll have on our lives. Mayhem. Marital breakdown. Murder. It should at least have been written in blood or come in the beak of a dark-winged raven.

It is a postcard. "Love from London" blazoned above a giant pair of pouting lips kissing a cherry-red heart.

At first sight it appears to be one of those "Please Come to Our Rave" flyers which get thrust through my door periodically. Now the chances of me, a world-weary, put-upon mother-of-two, going to a rave are slim to none, but heck it's nice to be invited.

I turn it over.

Dearest, sweetest Declan – it begins. My eyes widen as I take in the blue spidery handwriting and race to the signature. 'Love from La La.'

A tiny blip courses through me as I beetle down the hall attempting to identify the exact emotion I'm feeling.

Jealousy?

No.

Anger?

Nah.

It's – I recognise it now – excitement. A blip of excitement forcing its merry way around my clogged up veins.

'Postcard for you,' I say nonchalantly, opening the door and stepping back into the kitchen, 'from La La.'

I had a blip when I first spotted Declan at Bubbles, a dingy disco located east of the pier in downtown Bognor Regis. It was Sandra Mason's leaving work party and I was nineteen years old. Sandra was tear-stained and puffy faced – partly from drink, partly emotion and partly because she always had a fairly puffy face. We'd given her a pretty good send off, bought her sexy underwear and filled an enormous padded card with witty farewells and humorous poems, all of them sounding a whole bunch better than my lowly "To Sandra, All best – Cath".

The fifth yawn of the evening had just wormed its way out of my mouth corner, when I spied Declan dancing under a glassy mirror ball, had the blip and knew immediately we were destined to become involved. I wasn't sure how. Perhaps he'd introduce me to a mate or better-looking brother. Not that he repelled me exactly, but spiky ginger hair had never been top of my "must haves" and the way he was swinging those hips in perfect rhythm with a blonde nymphet, well, they looked set for life. In and out they gyrated to *Unchained Melody*, his large hands caressing her tanned shoulder blades. I found out much later she was his long-term girlfriend, Lucy. Juicy Lucy, I labelled her. Not very original maybe but it inevitably served its purpose of getting right up Declan's nose.

They made quite a couple. Lucy laughing, licking her glossy lips, and my future spouse leering lovingly at her, beads of sweat running down his freckled brow. I was entranced for a good few seconds before being beckoned back to earth by Sandra, who wanted an all-embracing photo of the girls from Credit Control. So, blocking out the blip, I pasted on a wide cheesy grin and darted across the room.

Declan?'

He sits motionless, his knife suspended in the Flora margarine, blue eyes gazing into the far distance, as he listens to a heated political debate on Radio 4.

'Postcard, darling, from La La.' I raise my voice, aware it'll take a more urgent tone to break that level of concentration. Either that or blasting out the latest match score. Arsenal 0 – Manchester City 2. He reminds me at times of De Niro in Awakenings, forever trapped in a catatonic state. I often wonder if I throw a ball at him whether he'd whirl round in his chair and catch it in one swift movement.

'What?' He finally looks up, granary toast perilously close to his open mouth. 'Not more bills, surely?'

'La La,' I repeat, handing the postcard to him.

'Who the hell's La La?'

'Sounds like a telly tubby,' I return to my half-eaten boiled egg, disguising my curiosity. 'Not sure which colour though? Ask Josh and Sophie about it tonight.'

Our two children have been despatched to school by Henrietta, a fellow mum. A ruse we'd come up with so we could have "quality" time with our husbands on alternate mornings. Knowing Henrietta she'll be using her time to bonk Neil senseless. Me – I just aimed for a halfway decent conversation and constantly missed.

He's silently reading.

'What does it say?' I add a pinch of salt to the last millimetre of yolk. Declan hates that I add salt to food, wants it banned from the house, which makes it all the more decadent and delicious.

He fishes in the drawer for his wire-framed reading glasses, perches them on the end of his nose, in a way that hides his boyish face and makes him look nearer fifty than his "recently passed forty-two".

He clears his throat. "*Dearest, sweetest Declan, I long to have you in my arms again. Ever yours.*" A tinge of colour slowly works its way up his cheeks. 'And there's a "Love from La La" at the bottom. Well, how about that?' He starts pacing the floor, a puzzled frown etched on his forehead.

'So who do you think sent it?' I ask eagerly.

'No idea.' The postcard's placed on the worktop. 'Practical joke, I guess.'

Forlornly I tackle the stack of plates lying accusingly in the sink.

'I seriously need a dishwasher,' I mutter, squeezing a generous helping of Fairy liquid onto a brown, greasy stain. 'Everyone's got one, even Patience Preston.'

Patience, mate of my closest friend, Raz, lives on her own in an immaculate flat.

'Hmm.'

'All she uses her fridge for is to chill vodka. Not a scrap of food's ever marred its spotlessness.'

'Hmmm.'

Sometimes my conversations went totally one way.

'She skips breakfast, buys herself wraps lunchtime and eats out each evening. And yet she owns a dishwasher. All I've got is an empty space waiting to be filled.'

'Patience can probably afford a dishwasher,' he says slowly. 'Because *she* has a job.'

My hackles raise a notch. 'Ah, but she doesn't have children to chase after all day, does she?'

'And nor do you. Now they're both at school till four.'

Another few notches of hackles are raised. 'Half three actually. And I have to leave ages before that to pick them up.' Rather than tromp through a well-planted minefield I decide to divert. 'Did you know Patience's mum owns a microphone once licked by Tom Jones?' Occasionally a little falsehood helped deflect the shrapnel.

It works, momentarily. 'Why on earth does Tom Jones go around licking microphones?'

'Dunno, maybe someone threw their knickers at it and knocked it into his mouth.'

He raises his eyebrow a fraction. 'Anyhow a dishwasher's not exactly a priority, is it? What with the roof space that needs lagging, windows needing replacing, boiler about to blow. Where the money's coming from, I don't know. My pockets aren't...'

His diatribe's thankfully interrupted by his ringing mobile. It's in his hand faster than Wyatt Earp with a smoking gun.

'Hi. Mm. Sure, sure. Sounds good. When? Ha, ha, ha. Have you asked Jessica-Ellen? Uh huh. Uh huh. Cathy? Nah she's cool. 'Course. Eight p.m. it is.'

'Eight p.m. it is,' I echo under my breath as I scrub furiously at last night's saucepan.

'So,' his voice is casual as he slips his phone into his pocket. 'Wonder who sent it then?'

'Maybe someone at work fancies you.' My chortle halts abruptly when I turn and catch his expression. He's not been in the mood for jokes lately, his sense of humour apparently absconding the morning of his fortieth birthday.

Besides he knows he's attractive. I made the mistake of telling him he was voted "Body of the Year" by the Tuesday Twice-Monthlies – the Restaurant Research Group I attend each fortnight. Henrietta likens him to a ginger Nicholas Cage with his high cheekbones and well-defined eyebrows. Raz adores his muscley arms, "sex on elbows" she calls them. And everyone everywhere tells me how lucky I was in nabbing him. As if I was a total pleb who lured him with some secret charm they could never quite see in me. I want to rage at them all, 'I was the one "nabbed" sisters. I was the one "bloody nabbed".' Of course being a coward, I never do.

He turns the card over. 'If that were true, you'd think they'd pop it in my pigeonhole rather than send it to my home, wouldn't you?' He drops his cup into my washing up bowl. 'Right, I'm off.'

I wipe my hands on my dressing gown as I follow him down the hall.

'You couldn't just take my watch to be repaired? On the bedside cabinet.' He retrieves his umbrella from the pot by the door.

'Sure, honey babe.' I stand on tiptoes to tweak his tie.

'Oh and my black boots need soles.'

'Consider it done.'

'And do get the kids to clear up those toys in the back garden.' His face takes on a pained expression, strange love cards already dismissed. 'Neighbours must wonder who they're living next to.'

'I'm on to it.' I resist the urge to snap into a salute.

Pathetic, isn't it? These seem to be our new roles in life. Declan barking orders, me acting the subservient housewife. Usually I'm not so wimpish but since Josh started school six months back, I realise I'm on extremely shaky ground even if it looks like the same old floor tiles. Casual mentions of spiralling debts, sharing the load or even carrying it for a change have been accumulating faster than Victoria Beckham's Hermes handbag collection.

Too bad that as the bickering increases so does my morbid fear of rejoining the workforce. Once lodged comfortably at the back of my mind, like a suspicion of woodworm you'll get around to dealing with later, it's morphed to become a monstrous bugbear between us.

Rattle of keys. He's already mentally in his office as he pecks me on the cheek. Smack of suit pocket to check for his wallet, quick comb of the hair to confirm it's up to R A Wilson Inc standards, and he departs for work. I wave serenely on the doorstep before dashing back inside to put on Coral Duster's Greatest Hits.

As Coral's dulcet tones wash over me, I head for the phone.

'Urgent sturgent! Urgent sturgent!' I can't disguise the thrill in my voice. Me with news? Something unexpected from the Cathy O'Farrell home front. I move aside Declan's raincoat and Sophie's puffa jacket, rub a hole in the dusty oval mirror and glance at my reflection. My eyes are so alive they're practically dancing. The whites are whiter than I've seen for ages, the iris a more attractive shade of green and my pupils have almost doubled. Even my hair, though badly in need of brushing, seems to have a few extra auburn glints.

'What's up?' Raz says excitedly.

I knew she'd be all ears. I don't call her "Nose-ache Nora" for no reason. Her name's really Rosa. Rosa Alison Zimmerman, but Raz was a pet name one of her ex's gave her and it had kind of stuck.

We met in the toilet of Johnson & Phillips Surveyors, both escaping for a clandestine ciggy and to get away from the oppressive atmosphere of the miserable men with their clacking rulers. During our regular smoke-outs we found we had much in common, i.e. sneaking off for two-hour lunches and rating the hotness factor of every guy we ran into. That was fifteen long years ago. We'd lived together, loved and lost together. We know each other better than we know ourselves.

She listens quietly, as I spurt it out in a waterfall of words. 'You think this postcard could be serious?' she says finally.

'Nah,' I giggle. Even my lips have a bee-stung feel about them. 'It's just somebody winding him up.'

'Sure about that?' Her imagination virtually scales the same heights as mine, except she's got minor sanity in her life – an office, desk, own direct line and, best of all, colleagues.

Colleagues. Thing I miss most about working. Especially male colleagues that I can banter with, groan at their silly jokes and amaze with clever solutions to their insurmountable problems. 'By gad you've got it, Cath!' They'd exclaim in awe. 'We've been struggling with that one ages' and I'd reply, 'No worries, lads,' and feel their admiring eyes on my bottom as they watched me leave.

Only that was before my bottom sagged to resemble Dumbo's and my pre-children brain cells were sparkling crystals, free from today's pea souper fog. Nowadays the only thing I could bring to the conference table would be the tea trolley.

Raz and I are both silent. I'm thinking about Declan and his endless meetings and oh-so-vital budget reports. Could he really sweep them all aside for unbridled, illicit sex? Raz, from the sound of things, is drawing on her first fag of the morning. I can almost smell the sweet aroma.

'You're obviously really really worried about it,' she adds. 'So...'

'I'm not *really* really worried about it,' I say, starting immediately to *really really* worry.

'I'm on my way.'

The sound of creaking and clopping, platform shoes on wooden stairs, reverberates throughout the house.

Made in the USA
Lexington, KY
26 April 2015